CROSSBONES

CROSSBONES

KIMBERLY VALE

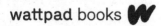

wattpad books **W**

Content Warning: brief emotional and physical parental abuse, death, drowning-related imagery, gore and blood, grief, torture

Published in Canada by Wattpad Books, a division of Wattpad Corp.
36 Wellington Street E., Toronto, ON M5E 1C7

www.wattpad.com

First Wattpad Books edition: October 2021

ISBN 978-1-98936-579-3 (Hardcover original)
ISBN 978-1-98936-580-9 (eBook edition)

Library and Archives Canada Cataloguing in Publication information is available upon request.

Printed and bound in Canada

1 3 5 7 9 10 8 6 4 2

Cover design by Laura Mensinga
Cover images © mihailomilovanovic, © wabeno, © cranach via iStock and © Luke Southern via Unsplash
Typesetting by Sarah Salomon

For the dreamers; follow your own compass.

THE
FROZEN GAP

INCENDIA

PORT
BARLOW

BALTESSA

SILVER SEA

CERULIA

RAVANA

GOLD SEA

SARVA

TERRAN

"Only the highest of valor can brave the seas.
Only the sharpest of wit can turn the tides.
Only the strongest of honor can sail straight on crooked seas.
Only the purest of heart can save a legacy."
—Captain of the Storm, First King of Bones

PART ONE

SEA AND FIRE

CHAPTER ONE
CSILLA

Port Barlow

Late Sunspur

I will not die today.

Csilla's unspoken words crowded her mind. She never dwelled on death—there was no reason to in the life she lived. Death came, it took, and it did not give back. She hadn't given much thought to how she would die, but she assumed it would be bloody and brilliant. *Not like this.*

As she walked through the crowd with her wrists tied tightly behind her, her fingers ached for the leather hilt of her sword. If she could, she'd fight until every Incendian soldier lay dead or until her last breath wheezed through her bloodied lips.

Around her, the weathered courtyard overflowed with unruly harbor-folk who'd normally be selling wares or watching the soldiers' demonstrations. On this day, however, they'd be witnessing her execution.

The soldiers marched before her, parting the path like a sword through the sea. To onlookers, she was a stain on their garments they couldn't scrub out, a plague they couldn't be rid of. Every time their eyes ran over the scars along her skin, the piercings that lined her ears, and her one blind eye, their anger flickered with fear and their shouted insults grew louder.

Csilla ignored them. The distant crash of waves and the briny scent of the sea was enough to calm the frenzied beating of her heart—for now. It was impossible to truly be calm when a storm was on the horizon.

Time was running out. The noose loomed across the courtyard.

If the Incendian Navy thought to humiliate her in her last moments, they would fail. She held her chin high and stepped with grace. No one would see her falter. No one would see her break. She'd show them only a girl who was proud of her pirate heritage, who preferred to die and be seen than to waste away, hidden in a cell.

"Filthy pirate!" a woman's voice yelled, her words slicing above the crowd's jeers like a sharpened blade.

Csilla glanced to her right, her good eye coming to rest on a woman whose worn face snarled at her. The woman wove through the crowd, following as the soldiers pushed Csilla forward. Then the woman stopped, slipped off her shoe, and hurled it, the shoe smacking hard against Csilla's cheek. She ignored the searing pain as well as the taunts and laughter that rose from the crowd.

Rage burned through Csilla like wildfire. They could rot in Limbo for all she cared. She stopped walking, pulled against the rope binding her to the soldier, and cut her sight to the woman. When their eyes met, the woman shriveled back, averting her gaze to the ground. It wasn't the first time Csilla had received this reaction, which was why she usually wore a scarf to cover her white eye, but today she embraced her difference. Today, she was glad the soldiers wouldn't let her wear it.

"*Sobel liitena shobenasku*," Csilla said, repeating the same words that had cursed her half blind. "*Sobel miitesa jaharren eto.*"

The woman's face went as white as merchant sails, her eyes growing wide and frantic as she realized Csilla's incantation was a curse. There was no magic in Csilla's veins to fulfill the venomous words, but the woman didn't know that. A glimmer of satisfying warmth spread through Csilla even as the soldiers dragged her forward, their fingers digging into the muscle of her arms and adding more bruises to her body.

"Witch!" the woman screamed. "Pirate witch! You'll waste away in Limbo!" The Harbor of Souls. Once a lost soul docked there in the afterlife, it never left again. It could very well be where Csilla's soul was heading today.

"See you there." Csilla locked gazes with the woman, her lip twisting into a smirk.

The sky was a blanket of clouds but the heat of the sunspur season still hung in the air. Sweat from the dense humid air gathered at the nape of Csilla's neck and traced down her spine like a river snake gliding over water. She wore only the filthy rags that the fort had *graciously* provided after they'd ripped her from the bed of her betrayer and stolen all her gear and armor. Though she hated the way the fabric scratched her skin, there was a twisted satisfaction in knowing that the soldiers, clad in their military trousers and multiple frilly layers, had to withstand the humidity. Sweat dripped down their temples, soaked their collars, stained their underarms.

One soldier shoved her forward into step again. The crowd

parted and Csilla's face went cold when the gallows came into view. She swallowed, her insides on the edge of heaving the small piece of bread she'd eaten yesterday. The noose swayed back and forth, a pendulum ticking down her last moments, and all previous confidence drained from her like blood from a fresh wound. The raised wooden scaffold with the dangling noose was a vision that reignited her darkest nightmares, her deepest unspoken fears. She shivered as she imagined her flailing body, her fingers clawing at her neck . . . her eyes, which would remain open long after her soul departed.

A soldier nudged her forward again until she was at the foot of the wooden stairs.

The world tilted—she blinked, but even in her good eye her vision didn't clear. A scream suffocated in her throat, her stomach turned to rock. She tried her best to remember her grandmother's training on the deck of the *Scarlet Maiden*: *Live fearlessly. Face every threat with a wicked smile and a sharp blade.* Yet as her gaze trailed up the scaffold, she struggled to lift her foot. Fear was an anchor that held her firm against the tide.

A drop of warm rain fell, splattering onto her cheek as she took the first step up and toward her death. By the time the soldiers corralled her directly in front of the noose, the clouds had opened up and showers poured down, cool against her skin.

Observers below pulled their hoods over their heads but Csilla embraced the rain. As the executioner looped the noose around her neck, she tilted her face back, letting the rain wash away the dirt and grime that had collected on her skin during her days in the cell.

The rope binding her wrists cut into her skin, but it didn't stop her from testing the strength of the soldier's knot. She wriggled her arms, attempting to free herself until a sharp blade pointed into her back, making her freeze.

"As issued by the king of Incendia," a soldier announced. His eyes trailed over the scroll as if he was reading the words, but the ink dripped in dark droplets from the edge of the rain-soaked parchment. He must've hanged so many pirates he knew the words by heart. His voice boomed across the open courtyard. "Any persons associated with piracy will be charged without trial."

Csilla scanned the upper level of the fort, searching for Rhoda or other Scarlet Maidens. She'd hoped her sister and her crew would come for her, like Csilla would do for them, but their absence proved that not everyone supported the youngest captain on the Sister Seas. Her crew had given up; and worse, they'd left her to die in this forsaken kingdom. Her gaze darted left and right, down by the stairs, by the doors, around the stage, anywhere, everywhere. Hoping she was wrong. Wishing she'd catch a glimpse of her sister's tightly woven braids or her friends' devious smiles.

But they truly hadn't come. It was a stab to the chest that left her knees trembling and filled her with a deep and cruel loneliness.

Then, her eyes fell upon someone in the crowd below, unhooded, rain dripping from his light hair with a smile that she knew too well split across his lips. The sight of him set her stomach on fire—an anger nearly strong enough to cover the ache in her chest.

In another time, in a place she'd buried deep within her memories, she would've been relieved to find his familiar sea-green eyes in this crowd, and perhaps, she would've allowed herself to get lost in them as he saved her from this unjust death.

But in this moment, in this turn of events, he wasn't there to rescue her. In fact, he was the reason she was facing death.

Flynn Gunnison—*her betrayer.*

It may as well have been him tying the noose around her neck. And after how he'd betrayed her trust, their friendship, and the possibility of what could've been between them, he had the gall to look her straight in the eyes. She lifted her chin. She would never let him see how much he'd shattered her.

She partly blamed herself for being so foolish, for letting the warm flame of his touch pull her into bed with him a week before. Maybe it was his charm. Maybe it was the rum. Whatever it was, the cost was her life.

Csilla's stomach twisted. She tore her gaze away from her betrayer as the soldier spoke once again.

"Csilla Abado of Macaya," he announced. "Captain of the *Scarlet Maiden*, conspirer against the Crown, pirate by choice, and pirate by blood, has been sentenced to hang by the neck until death."

The soldier rolled his drenched scroll back up even though it tore at the edges, then retreated down the stairs. No one cheered. No one clapped. The pattering of rain continued, seeping through Csilla's clothes, dripping off the tip of her nose. The fall through the gallows would break her neck, and if by some chance that didn't kill her, she'd choke to death soon after. This didn't stop her fingers from digging desperately at her neck for a grip around the rope.

Csilla closed her eyes once more, sending her last prayer to the Sea Sisters. She asked Anaphine to guide her soul with grace through Limbo and into the After. She prayed to Talona for strength for herself in her last moments, and even though they'd abandoned her, she prayed for her crew and for Rhoda, who had to go on without her. Finally, she pleaded for Iodeia to avenge her and smite Port Barlow with vicious waves taller than any tower they could build, taller than the Obsidian Palace in their capital city.

Maybe Csilla's dying wish would stop Incendia from encroaching any farther on the island kingdom of Cerulia. If the Incendian king had his way, the pirate fleet of Cerulia would be buried at the bottom of the sea, along with everything they stood for. Except for the gold. The greedy king would keep every coin for himself.

The footsteps of the executioner echoed behind her, thick heavy slaps against the creaking platform. Her chest fell in heavy pants and she counted every last breath. Her hands clenched into fists, her fingernails cutting crescents in her palms as she held on to every last second.

Then the lever clicked, and the wood below her dropped.

Everything stilled for a moment, a breath taken before the leap.

Csilla's heart fell first, then her legs followed. The blur of the crowd and their angry screams made her wish that the force *would* break her neck. A quick death. This hungry mob didn't deserve to watch her struggle for air.

It was just a blink of time, but in that moment, memories wisped through her mind, blowing past her like leaves in the wind. The flowered jungle treetops of Macaya. Her grandmother's sharp and commanding bark on the deck of the *Scarlet Maiden*, still able to be heard over the sea's crashing waves. The sparkle in her mother's deep-brown eyes even as she lay in her bed, frail and dying. And Rhoda's softness with her, which she never gave to anyone else.

All of it there, a beautiful painting, then a faint whir cut through the air above her and instead of jolting to a violent stop, she kept falling, the rope never tightening around her neck. She hit the ground hard, her legs crumbling beneath her weight, her head knocking into stone.

A thick tang clouded the air around her, making her throat itch. Maybe she'd died and the fall had broken her neck. Was this what death smelled like?

She opened her eyes but the cloud wouldn't clear from her vision. She blinked several more times before realizing it wasn't her eyesight—it was smoke. That was what she was choking on. Somehow, by some miracle, she'd escaped death this time.

Her left ankle throbbed unmercifully as she tried and failed to sit up with her hands still bound. Biting her lips shut to keep from groaning, she rolled onto her knees, careful of her ankle as she gazed out from under the gallows.

The crowd before her was a frenzied mob. Women screamed, tripping over their muddy skirts, clawing at each other to escape the possible danger first. Most of the men attempted to run for the fort gates, too, their eyes wide as they searched the area for threats. Soldiers swarmed in from their positions throughout the inside of the fort, their swords at the ready. They tried to reach Csilla but the panicked crowd's momentum pushed them back.

Csilla glanced at the end of the noose that still hung around her neck. The rope laid limp on the stone, severed and frayed. The smoke around her thinned, and her gaze trailed up the wall to see a small dagger wedged between two stones. There was only one person who could throw a dagger with enough accuracy to cut a rope. The same person who used to practice throwing her daggers at Csilla's dolls when they were children.

Her sister.

The weight that'd been suffocating Csilla was gone and she

could breathe easy again. She should've known Rhoda would be too dramatic to take out the guards as they escorted Csilla to the fort, or to break her out of her cell the night she got arrested. It was just like her sister to wait and make a scene out of saving her so that she could be applauded for the show later. Rhoda might've been brash and selfish at times, but they were family and all each other had left. Csilla should've never doubted her, but Rhoda could have at least saved her *before* she was dropped through the gallows.

"Csilla," a harsh whisper sounded from behind her as a blade cut her wrists free. "Get your lazy ass up. We've got a grand escape to make."

Csilla pulled the noose from her neck then whipped around to glare at her elder sister, wincing as she forced her body to stand, her ankle buckling beneath her. "We won't be going anywhere fast. My ankle's shot to hell."

"Don't be such a baby." Rhoda trudged toward her, eyes widening as she glanced to the side. Then she reached behind her back, withdrew a dagger from her leather belt, and threw it in Csilla's direction. The blade whizzed by her ear, followed by a thud and gurgle from over her shoulder. Rhoda had taken out a soldier, but Csilla still wasn't happy with her.

"You couldn't warn me?" Csilla asked as her sister yanked her dagger out of the guard's chest, wiping his blood off it with the crimson scarf that dangled from her belt. Csilla finally managed to stand alone without her sister's help and placed most of her weight on her right foot, allowing only the tip of her left boot to touch the ground.

"Are you finished griping, little cub?" Rhoda asked back, adjusting her daggers, then reaching for her cloak's tie and unraveling the knot. She pulled the scarlet cloak from her shoulders and draped the fabric around Csilla, lifting the hood over her soaking hair. Rhoda pulled another hood from her blouse and covered her own two braids before wrapping an arm around Csilla's waist and moving them both forward.

"Thank you, Rhoda," Csilla said as her sister helped her limp to the edge of the gallows' shadow.

"You didn't really think I would leave you to hang, did you?" Rhoda asked, the taunting sneer gone from her tone. She leaned forward, turning her head left, then right. "You're my sister. I'll always be there to rescue you when you get yourself into trouble." Csilla took notice of how she didn't address her as Captain; she likely never would.

Csilla braced herself as they left the cover of the platform and pushed into the chaotic crowd toward their escape. Soldiers still fought to get through the swarm of people while others searched for the one who had cut the rope. Smoke continued to clear, and the soldiers took the opening to shoot straight for the gallows, where Csilla and Rhoda had been a moment before.

"She's escaped!" a soldier yelled from behind them. "The pirate has escaped!"

Rhoda picked up her pace, practically dragging Csilla along. Csilla put as much weight as possible on her left foot, trying to ignore the sharp pain that shot up her leg with each step. *I will not die today*, she repeated over and over in her head. *Rhoda will not die today. I will not die until Flynn Gunnison has paid for what he's done.*

"Where are the others?" Csilla whispered to her sister.

"The twins are here," Rhoda whispered back. "They have more smokers ready if we need them. The rest are with Nara and the ship."

Csilla nodded, gripping Rhoda's waist tighter as she bit back her cry. Her ankle twisted again beneath her. The world spun, her vision spotting. She needed water. She needed food. She couldn't remember when she'd last had a good meal. But she didn't dare give up hope or Rhoda would use her instead of her old dolls for target practice. Just a bit farther and they'd be home free. If they could just get through the open doors and to their ship, then she could rest her ankle as long as she needed to.

"Find her!" someone yelled. "Find her allies! Do not let them leave this fort alive!"

Soldiers swarmed through the crowd, a few brushing past her in the chaos. Csilla always preached to her crew to remain calm in the worst of situations, to raise their chins against the biting wind, to grit their teeth and breathe deep when they wanted to scream and give up. Her girls never surrendered, never raised a white flag.

But there she was, their captain—her ankle throbbing, her spirit broken, tears pricking at the corners of her eyes like a weak little doe.

A soldier combed through the rushing men and women and stopped directly in front of Csilla and her sister. His brow turned down and his curious eyes flicked between the two them, their faces shrouded in shadow.

"Remove the hoods," he ordered, stepping even closer when they tried to shuffle past. When they didn't comply, he pointed his sword at Csilla. "I said, remove the hoods."

Rhoda sighed, then a hiss filled the air. Thick, white smoke rose in plumes from multiple spots in the crowd, unleashing more screams and yells among the harbor-folk. Smoke engulfed them almost immediately, shielding them from sight. Rhoda used the opportunity to hoist Csilla's arm over her shoulder, taking some relief off her ankle. Another body pushed in at Csilla's right, lifting her other arm. The scent of the mint leaves that Serafina liked to chew calmed Csilla's heart a beat.

Soldiers yelled orders but their confusion made them incapable of doing anything. They were birds flying blind. Smoke billowed up into the sky and out of the gates of the fort, masking their group as they continued forward through the sea of people. Soldiers yelled from behind, their curses fading the farther Csilla and her crew trekked down the hill to the harbor.

Cutting from the crowd, Rhoda and Serafina guided Csilla down a side path. Serafina's twin, Rosalina, darted in front of them, her dark ringlets bouncing as she led the way. She placed her hand idly at her back, ready to unsheathe her hidden blades if need be. If it came down to it, by Maiden's honor she would protect Csilla before her own blood.

A small farmhouse stood in a field off the path, surrounded by tall grass and little white flowers. Csilla thought someone stood in the open doorway, long dark hair blowing with her skirts as she watched the Maidens run like the wind toward the sea. She knew the watching stranger didn't matter in the scheme of things, but something in the back of her mind made her glance over her shoulder at the girl before they rounded the hill.

The sea finally came into view, followed by another glorious sight—the *Scarlet Maiden* with her crimson sails flapping, ready for departure. Csilla had never been so delighted to see her ship, even when she had set foot on it for the first time as captain. The deck had been her home since she was a little girl, more a home to her than anywhere else in the world. She needed the scent of the wood, the wind blowing against her cheeks, and the sun on her skin out in the open water.

Hidden by a short peak of land, the ship was unable to be seen from the busy harbor and its nosy inhabitants. Csilla and her girls neared the edge of the cliff, the *Scarlet Maiden* waiting below in the water.

Csilla peered down at the waves crashing against the jagged rock. Freedom was within reach, but first a high drop off a sharp and terribly intimidating cliff. "You just *had* to make this escape as dramatic as possible, didn't you?" she asked Rhoda as she cocked her brow. She remembered the time Rhoda blew up a military ship at a trading harbor just because she could.

"Oh, shut up about it," Rhoda grumbled. "We jumped higher cliffs than this in Macaya when we were kids. Now, do you need me to throw you over, or are you going to be a big girl and get your ass in the water?"

Csilla shot her own daggers at her sister with her eyes and moved back to make room for a grand swan dive. The sound of someone clapping stopped her as she bent at the knees.

"Well done," a familiar voice rang out behind. She would recognize that smooth honey tone anywhere. It was the same one that had coaxed her into bed, along with the soft eyes and even softer lips.

Csilla spun around to glare at the captain of the *Anaphine* and the one she'd almost let shatter her. She'd never developed a liking for killing, despite how many had died by her sword, but she would enjoy ripping Flynn apart piece by piece.

How could she have let him lure her to this in the first place? She'd been so gullible, so naive; she'd never make the same mistake again.

"You son of a—" she started.

"Ah, ah, ah." Flynn cut her off. He smiled and wagged his finger at her. "Our mothers have nothing to do with this, so please leave mine out of it. I could rattle off nonsense about your mother, but I'll bite my tongue for your sake."

There were shouts in the distance, coming closer every second. If she could somehow drag him with her to the *Scarlet Maiden*, she would, but she'd be lucky enough to get to the ship herself with her brokenness.

"I'll kill you, Flynn Gunnison." The words tasted delicious on Csilla's tongue. "When you least expect it, I will be there, waiting in the shadows. *And I will end you.*"

Flynn chuckled, as if knowing she wouldn't follow through on her threat. "You can hate me all you want, but I count on seeing you again very soon." Her stomach twisted at the reminder of a time when she would've been excited for that moment, but now she only felt the thrill of avenging his betrayal.

Without another glance at him, she turned around and flung herself from the cliff. Her hood fell away and the wind cut through her hair, billowing her cloak behind her, and when she hit the water, it engulfed her like a blanket. She came up for air, glancing back at the cliff as her crewmates made their own leaps.

Flynn stood at the edge, waving good-bye. For now.

CHAPTER TWO
KANE

Baltessa

Early Redwind

The crack of Kane Blackwater's knuckles against his opponent's nose was like the starting pistol before a race—the echo of it brought the gathered crowd to life. Surrounding men exploded into a cacophony of curses and guttural yells as they elbowed each other aside for a clear view down into the fight pit. He'd once been up there, years ago, hungry for violence.

In the basement of Grisby's tavern, it was easy to get swept away in the vicarious thrill of watching two people clash—fist to face, knee to gut. Even Csilla and Rhoda Abado had jumped into the pit for a bit of fun, but Kane was most often the one doing the beating, putting on a show, filling his leather pouch with gold pieces each time he visited the island capital of Baltessa. Tonight, his pockets would be brimming with Cerulian gold.

Blood trickled from his opponent's nose, rolling over his

upper lip. Kane pitied the man—Silas, he believed—because there were only more blows to come. Giving the crowd what they paid Grisby to see would be as simple as shooting fish in a barrel. Kane's knuckles might be busted and bloody by the end, but at least with the gold he would finally be able to pay off his debt to Dominic Rove, captain of the *Bonedog*. Making deals with him was like bargaining with a snake, and Kane had made one rotten deal too many. Things he'd like to keep buried in the bottom of the Silver Sea.

From above, men roared and stomped their feet in approval, rattling the wooden boards that walled the fighting pit, the ruckus causing dust to unsettle and cloud the air. Kane's eyes watered, and he rubbed his face with the back of his hand, smearing dirt across his cheek. The movement stung a little, his skin still tight from the sun after his voyage here.

"Get him, Silas!" someone yelled. "Don't just stand there!"

Silas bared his teeth and lunged forward, swinging his fist toward Kane's face. The man was all rage and no prudence. Kane stepped aside, smirking as the man blew past him like a rushing boar. Raspy jeers and laughter rumbled from above. Silas growled as he turned back to face Kane. Another swing, another miss. Kane countered and jabbed, grazing Silas's cheekbone and knocking his chin.

The man stumbled back and Kane saw an opening. With a wide sweep of his arms, he used the strike his father had used on him during their brutal training sessions, catching Silas in the ribs with a blow that cracked them and caved in his side. Kane hooked his punch wide again and put his weight into it. His fist connected with Silas's jaw. Blood spewed from his mouth and his body jerked to the side like a broken piece of wood.

Cheers erupted again.

But Kane wasn't quite finished yet.

He took two steps back and the crowd hushed. He surged forward with a roundhouse kick so spot on that Silas didn't stand a chance. The thud of the man's face hitting the floor echoed in the musty basement.

One breath.

Two breaths.

Shit. Had he ended the fight too soon?

He clenched his fists and rolled his neck to ease some of his tension. He could care less if the surrounding men enjoyed his brutality or not—he just needed the damned gold. Someone started clapping and his tight muscles eased.

One breath.

Two breaths.

The basement erupted into an ear-splitting roar of approval—the loudest Kane had received yet from his fights.

Thank the goddesses.

Grisby's payout would be hefty tonight. It would be enough to stop Dominic Rove's Bonedogs from breathing down his neck for repayment on his last . . . loan. The hated captain always collected his debts. If Kane was any other man, Rove would've been murdered in a dark alley by now. Kane's surname had saved him too many times to count, for the Blackwater name was renowned through the history of captains. As the captain of the *Iron Jewel*, Kane was favored by the ruler of the Cerulian Islands—the King of Bones.

Kane lifted his bloody fist, acknowledging the men who praised him. He imagined the crowds cheering for him, just like this, if he was ever the one on the throne, if he was the one wearing the Bone Crown. It was a pretty thing, crafted from the bones of an ancient enemy and dipped in liquid gold, known throughout the world, no matter which elemental deity you prayed to.

With a vision of the crown on his head, he quickly got swept away in dreams that would never come true. If he was the King of Bones, he'd cast Dominic Rove out of the kingdom and revoke his title as one of the five fleet captains. The sorry sea whelp didn't deserve his place behind the gold-crested wheel of the *Bonedog*. He bought his way with deals made in the dark, his crew's hands filthy with blood while his own remained clean.

But there was little chance of Kane ever becoming king. With the Cerulian king alive and Kane bearing no royal blood, striking against Rove was just a figment of a desire that would never be fulfilled. Relishing in this moment, pretending the applause was for his dream, was the closest he would ever get.

Then he heard it.

It was faint at first, like the hum of a crewmate drowned out by the flap of sails at sea. But as voices quieted, the sound became clear. The deep toll of a bell rang in the distance. The tune was different than the ones he'd become familiar with—yet somehow, he knew the song in his bones.

"The king!" someone shouted, startling Kane. "It's the king!"

His face went cold. The king. The bell. No wonder he hadn't recognized the toll. He hadn't heard the Blood Bell since he was a child.

Kane rushed to the rope ladder that dangled from the top of the pit, leaving Silas groaning on the ground. He would need his nose reset, and he might not be able to get out of bed for a few days, but he'd be fine. It wasn't Kane's fault the imbecile didn't realize just who he was up against. Most sane men wouldn't enter the pit with the captain of the *Iron Jewel*, but some saw his youth and thought they could get one up on him. They were always mistaken.

Once out, he motioned to a drunken Grisby in the corner—he'd be back for his payout—and followed the current of men as they moved up the stairs and into the tavern. Kane tried to listen in on flurried conversations, but keeping up was near impossible.

"Was it murder?" one man asked his friend. "It's so sudden."

"Who will take his place?" asked another.

"No heir? But what about the last Storm? Did they ever find her?"

Loud voices merged into one indecipherable hum. Kane rushed out the doors and into the city.

It was like stepping into a memory.

He had stood in this same district as a boy of nine. Still as a statue. Welded to his father's side even though he wasn't wanted there. Kane remembered glancing up at him from between the strands of his black hair. They'd stopped in the middle of the market, which was odd. Nothing could stop his father from finding a good deal in Baltessa. He was like a hound sniffing out gems among the piles of rubble. But the clang of the Blood Bell ended his hunt so abruptly that Kane had been scared for a brief moment.

"Captain?" a small Kane had asked as he'd tugged at his father's hand, trying to pull him from his frozen state. "Father, what is it?"

Kane didn't receive an answer from him. He never received much from his father besides brutal training and two meals a day from the age of six. Kane had learned to quit asking for anything a long time ago. He didn't dare repeat the question; instead he followed quietly behind his limping father.

Now, Kane didn't follow anyone—he set the course. As he made his way through the streets he couldn't help but notice how the spirits of Baltessa were the same as that day over ten years earlier. Sad faces blurred into a sea of despair for a king they'd never personally known yet who was their best protection against the encroaching Incendian kingdom.

As he walked, Kane's hand warmed, remembering the way his father's callused hand had gripped his like he was holding on for dear life. When Kane had glanced up all those years ago, his father was watching him, his eyes shining with despair and regret—too many things for a boy like him to understand at the time. His father didn't have to say it aloud. He had been thinking about the death of the woman they both loved most in the world.

Kane always thought of her when he encountered death— even now as the Blood Bell announced the death of the pirate king.

The bell still clanged in its perch above the city's copper spires and stone streets. Darkened windows lit up like beacons in the night. Curtains swept to the side and shutters opened as people mirrored Kane, their eyes searching for the tallest tower. Between the tolls rang a new sound—a chorus of crying. It echoed through the air, snaking between the spires. A song of mourning.

Kane should have felt an inkling of despair for his king, but the truth of the whispers circulating through the narrow alleys and clustered streets left him feeling something he hadn't felt in many, many moons. Hope.

The king had no child—no heir.

There was no son to take his place, no Rathborne to continue the bloodline. The king could've still conceived children, he'd still had time. His death was so sudden that Kane wondered what the cause had been—a blade in the night? There was little time to wonder, and if there was a traitor in their midst, he'd sniff them out as soon as a larger, more impending problem was dealt with.

The Bone Crown now belonged to no one. There had to be a king to rule the islands—to keep the people safe against Incendia, who would see their ways burned to ashes. The flame-worshipping kingdom would turn the islands into ports for their navy. They'd collect every gold piece for themselves and enslave the free islands to perform the daunting tasks of building their marvelous cities and palaces, just as they'd done when they'd left their western kingdom and crossed the Frozen Gap, taking the eastern land. Now they wanted to expand once more.

If Kane was king, he'd never let the Incendian Navy close enough to even glimpse one of the islands.

While the rest of the Baltessans hung their heads in despair, Kane held his chin high as he strode through the market. It should've been empty since all of the stalls were closed up for the night, but there were more people swarming the area than Kane had seen before. His mind wandered to the other four captains, including his old friends Csilla Abado and Flynn Gunnison. They'd all be wondering the same thing as him when they heard the news: Who would their next ruler be?

More citizens poured into the streets, but Kane took a sharp right and darted back to the inn where he and his crew were staying. There was too much to get in order—and too little time to do it all, especially for what would be coming next after the king's funeral. His hand twitched for the familiar feel of his father's compass in his hand, the one he'd left on the nightstand in the room he'd rented. If he could just hold it for a moment, rub the weathered scrapes along the side with his thumb, he'd be able to think clearly and piece his plan together, like his father would have done.

When he stepped into the room, everything seemed in place. In the fireplace was the faint ember of a fire he'd forgotten to put out, casting the room in an orange glow. The doors to the balcony were still open, curtains curling in the night wind like waves in the light of the moon.

"Kane?" a soft feminine voice asked.

Shit. He'd forgotten he'd left Clarissa in his bed before running off to Grisby's for gold and blood. He thought she would've been gone by now—or at least, he wished.

"Where'd you run off to?" she asked. He glanced over at her then, still in his bed. Her amber hair fell over her shoulders as she sat up, covering herself with the sheets. "When I woke up, you weren't here. And the Blood Bell. Did you hear the Blood Bell? I was worried you—"

Kane scrubbed his hand down his face. "You need to go," he said, aware of how cold he sounded, wishing she'd listen just for once.

"Go?" she asked, her face melting into a forced pout. Her hazy emerald eyes shimmered with crocodile tears. "Go? Is that how you're going to treat me? Like I'm one of Grisby's whores?"

Kane could've thrown his head back and laughed. This trick worked on traders and new recruits, but not on Kane. "You knew what this was. You knew there were no strings attached." He sighed, ready to be alone so he could get his mind right. "You said you wouldn't linger, so don't feign ignorance with me."

Clarissa straightened in the bed, her gaze down at the sheets. "I just thought that . . ." Kane knew the game she was playing— she was an innocent girl being treated unfairly by a beast such as him, but she was beastly too; her claws were just hidden. "I thought that maybe you and I would . . ."

"What?" Kane asked, taking a step closer to the bed. "You thought that I would pronounce my love for you? That I would whisk you away on my ship?"

Clarissa tore her gaze away from him, her cheeks flaming. Kane knew the blood rushing to her skin was not from embarrassment but from hidden anger. "We've been doing this for years, Kane." Her voice quieted to almost a whisper. "I know it started out as just a fun roll in the sheets every time you docked but you can't blame me for falling for you." He imagined many men would fall victim to this act, but he knew better.

"Oh." Kane watched her carefully. "So now you've suddenly fallen in love with the captain of the *Iron Jewel.*"

Clarissa nodded, her lips curling into a pathetic frown. Kane might've believed her if it wasn't for the feline glint in her eyes. He neared the edge of the bed, noticing her breath hitch with his movement. Settling one knee on the mattress, he leaned forward, and laid one hand on either side of Clarissa's face. She arched her back as he bent toward her, so close that her quick breaths were on his face.

"Oh, Clarissa," he whispered, tracing the tip of his nose down her cheek. She shuddered beneath him. "How convenient of you to declare your feelings for me after you hear the Blood Bell."

Clarissa went still beneath him, but his voice remained low and seductive.

"Did you truly think that I wouldn't connect the dots?" he asked, pulling back to watch her green eyes widen as she realized she'd been caught. "We all know that the Blood Bell signifies the death of the pirate king. We all know that our king has no son."

He lowered his head, whispering the next part in her ear. "Tell me, Clarissa. What happens when there is no heir?"

Clarissa tilted her head to the side, exposing her neck as Kane blew across her skin, making her shiver. "The Trials," she answered with a rasp. She cleared her throat. "The Trials begin."

"Do you think that I will win the Trials?" A light kiss on her collarbone.

"Yes," she said, breathless.

"Will I make a great King of Bones?" His fingers traced softly down her jaw.

"Yes," she whispered.

"Do you want to be my queen?" He leaned farther into her, brushing his lips against hers.

"Oh Goddess, yes," she moaned.

"Do you really think I am that stupid?"

"Yes! Oh yes! Yes—" She stopped, clearly realizing that Kane's question was not the one she'd assumed he was going to ask.

Clarissa put her hands on Kane's chest and shoved him away. Her sharp fingernails dug into his skin, but he didn't flinch—he'd felt much worse.

"You're a cod, Kane Blackwater," she hissed, snatching her dress from where Kane had thrown it. She slipped out of the bed and snatched her sweater from the coatrack, pulling the fabric over her curvy frame, huffing and puffing the entire time.

"You're right," Kane answered, lightly grabbing her wrist before she could run out of the room. "I am a cod, a scoundrel, all the terrible words you're thinking in your head right now. So get out of my room and go find yourself a love who sets your heart on fire and stop wasting your time on ashes like me. Don't wait for me, because I won't be waiting for you."

Clarissa raised her chin defiantly at him, but Kane knew she understood. They were both raised to take what they wanted and offer no apologies. It was one of the first things his father had beat into him.

As she trudged to the door, the strap of her dress hanging off her shoulder, she stopped and stared Kane straight in the eyes. "I wish I'd never met you," she said through her teeth. The blow should have hurt, but it didn't. Nothing really hurt anymore.

"You should be thanking me," he said, crossing his arms over his chest as he eyed his father's open compass on the nightstand. Good. Right where he left it. "I've taught you one of the most valuable lessons in this life."

"And what is that?" She pursed her lips, waiting for his answer.

"Never trust a pirate."

CHAPTER THREE
LORELEI

Port Barlow

Early Redwind

Lorelei stood at the cliff on the hill's crest, watching the sea toss and turn in the distance. The view from the farm had always been the most redeeming quality of Port Barlow. The cool breeze of the early redwind season played with her hair, making strands slip out of her braid and tickle her neck. While her mother baked fresh rolls, Lorelei left the small cottage and did the same thing she did every morning—stood, watched, and dreamed.

She dreamed of seeing nothing but the dark blue of the sea surrounding her. She dreamed of waking up to the sound of waves washing against the ship she would travel on. She dreamed of the wind and the sky above her and the endless sea of stars that reflected in the water.

But that was all they were—dreams.

She would never drift across the sea in hopes of finding

someplace new. She never had, and she never would. It wasn't her fate to storm the seas—it wasn't her legacy. Her destiny was here, on the farm with her mother.

Lorelei sighed and tucked her hair behind her ear even though the strands fought against her in the wind. Goddess, she missed her mother. She'd just seen her before she left the cottage—hunched over, kneading dough—but in the past year her mother had deteriorated from the woman she was in Lorelei's memories into someone consumed with madness. Lorelei missed the sound of her mother's gentle voice and the cinnamon scent of her hair from the soap she used to make herself. She missed the stories of beautiful mermaids, ice dragons that lived up north, beyond the Frozen Gap, and most especially the legendary Captain of the Storm, a mortal pirate whose goddess-given sea magic won an ancient war. Mystical tales that seemed so real it was almost as if her mother had lived them. But that was an illusion, the art of great storytelling. Her mother had always run this farm, and so Lorelei buried the way the sea sang to her, reached for her, called to her, because she would run the farm one day too.

Lorelei could very easily catch the first ship out of Port Barlow and head somewhere new. She'd once seen a map that had slipped out of one of her mother's old books. She still remembered the jagged scar of islands cutting between the Silver and Bronze Seas—the jungles of Macaya, the lively sister islands of Sarva and Ravana, the ruins of the Lost Isle, and other islands, with the capital, Baltessa, at the very center. *Cerulia.* During one of the tales her mother used to tell years ago, she'd told Lorelei the island kingdom of Cerulia was a welcome home to anyone wishing to escape the bitterness of the land kingdoms. Maybe in Cerulia Lorelei could find a witch that could help cure her mother's mind, erase the imaginary voices she was certain whispered to her from the fire. Maybe Lorelei could find her father, the man her mother barely spoke of but murmured about in her sleep.

Jack was his name. Her mother's croons in the night echoed off the walls in their small cottage. Although she never delved too far into details of the man she loved, from the bits and pieces she'd told, Lorelei had put together that her mother never wanted to leave Jack behind but left because of a great fear of something from which even he couldn't protect her . . . of course she never said exactly what. Lorelei could sail away and find him, bring him back, and make their lives whole again. Even though she'd never met him, she could look into his eyes and know who he was—they shared the same blood. He could be the piece that was missing from Lorelei's life. Perhaps his return could fix her mother.

But each time thoughts of leaving drifted into her mind, her heart tugged, pulling her away from the dreams and back to the farm where she belonged.

Lorelei gripped her skirts and turned away from the sea. She should be ashamed for even thinking about leaving her mother. Especially now, when she faded with each day. But being around her was suffocating, and Lorelei needed the stolen moments by the sea to breathe freely.

Lorelei headed down the hill. The bustle of the harbor would be enough to distract her wandering heart.

As she trudged down the path, the sea continued its siren call to her, but she ignored them. Harbor-folk milled about the docks and roads winding between the short, squat buildings. Even though she didn't know most of the people very well, she enjoyed watching them, like the way others took pleasure in watching birds. Some kept to themselves and nodded politely as Lorelei passed.

Most remained quiet—ears piqued to private conversations, eyes searching for careless decisions with damning consequences. They buried themselves knee deep in everyone's business. Some still gossiped about the captain of the *Scarlet Maiden*'s escape over a month ago.

She still remembered the thrill of seeing them escape through the field in front of the cottage. The limping girl was the only one who noticed her standing in the door, and even then it was enough to make Lorelei shrivel back into the shadow of the doorway.

At least their escape had given the harbor-folk something to talk about other than her mother. It was already bad enough the entire harbor had noticed their absence throughout the years at the Flame Festivals and the executions at the fort. Sometimes Lorelei wondered if they knew about her and her mother's secret prayers to the Sea Sisters before eating dinner or about the Cerulian gold necklace her mother kept tucked in the collars of her dresses at all times. Maybe it was time to finally summon the courage to demand that her mother tell her the truth about her past, about where she really came from—to see if the fantastical stories held a figment of truth in them.

"Lorelei Penny," said a warm, familiar voice from behind her. "You're down earlier than usual."

She turned to see Luis smiling at her from the door of his father's butcher shop. His light-olive skin glowed in the morning sun and his wavy, dark hair flopped as he strutted across the narrow street toward her. She had to crane her head to look at him, but she was used to it. He had always been taller than the rest of the kids by the docks when they were growing up.

"Don't tell me you rushed down to the harbor to see me." Luis winked. If only it was that easy—to be a love-struck girl with no worries except which arm she belonged to. How could she fantasize a future with anyone when her mother whispered angry words to the fire at night?

Still, it didn't hurt to flirt. She'd play his little game.

"I couldn't leave the cottage fast enough." She giggled behind her hand.

"Don't tease me, Lori." Luis clutched at his chest playfully. "My fragile heart cannot bear it if it isn't true."

"Perhaps your heart needs armor then."

They stared at each other for a moment, neither of them blinking. Luis cracked first, his chestnut-colored eyes sparkling, his lips curling up until he burst into a handsome grin. He crossed his arms over his chest as his laughter echoed down the harbor streets.

"You laughed first," she said with a smile of her own. "I win. Again."

"You only win because I let you," Luis argued. He cleared his throat. "What kind of gentleman would I be if I didn't?"

"Are you going to be so gentlemanly to pirates after you enlist in the Incendian Navy?" Lorelei asked. She'd given Luis an earful about enlisting when he'd first shared his plans with her, but since the recent escape there seemed to be no stopping him. "Are you to become a Scout too? I swear those men have no souls left in them. They set fire to that small trading port in the northern harbor just a few moons ago."

"Oh, come on, Lori, they were aiding fugitive pirates." He rubbed his temple as if the matter gave him a headache. "We've already talked about me enlisting. Do we really need to talk about it more?"

"We did, didn't we? Yet your father told me two days ago that you're still following through with it." She poked him in his meaty chest. "You told me you'd think about it."

"I *did* think about it, and I made my decision."

"Well, your decision is asinine." Her stomach twisted to learn he had committed to what she hoped she'd changed his mind about.

"And it's *mine* to make. Not yours."

Harbor-folk slowed their paces as they passed by, their eyes wandering to the quarrel in the middle of the road. Luis noticed this, too, and quieted his voice.

"I don't understand why you're always so enamored with Cerulia." He brought his face closer to hers as he continued. He smelled of embers and charred wood from hours of smoking meat at his father's shop. If he became a Scout, he'd smell even more of fire and destruction. "Pirates cause nothing but trouble. They steal. They murder. They sink entire ships of weapons needed to protect our people."

"Protect our people? From what?"

"From *them*."

Lorelei rolled her eyes. "Do you believe every story drunken sailors tell in the tavern? Half of *them* have killed men with their own hands. I'm disappointed that you deem them reliable sources."

"A soldier died during Csilla Abado's escape. He was a husband and a father. Her crew made a mockery of the navy. What other proof do you need of their wickedness?"

"Why were they hanging her in the first place, Luis? What was her crime? Being one of them?"

Luis shifted uncomfortably. "Their way of life promotes violence and chaos."

"Generalizations like that lead to hatred and hatred to—"

Luis's sigh interrupted her. He turned his head away and narrowed his eyes, as if something in the distance would help him come up with a reply. He clenched his jaw and looked back. "You're only seventeen and naive. You'll understand one day."

"Pardon me?" She gritted her teeth as anger built in her chest. "Don't act like I'm a foolish child. You're only two years older than I am, and we've been friends our whole lives."

"Lori." Luis ran his hand down his face. His ears flushed red. "I'm sorry, I—is that your mother?"

Lorelei drew back, her face twisting in confusion. Luis wasn't looking at her, but instead over her right shoulder. She'd rather stand and argue with Luis until the sun went down than face her mother in public. The last thing they needed was more gossip being spread.

"Lorelei!" yelled her mother. It was a frightened cry that was too familiar to Lorelei. She often heard the anguish in the quiet of the night.

"Good luck," Luis said with wide eyes.

"Lorelei!" yelled her mother again. There was slight relief in her tone, but it still oozed of paranoia and fear.

Every pair of eyes in the harbor latched onto Lorelei, waiting for her to react, to do something so deliciously terrible that they could talk about it for weeks.

Dear Goddess, please just smite them now.

Luis's eyes widened then fell on Lorelei. "I should get back to my father."

"You're a terrible friend," Lorelei growled at him. "Don't you dare leave me."

Luis ignored her and put his hand to his ear. "Do you hear that? Sounds like he's lifting a cow, or a boar, or something . . .

heavy." He turned and bolted, giving Lorelei a small wave over his shoulder. *Traitor.*

She cupped her hands around her mouth and yelled after him. "I won't miss you when you leave!" Another lie. Port Barlow would be even more boring when Luis left for naval training.

A hand gripped Lorelei's shoulder, ripping her from her thoughts, forcing her to turn around and face the owner. Lorelei's stomach dropped, her heart twisting in her chest at the sight of her mother. Eyes shimmering with tears. Dark-brown hair a tangled knot. Face red and blotchy from crying. *A complete and utter mess.*

"Where were you?" her mother asked, her bone-thin hands and sharp nails digging into Lorelei's shoulders, shaking her. "Where *were* you?"

As Lorelei stared into her mother's broken eyes, she realized that she might never be able to pick up the pieces. If anything, she only added more cracks.

Lorelei glanced left, then right at the harbor-folk who had gone still in the streets. With curled lips and beady eyes they watched the trembling woman in her dirty clothes and matted hair. They regarded her mother as if she was a rotten tomato on the vine, like her madness would spread to them if they got too close.

She shouldn't have let this go on so long; she should have gone to her mother the moment she heard her name being called. Then the others would have less to gossip about. Goddess, she was the worst daughter in the kingdom.

She'd just wanted one breath of fresh air, of a somewhat normal life. And it ended up further worrying her mother.

Gently, Lorelei shifted out of her mother's grasp and wrapped her arm around the woman's shoulders, pulling her into her side.

The harbor-folk watched, their burning gazes labeling Lorelei the daughter of madness—the maiden likely to spiral into insanity after her mother.

"What are you all looking at?" Lorelei asked, unable to hide the tremble in her voice. "Don't you lot have something better to do?"

She damned their judgmental gazes and walked with her shaking mother pinned to her ribs. For now, what mattered most was shepherding her mother out of the harbor before she had a fit. Lorelei would let her guilt wash over her later.

"Where were you?" her mother asked again as the crowd thinned out and the path up the hill loomed ahead.

"I just came down to see Luis," Lorelei answered, loosening her hold on her mother. She'd stopped shaking and the red blotches had faded. Now, her face was pale and ashen.

"You didn't tell me."

Because she wouldn't have allowed it. "I was on my way back—"

"You must be careful." She cut in with a harsh whisper. The sea wind whistled in Lorelei's ear, muffling her words, but there was no mistaking what she said. "The fire glows brighter when he talks to me. He wants to kill the heir. That's all he needs to regain his power. That's why you have to stay safe, Lorelei."

"Who? What does this have to do with me?" Lorelei gently grabbed her mother's hand and pulled her to a stop. She knew her mother held no passion for Incendia or the fire gods, but this was different. "There are no voices in the fire, Mother. There is only you and me." *Or at least there used to be.*

"Oh, my sweet Lori." Her mother's face changed for a moment, her eyes sparkling with emotion, her cracked lips curving into a frown. She opened her mouth to say something else, but then she froze as if someone had interrupted. After a few moments, her lips snapped shut and she yanked her hand away, as if Lorelei's touch was a flame. "Don't sneak off again. Dark tides are rising. If you aren't careful, you'll drown."

CHAPTER FOUR
CSILLA

Sarva

Early Redwind

A sword had never felt so good in Csilla's hand. This particular blade was her favorite, not just because of its perfect balance and grooved handle, but because of the throat its steel was pressed against at that moment.

The *Scarlet Maiden* had docked in Sarva only an hour ago, and Csilla hadn't even had time to order a pint of ale before she saw Flynn Gunnison eyeing her from a corner booth in the back of the tavern. He was either incredibly stupid or his balls were made of brass. Either way, he was a dead man. All it took was a snap of her fingers, and the group of Maidens yanked him into the back alley and forced him onto his knees in front of her.

Outside, in the lane between two buildings, a rotting pile of trash in the corner had grown to epic proportions. Shutters dangled from windows at awkward angles and forgotten garments hung from clotheslines strung between the buildings. Smoke from stale tobacco lingered in the air, scratching at Csilla's throat. A rat skittered by but she didn't tear her gaze away from the traitor at her feet.

"Well, well, well," she mused, shifting her weight onto her hip as she gazed down at him. "Tell me why I shouldn't slit your throat, Flynn Gunnison."

If she inched her sword up higher, she could cut off the smirk that tilted at his lips. But then again, those lips might be the only redeeming quality about him—when they were sealed tight, *or pressed against her collarbone.* Csilla banished the last thought from her mind. Flynn didn't have to speak a word to get under her skin. He was there, scratching at the surface, just by gazing at her with that spark in his sea-colored eyes. A strand of hair fell loose from his hair tie, its shade reminding her of wet sand.

"I could give you many reasons as to why you shouldn't kill me," he replied. His voice was smooth and warm but his grin was full of mischief. "The question is, which one do you prefer?"

"Don't play games with me," Csilla spat out. She curled her fist so that her sword angled dangerously against the artery in his neck.

Flynn swallowed as his eyes drifted down the steel. "Play games with you? I would never." Lies. Everything he said was a damned lie.

"Why are you here?" With each word, she pressed the blade farther into his skin. All it would take was one sliver of movement to make his blood spill, then his dead body would be forgotten like everything else in the cluttered alley.

"The Incendian king has issued a bounty for you. They've sent the best Scouts from the Obsidian Palace." His eyes watched hers, waiting for a reaction, Csilla was sure. The Scouts were rumored to find what they were searching for. Always. No matter what stood in their way. The thought of them hunting for her made her stomach turn over, but she gave Flynn no inkling that his words frightened her. He continued, "It is safe to assume that he did not find Rhoda's escape tricks very entertaining."

Rhoda snorted from behind Csilla. "They're lucky that I let most of them live," she retorted. Csilla didn't need to turn around to know that Rhoda had crossed her arms over her chest.

"The key word there is *most*," Flynn replied, glancing around Csilla. "Not all survived the wrath of your blade."

"Would you like to feel my wrath?" The sound of Rhoda unsheathing one of her daggers echoed in the dark alley. "I'd be more than happy to give you a taste."

"I've already tasted your sister's lips—"

Csilla's fist cut off his words, her knuckles colliding with his face. "Enough!" she commanded. Her cheeks warmed as she took in Flynn's cocky blood-toothed grin. She inhaled a deep breath, trying to hold her now-shaking sword steady as she placed it against his neck once more. "So, Incendia has a bounty out for me. What does this have to do with you? Why are you here? Did you track us? What in Sisters' name do you want from me?"

"Slow down." Flynn dragged out the words. "I am but one man. I can answer but one question at a time."

"Maybe we should be like Incendia and feed him to the Brothers of Flame," Nara said. Murmurs of agreement rose from the other Maidens, including a snort from Serafina. "The molten men would burn away that sarcastic smile of his."

"But I haven't gotten to the best part!" Flynn whined, his eyes shining at Csilla like a pup.

"You have ten seconds," she said quietly. "Rhoda, count." She glanced over her shoulder at her sister, who nodded with a devilish smile. Csilla bent forward, letting her face linger dangerously close to Flynn's. She whispered so that only he could hear, a promise between two lovers. "I don't care if you're one of the pirate fleet or that you captain the *Anaphine*. If you don't spit it out by the time Rhoda gets to ten, then I'll cut out your tongue *before* I kill you."

Somewhere in a forbidden place in Csilla's heart, she hoped she wouldn't have to fulfill her threat.

He smirked the same smirk that had drawn her to him the day they'd met as children during recruit training. "I recall you *loving* the things I did with my ton—"

But he always had to ruin everything with that mouth of his. Csilla pressed the blade farther into his skin, shifting just enough to draw a line of blood.

"One!" Rhoda started.

Flynn rolled his eyes before taking a deep breath. "Incendia issued your bounty the day after your escape."

"Two!"

"Scouts have been ordered to kill your crew on sight and—"

"Three!"

"I swear, she is counting too fast." Flynn's eyes narrowed.

Csilla shook her head. "You're wasting time. Ticktock, ticktock."

"Four!" Rhoda yelled again, her voice rising in excitement.

"They've been ordered to bring you back alive," Flynn continued.

"Five!"

"To make an example out of you."

"Six!"

"Come on, Rhoda! That wasn't a full second!"

"Seven!"

"I left Port Barlow the moment I heard so that I could warn you." Flynn's eyes searched Csilla's face, but she revealed nothing. He hadn't answered every question yet, and she enjoyed his squirming.

"Eight!"

"What *else*?" Desperation poured off Flynn, which was exactly the emotion that Csilla wanted to see. Make him feel the same thing she had when the noose was around her neck.

"Nine!"

"Did you track us?" Csilla prompted.

His response was a slur of words, but she caught every one. "I headed here because we *all* come to Sarva to celebrate!"

Csilla lowered her sword. He was right: even the *Scarlet Maiden* had docked in Sarva to celebrate Csilla's escape from death.

"Damn you, Csilla!" Rhoda shrieked. "I wanted to see you cut out the bastard's tongue!"

"Another day," Csilla said. A secret flood of relief washed over her.

Flynn wiped the blood streak from his neck and straightened his spine. "The Sea Sisters must favor me today."

"The only thing that favors you today is pure luck," Csilla replied.

"How is that ankle of yours, by the way?" Flynn asked, tilting his head to the side as his eyes trailed down her body. Always the master of distraction. "Does it still hurt?"

Yes, it still hurt, and she tried her best to hide her limp, but Csilla wasn't going to admit that to him. It was his fault that it hurt in the first place. She had attempted to let it heal properly, but staying in bed and hiking her leg up while she watched her crew do all the work for her didn't sit well in her gut. A useless pirate was a restless pirate.

She sheathed her sword and crouched in front of Flynn. Reaching up, she adjusted the crimson scarf that she wore over her blind eye. "Where are the Scouts now?" she asked, dropping her voice an octave.

"They're in Sarva," he replied. His voice was smooth, as if he hadn't panicked just a few moments before.

Csilla's gut twisted. It was a trap. Another *damned* trap. Her hand snatched his vest. She tightened the leather in her fist as she pulled him forward. "And where are your men?" she asked, trying to keep her voice from shaking. If one of her girls died because of him—she couldn't even fathom the pain she would make him endure.

"Right now, one of my men is taking out the snipers that have their rifles pointed at Rhoda."

Csilla shoved Flynn to the ground as she spun around toward the Maidens, who all jolted to attention. Her heart stopped as her eyes locked with her sister's. "Rhoda!" she screamed, her agony rippling through the air.

But instead of gunfire, there was the comforting sound of men choking on their own blood. Movement above the alley caught her eye, and her gaze trailed up to see two bodies falling from the rooftops. They landed with a thud on the ground, blood pooling across the stones. On the bare skin of their forearms was a branded emblem of flame and sword—Incendia's.

"You're welcome!" called a voice from above. Even in the night's shadow, Csilla recognized the smug smile of Arius Pavel, Flynn's first mate.

"I hope this means you can reconsider your quest for vengeance against me?" Flynn mused. "After all, I did just save your sister's life."

"Correction," Csilla replied. "*Arius* just saved Rhoda."

"Details, details. I hope you—"

Flynn stopped, hearing the same sound that made Csilla perk her head up. Squawks rang through the air, signaling the gulls' arrival. Two white birds swooped down, quieting as they reached the two captains. Small, rolled parchments were tied to their legs.

The last time Csilla had received a message by gull, it was the scribbled note from Flynn that lured her to Port Barlow. The memory of the excitement she'd felt at his summons was now stained with regret at his betrayal. Her fingers trembled as she untied the twine and let the parchment unravel in her palm. She read the written words over and over, not fully understanding their meaning until the fifth or sixth time. Then it hit her, so sudden and fierce, she almost fell to the ground.

Flynn's eyes lifted to Csilla just as she let hers drift to him. Their pieces of parchment held the same words—the words that repeated in her head as they both watched each other silently.

Captains of the Fleet,

The King of Bones is dead. The Trials will begin at Crossbones on the eve of late redwind. Captains must be present with their first mate before the starting pistol or must forfeit their claim for the Bone Crown and the golden throne of Cerulia.

A hearty celebration for the late King Rathborne will be

*held in three nights for any crews close enough to make
port in Baltessa. Crown officials will assume control of
governing duties until a new King of Bones is chosen.*
—General Lockhart

Csilla took notice of Lockhart's choice of words—King of
Bones, not *Queen* of Bones. There had never been a queen of the
Cerulian Islands or the pirate fleet. It should've been the last Storm,
the woman with legendary blood in her veins who ran away on her
wedding day, never to be seen again. If these men wouldn't allow
a woman to sit on the throne by blood in her veins, then Csilla
would take it for herself in the Trials.

"Well," Rhoda prompted, her voice holding an edge. "What
does it say?"

"The king is dead," Flynn replied while keeping his eyes fixed
on Csilla.

"*What? How?*" Rhoda's voice rose an octave. "An heir? Did
they ever find an heir?"

"The message didn't say how he died. And no, they never
found the Storm, so how would they find the heir?"

The alley suddenly felt too narrow, the air too thick. She hadn't
smelled the pile of trash before, but now its stench poisoned her
stomach.

"She's got to be out there somewhere," Nara said over Csilla's
shoulder. "No one can disappear without a trace like that. What if
they had a child? What if that's why she ran away?"

"She most likely died at sea after she stole one of Rathborne's
ships." Flynn stuffed the parchment in the pocket of his pants.
"There's no heir. The note also said—"

Rhoda rammed her knee into Flynn's side. Csilla grimaced

at his groan, but Rhoda shrugged. "What? He deserved it." She ended his sentence for him, stealing the stage for herself. "What did the rest of the note say?"

"The Trials begin in two moon cycles, on the last day of redwind. The throne will seat a new bloodline come frostfall."

The Trials—the dangerous hunt created by the first king, the Captain of the Storm, for this very purpose. The last Trials were held nearly a century ago, a Rathborne captain from the *Wavecutter* taking the crown and blessing the kingdom with a line that produced plenty of sons over the generations. Until their line dried up.

The words washed over Csilla like cold water, bringing her to life, filling her every sense. She suddenly had much more energy than before. She could do anything, slay anyone, with both eyes blinded.

"The other captains must know by now," Nara said, pacing the alley. "They'll all stake their claim for the Bone Crown. Csilla, do you realize? If you compete in the Trials and win, you'll be the first pirate queen the world has ever seen, *the first Queen of Bones.*"

"The Scarlet Maidens will become a true legacy," Rhoda mused, but only Csilla heard her next words as she muttered them under her breath. "It should have been *me.*"

The Scarlet Maidens burst into excited chatter. Serafina and Rosalina were huddled close, their whispers curiously unheard by the others. Some whispered behind the backs of their hands. Nara had suddenly gone quiet, making Csilla ever so curious as to what was running through her mind.

The most frightening part about it all was that she was blind to the opinions of the ladies in the alley with her. They were all so different—a sea of different colors and shapes, varying strengths and weaknesses, a mixture of soft hearts and sharp glares. While Csilla put complete trust in Nara and the twins, she still wondered whether other Maidens would rather have Rhoda standing in her place. They all knew her older sister desired to be captain more than gold or the richest tobacco in the islands. They'd also all witnessed Rhoda beat the hell out of her during a duel on the deck of the *Scarlet Maiden*.

While the words of the written message ignited an array of reactions among the Maidens, they only sparked a deep fear inside of Csilla. Failure seemed to follow her like her shadow. She'd failed to escape capture in Port Barlow. She couldn't keep her mother alive when she fell ill. She didn't know why, but she glanced back at Flynn, who was already observing her reaction. She found herself wondering if the same doubts also ravaged through his head.

Not that it mattered.

"It looks like fate is on your side today, Flynn Gunnison," she said, rolling the life-changing parchment paper up and stuffing it into her coat pocket. "You live to die another day."

CHAPTER FIVE
KANE

Baltessa

Mid-Redwind

Kane was the youngest captain present at King Rathborne's funeral. He wouldn't have felt as out of place if Flynn and Csilla had bothered to attend, but neither they nor their crews were anywhere to be seen. The young captains were thought of as children by the elders, but at least the three of them together were a strong tide against their judgment. But now he was a pool on his own, isolated from the rest of the sea, as usual.

He didn't think to worry about what kind of trouble Flynn and Csilla might be in because that was the entire point—*trouble*. Just as long as it wasn't between the two of them, then they'd be fine. They bickered enough as it was. Kane rubbed his thumb along the edge of his father's compass, deep in thought as he lounged in his chair among the lavish party going on around him.

He remembered he used to secretly long for their friendship, but when the two of them couldn't stay away from each other, it was clear Kane would just have been a third wheel. He remembered the first time the three of them met at the last king's funeral ten years earlier. They were all children then, Kane on course to inherit captainship, Csilla always a step behind her sister, and Flynn just a recruit with the hope of adventure twinkling in his eyes. Kane only watched them, not speaking to them because his father had trained him to perceive the two as a threat.

"Don't let their age fool you," the man had whispered harshly in Kane's ear, the reek of rum on his breath still lingering in Kane's memories. "They'll turn on you faster than a pirate spends their gold."

He followed his father's orders. The only thing that would stop him from completing his duties would be a run-in with dragons or with a kraken. So, he kept Flynn and Csilla close during their two years of training before they joined their crews on the seas, but not too close, always the third wheel to the pair of them. He'd found it odd how they unknowingly searched for each other in the crowd of recruits, like flowers searching for sunlight among an overgrowth of weeds. He'd never admit it to anyone, but he'd secretly wanted a garden of his own.

King Rathborne's funeral at the palace was just as extravagant as those of the Rathbornes before him. Gold pieces scattered across every table, a drink in every hand, off-tune shanties drifting through the evening air. There weren't as many tears as Kane had remembered—this funeral was more of a celebration of the man's life. Truthfully, they all needed this moment away from the bloodshed and turbulent seas. Brotherhood between crews was rare, but witnessing them all come together to celebrate the life of King Rathborne was a sight to see.

The festivities were so immense that wooden tables were scattered through the main hall, into the foyer, and out into the courtyard. Kane and his crew preferred the outdoors, where they weren't blinded by the palace decor, and where, even from the center of the capital, there was a scent of brine on the breeze. The sea ran in all pirates' veins—his father taught him that a true pirate could find their way back to the water from anywhere, even if stranded in a desert.

Kane scanned the courtyard from his perch on a comfortable chair he'd stolen from the main hall. The crews of the *Scarlet Maiden* and the *Anaphine* were still missing from the bunch, but he recognized the other crews that were scattered about. The men of the *Bonedog* lumbered around, snagging drinks that didn't belong to them. A few members of the *Wavecutter* crew had stolen the stage from the band and were attempting a rendition of a depressing sea song about a barmaid in Sarva. At events like these, all qualms against each other were put aside. But this wasn't just a celebration of the king—casting away differences would be a difficult task tonight. This king had no heir to take his place. Soon, they would all be at each other's throats, vying for the crown when the Trials began. To be the one who ruled the islands, ruled over the sea. No one crossed the Silver, Bronze, or Gold Seas without the king's knowledge, meaning he controlled the most valuable thing in this evolving world—trade.

"Perhaps someone wanted the king dead," came a voice from one of his men. Doan was quiet, sure to be unheard by other crews. "Perhaps someone wanted to initiate the Trials. I've heard whispers in the market." The men around him murmured in agreement. There were so many fewer than there used to be.

When Kane's father died a year ago and Kane inherited the

ship, he'd nearly succumbed to mutiny—dueling Jarnis the Brute was the only way to keep the ship. Kane won by some miracle, and although he lived to tell the tale, his chest would never fully heal from the deep slash of Jarnis's axe. His fight gained the respect of the crew that remained, and the rest, for all he knew, had followed Jarnis across the sea.

Maybe he could be thankful he had a smaller crew now. Maybe he'd try to relax a little bit with his goblet and his wine. No pestering. No looking over his shoulder since he'd paid off Dominic Rove with his fight winnings. Kane leaned back in his chair and crossed his ankles on the edge of the table. Perhaps he could *attempt* to enjoy the celebration, even if only briefly.

Fate's coin flipped, as it always seemed to do when his life was concerned.

Kane sensed the man behind him before the voice scratched in his ear. "Well, look at what the tide washed in."

Kane didn't have to waste his energy by turning to look at the man. He'd know that slithery voice anywhere. He lounged back farther into his chair and kept his gaze ahead as Rove rounded the table. Just when Kane thought he had rid himself of the dirty dealer. Rove cast a wicked smile in his direction, one gold tooth shining through his combed moustache. His salt-and-pepper hair was pulled back from his meaty face and he wore a new leather cocked hat that he had most likely purchased with Kane's gold.

Rove was not alone. Behind him, a boy followed his every move like a shadow. While his ivory freckled skin painted his youth, he stood almost as tall as the *Bonedog* captain. The boy glanced at Kane, blank of any expression. Beneath his mop of curly auburn hair, his eyes of gold glimmered in the sun, like two drops of stardust had kissed his face. Kane had never physically seen a witchblood since most remained in the southern kingdom of Terran. No number of stories could have prepared him for those startling golden eyes and the magic gifted by the earthen deities the Terrans worshipped, but he tilted his head to the side and tried to look unimpressed with Rove's new boy-shadow. Kane's gut twisted. Parading his newest capture in front of Kane was Rove's full intent, as sickening as it was.

"Where are all of your little friends, Blackwater?" Rove asked, the rasp in his voice creeping up Kane's spine. If a snake could talk, it would sound like Rove. The *Bonedog* captain knew Kane didn't keep *friends,* but he would remain unrippled by Rove's taunts.

"They couldn't make it," Kane replied with a shrug. "Said something about how they'd rather die a slow and painful death by mermaid venom than have to see your ugly mug."

Rove didn't respond but his moustache twitched.

"Who did you pay for the witch boy?" Kane asked, keeping his face empty as a blank page. With a wave of his hand, Kane dismissed his lingering crew members. They wandered into the crowd, some of them drunkenly stumbling as they struggled to stay upright.

"The Ruin Witch," Rove answered, plopping into the wobbly chair across from Kane. The boy stood closely behind. "And who said I paid her?"

"The Ruin Witch? Csilla Abado said she gives nothing for free." Kane swirled his finger around the edge of his goblet, contemplating whether to grip his hidden knife under the table. Csilla never lied.

Rove rested his elbows on the wood between them and leaned forward. "She did not give. More like . . . I took. But she didn't put up as much of a fight as I thought she would. She practically gave him to me. Made the trip to the Lost Isle much easier than it could it have been." His voice quieted as he hunched even farther over the table. "She controls the trees—I swear it. I heard their whispers and saw their snaking vines. The witchbloods really are blessed by the earth gods."

A dark thought crept into Kane's mind. *Would have been nice if one of those vines had looped around your neck.*

Kane took a swig of his wine to drown out the curses rising to his tongue. "How hasn't he killed you with his magic yet? He looks like he wants to. *I* want him to."

Rove chuckled as if Kane had made a joke. "See that 'round his neck?"

A bronze band rested on the boy's collarbone. It didn't look out of the ordinary.

"Bought it off a trader in Sarva. Cursed by a different witch. Keeps him under my control. Cost me quite a bit of gold too." A smug smile twisted at his lips. "Before you get any heroic ideas, it can only be removed with magic."

Kane sighed. "Why are you here, Rove? What do you want?"

Rove wrinkled his brow, feigning confusion. "Why, I'm here for Rathborne's funeral. Same as you. Always so accusatory. Perhaps this is why the others haven't accepted you yet?"

Kane slammed his goblet on the table. Wine spilled over the edges and dripped onto his hand. "Why are you *here*? At my table. Why aren't you with the rest of your Bonedogs?"

Pushing his elbows back, Rove leaned back in his chair, making himself more comfortable, although Kane was sure he made it very clear that the rival captain wasn't wanted anywhere *near* the table.

"I just want to talk," Rove said lightly. "I have a deal for you."

Kane narrowed his eyes. "Don't waste your breath. I want nothing more to do with you or your filthy gold. You may polish it clean, but you can't scrub out the stench of you."

"You might change your mind after you hear what I have to say."

Kane thought back to their previous transactions—the bodies he'd tossed into the sea, the men he'd silenced in the shadows of the night, the grisly secrets he'd kept all for gold, all to rebuild the *Iron Jewel* into the glory he remembered as a child. But he was trying to do better now—be better. Those days were over and he'd paid back his debt.

Rove took Kane's silence as a chance and cleared his throat. "I need you to put down two women in Port Barlow. I'll make it worth your while in gold."

"I don't want your gold." Kane stood abruptly. Slamming his hands down on the table, he leaned forward. He enjoyed the way Rove shrank into his chair, his moustache quivering slightly. The man may swim in jewels, but his wealth couldn't buy him bravery. "I paid back my debt. I want to be free of you." Kane glanced at Rove's boy-shadow, feeling regret for his choice of words.

Rove glanced over his shoulder and hushed his voice. "You do this for me, and I'll keep my distance."

Tempting.

"Two women?" Kane asked curiously. This was different. Although Rove was inherently greedy and a bad man in general, killing women wasn't frequently a part of his plans. "Why?"

"Not your business, Blackwater." Rove combed his fingers through his beard. "But I can see you're torn. Is your stone heart crumbling? What would your father say of your weakness?"

Kane was two breaths away from launching himself across the table and damning any ounce of respect he might have gained from the elder pirates. While he'd rather see Rove dead, he also didn't want to be known as the loose cannon, exploding at any given moment. Respect was earned. Another time, another day.

"So serious," Rove grumbled. "Fine. I'll say my final piece. The Trials will start in one moon, and I know how badly you want to win—how badly you want to beat *me*. But you won't have the chance to do that if those two women still breathe."

Rove was right about one thing. Defeating him would be more gratifying than becoming the King of Bones and wearing the Bone Crown. But there was more to Rove's answer. Something hidden within his cryptic wording.

"Why are they so important?" Kane asked. "What do they have to do with the Trials?"

"You're getting nothing more from me." Rove pushed his chair away from the table, nudging the boy behind him. "If you're interested, I'm staying in the guest quarters. Come at nightfall—alone—and we will discuss further."

Kane didn't accept or decline the invitation. He decided he'd see where the wine and the wind took him. If he made an appearance, it would be for information—nothing more. The last thing he wanted to do before the Trials was find himself tangled in another one of Rove's webs, especially if it meant murdering innocent women.

Cheers erupted from a few tables away, cutting the silence between the two captains. Kane glanced at the group. Two men had their elbows on top of the surface, both of them straining in an arm-wrestling match. Others gathered around, tossing their bets on the table, coins clinking over the men's grunts.

Kane glanced back at Rove, but he was gone, sliding through the crowd like a snake in the grass. The boy followed close behind but dared to look over his shoulder at Kane. Their eyes connected, and Kane vowed he'd find a way to end Rove *and* free the boy of him.

Perhaps he *would* pay the Bonedog a visit.

—

Kane stood alone in the darkened hallway of the guest quarters. The celebration still carried on down in the courtyard. Music drifted through the open windows. The moon's rays shone a path of light down the floor like a long, illuminated rug.

He was a shadow against the wall, hiding in an alcove behind a sculpture of Talona, Water Goddess of Strength—which was precisely what he needed. Patience slipped away with each moment that passed.

A shadow twisted at the end of the hallway. Kane pressed his back against the wall, unmoving as footsteps echoed toward him. They fell closer and closer until they stopped and a knock on a door followed. Kane inched his head forward, peering over the shoulder of the statue of Talona.

Jarnis the Brute stood before a wooden door. His pale, bald head shone in the moon like marble. The door creaked open and light spilled into the hallway, only reaching up to Jarnis's abdomen.

At the sight of the traitor, Kane touched the jagged scar across his chest. It still ached in cool weather, when his skin tightened in a chill. Kane hadn't felt Jarnis's axe slice through his chest that day. He'd been dreadfully numb, wholly believing that the blow had been fatal and his lifeblood would stain the ship's deck. It was in the days after the duel that the pain began. It was a blur of fire and cursing.

Rove appeared next in the doorway. He motioned for Jarnis to enter the room, then stuck his head out into the hallway, glancing left, then right, before closing the door.

Damn.

He couldn't hear them from out in the hallway. He could try to listen through the door, but that would be too close, too risky. Then his eyes fell on the open window and the ledge on the other side of the ruffling curtains.

As quietly as he could, he dashed away from his spot in the shadows and shuffled to the window. He braced his hands on the frame and lifted himself onto the ledge, careful of where he placed his feet. Slipping the rest of his body through the window, he flattened his arm against the stone wall of the palace while still gripping the inside frame so hard he was sure the bones in his fingers would crack.

The wind whipped fiercer from this height, swiping at Kane's clothes, blowing his black hair across his face like a mask, making him wish he'd tied it back for the party. The music from the celebration below taunted him, begging him to look down and be suffocated with fear at the sudden realization that he was standing on a ledge on the outside of the damned palace. Truthfully, he was insane for doing this. One wrong move would mean his early death and a week's worth of scrubbing his bloodstains from the courtyard.

He closed his eyes, taking a deep breath before sliding his feet farther along the ledge. His stomach was pressed against the wall, his fingers digging for a hold that didn't exist. Just a little bit farther and he was able to grip a statue of a golden sea serpent that curled out of a groove in the smooth cream-colored stone.

Kane craned his head to see another open window just on the other side of the serpent. Slipping through the space between the statue and the wall, he inched closer, his ears piqued, his heart thrumming in his chest.

Then he heard their voices.

"Did he come?" Jarnis's deep voice rumbled.

Rove shushed him. "Lower your voice," he said quietly. "No, he didn't."

"I told you he wouldn't. He enjoys women too much to kill them."

"The man loves gold just as much. He would have made the deal had he come tonight." Someone shifted, knocking against something with their chair. Rove's voice was so quiet, Kane could hardly hear him. "With or without Kane, the Storms must die. The heir cannot be alive when the Trials begin. While I travel to Port Barlow, I need you to secure my claim at the Trials. Do you know the way to Crossbones?"

The men's hushed voices blended together as Kane's head struggled to stay afloat a whirlpool of secrets. He pushed back against the wall, the wind still whipping his hair around his face, the realization of what he just heard making it more difficult to grip the golden serpent.

Heir. There was an heir, and the Storms were still alive. Somehow descendants of the first King of Bones, the Captain of the Storm, still walked the earth. Throughout the years he'd heard whispered rumors in the Baltessan markets of a girl child whisked away under the mask of night, but he didn't realize they'd been any more than that: rumors.

The Trials were illegal—there was already a Queen of Bones.

If this heir knew who she was, if she announced a claim to the

throne before the Trials began, his desire to win wouldn't matter—
she would take the Bone Crown from him because of the blood
running through her veins.

His hopes and wishes gone, just like that. With what he knew,
though, he could either make them disappear or let Rove fulfill
his own plans—but what he couldn't do was sit around and wait.

CHAPTER SIX
CSILLA

Sarva

Mid-Redwind

Csilla believed there was beauty in the slum that was Sarva.

The buildings were shoddy, the roads were mud instead of dirt, and there always seemed to be a cloud of rain, but across the Coral Bridge, the island of Ravana was a stark contrast. The white buildings of the wealthy always glistened in the rain, taunting Sarva like a privileged elder sibling. But while Ravana shone like a diamond in the sun, Sarva was a hidden gem.

As Csilla made her way to the tavern on the corner, her boots splashing through puddles, she peered into the open market stalls that lined the street. She'd already purchased a new, handcrafted wind chime for the window of her cabin from one vendor and a crate full of ceramics from another. The scent of savory pork hash from another stall was enough to make her want to throw all her gold away on just a small bowl of it.

The biggest difference about this market, compared to the markets of Incendia, were the people who walked the streets. Csilla passed by an abnormally tall man with black tattoos that wound around his arms, making him look like he had stripes. She saw a woman with a smoothly shaved head and plugs in her earlobes that stretched nearly to her shoulders. There were a few women who wore skirts like the Incendian women, but there were others who wore trousers like Csilla and the other Maidens, and a man who donned a wig and skirts of his own.

Sarva made Csilla feel free, which was why the crew lingered on the rain-shrouded island for a couple of weeks instead of heading for Crossbones the moment they'd received the message from Lockhart. Soon, when she was tired and bleeding during the Trials, she'd be wishing she was back here.

Csilla stepped inside the tavern, removing her dripping overcoat as she made her way to an empty table near the wall. She draped her coat over the back of an empty chair and gave a small wave to one of the barmaids who'd served her before. Csilla watched the door as she waited for Rhoda and Nara to arrive, but she was served a short glass of rum before they made their entrance.

Csilla took a long swig of rum, letting its warmth run down her throat as if it would soothe all of the broken things inside of her. She wasn't one to lie to herself—she had demons she needed to face, but she'd face them when she was ready. There was no reason to pretend her life was devoid of all obstacles. There was no sense in fogging over every dark piece of her like they didn't exist.

But maybe the rum would clear it all for just one, small moment.

Csilla gagged. She swallowed again, trying to clear the taste from her mouth, and pushed the cup away with one finger. The liquid bravery didn't settle well with her anymore. Not since that night with Flynn.

"Aren't you too young to be drinking, girl?" a voice scratched in her ear. She'd chosen this specific tavern to avoid drunken imbeciles. They usually confined themselves to the western side of Sarva.

There was no legal drinking age in Cerulia, but this didn't stop some from sneering at Csilla about her presence. If she'd been a boy, the man wouldn't have even asked her the question.

"Turn around and walk away," Csilla said without looking in his direction. Unease slithered up her spine. He stood to her left, on her cursed side, hidden from her. If he'd been on her right at least she'd know his size based on his shadow.

The man chuckled. "I don't take orders from little girls. Why don't you run home to your mother?" He was suddenly so close— his voice in her ear, his stench surrounding her.

Csilla whipped around to face him. Her blood boiled hot not only because of the line he'd crossed, but because she'd let him get so close without seeing or feeling him. She hated that she was blind to it. And he'd spoken about *her mother*.

He was just as she imagined—greasy, balding, missing teeth. His cocky smile faded when she looked him in the eye. She made sure he was watching her when she skillfully unsheathed one of her hidden blades and pointed the tip against his stomach. "Insult me again and I'll gut you from navel to nose like the pig you are." The blade became a feather that she lightly traced up his chest. "It would be so easy." Her voice was so smooth that even she believed her lie.

The man's throat bobbed as he backed away.

"A wise decision," Csilla said, nodding. "Although, my hounds will be upset they won't have a meal tonight."

Color drained from the man's face as he gulped down a long, shaky drink of his ale. Without taking his eyes off Csilla, he set his empty cup on the table then stumbled to the door.

A stool scraped against the floor and Csilla shifted to the sound. Nara sat down at the table, her smoky eyes watching Csilla curiously. Her silky black hair cascaded over her shoulder as she glanced over at Csilla.

"When did you buy hounds?" Nara asked, arching her eyebrow.

"I didn't," Csilla replied. She tucked her knife back in its leather sheath at her back. "Where are the twins tonight?"

"Serafina found a merchant who sells some special fuse for the smokers they've been making." Nara took a long swig of ale, then tucked her hair behind her ear. "Rosalina is visiting that rich pretty boy in Ravana who owns all the trader ships in the east dock."

Csilla smiled at how different the twins were, almost as different as her and Rhoda.

"You were much more gracious with that lard than I would have been," Rhoda chimed in as she took her place at the table. "I'd have ended the ass the first step he took at me."

Heat crept up Csilla's neck. She should've done the same, if she had seen. If he'd lunged to attack her, she wouldn't have been able to defend herself. This hole in her armor was a blow she couldn't ignore.

If she could hardly defend herself against an old drunk, how could she expect to win the Trials, where she'd be battling against the greatest pirates of Cerulia?

"Csilla?" Nara asked, her voice dropping. "Is something wro—"

"I'm fine," Csilla cut in, looking away from the two pairs of eyes that tried to see past her facade. She didn't need or want their pity. She'd brought weakness on, cursing herself more than the Ruin Witch's magic that had taken the sight from her eye in the first place.

She would continue to tell her Maidens she was fine. It was her job as captain to be fine, even though she wasn't.

But maybe there was a way she could be.

—

Returning to the Lost Isle was not the brightest of ideas. The fog blanketing the surrounding waters only made her nerves twist tighter in her stomach. Somewhere inside the mist, the Lost Isle rested in front of her, just as mysterious and intimidating as the first time she'd set her eyes on the overgrown vegetation.

Legend told of a glorious past back when the isle wasn't lost, when it was called Alannis; a joined city between Cerulia and Terran, the southern earth-worshipping kingdom—two kingdoms living harmoniously together on one island. If Csilla looked close enough between the treetops, she could see the marbled ruins of the city lost to the ancient war between the gods and goddesses. Bits of faded white marble peeked through the sea of jungle, greeting Csilla like an old friend.

"We shouldn't have come here," Rhoda whispered at Csilla's side. "Your last visit didn't end so well."

Rhoda was right, as always. The last time Csilla had traveled to the eastern island ruins, almost a year ago, she'd come alone in a desperate last attempt to save her mother. Not wanting the Maidens to know the truth of her frequent ventures to the witch who dwelled in the mist and tangled vines, she saved face, and lied to the Maidens, claiming the Ruin Witch had cursed her blind for stepping foot on the Lost Isle. Any display of weakness was as good as a curse in front of the women who still debated which Abado sister would have been a better captain. Even though she'd been their captain for three years now.

Csilla shivered, but not because of the chill in the air. Rhoda gripped her shoulder, a clear attempt to try to ease some of the weight she was carrying, but the anchor still lingered. Csilla shrugged away from her and wrapped her arms around herself.

Flynn's impeccable shot with a pistol would've come in handy if dealings went sour during this stop. Truthfully, she wished on the smallest of stars that she'd forced him into captivity while she had him kneeling under her blade. She would have appreciated his support before—before his betrayal, before she became captain, before burdens piled on top of her in heaps. A time when they had been friends. Friends who argued more than anything, but friends nonetheless. Perhaps it had been a mistake to let him go.

She shook her head clear of him.

"The pressure of the Trials is too much for you." Rhoda stepped closer, her arm brushing against Csilla's. "Let me help you. Let me take some of this responsibility from you before it smothers you."

Where had this compassion been when Csilla had been named heir? She briefly wondered whether Rhoda's concern was genuine or if it was a ploy to steal the captain's sword from the belt at Csilla's waist. She remembered the day she'd held the blade for the first time, the day that everything changed.

Her flesh had healed from that day, but *she* hadn't. Not fully.

Csilla was sixteen at the time, Rhoda nearly twenty. Anyone with sense would have placed their bets on Rhoda to win. Hell, Csilla knew she was in for a beating the moment the words left their grandmother's mouth.

The old woman, with eyes of steel and a glare that could make a grown man tremble, ordered Csilla and Rhoda to the middle of the deck amid the surrounding Maidens. As she leaned forward, bracing herself with a cane that was used more for bruising than walking, she gazed at them both, then nodded.

"My granddaughters," she said, her voice thin and raspy from years of shouting commands across her ship. "You have both proven yourself to be extraordinary Maidens. With my time in this world closing, one of you must take my place as captain of this ship, this crew, and this legacy."

Beside Csilla, Rhoda raised her chin.

"Every ship has their own way of choosing their captains," their grandmother continued. "The Bonedogs buy their way to the wheel. The Sons of Anaphine elect their leader. And like the Blackwaters of the *Iron Jewel*, our ship is passed down through our bloodline."

Csilla glanced at her sister then. Rhoda was on the verge of smiling, the corner of her lips curling slightly. Csilla knew Rhoda would be named captain. She was the eldest, after all, and she deserved it. Rhoda had trained harder than any recruit Csilla had seen. During training in the capital, she'd beaten every recruit in hand-to-hand combat, including the boys, and pummeled any-one who teased Csilla, the youngest and smallest one present. Rhoda even threatened Flynn for not keeping his eyes where they belonged, which was off her sister.

"But unlike the Blackwaters," Csilla's grandmother said, drawing her attention back. "I will not name my heir as the eldest successor."

Silence.

Even the waves were quiet.

"What?" Rhoda asked, her quiet question a shout among the hushed Maidens.

"Instead, you will duel."

Surrounding Maidens gasped, but Csilla didn't. She'd forgotten how to breathe. She found Nara's gaze across the circle, her friend already watching her closely. Even though Nara's face held no expression, her obsidian eyes held a sadness in them, even a subtle fear. The twins stood close behind her, their faces identical except for Serafina's, chewing her mint leaves.

Csilla expected a flurry of curses from Rhoda and demands as to why their grandmother made this decision, but Rhoda was silent as she stared across the space between them and their grandmother, her jaw muscles working beneath her skin.

"Grandmother," Csilla said, her mouth suddenly dry. "You want us to duel?" Perhaps she'd heard her wrong.

"Yes," she replied. "As captain of the only all-female crew on the Sister Seas, you will face much adversity and with it, you must have strength. So, which one of you is stronger?"

Rhoda answered by sliding her sword from its sheath at her waist. Csilla's face went cold. Her sister backed up before she charged forward, allowing Csilla time to draw her own sword and block the first strike. The crowding Maidens backed away, the circle growing wider as the two of them clashed in the center.

Csilla pushed against Rhoda's steel, the tip of her sister's sword coming dangerously close to drawing blood at Csilla's cheek.

The fear that clenched Csilla's gut in that moment was unlike anything she'd ever felt. She'd been scared of losing her frail mother for years, dreading the hole that her death would carve into her heart. She'd been intimidated by recruits during sparring sessions. But as the fire in Rhoda's eyes burned hotter, Csilla's blood pumped cold, making her hands shiver and her teeth chatter.

Would Rhoda really hurt her if it meant becoming heir?

Csilla received her answer when Rhoda pushed forward, sliding her sword down and slicing Csilla's right thigh. She nearly dropped her sword at the searing pain, but if she let that happen, only more fire would come. So she gripped the hilt with everything she had and raised the cutlass just in time to block Rhoda's next blow, her hand aching at the tremors that shot through the steel and into her bones.

Again and again Rhoda struck and Csilla could barely keep up.

She could have fought back. She could have raised her sword in an offensive stance the moment their duel commenced. But she didn't—she wouldn't.

Bleeding from her leg, arm, and the back of her hand, she stumbled away from Rhoda, nearing the edge of the circle of Maidens. With the strength she had left, she lifted her sword above her head and threw it down onto the deck. The clatter stopped Rhoda dead in her tracks. She froze midattack, her blade glinting against the sun as it hovered above her.

"I will not fight you," Csilla said, her voice weak and shaky. "I *refuse* to fight you."

"Don't you dare back out," Rhoda whispered harshly across the space between them, as if her words were only for Csilla to hear. "Fight me. *Please*." Her gaze was desperate, begging for Csilla to give her a chance to prove her strength to their grandmother.

But Csilla made no move to retrieve her sword.

"Fight me!" Rhoda screamed. Csilla had always envied the angles of her sister's face, the way the sun would shine on her cheekbones. But on this day anger darkened those features, making them sharp and cruel in a way Csilla had never seen.

"Csilla," their grandmother cut in. "Why will you not duel?"

Every pair of eyes latched onto her, trying to see past the armor she wore, trying to witness the turmoil that ravaged inside of her. But she would not let them see her for what she was—a little cub among fierce wildcats. Her chin wobbled, and she clenched her jaw to force it to stop. With a deep breath, she answered her captain's question.

"Rhoda is my sister," she said, her voice sounding like a damned child's. "She is my blood. I will not fight her for a title or a ship. Make her your heir. Let her be captain. It's what she wants more than anything. It's what she has trained for her whole life. But I will not spill the blood of one I love for power."

Rhoda's rage-fueled glare softened at Csilla's words. She lowered her sword slowly, breathing a sigh of relief.

Their grandmother watched Csilla closely through narrowed eyes. Csilla was sure she'd made the biggest mistake of her life when she opened her trap, and would be punished for it with the cane her grandmother gripped.

"Csilla Abado," her grandmother said. "Daughter of Soleil Abado. Youngest descendant of the Abado bloodline. You have disobeyed a direct order from your captain."

Csilla braced herself for whatever punishment her grandmother saw fit, and her pain would be witnessed by the rest of the Maidens to make an example. Loyalty was one of the

Scarlet Maidens' most important morals. Not even family of the captain could drift by without punishment. Csilla just hoped it wouldn't hurt too bad.

"But in your defiance," her grandmother continued, "you've proven more strength than I thought you could muster. It is in you that I see our legacy flying high above the other ships' flags. It is in you that I see the next captain of these women. I state you, Csilla Abado, as my successor."

It was then that Rhoda unleashed a flurry of screaming curses, some that Csilla had never even heard before. And when her fury finally subsided enough, she spoke, her voice on the edge of cracking, her eyes filled with unshed tears.

"I've been strong for you, Grandmother." Rhoda wiped furiously at her eyes with the back of her hand. "I've trained night and day. I've put in more work than any other woman on this ship. I've become a weapon—for you! I am what you made me!"

"Your hard work does not go unnoticed, Rhoda." Their grandmother's voice was eerily calm. "But strength can be defined in many ways. Csilla is strong where *you* are weak. You let your emotions control you, until it is no longer you who makes the choices, but your rage and jealousy."

"I . . . I . . ." Rhoda fumbled over her words, her gaze flicking to the deck, then back to their grandmother. "I apologize for my rashness." She wiped again at her eyes, then the tears stopped flowing and she breathed in deeply through her nose, composing herself once more.

Rhoda clasped her hands behind her back and bowed her head toward their grandmother. Only Csilla was close enough to hear her mutter, "It should have been me," before she turned on her heel and walked away. The Maidens parted, letting her pass, their faces a mixture of disbelief, pity, and in some, a hint of anger.

It was weeks before Rhoda would look at Csilla, and it took the rest of the frostfall season for her to acknowledge her presence. But when their grandmother passed into the After, only two moons after she'd declared Csilla her heir, Rhoda buried her contempt and acted as if the duel had never happened. They were all each other had left. Better to stick together than let tides of jealousy keep tearing them apart.

Rhoda never asked for forgiveness, but she didn't have to. Csilla forgave her for her faults regardless.

And now, as both of them stood at the railing of the ship, Rhoda watched her with pleading eyes, waiting for Csilla's reply to her offer of bearing the burden of responsibility.

Csilla's responsibility.

"*I* was chosen, Rhoda." Csilla would have gladly given her older sister the reins before. "It has to be me who competes in the Trials if I want any one of those men to truly respect me."

"I know, little cub." Rhoda draped her arm over Csilla's shoulder and pulled her close. Her deathlike grip allowed no wiggle room. "I just don't want to see you die is all." Even though there seemed to be a slight disappointment in Rhoda's tone, Csilla ignored it.

She didn't reply as she gazed into the fog-shrouded canal that rested in the split between two cliffs. The jagged edges pushed in on her, suffocating her already—and she hadn't yet left the safety of the *Scarlet Maiden*. Vines dangled like the ropes that had been looped around her neck a couple of moons ago. "That's why we need an upper hand," Csilla assured her sister, but truthfully, she said it more to herself.

Rhoda dropped her arm from Csilla's shoulder and gripped the rough wooden rail. "They underestimate us. That's *our* upper hand."

"Think about Blackwater and his crew, or Flynn and his. Rove's Bonedogs could easily wring our necks. My ankle still aches. I'm half blind. What am I against them?"

A fragile bird facing one hell of a storm.

"Are you finished?" Rhoda asked, giving her a shove. "That must be the most ridiculous thing you've ever said, Csilla." She crossed her arms over her chest. "Listen. I'm only going to say this once, but Grandmother chose you as captain for her own reasons, even if I don't necessarily agree with them." Of course, she didn't. She paused for dramatic effect. "But I can't deny that I have seen some good things coming about since you took the reins. Not as much as what I could've done, but that's beside the point."

"I did nothing but step in after Grandmother passed away." Csilla turned away and headed to the dinghy attached to the port side of the ship.

Rhoda quickly followed behind her. "You're right. You didn't do much at first, but your lack of discipline gave us the freedom *she* never did. You let me practice my daggers whenever I wanted, and encouraged Rosalina and Serafina with their experiments. Thanks to you they created those smokers that helped with your escape. And Nara actually smiles sometimes. She *smiles.* All of it, all of who we are and the threat we are to those men—it's because of you, even if it bothers the shit out of me. Just think what it could mean if we, a crew of young women, won the Trials? If we had a pirate *queen.*"

Csilla let Rhoda's words sink in as she fiddled with the ropes that lowered the small dinghy into the water. She couldn't allow

Rhoda to come with her; if she did, she'd learn the truth about Csilla's weakness and how she'd really lost the sight in her left eye. Maybe Rhoda had a hunch, considering that she knew about the vials of medicine Csilla had received for their mother. Maybe letting her come wouldn't be such a bad thing in case the witch didn't like that Csilla kept returning, asking for more magic to be done in her life.

"You didn't always praise me," Csilla said before she climbed over the wooden railing and into the small rowboat. "In fact, I vividly remember you trying to kill me when Grandmother ordered us to duel."

A wicked smile curved at Rhoda's lips. "You can blame my competitive heart. I'm the eldest. The ship *should* have been handed down to me. Also, you were only sixteen and were the youngest proclaimed captain ever. I was jealous."

"Reasonable," Csilla said. "Can you lower me down, please?"

"Let me come with you." Rhoda gripped the rope so tightly that her knuckles whitened. Csilla's heart warmed as Rhoda's eyes glistened and she stuck her lips out in a pout.

She couldn't resist. "Fine. Get in."

Rhoda leapt over the railing and into the dinghy, making it rock back and forth with her sudden weight. "Thank you!"

"Don't thank me yet." Csilla cocked an eyebrow. "When we get back, you're peeling potatoes."

With a groan, Rhoda lowered them down to the water. "You'll be the death of me, Csilla."

Csilla smiled as she stood at the front of the boat and Rhoda grabbed the oars, rowing them away from the ship and into the unknown.

CHAPTER SEVEN
CSILLA

The Lost Isle
Mid-Redwind

It was too quiet as their boat approached the island of ruins and followed the narrow river that wound through the land, wild and unpredictable. The farther Csilla and Rhoda rowed, the closer the trees skirting their passage became. Thick moss-covered vines hung so low that they brushed Csilla's shoulders and made her duck so that she didn't get tangled in them. The element of earth was stronger here than anywhere else north of Terran, where the endless forests made a sea of their own.

Nerves bubbled like boiling water in her stomach, making it hard to sit still. Every instinct begged her to turn around and head back to the ship, but her heart told her that this was the right move. It was a gamble, but she'd been playing this game from the moment her grandmother placed the captain's sword in her hand.

The trees rustled to her left. Csilla whipped around to face the threat. There was no one there. The canopy above shook, leaves hissing with unspoken secrets.

"She knows we're here," Csilla announced quietly.

"How can you tell?" Rhoda's brow curved down in confusion.

Csilla pointed up. "They're whispering to each other."

Rhoda's face went pale as she tore her eyes away from the trees and to her boots. It was good she was scared. Perhaps she wouldn't be reckless.

They rowed a few more minutes, and Csilla thought she would burst from the tension coursing through her. She had visited the Ruin Witch many times before her last trip, and each time she had entered this place with hope. But now, as she came to the Lost Isle asking for something more than just medicine and healing magic, she feared the cost. Each dealing had cost her something—first, one of the dolls her mother had sewn, then her favorite sword, and the last price had been her left eye. Fear of the unknown ate away at Csilla like a rat clawing a hole through a wall. What would Rhoda think of the truth of her dealings with the witch? What would the witch ask for this time, and could she pay the price?

The river continued to narrow until a small dock came into view. The familiar sight of it raised the hairs on Csilla's arms, and though the air was thick with humidity, a chill swam down her spine.

The witch's curse rang through her head.

Sobel liitena shobenasku. Sobel miitesa jaharren eto.

Csilla never asked what the ancient words meant, but they were seared into her mind, repeating constantly during the darkest of nights.

The memory of that day twisted her gut once more. She

couldn't shake the memory of the Ruin Witch's stare alight with the dark magic, or how her own eye burned like fire as her iris faded into the white of the blind. The headaches from adjusting to her new vision were unbearable at first, but a merchant in Sarva had sold her an herb that helped ease the pressure in her head. It was the trauma of the spell that hurt Csilla most now, and that was the hardest problem to fix. And the worst part of it all was that she'd willingly given her eye. A weakness that couldn't be fixed—that's what Rhoda would say about it.

"You look like you've seen a ghost," Rhoda whispered.

Csilla blinked, realizing that they had stopped at the dock. The compass she'd been holding had fallen from her hands, and she hadn't heard its clatter at the bottom of the boat. She'd only heard the memories of the harshly spoken curse.

"Let's just get this over with," Csilla said, refusing to address her sister's concern. Rhoda followed her from the boat, the sound of her unsheathing her sword ripping through the air. "*Shh!*" Csilla chided, not wanting the trees to tell the Ruin Witch anything about a pirate wielding a sharp sword.

They didn't need to trek very far into the jungle to be lost among trees with trunks thicker than the masts on the *Scarlet Maiden*. Behind Csilla, Rhoda forged a path with her sword, hacking at shrubs and vines, but Csilla gently pushed them aside, not wanting to anger the plants—or worse, the witch. Telling Rhoda to lower her sword was worthless. Csilla would only receive a growl in return.

They pushed through the last of the suffocating vegetation and into a narrow clearing. To their left stood a small shack, not much bigger than the one in which she and Rhoda had grown up in Macaya. A garden stretched between the home and the edge of the trees. A fire pit sat closest to them, the flames extinguished, smoke rising from the ashes. So many things—the scent of the burnt wood, the thick humid air, the songs of birds in the canopy overhead—reminded her of home, of Macaya, of her mother, and the grave that Csilla couldn't keep her from, no matter what she'd given up.

"You must be a fool to come back here, Csilla Abado."

The lyrical, female voice sounded from behind them, making both Csilla and Rhoda spin around. Rhoda pointed her sword at the greenery, ready to attack. But Csilla remained still. She knew the voice of the Ruin Witch all too well.

The witch emerged from the shade of the trees and into the sunlight of the clearing. Despite the many years, the witch's cream-freckled skin seemed ageless. It was as if she remained young while the world around her withered. Her golden eyes were always startling, no matter how many times Csilla saw them. All witchbloods had eyes of gold, but the Ruin Witch's were the only ones that shimmered when she moved. Her red-gold hair was twisted into a mess on her head and a scarf woven of green and amber kept any strays pulled back from her face, revealing the depths of her hollow cheeks.

Csilla stopped and took in a breath. "Were you following us?"

"Your sister is so achingly loud," the Ruin Witch replied. "I was curious if she looked anything like you or your mother."

"But you knew we were coming," Rhoda butted in, making Csilla cringe. "So why waste the effort of tracking us?"

"Rhoda," Csilla cut in. "No more."

"I will answer her question, Csilla," the witch said before turning her attention to Rhoda. "I didn't waste my effort on tracking you. I just wanted to see you for myself *before* you opened that mouth of yours." The Ruin Witch touched the tip of Rhoda's sword with her sharp fingernail and pushed the blade aside. "Let me just say that I prefer you with your mouth closed." She brushed past the two of them and left the trees behind.

Csilla watched her go. Perhaps there was a chance they'd get the help they needed here. That small shred of hope melted away the bitter, cold fear that had iced her veins.

The inside of the Ruin Witch's home was just as cluttered as Csilla remembered. Shelves spilled over with vials of different colored powder and liquids, the feet of animals, and assortments of candles, bowls, and pots. A fire lit the hearth at the far edge of the shack, filling the small space with a spicy aroma. Csilla's stomach growled in response.

"What brings you back to the Isle of the Lost, *Captain* Abado?" The Ruin Witch settled herself in a chair draped with a tattered Incendian Navy flag. Csilla briefly wondered how she'd gotten it and if any men had survived. The witch's long fingernails tapped the wooden armrest as she watched Csilla. "Are you not content with the last gift I gave you?"

"The last thing you gave her was a blind eye," Rhoda cut in. "You call that a gift? I'll give you a gift. I'll take my sword and shove it right up your—"

Muffled sounds of protest replaced Rhoda's voice. Csilla spun around to see her sister with wide, panicked eyes and lips that would not open. Heart pounding in her chest, Csilla turned back, ready to confront the witch. She shouldn't have let anyone come with her. Especially Rhoda, who could never keep her mouth shut. What was Csilla thinking in bringing her here?

Rhoda moved to attack the witch, but magic was faster than might. Csilla blinked and a knife from the cutting board flew across the room and stopped before Rhoda. The tip of the blade rested dangerously close to her eye.

"Don't worry," chided the Ruin Witch. "It's only temporary. As soon as she leaves the Isle, she'll be able to unseal those sharp lips of hers, even though it will hurt like nothing she's ever felt. But if she moves again, then so does the dagger." She shot Rhoda a warning glare. "Now, let us continue. Just the two of us this time. I see you haven't told your sister the truth about your eyesight."

"There's nothing to tell," Csilla replied. Rhoda's eyes burned holes into her back, but she refused to turn around.

"You can lie to your sister, but do not lie to me, girl." The Ruin Witch narrowed her gaze. Her fingernails stopped tapping. She stilled as if waiting to see what Csilla's response would be next.

Was this a test?

Csilla remained silent for a moment, thinking of what she should say. She did not want to offend the witch or anger her in any way that might make her take something else from Csilla. She sorted through the possibilities of what the witch could do to her. She might take her other eye or her sense of hearing. Maybe she'd rip her heart out of her chest or even worse, she could curse her with a death so painful even the gods and goddesses would shudder.

"I did not lie about the curse," Csilla answered, deciding to be honest. "But I did not share the details of our last meeting."

"And why not?" The witch arched one eyebrow.

"You know why." Csilla glanced back at Rhoda.

"When you take from the earth, you must give something in return. It's how my magic works. It's how all witchblood magic works. You cannot fathom the things I gave to the earthen deities for the power I have. Your sister should know what you gave." The witch waited, head tilted in anticipation. Finally, Csilla nodded and the witch continued. "Each time you came to me, begging me to aid your frail, sickly mother, you paid." She looked past Csilla to Rhoda. "Your sister eventually sacrificed her eye for more time with your mother." Her gold eyes returned to Csilla with force. "Even then, it wasn't enough, was it?"

Csilla clenched her jaw and took a deep breath through her nose. "My love for my mother was a weakness. I needed to remain a strong leader for my crew. Instead, my weakness let them down. So many doubt us, and we need strength now more than ever." As she said it, Csilla resisted the urge to tug on the scarf covering her damaged eye. "*I* need strength." She had to prove to Rhoda that their grandmother didn't make the wrong choice—she needed to prove it to *herself*.

"It's never enough with you pirates." The witch's voice raised, echoing around the small shack. "You take, and you take, and you take because your towers of gold coins will never be tall enough to satisfy the greed that festers inside all of you. You may not be conquering lands like the Incendians, but how long until that begins, I wonder."

Nerves bubbled under Csilla's skin, making the hair on her arms stand on end. "I *was* grateful. I still *am* grateful for what you did for my mother. If it wasn't for you and your magic, she would have died many years before she did." Csilla first came to the Isle when she was fifteen, hands trembling the whole time while she traded one of her mother's handcrafted dolls for a vial of murky liquid that strengthened her mother's bones. But it was only temporary. Csilla had to give more each time she visited.

"You should have just let her go, Csilla Abado of Macaya." The Ruin Witch leaned forward in her chair, bracing her elbows on her knees. "Your greed lured another captain here. One so selfish and cruel that the trees curled their branches away from him. He came onto my land with his crew and he took my Borne."

Csilla remembered Borne. He was a beautiful boy who had always begged her to play with him when she'd visited the witch. He had to be around thirteen years now, and it made Csilla sick to think of the gentle and kind witchblood being taken against his will.

"I could have stopped them," said the Ruin Witch quietly, as if it was a dark, delicious secret she was telling. "I could have melted their flesh and blown their bones into the wind like ashes. It would have cost me much, but I could've done it. You see, I had to let my Borne go. I've seen his fate and it lies at Crossbones." Her voice faltered. "I have the power to do amazing things, yet I had to watch them take away one I love. Do you know how that feels?"

"I do not know what that feels like," Csilla answered. "But I do know what it feels like to stand by, helpless." She hoped the Ruin Witch might pity their connection. "Sometimes what we do isn't enough. Sometimes fate wins this crooked game of life and death."

The Ruin Witch's eyes sparkled again at Csilla's words. "I've read *your* fate since we last met, Csilla. If you follow the path, you will be rewarded."

"Rewarded?" Csilla cocked her eyebrow skeptically. "How?"

The Ruin Witch swatted the air, and Csilla felt the sting of a hard slap against her cheek. She shut her mouth and rubbed her face as the witch poured out even more cryptic words. "You cannot know your fate to follow the path for there is no map. You make your own path with the choices you make, and you shall receive the reward you reap. Some choose the shaded passage, like the man who stole my boy, his mind clouded with dark desires. His fate will not be kind."

"Who was it?" Csilla asked, her voice cold as steel.

"Dominic Rove."

The name didn't surprise her, but the mention of him was still enough to set her insides ablaze. "Are you certain? Rove?" Csilla spat out his name like a bad taste. The man was a coward. What gave him the gall to step foot on the Lost Isle?

"Do you take me for a fool?" The witch cocked her head.

"Why would he take Borne?" Csilla mumbled to herself. "It doesn't make sense. Rove is only interested in gold."

"Dominic Rove wants what he doesn't already have. He may be a mess of a man, but he is as cold and calculating as they come. He was one of the only few who knew Rathborne had a daughter somewhere out in the world."

"A daughter?" Csilla's eyes grew so large she feared that they might fall right out of her skull. The reality of the various revelations came crashing down. Csilla knew that behind her, Rhoda was cursing up a storm on the inside, the magically hovering dagger keeping her silent.

"Not just a Rathborne daughter." A sinister smile spread across the lips of the Ruin Witch. "But also the daughter of Genevieve Storm."

Csilla's throat suddenly felt dry. Her voice scratched when she spoke. "That means . . . that means . . ."

"She is the truest heir since the original Storm bloodline."

"How?" The question spewed from Csilla's lips like vomit. "How do you know this? Who else knows?"

The Ruin Witch shrugged her shoulders. "I do not know what others know. I only have knowledge of what the trees have whispered to me. Come closer, Csilla. I do not want the wind to hear and carry out these secrets to the rest of the world."

Csilla released the wood table from her grip and stepped forward. She came toe to toe with the witch and crouched in front of her, looking straight into her golden eyes among her sea of freckles.

"The world is trembling with flame and darkness again. If it is not stopped, it will devour the sea and all of us along with it. *Cerulia will fall.* A sinister and blazing fire has reawakened because of the girl, and it will do whatever it can to end her. I see inside of you. I know the real reason you want the throne, but there is too much at stake—it *must* go to the true heir. The sea needs her. The Sea Sisters need her. And she needs *you.*"

"Me." The room tilted as Csilla's face grew cold with sweat. "Why me?"

Rhoda's muffled yells grew but Csilla and the witch ignored her.

"For the same reason I helped you with your mother. For the same reason your grandmother named you as her heir instead of the loudmouth back there. For the same reason that I allowed you to step foot on the Lost Isle again. Consider it a part of your path to fate."

"My ankle is shot to hell, and I can't see out of my left eye." The memory of the pain sent a shiver down her spine. "Why would you have any faith in me?"

"Soon you will view your curse as a gift. Does it not help you gain awareness of your surroundings?"

It makes me weak, is what Csilla wanted to say. "Yes, I suppose you could say so," she half lied. "I rely on my hearing much more than I used to, even if I'm still horrible at it."

"Good," the witch said with a rueful smile, as if she knew the guilty thoughts that ran through Csilla's mind. "You need to not only be careful of your surroundings—you must be careful of those around you, even the ones to whom you think you could trust your life."

Even with her lips bound, it was obvious from Rhoda's grunts that she thought this was all a farce. The witch's eyes darted behind Csilla to glare at her. "Even blood can turn against blood when power is involved."

Csilla wanted to defend Rhoda. She was her blood and Rhoda would never betray her, but crossing the Ruin Witch was too much of a risk. The witch was aware of Rhoda's history—she was aware of *everything*, it seemed. But the witch didn't know Rhoda like Csilla did. She hadn't heard the way Rhoda had cried for days when their mother had finally died or how she'd helped take care of the wounds she'd caused during their duel. Csilla trusted Rhoda with every fiber in her body and a witch's cryptic words wouldn't change that.

The Ruin Witch rose from her chair. "Now I will answer your burning question as to whether or not I will aid you in the Trials."

Csilla held her breath, leaning forward on her toes as the witch held her answer in front of her like meat dangling in front of a beast's mouth.

"It would be cheating," came the witch's answer.

Muffled protests sounded once more from behind Csilla.

"Let me finish, Rhoda," cackled the witch. "It *would* be cheating, but I'm not one to follow the rules."

She reached inside the pocket of her amber-colored dress and fished around until she found what she was looking for. When her hand revealed itself again, from her fingers dangled a white feather attached to a golden hook. As the feather spun, light reflected from it like the sun sparkling on the sea. Csilla watched it spin, the walls of the shack shrinking around her the longer she looked.

"Do you know what bird this feather is from?" the Ruin Witch asked as it shimmered between her fingers. When she received no answer, she continued. "It is from the zhacia."

"The bird is just a myth," Csilla replied in disbelief. Rhoda used to tell her scary stories about lava monsters when they were kids, but sometimes, when she was in a pleasant mood, she'd tell about fantastical creatures like the zhacia. The zhacia were hunted for their eggs, which shone like jewels, but what good were their shimmering feathers? *If* the witch had found a real zhacia.

"According to Incendia, I am also just a myth." The Ruin Witch gave a rueful smile, then held the feather higher. "I prepared this earring this morning when the trees told me you were coming. You want to be as strong as your grandmother believed you to be. So take this and see for yourself. As long as you wear this feather, luck will come your way when you are most in need . . . but its magic will run dry."

"What's the catch?" Csilla asked.

"Catch? I don't know what you mean."

"You said yourself earthen magic only deals in payment. When I use up the magic and all my luck is gone, what will I lose?"

"That's not my decision to make. Ask yourself if this is a risk you're willing to take."

If she didn't snatch the opportunity, Rhoda would scold her for it later, and something inside her wanted to take it regardless of the consequences it may hold. This feather could be the thing she needed to propel her into the greatness that was expected of her—not this half-blind, hobbling version of herself.

Csilla stepped forward. She held her palm open, and a knowing smile curled at the Ruin Witch's lips as she placed the feather in Csilla's palm. Somehow, it was cool against her skin. She curled her fingers around the softness of it, and let her gaze trail back up to the witch's golden eyes.

"Protect the heir. Should she choose to claim her birthright, there will be some who refute it. Some will try to kill her. *You* might want to kill her for the power she holds. But hold your blade for the ones who mean to turn this world into a blaze of fire and its shadow."

"How will I know who she is and when she needs me?" Csilla asked, wondering if this was just a trap to take more away from her. "You've told me nothing else about her, except that she is a Rathborne and a Storm."

"You will know when the moment comes, the decision that you must make. Consider this the start of your path to fate, Csilla Abado. Which direction will you take?"

"I plan to take the throne for myself," she answered, hoping her sister heard her. She carefully tucked the feather earring into her coat. She straightened her spine and kept her voice calm and steady even though her heart was on the edge of bursting from its cage. "If the girl should need my protection from this darkness you speak of, I'll offer my blade, but the throne is mine and will belong to the Scarlet Maidens." Hopefully the heir stayed hidden long enough for her to take the throne. It was the only way to prove her strength.

The Ruin Witch nodded, a wicked gleam in her eyes. "Just remember who your real enemies are, Csilla Abado."

CHAPTER EIGHT

KANE

Iodeia's Belt

Mid-Redwind

Kane stood on the shores of one of the many small, wild islands in Iodeia's Belt, with his boots in the sand, staring out at the sea. The breeze ruffled his hair and blew his leather coattails, but he remained still. Calm and collected on the outside, but a raging storm on the inside. He'd made the crew anchor off the shore of the island, despite their curses and groans. His feet needed to be on steady land so that he could think clearly. So there he stood, motionless at the foot of the tide, a flesh and bone statue in a vividly moving world.

Even though Kane had grown used to the rocking motion of the sea, he couldn't stomach the sway when his mind was a flurry of jumbled thoughts and choices. Just when Kane thought he'd have the upper hand in the Trials with his strength and brutality, the realization of a secret heir turned every coin on its head. It was just his rotten luck.

He remembered his father's luck and how grand it was, how he could scavenge the smallest trading ship traveling from western to eastern Incendia and find a small case of rubies worth more than three *Iron Jewels*. It was when Kane was around that Castor Blackwater's luck seemed to run dry, and Castor thought of Kane as a curse because of it. *A black spot of a Blackwater*, he'd always say before thwacking Kane on the back of the head. Even after his father died, Kane found he could still disappoint his old man in some way. Kane often felt the presence of Castor's narrowed eyes watching him during every choice made, especially now, as he debated his next course of action.

The *Iron Jewel* could sail west and arrive at Crossbones with plenty of time to prepare and for Kane to select a first mate to compete in the Trials. Or they could sail east toward Port Barlow and he could stop Rove from murdering two innocent women. Entangling himself in Rove's mission to silence the heir was not on his list of priorities, and being a hero wasn't something rooted in his nature, but there was a tug inside him that pulled him toward Port Barlow. Perhaps it could be his first true step away from the shadow that followed him.

The men of the *Iron Jewel* scoured the jungle behind him, searching for fresh fruit to bring on board when they set sail again. There was nothing like sweet nectar after days of potatoes, salt beef, and hard biscuits. But Kane made no move toward the trees.

A peculiar sound traveled on the wind, a scent of faded embers lingering with it. It was so faint Kane hardly noticed it at first. Soft like a whisper, yet harsh like a hiss. Kane glanced over his shoulder, supposing a snake or spiked lizard had crept up on him from the jungle. But there was nothing to be seen except the pale sand.

Odd.

The sound continued to rise in crescendo, and Kane looked in every direction but found nothing. Then he noticed the sinking black spot in the sand to his far left. He'd thought it was a rock the first time he'd glanced at it, but now he could see that wasn't the case. The sand seemed stained, as if it had been burned.

Suddenly, it moved, rippling out like water.

Kane stepped back, his eyes widening as the black spot rose up and down, as if it was breathing. With each rise, the stain reached farther, spreading like wine on cloth, stretching as wide as the deck of a small merchant ship. He realized then, the sound he heard was not a whisper or a hiss; it was the sizzle and pop of oil against a fire.

Then came the screaming.

It rose from the jungle, from the direction of his men. Kane whipped toward the trees. Thick black smoke rose between curved trunks and vines. Birds flew from the canopy up to the sky. He smelled more embers now that the wind blew in his direction. Kicking up sand behind him, he ran in the direction of the jungle, hoping his men were okay while wondering what had started the sudden fire.

The stretch of beach in front of him blackened, blocking his path like a slash made with an ebony sword. The toes of his boots buried themselves in the sand as he came to an abrupt stop. His knees remained bent, his hands splayed at his sides, ready to defend himself from whatever witchcraft the burnt sand may be.

This had to be another one of Rove's tricks, another deal he'd made with a witch.

His men's screams continued from the jungle and Kane refused to let them die while he stood idle. He took a few steps back, ready to make a leap over the stained sand. Then the grains of sand rolled away as fiery magma emerged from the depths below.

Kane froze, watching with his jaw slack as a figure took shape in the molten lava: a head, shoulders with thick arms, and a body that stood taller than any man Kane had ever seen in his travels around the world, at least the size of two men.

The manlike creature stood still, yet moved. The lava pulsated a blazing orange, hardening, cracking, and fissuring again. Obsidian formed plates of thick armor along its body and a long sharp spear slowly grew from its arm. Two eyes looked down on Kane, emptier than a moonless sky, darker than death, more hollow than a man without a heart.

No. It couldn't be. Yet there it was in front of him, more terrible than he could have ever imagined.

A molten man.

These creatures had been created by the Brothers of Flame, the three gods of fire and destruction, during their ancient battle against the Sea Sisters. The molten men were nightmares made real, lava come to life, mindless puppets of fire and destruction. With the help of the first Cerulian king—the Captain of the Storm—the sea goddesses vanquished the fire gods and imprisoned them in Limbo thousands of years ago, and all the elemental deities had been sleeping since, cutting their connection to the mortal world. The molten men should have disappeared with them all.

What kind of troubled waters were brewing if these creatures and the gods and goddesses had returned? Kane didn't have time to wonder. He unsheathed his sword and gripped its hilt tightly with both hands. Kill and destroy first. Solve riddles later.

Blackwater.

A dark whisper lingered in his mind. A shallow rasp filled his every breath.

SSSon of the Iron Jewel.

"Who are you?" Kane asked. He watched the molten man carefully.

I am the flame. I am the warmth of thisss world.

Kane blinked. Not the answer he was looking for. "What have you done to my men?"

SSStay away from Port Barlow. Do not set sail for Incendia. Let the heir die or I'll ssslaughter them all. The voice dripped with malice, surrounding Kane, pushing in on him from every direction. *Join me and I will ssspare their livesss. The Bone Crown can be yoursss. You can rule over your tiny sssea kingdom. Anything you desssire, I can give it to you.*

Kane's fingers wrapped even tighter around the hilt of his sword. "I am the captain of the *Iron Jewel*, and I will be bought by no one." Not anymore.

The air seemed to still as the molten man began to move again. Its empty eyes turned to slits and the molten lava beneath its obsidian armor glowed brighter than before. Its jaw unhinged as it unleashed a roar that made the ground below Kane's feet tremble.

But Kane did not retreat.

He raised his sword and took one step closer.

Then the molten man stormed toward him, leaving scorched footsteps in its wake. Magma flung off it in droplets, the sand sizzling where it landed.

Kane met the creature's first strike with his sword, stopping the creature's spear from stabbing a hole right through his face.

He'd thought his blade would slice right through its arm, but the place where steel met obsidian shell was hard as stone.

Stepping back, Kane sliced from the left and scraped against the molten man's side armor, leaving only a faint scratch as proof of Kane's attack. Then he aimed for a crack in the armor along its arm, but when his blade met the magma, his sword only came away smoking. A moment longer and the steel would've started to melt.

Worry wasn't a feeling Kane would say he was accustomed to. He brazenly faced his obstacles, doing whatever he believed he had to do for the betterment of himself and the *Iron Jewel*'s legacy. But as the molten man attacked again and the clash of his sword on stone echoed over the tide behind him, worry was like a blanket that smothered him on a humid sunspur night.

There was nothing he could do against this creature.

Again the molten man advanced and again Kane deflected it. The scrape of his blade against its armor raised the hairs on his arm. It would be a sound that would haunt him—if he left the island alive, and if he was lucky enough to survive, he swore he'd make that first step toward the light. He'd chase that idea of doing better, being better. He would put aside his vendetta against Rove and he'd do what he could to save the heir. She certainly held some importance to this fire god, and if he wanted her dead, then Kane wanted her alive.

Saving the heir meant saving them all. Living was suddenly as dire as breathing, but with the invincibility of this creature and the sea behind him it seemed his chances of fixing the wrongs he'd done in this world were slipping through his fingers.

If he died here, he at least hoped the tide would carry his body out to sea.

Then a realization hit him so fiercely he almost stumbled back into the water. Why hadn't he realized it before? The Captain of the Storm hadn't defeated the molten men with his steel; he'd used his goddess-given magic to vanquish them.

The tide rose, washing at his ankles. Kane glanced down at the water, clear as a glass bottle. He took another step back, then another, until the tide was halfway to his knees and his pants were soaked. The molten man lumbered after him. When the edge of its foot met the waves, a faint sizzle split the air, followed by an ear-splitting screech. Smoke plumed from beneath the creature as it retreated to the safety of the beach.

Now Kane could have his fun.

He dipped his sword into the sea as he went on the offensive once more. Weakened from the water, the creature could not get away quick enough. Kane planted his feet in the sand and swung low. Droplets of water flew from the steel of his blade.

The molten man roared as Kane's sword sliced clean through both of its legs as if the Sea Sisters had blessed his blade when the water touched the steel. A furious hiss scratched its talons down the walls of Kane's mind as the creature toppled onto its side. Behind it, the jungle was in flames, his men only ashes in the wind now. *May the air goddesses guide their souls back to the sea.*

The creature's screech carried over the crackle of the jungle fire as Kane went back to the tide. He dipped his sword into the water and turned back to the molten man crawling away from him, a streak of blackened sand in its wake. The stumps of its feet crumbled into ashes, blowing away like snow in the wind.

You haven't won, the voice in his head whispered weakly. *The heir will die. She will fall and when the lassst drop of blood leavesss her body, I will rissse. Incendia will fall to its kneesss before the one they worship, and when we conquer the SSSea SSSisters' pearl of Cerulia, you will be the firssst one I come for.*

"Not if I can help it," Kane said as he lifted his sword above the broken molten man. Water dripped down his hands. "But if the day comes, I'll be waiting for you." Arcing his sword through the air, he brought the blade down on the molten man's neck, separating its head from its body in one effortless swoop.

The fire in the jungle was suddenly extinguished like the wick of a candle, but the scent of burnt wood and charred flesh still hung on the breeze. Kane swiped his forehead with the back of his hand and turned his gaze toward the eastern horizon, knowing where the sea would take him next.

CHAPTER NINE
LORELEI

Port Barlow

Late Redwind

Scoundrels.

Thieves.

Pirates.

Whispers danced through the harbor, drifting on the sea winds as Lorelei strolled to the docks. She'd expected the hushed words to be about her mother and the last time she'd shown her face, but they were not.

The farther she pushed through the bustling crowd, the more she noticed all eyes pointed toward the sea. As Lorelei tried to peer around the crowded area, she nearly dropped the fresh wheat rolls she'd made to sell to the docked sailors, and she didn't dare waste a single one of them—money was hard to come by now that her mother hardly left the house. Her mother's rolls were softer, but instead of kneading dough each morning like she used to, she only read through the piles of old books by her bedside, swatting Lorelei away anytime she tried to come close enough to see what her mother was so engrossed in. Grasping the basket handle tighter, Lorelei rose to the tips of her toes, hoping to see over the heads of surrounding harbor-folk.

If she could just glimpse the colors of the sails, she would know. Anything other than white would mean her suspicions were true: pirates had come back to Port Barlow.

If the sails were red, the ship belonged to the *Scarlet Maiden*, the swiftest vessel on the Sister Seas. Lorelei once heard a sailor say the crew's founding captain had dyed the cloths with her victims' blood. Lorelei knew better than to believe every tale she heard, but she still hung on to the magic of the myths from across the sea.

Gray sails would belong to the *Wavecutter*. The magicked steel on its bow was whispered to be able to cut through the layer of ice on the Frozen Gap during frostfall. She wasn't sure if the stories were true but seeing the ship with her own eyes would be *something*.

Blue sails would belong to the *Anaphine*, named after one of the Sea Sisters, and one of the only ships stocked full of heavy shots. Lorelei had never seen a ship with guns, but perhaps today was the day.

The crowd parted like the curtain before a show, only the sight before her deflated her excitement.

Her stomach dropped, the basket of rolls almost falling with it. Her face went cold. There wasn't just one ship. There were two. And the sails weren't red or blue.

One had sails the color of rich cocoa. Its masts and railings were etched with gold, on its flag an emblem of two crossed bones with a blade cutting down through its middle. The wealthiest crew on the seas, the *Bonedog*—it had to be.

The other ship had sails darker than a starless night and wood like shadows. The *Iron Jewel*. Why the fresh hell were harbor-folk still milling about? Did they not realize? Were they purposefully acting clueless to not draw attention to themselves?

She found herself searching the crowd for Luis, forgetting that he'd left for the Incendian capital for training with the rest of the soldiers. The trading harbor of Port Barlow was left defenseless and vulnerable.

Lorelei's heart thumped quicker in her chest as she took a step backward, her eyes locking on the black sails she'd heard many stories about. This crew wasn't like the others she'd fantasized about as a child, staring out at sea, waiting for the day when she would have a ship and crew of her own.

Lorelei had never seen the rest of the world, aside from the visions in stories, but it didn't take much to know good from evil. When she looked upon those black sails, it was as if evil had reached out and touched her with its scaly, dirty fingers.

She should've darted for the farm the moment she heard the whispers of pirates. Luis said nothing good came of them. She knew she should be running, so she wasn't sure why she stood still and stared. *Why am I so fascinated by them?*

Her thoughts cut short when she saw what could only be a pirate.

His footsteps echoed across the wood as quiet harbor-folk shrank away from him. Lorelei's gaze first fell on his scuffed leather boots, then trailed up his loose trousers and the ornate belt that buckled at his waist. He wore a simple black waistcoat with a white blouse underneath, ring-clad hands clenched in fists at his sides. His hair was dark and pulled away from his face by a black scarf, but a few black strands remained in front, nearly long enough to brush against his angled jaw. He looked young, yet his eyes and the set of his brow made him seem as if he'd seen more than any old man in the harbor, maybe even in eastern Incendia. She avoided eye contact with him as his gunmetal glare traveled across the harbor with unnerving thoroughness.

He must have been searching for the rest of the pirates, wherever they were. He was the only one to be seen. Perhaps the rest were smarter than this one and were being more inconspicuous.

Lorelei briefly wondered if had the soldiers been present, would they have arrested him on sight or would they have provoked him? They'd never issued a public address on Csilla Abado's crime and the harbor-folk had been too swept away in their gossip to notice the oddity, which meant the Incendian soldiers had to have arrested the *Scarlet Maiden* captain at night when there were no witnesses to cry foul play. With all the harbor-folk out today, odds were the soldiers would wait until the pirate was alone before making their move, *if* any of them returned before the pirates set sail again.

She flicked her gaze over the *Iron Jewel* and the *Bonedog*, watching for movement, for hints of where the remaining pirates were. Nothing. Only sails flapping and ropes swaying in the wind. Either they were all hiding belowdecks, waiting to be investigated and to launch a sneak attack, or these were ghost ships. The last thought seemed unlikely.

When Lorelei turned her gaze back to where the pirate on the docks had been, he was gone. *Damn.* She'd let her mind wander too long. Perhaps her blue eyes weren't the only thing she'd inherited from her mother.

She shouldn't have even wondered where he'd disappeared to. She should have quickly sold the wheat rolls in the basket she still gripped and headed home. That's what her mother would want her to do. If she knew that Lorelei had lingered in the harbor while two pirate ships were docked, she'd lose her ever-loving mind—what was left of it anyway.

As curious as Lorelei was, it was best if she moved along. She shifted toward the fishermen grouped at the other end of the boardwalk. They were huddled close together, whispering to each other, taking turns glancing across the way. Following their line of sight, she spied the pirate slipping through the doors of the harbor's tavern.

Again, she should have gone on her way. She should have forgotten about the reappearance of pirates. But curiosity won, as it always did with her. It pulled at her like a string that she couldn't cut.

Turning away from the fishermen, she hurried across the boardwalk and onto the dirt path, lifting her skirts as she avoided the mud puddles. She took a deep breath before stepping through the door and into the tavern as a group of men exited hastily.

Tobacco smoke immediately burned her eyes and scratched at her throat. She fanned the smoke away from her face, then quickly stopped and gripped the handle of her basket again, realizing she should be trying her best to fit in. The basket of rolls didn't help any. Glancing to her left, she noticed an empty table next to the door and set the basket down, making sure no one was watching her. They were all too preoccupied with eyeing the pirate who'd made himself comfortable at the bar.

The surrounding men and barmaids kept their distance, as if he was a plague they'd catch. The man tending the bar, Gregor, had his rag inside a mug, scrubbing like there was a stain that wouldn't come off, refusing to glance at the pirate in front of him. Gregor wasn't one of Lorelei's favorite folk in Port Barlow, and for some reason, she liked him and his scraggly hair even less now.

Lorelei took a step closer and leaned against a wooden post. Half hidden, she looked on, growing more and more curious about what the pirate's intentions were, regardless of the supposed danger she was putting herself in. For the first time she felt the thrill of excitement. She debated moving closer to see if the feeling would expand.

The tavern was so quiet that she could hear him clear his throat. Gregor had to have heard him, too, but he continued to ignore him. When the pirate slammed his fist onto the bar, Gregor stopped scrubbing the mug, his gaze slowly trailing up.

"Can I help you?" Gregor grumbled.

"Pint of ale," the pirate answered. "A dark brew, if you have it."

Gregor tossed his rag back onto his shoulder. "My tavern doesn't serve pirates."

"Not even for gold?" The pirate dipped his hand into the pocket of his black waistcoat and pulled it back out, something shining between his fingers. He placed a few gold coins on the bar and slid them toward Gregor, whose eyes had gone wide. The pirate kept one coin, flipping it between his fingers and over his knuckles with such fluidity it could have been magic.

The barman glanced around his tavern at the harbor-folk who watched their exchange. Lorelei knew what he was thinking from the panicked look in his gaze. The folk might have new gossip to whisper about—Gregor, the bartender who accepted gold from a pirate because he secretly loved them and wanted to be one himself.

Gregor's hand hovered over the gold, and for a moment, Lorelei thought he would take it. But instead he pushed the coins back to the pirate. "Perhaps you should travel farther north. I hear the ice miners in Ventys don't mind pirate stench so much."

Gregor was more ignorant than Lorelei had thought. He should have taken the gold. With even that much he could have fixed up the tavern, patched the holes in the ceiling, and nailed down the crooked planks in the floor. The folk wouldn't whisper about him if they had a nicer place in which they could drink away their problems. Lorelei would have snatched up the gold in a heartbeat. She found herself wondering just how much gold the pirate had in his pocket and if it would be enough to buy her and her mother a way out of this harbor town.

Even the few pieces with which the pirate had tempted Gregor could afford Lorelei provisions for the bitter frostfall season. But not only had Gregor refused the gold; he'd insulted the pirate who now rose from his bar stool.

Up closer, the pirate was much taller than he'd appeared to be on the dock. He swiped the gold from the bar and dropped the coins back into his pocket.

Surprisingly, he did not react to Gregor's insult. "I'm searching for a woman by the name of Storm."

"Never heard of any Storms," Gregor sneered. "And even if I had, I wouldn't tell you about it."

The name felt strangely familiar to Lorelei, as if she'd heard it in an ancient story or song.

"Then maybe you can help me find someone else," the pirate proposed.

Gregor curled his lip in response.

"My ship is not the only pirate ship docked in this harbor.

There is another captain, one who would be much less forgiving about that ice miner comment of yours. Have you seen him? Wears his weight in gold? You can't miss him."

"No," Gregor answered. "Haven't seen him."

"Then I'll make my leave." He turned to leave, but Gregor's next words stopped him.

"And don't come back, *pirate*."

"The name is Blackwater," he replied. The change in his voice sent a chill down Lorelei's spine. "And I'll return for my ale later. I'll get it, one way or another."

Blackwater.

Lorelei remembered *that* name from the stories she'd heard. A bloodline of brutal men, the name of every captain of the *Iron Jewel.*

Gregor swallowed as Blackwater turned back around and stalked toward the doors of the tavern. As he neared, Lorelei's heart quickened. While she'd been focusing on their conversation, she couldn't ignore the fierce pull of the gold buried in Blackwater's coat pocket. It could change her life—her mother's life. Maybe she could find a doctor to rid her mother of the voices in her head.

With each step that drew Blackwater nearer, her blood pumped harder. Her fingers trembled at her sides. She could very well die for what she was about to do, but if she could make their lives better, then the risk would be worth it.

Biting her lip, she pushed away from the wooden post and stepped into Blackwater's path at the last moment. With no chance to react, he barreled into her. She slid her hand into his pocket as he caught her in his arms and they stumbled together. She dropped his coins into the pocket of her skirts as they regained their balance and he stepped away from her.

Blackwater's dark gaze locked with hers as he braced her shoulders and mumbled what might have been an apology. Then he hurried away, harbor-folk whispering in his wake.

A hand came to rest on her shoulder after the tavern door slammed closed, making her flinch. Lorelei turned her head to see one of the barmaids watching her with concern in her eyes. "Are you all right?" she asked, giving Lorelei's shoulder a squeeze. "I'm surprised he didn't knock you to the ground."

Lorelei couldn't remember what she mumbled in return to the barmaid because the gold was burning a hole in her pocket. As soon as she could, she slipped out of the tavern, forgetting about the basket of rolls she'd left on the table. She buried her hand in her pocket, fingering the gold coins, as she wove through the harbor-folk skirting the muddied path.

She couldn't reach the trail up the hill fast enough. When she finally breached the current of people, she took a breath of fresh air, then bounded up to the cottage. A breeze blew the long grass that grew on both sides of the worn path. The smooth waves that rolled through the fields reminded her of the sea, calm yet restless, as the skies above started to darken and the wind picked up.

Her heart still raced from her thievery as she burst through the door of their small cottage. She'd committed a crime for the first time, a crime against a pirate no less. She stopped two steps into the room. She'd been so blinded by the idea of what the gold could buy she hadn't even thought of the repercussions, besides death, in that moment. The pirate would likely hunt her down once he realized he was missing half the gold from his pocket. Then he would kill her mother while he made her watch. All the terrible things Luis had said about pirates moved to the forefront of her thoughts.

Lorelei was so deep in her mind, she didn't hear her mother asking where the basket was or what she was playing with in her pocket. It wasn't until her mother shoved her hand into Lorelei's pocket and pulled out a shining coin that Lorelei returned to the present.

She didn't have to explain where she'd gotten the gold.

"Pirates!" her mother yelled, dropping the gold like it was fire in her hands. The coin clinked and rolled across the floor. "They're here? In Port Barlow?" Her voice was shrill, on the verge of cracking. Her blue eyes were the widest Lorelei had ever seen them.

"Mother." Lorelei sighed, dropping to her knees to pick up the coin. "Calm down. Everything is fine. With the gold we can stock up for frostfall, or patch the holes in the roof, or both. We could even travel somewhere new. Maybe across the sea—"

"What color were the sails of the ship docked?" her mother interrupted. "Was there more than one ship?" She reached down and grabbed Lorelei's arms, pulling her to her feet. Her gaze was frantic, her cheeks reddening. "Who did you get the gold from?"

Lorelei's mouth suddenly went very dry as she observed her mother's panic. Her tongue twisted, along with her gut.

"Lori!" Her mother shook her shoulders. "What color were the sails?"

"Th—There was a ship with brown and one with black," she answered.

Lorelei thought she'd seen madness in her mother's eyes before, but that had only been a taste of it. Placing both hands on either side of her mother's face, she forced her mother to look at her. "Mother," she said softly. "Please, calm down. You're scaring me."

"And you *should* be afraid!" her mother yelled, gripping Lorelei's wrists and pulling her hands away from her cheeks. "He's found us. The fire must have led him here."

Lorelei sighed at the mention of fire. It was a false alarm. Just another one of her mother's fits.

But then her mother looked past her, to the window. Her breath caught, her eyes widening as her chin shook. A crack of thunder rattled the boards of the cottage. That was odd. The sun had been shining through holes in the clouds on Lorelei's way home.

"He's here," her mother whispered.

CHAPTER TEN
LORELEI

Port Barlow

Late Redwind

Lorelei's mother dashed to the rug in the center of the cottage, leaving Lorelei frozen with fear. In one swift movement, her mother threw the rug back to reveal a small door that led under the floorboards. They'd gone in only once, years ago, during another one of her mother's false alarms, and Lorelei didn't want to go back in there. Just the thought of the musty darkness was enough to make her skin crawl.

But her mother's desperation was different this time. The way her eyes glistened unsettled Lorelei's nerves. Unease crept up her spine.

"In," her mother demanded as she pulled open the trap door. "Quickly."

Lorelei didn't dare argue. She ran on her tiptoes, trying to be as quiet as she could, almost falling down the steps leading into the dark. She turned to help her mother in after her, but her mother didn't move from the door. Instead, she crouched, tears dripping over her cheeks as she looked at Lorelei.

"Aren't you coming?" Lorelei asked. Her voice trembled like she was cold, but sweat beaded at her temple. She reached for her mother, placing her foot on the bottom step.

"No." Her mother held out her hand and stopped Lorelei. "Stay quiet. Stay hidden. No matter what happens. Do you understand?"

She didn't reply, confused.

"Do you understand?" her mother asked again, more frantically. "No matter what happens."

Lorelei nodded weakly. Words left her once more as she tried to hold on to every thread inside of her so she wouldn't fall apart at the seams. This was no false alarm. Danger truly was on the horizon. Guilt knotted in her stomach for ever doubting her mother or the stories she'd told her.

Her mother paused for a moment, watching Lorelei's face as if she was capturing it in one of her paintings. "When you feel lost, my sweet Lori, follow the storm inside of you."

Lorelei bit back her tears, closing her eyes and listening as her mother shut the door and slid the rug back over it. Silent and waiting, just as she'd asked.

The door of the cottage slammed open, rattling the floorboards above her. Footsteps entered their small home like thunder ripping apart a peaceful night.

"Where is she?" a gruff voice asked. "Where is your girl?"

"I don't know who you're talking about." Her mother's voice trembled. "I live alone. I have no girl."

"Liar," he growled. A shadow swept across the cracks above her.

"Are you frightened? I can practically smell it. You're terrified."

At first, Lorelei had been scared that her ridiculous idea to pocket the gold had led the Blackwater to her home, but it wasn't his voice. It must have been the other pirate, the one Blackwater mentioned he was looking for.

"I recognize you, you know, from sixteen or seventeen years ago," the man continued, his shadow stopping in front of her mother's. "Don't you remember me too?"

Silence.

"Aye," he grumbled. "You remember."

"You can't forget a Rove," her mother hissed.

"And I certainly never forgot you, Genevieve."

Lorelei froze. He knew her mother's name.

"I know your secret," Rove continued. "You've hidden her. That would've been the smartest thing you could've done when you ran away. Or maybe you've sent her away. No matter. I will find her, and I will kill her."

Lorelei's rapid heartbeat was an ache in her chest.

"I have no daughter," her mother replied, her voice even and firm, unafraid. It was the clearest it had been in years.

"Liar." Rove's words became a low rasp. A sword unsheathed sickeningly slowly, raising goose bumps on her skin.

She wanted to burst out of the door. She wanted to scream for the pirate to take her and leave her mother alone. But she remembered what her mother had asked of her and she honored her word.

Her mother didn't beg. She didn't plead for him to spare her life.

There was a squish, like the sound of when her mother was cutting tomatoes for stew, then a thud against the floorboards.

As Lorelei gazed up, searching for answers to what had happened, something dripped onto her face. She touched the drop with the tips of her fingers and brought her hand down into a stream of light that flickered through the floorboards' cracks. She realized what it was.

Her mother's blood.

A cry rose in her throat, and she quickly slapped her hand over her mouth. She prayed to the Sea Sisters—Anaphine, Talona, and Iodeia—to keep her quiet, keep her still, keep her alive for the sake of her mother's sacrifice.

It was as if the goddesses heard her prayers. She was as silent as the falling snow. She was as still as the mountains. Despite the emotions ravaging like a hurricane inside of her, she stayed quiet and she stayed alive as Rove destroyed the inside of the cottage, searching for her.

The room above erupted with sounds of glass breaking and shelves falling, the ripping of curtains and the rumble of his boots stomping across the floor. It tormented her as she sat in painful silence. Then, after what felt like hours, everything settled as the clomp of his boots faded toward the door. He spoke once more, his sudden words chilling her bones.

"If you're in here, girl, I'll let the fire find you. If not, I won't stop searching the seas until your blood spills."

Then the cottage fell silent.

Lorelei's thoughts didn't linger on the meaning behind Rove's last words. Instead, she counted her breaths, waiting for the pirate to burst back in with his crew. But he didn't return.

She ran up the stairs and pushed against the trap door with her shoulder, the rug on top of it weighing it down. Gritting her teeth, she placed both palms against the wood and shoved with her legs until finally it opened a crack. She peered out, checking if the coast was clear.

Then she saw her mother in a puddle of blood.

"Mother!" she cried, heaving the door aside enough to crawl to her. She cradled her mother's head in the crook of her arm and brushed her hair away from her pale face. Blood soaked Lorelei's clothes, her hands, the tips of her long hair, but she didn't care. Her heart was cut into ribbons of memories and regret. The longer she knelt, holding her unblinking mother, waiting for her to come back, the more it hurt.

She couldn't breathe. She couldn't think. She couldn't open her eyes and face the brutality of this night and the damage it had reaped. What was stolen . . . and what she'd never get back.

She was alone in this world. Truly and utterly alone.

Then came a voice.

Loreleiii.

It was a shout in the quiet cottage, but now all she could hear was the crackle of the fire. Lorelei's spine straightened and her heart beat frantically in her chest. She held her breath as she listened, but nothing more came. Unable to shake the feeling that someone was watching her, she carefully rested her mother's head back on the floor and rose to her feet.

"Who's there?" she asked, her voice echoing in the small room. She curled her hands into fists to keep them from trembling.

She didn't want the voice to reply. She had her suspicions of where the whisper had come from. She glanced at the fire, which seemed to be bigger than she last recalled. Had her mother been right all along?

The fire sizzled faintly.

Its orange glow filled the cottage. The crackle grew.

Lorelei fixated on the hearth. Tendrils of flame snaked up with a life of their own and she stumbled backward.

A scream caught in her throat.

The fire grew higher and higher.

She needed to run but watched in horror as the flames licked up to the roof of the cottage, her chin wobbling, her eyes burning with tears.

The flames spread.

They devoured her mother's old paintings of ships and the seas they'd traveled on.

She blinked and their wardrobe was gone.

The life she knew began to turn to ashes and there was nothing she could do to stop the wildfire.

Smoke smothered the air, making Lorelei choke and cough. She fell to her knees, tears freely streaming down her face as she scrambled for her mother's still body.

If there was one thing her mother taught her, it was to never give up.

Lorelei pushed onto wobbly knees and bent over her mother. She grabbed her under her arms to drag her toward the door. The body didn't budge. Planting her feet again, she yanked harder, moving her just an inch. The small movement wasn't enough. She couldn't let the flames consume her mother—they had already taken over her mind. But there was no time. The window to save herself was closing quickly.

With a choking sob, she let go of her mother, bent down, and kissed her forehead. "Good-bye, Mother," she said, wiping a bloodstain from her mother's lips. No more of her mother's stories, no more of her dreamy sighs, no more of the soft pull of her fingers weaving braids in Lorelei's hair.

Lorelei pried herself from the floor and stood and ran for the front door of the cottage. She yanked on the doorknob, screaming in pain as the brass handle burned her hand. The flames pushed closer. They'd engulf her in seconds.

Fire brushed her arm like the slice of a sword, searing her skin. She gritted her teeth, ignoring the forming blisters, and grabbed the handle with the skirts of her dress. She threw the door open then tossed herself out onto the grass, choking on the fresh air. Her chest heaved up and down as she coughed and crawled away from the burning cottage and everything she'd ever known.

The flames roared behind Lorelei. The house creaked and groaned as the roof caved in, but she didn't look behind her as she continued to crawl away. Her arm ached like the fire was still there, burning her skin, but she still kept going. She didn't stop crawling until the grass turned to rock and the ground beneath her dropped away.

She was on the edge of the cliff.

Lorelei gazed over. Watching the waves crash into the wall of rock, she let their sound wash over her, drowning out the burning home and the memories of her mother that were vanishing with it.

A sob escaped from her open mouth. Digging her fingers into the ground, she curled in on herself, the pain of losing her mother hitting like a tidal wave, pummeling her over and over, until her eyes were raw and her throat ached.

This was her fault. She could have prevented this. She could have believed her mother's claims about the voices in the fire. The moment she'd seen pirates in the harbor she could have gone home and warned her mother. There was so much she could have done but hadn't.

Slowly, she lifted her head, letting her gaze trail over the waves that shone with the last bit of sunlight left in the sky. The water shimmered, glittering like the same gold pieces Blackwater had placed on the bar top.

As Lorelei's gaze trailed down to the harbor, something caught her eye. She squinted through her swollen eyes to see the brown sails of the *Bonedog* drifting away. Her heart went frigid. If she hadn't waited so long under the floorboards perhaps she could have snuck on board and stowed away. Then when night fell, she could have crept across the ship and slit Rove's throat in his sleep.

That chance was gone, but there was another ship still docked. The *Iron Jewel*.

What were the odds of Blackwater being docked on the same day as the *Bonedog*? He had to know something, and he didn't seem to have a liking for Rove. Maybe he would help her if she begged him to.

No. Lorelei was done asking permission. She wiped her raw eyes with the back of her hand. She had failed her mother once, and she wouldn't fail her again. The last thing her mother had told her was to follow the storm when she felt lost, and it was inside of her right then, a ravaging beast that needed to be fed.

With ice in her veins and blood in her eyes, revenge was a goblet of rich wine that she'd savor until the very last drop.

PART TWO

SILVER AND GOLD

CHAPTER ELEVEN
CSILLA

Crossbones
Late Redwind

The *Scarlet Maiden* had been the third ship to arrive at Crossbones. Csilla assumed they'd be the last, considering their detour to the Lost Isle, but two crews were still missing. Perhaps the *Iron Jewel* and the *Bonedog* had also sought an advantage like Csilla had, but it was odd that Kane hadn't arrived by now. With his ethics, she thought he'd be the first to arrive, his men already having made camp and training just to intimidate the other crews.

The voyage to Crossbones made Csilla wish they'd never stopped at the Lost Isle. Once they'd set foot on the ship and they were able to pull Rhoda's lips apart, a dark part of Csilla regretted that the curse hadn't lasted a bit longer. When Rhoda opened her mouth about something, she didn't stop until her tongue was dry. The heir was nearly all they spoke about at sea. Rhoda's barking arguments made Csilla cringe, yet her words held truth.

You're going to trust the witch who blinded you?

Who cares if she's a Storm?

This is our chance to finally rule these men. Don't let her take this away from us.

The constant hammering of Rhoda's opinion was enough to make Csilla want to scream. She was glad to be off the ship. Rhoda wouldn't dare talk about the Storm among the other crews because if an heir became known before the starting pistol shot, the Trials would be forfeit, even if the heir was a girl. The Cerulian crown officials would choose what happened then.

The zhacia feather hung from Csilla's ear—a weight reminding her of her promise and the Ruin Witch's words. She'd handled the earring with care when the witch had placed it in her hand. She hadn't worn it at first, and instead stared at it from her bed as it lay on her nightstand in her cabin. Then finally, she'd tried it on and decided she quite liked the way the feather shimmered flecks of light onto her jaw and neck.

Protect the Storm.

Consider this the start of your path.

Which direction will you choose?

Yet there Csilla was, still at the center, choosing neither course. What she really needed was to relax and focus on what was directly ahead of her. The heir wasn't at Crossbones. The witch said she'd know when the moment came and what she would have to do, and the only thing her gut was telling her was that she was hungry.

Rhoda and Nara flanked her sides on one of the logs around the fire. Serafina and Rosalina were off smoking stolen tobacco somewhere. Rhoda had been prattling on about something meaningless, which was why Csilla had escaped inside her mind, but then Rhoda reeled her back in.

"I heard the most interesting conversation while I was sharpening my blades earlier today," Rhoda said, lowering her voice with each word. "Jarnis the Brute was bragging to some lowly member of the *Wavecutter* about how the Bonedogs have sealed the win."

"Imbeciles," Nara sneered. Csilla had grown to enjoy her friend's company more than Rhoda's recently. She'd always admired Nara's skills with a bow and the deadly silence of her glares. If she trusted anyone else besides her sister to be her first mate in the Trials, it would be her.

"Did he say anything about where Dominic Rove is exactly?" Csilla asked. "And what about Kane?"

Rhoda groaned. "I hope Kane never shows up. He's so dreadfully serious."

"And you'd rather Rove make his appearance?" Csilla couldn't believe her sister's words.

"Will you stop questioning me? I'd be happy if both their ships sank—less competition." Rhoda lifted an eyebrow at Csilla. "I haven't even told you what I heard Jarnis say."

"Go on, then."

"The Bonedogs are going to attack the *Iron Jewel*. Heard Kane followed them across the Silver Sea with his own secret intentions and they're going to sink his ship so he can't make it to Crossbones. Who knows? Maybe he'll drown." Rhoda shrugged.

"Mutiny." Csilla hadn't realized she'd spoken so loudly, but her fingers were starting to tremor.

Voices around them hushed, eyes latching onto Csilla. Heat rose to her cheeks as she avoided their curiosity. She ignored them, looking down at her feet in the sand until conversation picked up again.

"The snake," Nara said under her breath, like she'd seen into Csilla's mind.

"We should stop them," Csilla whispered. "We could take them by surprise. They'd never see us coming and it would all backfire on Rove."

"Just let them sink each other," Rhoda replied, waving her hand dismissively. "That's two fewer competitors. You'd only have to beat Tomas Stone, who can barely keep his lips off his flask, and Flynn, who we can arrange an accident for." The *Wavecutter* was one of the sturdiest ships on the Sister Seas, yet had a drunk at the helm who could barely walk straight. Beating him alone wouldn't feel like winning anything.

Csilla's dinner threatened to creep up her throat, and her face grew cold. "There is no honor in that."

Rhoda scoffed and pulled one of her daggers out of her belt. She twisted the handle in and out of her fingers, the blade dancing in circles around her hand, yet she never cut herself . . . only other people. "Honor is earned, Csilla. If you lose the Trials, how much honor do you think you'll have then?"

"Grandmother always said honor is—"

"Who cares what *Grandmother* said?" Rhoda seethed. The glare from the fire sparked in her dark eyes. Then she shook her head, as if she was trying to clear it of something, but when she looked back at Csilla, her gaze was like troubled water, restless and unpredictable.

Csilla glanced away from her, breaking quickly under the tension. She cleared her throat before she spoke, her voice sounding much more feeble than her sister's. "I understand your strategy, Rhoda. However, remaining at Crossbones with the knowledge of another captain in danger does not sit well with me. Did you forget Kane is the same boy who sent us a crateful of fresh fruit and flowers when he heard of our mother's passing?"

The troubled water in Rhoda's eyes puddled at the mention of their mother, but then she blinked and it was gone, her sharp glare returning. "I don't trust him, and you shouldn't either. Do you even trust me?"

"Of course I trust you, and if you were in danger, I would come to your aid as well. The difference between you and me, however, is that I would help you before you were about to hang by your neck."

Nara sucked in a breath and the three of them sat in a silence as thick and heavy as their ship.

"Go ahead and do what you want, Csilla." Rhoda bared her teeth. "But don't damn the *Scarlet Maiden* in the process. Remember that I'm your *elder* sister, little cub." Her nickname suddenly wasn't as endearing as it had been when they were kids. "The only reason I'm not your captain is because Grandmother was jealous that I could be better than her one day."

"That's a load of rubbish." Csilla couldn't believe the audacity of Rhoda to speak ill of their bloodline, their previous captain. Rhoda had always been an envious person, but it was usually buried deep within her. She'd never been that outspoken before. "Any other captain would have thrown you overboard for your reckless entitlement. You should be thankful that I haven't."

"But would you do that?" Rhoda's gaze darkened. "Would you actually throw me overboard, Csilla? Do *you* have the strength and the guts to get rid of me if I say the word *no*?"

Csilla bristled at the question, finding herself unable to truthfully answer. "You don't want to help me, fine!" Csilla yelled, suddenly uncaring that other pirates' eyes landed on her. No choice she made was ever good enough for Rhoda, no thought was right. She couldn't sit still any longer. She had to move—she had to do something to clear her mind and decide what move she should make next.

Csilla stood abruptly from her seat, accidentally nudging Rhoda as she stood up. Rhoda said something foul as she walked off, but Csilla ignored it and kept going.

She stopped a little way from the fire and slipped off her boots. Holding them by their laces, she tossed them over her shoulder and continued to walk, letting the cool white sand sift between her toes. The full moon reflected against the sea, twinkling and shimmering like fine jewelry as the waves washed up to the shore.

"Beautiful, isn't it?" came a voice from behind her, making her stop and brace herself.

Csilla recognized Flynn's voice the moment he started speaking, her heart flaring with anger that he'd followed her. She'd heard his footsteps racing through the sand as he tried to catch up with her, but she hadn't turned around then and she wouldn't face him now. Seeing him in the light of the moon would be her downfall, and tonight was not a night that she could allow herself to fall victim to his beauty and charm. In another world, where the responsibility to prove herself didn't loom over her like a dark cloud, maybe she would have let herself succumb to him a long time ago. If she'd have allowed it, they'd have gotten together much sooner than they had, considering that Flynn had been flirting with her since they'd been children. He was practically a professional at this point.

"Are you following me?" Csilla asked, refusing to acknowledge his question. She hoped he hadn't seen her storm away from Rhoda. "I left the fire to be alone, not to be followed and pestered by you."

Then he was there in front of her. She hadn't sensed his presence drawing closer to her, which was terrifying. She couldn't let her guard down around him, especially since it had only been three moons since his betrayal. Taking a step to the left, she tried to dodge him, but he stepped with her, blocking the path.

"Drop the act, Csilla," Flynn said, his voice teetering on the edge of annoyance. "It's just you and me on this beach. Stop acting like you can't stand to be around me when we both know it's the opposite."

Csilla took a step closer so they were mere inches apart. She had to tilt her head to look up at him. Again, she thought back to the possibility they'd once had, the idea of what they could have been if she didn't have to hide her weaknesses like they were secrets. Love was a weakness in this world. The one moment she'd let herself give in to that warmth, she'd found herself with a noose around her neck.

A true pirate like her grandmother wouldn't waste time with this conversation. They'd gut the traitor on the beach and leave them for the vultures, but Csilla couldn't do that. Maybe she really was as weak as they all thought. "Once upon a time, you would've been right," she told Flynn. "But after what you did to me, I want nothing to do with you. Ever again." She bit out the last few words, hoping she made her point very clear, despite the way her heart sank when she said it. Csilla wished she could wipe herself clean of the part of her that still held on to him.

For a moment Flynn looked wounded, but then he quickly covered it up with that sly smile of his. "If you mean to hurt me with your words, then you should try harder."

Csilla let out a grunt of frustration. "You are so infuriating." She shoved his chest but he didn't fall backward like she'd hoped he would. "I can't believe that you even have the nerve to look at me. Do the others know you turned in a captain to the Incendian Navy? That the Scouts' hunt for me could lead them here? Incendian Scouts, Flynn. Men who move with unnatural quickness and hunt like wolves. There are whispers that some of them can even wield flame like those wretched gods they worship. What would the pirate fleet think of *that*?"

"You have no idea what really happened in Port Barlow, Csilla." The smile had fallen from his face. "Even if I said that I wasn't the one who turned you in you wouldn't believe me." For a moment, she believed the sadness in his sea-colored eyes, but then she remembered the way those same eyes had gleamed at her as she stood at the gallows with a noose around her neck.

"Then enlighten me. Tell me your story of woe, *Flynn Gunnison*. Tell me how, when I felt safe in your arms that night, you had intentions of betraying me the whole time. Tell me how the soldiers bullied you into giving me up, or maybe they paid you well." She stood on the tips of her toes, bringing her face so close to his that he would feel the livid fire on her breath. "Hell, maybe you did it just because you *wanted* to."

Flynn silently watched her for a moment with narrowed eyes, strands of his sandy hair wisping across his face in the sea breeze. "Would you even believe me?" His voice a whisper. A whisper she couldn't trust, but her heart wanted to. Then without warning, he grabbed her face and tugged her to him. His lips were molten against hers, warming her skin, heat spilling down her spine. She needed to pull away but she couldn't. She let herself melt against him.

Flynn was painfully correct. She didn't hate him, especially when his kiss crumbled down every wall she'd built around herself.

His hands trailed down her neck, over her shoulders, and grazed her hips. Wrapping his arms around her waist, he pulled her in so close that his warmth radiated from beneath his thin shirt. Csilla could easily rip the fabric and scrape her fingernails down his chest if she dared. The further Flynn pushed the kiss, the more desperate she became until she was standing on the edge of making a very dangerous decision—whether or not to pull him down into the sand with her and escape the madness of the world.

When Flynn groaned against her lips, a soft euphoric sound, she froze. He stilled in response, hanging on her last breath.

What was she doing? This was the same position she'd found herself in the night before she was captured. She wouldn't let him trick her again, despite the way his touch set her body aflame.

Csilla yanked herself out of Flynn's grasp. She stumbled backward into the sand, her legs still weak from the kiss they'd just shared. Flynn reached for her like she needed help. She slapped his hands away and rose to her feet.

He stepped forward. She stepped back. The never-ending dance of their relationship.

"What's wrong?" he asked, as if the complex question had a simple answer.

Csilla shook her head, remembering the first rip he'd left in her heart. "The last time you kissed me I ended up with a rope around my neck. You didn't just sell me out, you *betrayed* me. We were *friends*, and that night, I thought maybe we were going to be more. But you wrought hell down on me and this kiss is not going to change that. I have much more important matters to attend to."

"Please, Csilla," he begged. He took two steps. In one breath, he was right back in front of her. "Let's talk about—"

"I don't want to hear a word. You're everything that I don't need right now—a distraction." Csilla turned around, eyeing the fire in the distance.

Flynn caught her arm and pulled her back to face him. His eyes, which usually danced with humor, were now completely serious. "Don't leave."

Not sparing him another glance, she ripped her arm away from him and trudged off, feeling Flynn's eyes on her as she left.

Playing games with Flynn should be the last thing on her list of priorities. There was a captain who needed her help and another who needed to learn a lesson. She headed to gather Nara, the twins, and other Maidens who chose to stand by Csilla's side, at her back, wherever she needed them. Rhoda wouldn't follow and that didn't matter. If she failed to do her duty as first mate to Csilla, then she was replaceable.

There was still time before the starting pistol shot when the Trials began. If things went wrong, they could return in time to compete, but she couldn't allow Rove to get away with this. She might be too late, but her heart told her different—there was still a chance.

The feather earring in Csilla's ear warmed as she made her choice. It made her wonder: What would happen if she chose wrong?

CHAPTER TWELVE
KANE

Port Barlow

Late Redwind

Kane stepped out of the tavern in Port Barlow, his blood boiling hot with rage when he spotted the empty air where the *Bonedog* should have been. Impossible. He'd searched the entire town for Rove and his mutts but his hunt had come up empty, so he returned for the ale deprived of him earlier in the day. Either the harbor-folk were all as dumb as the fish they reeked of, or Kane had scared them silent, which he was used to. Perhaps he should try to smile more during a conversation, but right now he felt only like ripping out someone's throat.

It didn't help that half his gold had been stolen from his pocket. Although he suspected the girl he'd barreled into at the tavern, she'd seemed terrified at the sight of him, so he didn't think she'd have had the nerve to steal from a pirate. Then again, no one else had been close enough to attempt thievery, except for the barmaid who'd followed him around the tavern tonight, but from the way her gaze lingered on him, she was interested in something else.

A delicate touch caressed the bare skin at his neck. "Where are you going?" a soft, feminine voice asked. He hadn't told her he was leaving. There was no reason to, not when the only information this barmaid had was of a mad woman who lived up the hill above the harbor.

"I have more important things to attend to," Kane replied, brushing the girl's hand away. It found its way back to his shoulder.

What a waste of time this venture had been. He could've been at Crossbones, preparing his crew for the Trials. He'd lost a lot of men during the island fire, had quickly replaced some with a shoddy lot from Sarva in desperation, was running so far behind he might miss the starting pistol at Crossbones, *and* he hadn't even found this supposed heir. Things couldn't have gotten any worse.

Up on the hill in the distance, he thought he saw smoke rising into the air, but under the shade of night it was hard to tell. Kane briefly wondered if the fire on the hill and Rove's departure were connected. If Rove had butchered the heir, and if the whispers he'd heard were true, then the fire god would be rising soon, if he wasn't already walking the earth somewhere.

Kane had to warn Cerulia. He had to get to Crossbones as quickly as possible.

Just when he was about to brush the barmaid away from him again and set sail, something down the path caught his eye. A girl stumbled in the moon's shadow, as if trying to remain unseen. She could've fooled any of the harbor-folk, but not him. As she drew closer, he recognized her as the thieving girl from the tavern. But now her dark hair hung in her face and her clothes were torn and stained with something dark.

Curious.

"Who is that?" Kane whispered in the barmaid's ear.

"Who?" she asked, leaning in closer to him.

"That girl creeping around in the shadows?"

The barmaid squinted, then a smile lifted at her lips. "That's the mad woman's daughter. Seems that she's just as much of a mess as her mother after all."

Kane didn't know why, but something inside him told him he had to ask. "What is her name?"

The barmaid curled her lip at him like it was preposterous he'd even be wondering.

"Well?" he urged.

"I'm not entirely sure. I think it's Lorelei? Lorelei Penny?"

His heart sank a bit when the barmaid didn't say Storm or Rathborne, but there was a chance they were living under another name, hoping to remain a secret. Perhaps Rove had found them and had failed to finish what he started, which explained why the world wasn't on fire and also why the bewildered girl was now tiptoeing in the darkness toward the docks. Perhaps he *had* inherited just a sliver of his father's luck.

Kane shrugged away from the barmaid, ignoring her pleas for him to stay. Curiosity piqued, and he followed the girl, who kept to the shadows and hurried down the dock on her bare toes.

She stopped and glanced over her shoulder, the moon painting her as a bloody ghost before she realized she was out in the open for anyone to see. Kane quickly ducked behind a stack of crates, hoping she hadn't seen him. From the twitchy way she moved and her quick breaths, Kane knew she was terrified.

When her light footsteps continued down the wooden planks, he rose up, peeking over the top of the crates. She stopped at the last ship docked—the *Iron Jewel*. With one last glance at Port Barlow, she quietly climbed one of the foot ladders onto his ship.

Well, this will be interesting, he thought to himself.

When Kane boarded the *Iron Jewel*, he expected her to be there. He assumed she'd be standing there, crying, begging him to forgive her for her thievery and to help her, but she was nowhere to be seen. The few crewmen who had survived the jungle fire— the ones who'd stayed on the ship—said nothing to him of a girl with wide eyes and a scarlet-stained dress sneaking around on deck.

Perhaps she truly was a ghost. She'd vanished into thin air.

Kane rushed the men to leave port, despite their complaints of it being nighttime. If she was on the ship, he'd let her come to him. She had a reason for creeping onto his ship and he was curious to know why, hoping she was the heir so that Cerulia wouldn't fall to flame. Or perhaps if she'd had a run-in with Rove, she now had a thirst for pirate blood and planned to murder Kane in his sleep. In that case, he'd sleep with a blade under his pillow.

—

Lorelei Penny did not show herself the first night. Or the second.

Each day as the sun arced over the sea, his thoughts trailed to the thief. Every morning, he gripped the grooved handles of the ship's wheel tighter, growing impatient with the girl, and each night he fell asleep angry that she might not even be on the ship at all.

Finally, on the third day, he awoke to the sound of shouts.

"Let go of me!" a female voice screamed, followed by scuffling.

Footsteps shuffled past the door of Kane's cabin. He sat up straight in his bed, scratching his head groggily as the noise continued.

"There's only one thing we do with stowaways on this ship," growled one of his men.

The thief.

Kane threw off the bedsheets and hurried to the door, not bothering to pull on a shirt or his boots. He flung open the thick wooden doors, his line of sight following the noise to the starboard side of the ship. His men had hoisted a plank through the railing and were pushing the girl up onto it.

"Stop!" Kane yelled, bursting forward.

The crew didn't hear his shouts above their own. Imbeciles.

The thief now wavered atop the plank as Kane hurried across the deck. The wind blew her dark, coffee-colored hair, ruffling the sleeveless shirt and trousers that were much too big for her small frame. He briefly wondered what happened to her bloody dress and where she'd gotten the new wardrobe. Her fingers were stickier than he'd assumed. Along her arm an angry red line marked her skin like she'd been burned.

Kane pushed aside the rowdy men. "Stop!" he yelled. The girl turned to look him square in the eyes. He expected tears, but there were none; only dark circles rimmed her gaze. "Come down from there this instant." He held out his hand but she didn't take it. Instead, she brushed past him and climbed down herself.

"What were you lot thinking?" Kane yelled at his crew. The two scrawny brothers he'd enlisted in Sarva shrank away from him.

It was one of his few original crew members, Doan, who

answered, his voice deep. "I tried to tell them not to, Captain. But they insisted it was the code of the *Iron Jewel*. Stowaways walk the plank."

Kane glanced away from Doan at the surrounding men, some he recognized as his own crew among the new faces. "That code was abolished when I took the place of my father!" he yelled, ready to pummel them all with his fists. "Did any of you notice the state she is in?"

Kane could have pummeled *himself*. He should have searched for her and not let her sneak around the ship for this reason. Mistakes seemed to have become part of his routine.

"Luis *was* right about pirates," Lorelei said. "You're all rotten." The fierceness in her voice surprised him, and he suddenly wanted to know much more about this *Luis* and the lies he'd fed her. He watched her gaze travel down his naked chest and the jagged scar that ran across it, then up at his face.

Lorelei's cool blue eyes watched him from beneath knitted brows, as if she was assessing how much of a threat he was to her. When he cleared his throat, a blush blossomed across her fair cheeks. Acting like she hadn't just been staring at him, she stepped forward, stopping directly in front of the pirates who blocked her path. They moved aside, letting her pass.

"Wait," Kane called to her, nudging aside his crew and following her. "We must speak at once."

"Yes," she replied, stopping but not turning around to address him. "But first I—"

The blare of a horn in the distance cut her off. The crew went as still as a mast without sails.

"Was that a horn?" Lorelei asked, looking in different directions. "What was it?"

Kane growled in frustration, digging his hands into his hair. His men's panicked voices carried to him. "It's the sound of very bad news, Lorelei."

"How do you know my name?" she asked, whipping around to face him breathlessly.

"There's no time for that. Go to my quarters. Lock the door. Do not let anyone in but me."

"Not until you tell me what that horn was." Now, there was fear in those blue eyes. *Good.*

"The *Bonedog* is approaching." He turned away from her and to his mishap of a crew. He should've seen this coming, considering what he knew. "Someone get me my boots, my belt, and my sword. The rest of you—" An explosion filled the air and moments later the force of a cannon shell's impact brought Kane to his knees.

CHAPTER THIRTEEN
LORELEI

Where the Silver and Gold Seas Meet
Late Redwind

Lorelei had never heard a sound so earth-shattering. The boom of the impact ricocheted in her skull. The burn on her arm from the cottage fire had been aching moments before, but now, as her blood raced through her veins, her skin was numb to it.

Shards of wood flew overhead as Lorelei dropped to the deck. Already the air was thick with gunpowder and smoke, fogging her senses, bringing her mind back to the cabin fire just days earlier. Even though there was presently no fire, she could feel it on her skin again, that vicious whisper in her head, the smell of her home burning with her dead mother inside. Burying her face in her hands, she tried to escape it, but she was still choking, aware of the chaos around her yet locked inside the cage of her mind.

"What are your orders, Captain?" one pirate yelled. He was near her but he sounded so far away.

"We must retreat!" yelled another. "We'll be outnumbered in battle."

"No," Blackwater said, his voice muddled like he was behind a closed door. "Blackwaters never run from a fight."

Lorelei pulled her face from her hands and glanced up at the pirate. His black eyes were set on the horizon, his brow lowered, his lips pressed together in a firm line. The front of his dark hair nearly covered one side of his face while the rest was pulled back in a hasty tie. The scar that cut across his tanned chest was as jarring as a piece of gold in a pile of silver. He was as terrifying as every tale her mother had ever told, but the longer she looked at him, grounding herself in the moment, the more the world came back to her, the nightmare in her head slipped away, and she was able to stand up like the rest of them.

"They haven't fired another cannon," Blackwater mused, then turned to face his crew. "They mean to board us, not sink us. We still have time to surprise those sea scum!" He pointed at the tallest man. "Doan. Bring up a barrel of gunpowder and a lantern, and make sure it's still lit. The six of you, load as many cannons as you can on the port side and wait for my signal."

"What'll be the signal, Cap?" one asked.

"You'll know." Blackwater paused for a moment and Lorelei's gaze fell on his crew. The men only shifted from one foot to another, their faces scrunched in fear and confusion. "Why are you all dawdling? You new lot stand in the place of many brave men. The *Iron Jewel*'s crew is renowned for bravery in the face of battle and I will expect no less from you. Stop soiling your pants and *move!*"

The pirates scattered around Lorelei as she stood in the middle of the deck. Some of them looked as if they barely knew how to hold a sword. She felt sick to her stomach at the thought that these were the hands in which she'd laid her life. Taking a glance past the chaos around her and out at the sea, she spotted the brown sails of the approaching *Bonedog*. The ship's gold engravings sparkled in the sun even from the distance, its flag, with its crossed-bone emblem, waving in the wind. Dominic Rove was on that ship. Was he waiting for her like she was waiting for him?

"Why are you still on deck?" Blackwater turned his attention to her. His eyes flashed with anger. "You need to hide *now*."

The truth was, she didn't want to hide anymore. She'd hidden while her mother sacrificed her life. She'd squeezed into an almost empty barrel of potatoes on the ship for a full day before she'd had the nerve to sneak out, find water to drink, and steal the clothes she was wearing.

She spotted a sword leaning against the thick wooden mast and rose from her knees to grab it. "No more hiding," she told Blackwater as she tested the weight of the blade in her hand. It was heavier than she thought it would be.

She glanced at Blackwater, his brows drawn together, already studying her. "I'd apologize for this, but you'll thank me later." Suddenly, he grabbed her by the waist and hoisted her over his shoulder like a sack of flour, the surprise making her drop the sword.

"Put me down!" she yelled, hammering his back with her fists. He walked across the deck, her strikes nothing to him. "You— You scoundrel! You cod! You crooked pirate!"

"I've been called worse," Blackwater rumbled. The crew ran in circles around them, yelling over each other to be heard, but Blackwater's voice remained calm. He tightened his grip around her legs, not letting her fall as she squirmed harder.

"You don't understand," she pleaded. She wanted to see the

face of her mother's murderer, she wanted to claw the skin off his cheek before she sank with this ship. "This pirate, this Rove, killed my mother! I will not hide from him. It's my right to face him before I die."

Kane stopped suddenly, and set her back on her feet. He kept both hands on her shoulders, knees bent so that he was eye level. He brought his face closer to hers as he eyed her closely, like she was a puzzle he was trying to figure out.

"Rove killed your mother," he said, lifting a brow. "What were you going to do when you saw him? Challenge him to a duel? Sneak up from behind and stab him in the back with the sword you don't have?" He nodded to the one she'd dropped on the opposite side of the deck.

Lorelei's chin trembled. She snapped her mouth shut, realizing he was right.

Blackwater sighed. "I know what it's like to have vengeance in your veins. It runs through mine too. If you hide and wait until this is over, I promise you you'll have it."

"I'll have it? You mean, you expect us to sail away alive?"

"I never expect to lose in battle. Doubt leads you straight to death's harbor. I don't know about you, but I don't intend to die today."

"Captain!" Doan yelled from behind Blackwater. "They're gaining! Where do you want the gunpowder?"

Blackwater glanced over his shoulder as he shouted his commands. "Make a trail from here to the center of the deck. Leave the barrel in the middle and order the men to take cover."

"Aye," Doan said, ambling forward with the barrel. He pulled the cork and let the gunpowder sprinkle on the wood at Blackwater's heels, leaving a trail as he walked backward to the center of the deck.

Blackwater leaned toward Lorelei, blocking her view, and reached around her to open the door to his cabin. He stepped forward, giving her no choice but to take a step back herself until she was inside.

"I'm going to have to ask you to trust me, Lorelei," Blackwater said, leaning in the doorway with his hand on the doorknob.

"Why would I, Blackwater?" she answered, even though she was the one who'd snuck onto his ship with intentions of asking for his help. "My mother told me to never trust a pirate."

"Your mother was right, but right now it seems I'm the only person you've got. Lock the door." He left without another glance.

Lorelei wanted to defy him. She resented hiding from the Bonedogs again, but she'd go with Blackwater's plan . . . for now. She'd held a blade only to cut carrots, never as a weapon. She cringed as she imagined sliding steel against skin and bone, and rubbed her sweaty palms against her trousers.

The scuffling of men went quiet and Lorelei rushed to the door, locking it with a soft click. She ducked behind the lower wooden half, pulled back a corner of the teal-colored curtain, and peered out the window with one eye.

The ship seemed abandoned. Even though the crew was small compared to what she imagined, it was strange to see not a single soul on deck. Her heart beat so loud, it thrummed in her ears.

The Bonedogs swung in on ropes, their shadows sweeping across the ship before the pirates followed, their boots clomping as they landed with swords drawn.

At least ten of them wandered the deck. Their clothes were cleaner and more uniform-like than those of Blackwater's disarrayed crew.

Lorelei waited impatiently for Blackwater to make his move.

Then she realized that he might not, that this could very well be a trap and he'd shut her in here as a present to Rove.

Something caught her eye. She wasn't sure how she hadn't seen Blackwater crouched to the left of the door, but now she could see the lantern casing discarded at his feet, its candle now in his grasp. The flame flickered in the wind but Blackwater protected it, shielding it with his other hand.

Lorelei glanced back at the Bonedogs with her heart in her throat. One man turned to the door and looked her directly in the eye. Her breath caught, her eyes slicing back to Blackwater, who lowered the candle's flame to the gunpowder at his feet.

The tip of the black trail ignited and the flame crawled along like a boat floating down a stream. The pirate who'd seen Lorelei rushed forward, but he was too far across the ship. By the time he was close enough to stomp out the crawling flame, it had grown too strong.

Then the fire disappeared into the barrel in the center of the deck.

The gunpowder exploded.

Fire shot out, taking down several Bonedogs. As body parts blasted from the area, the cloud of smoke mixed with the hazy mist of blood. Splinters of wood flew in all directions, finding targets in chests, backs, and necks. It was gory and raw, yet Lorelei couldn't look away. She held each and every Bonedog responsible for the death of her mother. The satisfaction of watching them writhe alarmed the deepest part of her, but fed the darkest corners.

As the howls of pain rose, the cannons below the ship fired. The force made Lorelei fall backward. She scrambled onto her feet amid the sound of ripping wood and the shouts of furious men. Peering through the window, she witnessed the crew of the *Iron Jewel* swarm out of the smoking hole in the middle of the deck. Blackwater leapt from his spot by the door and joined his men.

The slaughter of the remaining invaders didn't last long. She'd never seen so much blood, so much brutality. Her hand trembled as she held the corner of the curtain aside.

The men cheered when the last Bonedog on deck fell still, but not Blackwater. His eye was to the sky, where more shadows swept overhead. He slashed out with his sword, gutting the first Bonedog who landed on the ship.

They swung from ropes again, dropping onto the deck. One after the other, after the other. The clash of swords reverberated through the room. She watched as more Bonedogs joined the battle. The number of strikes lessened as Blackwater and his men were surrounded.

Lorelei shook so hard it was impossible to breathe. She could no longer see Blackwater or any of the crew of the *Iron Jewel*, only the backs of the Bonedogs as they closed in on the group.

All hope was lost.

No. It couldn't end like this. Lorelei couldn't have left Port Barlow for nothing.

She was in the captain's cabin. All she needed to do was look for a weapon and she'd surely find one. Ignoring the wardrobe and large bed on the right, she went to the desk and the cabinet behind it. She bumped her hip hard on the corner of the wooden desk, but she muffled her cry and pushed on, reaching for the cabinet doors.

When she opened them, she blinked at the number of blades, swords, and guns lining the inside. *Jackpot.* She didn't know how to load ammunition and she stood no chance in close combat, so she grabbed one of the lighter-looking swords on the rack. Wrapping her hand around the leather sheath, she pulled the sword out, mesmerized by the way the steel glimmered in the light.

The sword wobbled as she held it in front of her, its tip pointing to the door. If the Bonedogs forced their way in and Rove came to finish what he started, she would fight. She would die fighting in the memory of her mother.

The doorknob rattled.

She stepped forward, tightening her grip on the hilt.

Suddenly, the door's window shattered. Lorelei jumped as the glass tinkered to the floor, and a bloody hand reached inside, grappling for the doorknob.

She squeezed the sword tighter.

The pirate opened the door and sauntered inside. Blood was splattered across his shirt.

"How cute," the Bonedog said, a smile twisting his face. "A little dove with a sword."

Lorelei swallowed and hardened her gaze.

"And what do you think you're going to do with that?" the man asked.

"Whatever I must," she answered, hoping her voice sounded strong.

The man reached for her, and she stabbed the sword forward instinctively, plunging the tip of the blade into his shoulder. He howled and stumbled back. One of his hands gripped his shoulder while the other reached for her. Lorelei dodged past him, the open door beckoning her, but the pirate grabbed for her again, scratching at her skin until he got a good grip, and he pulled her back into the cabin.

A scream bubbled up her throat but was blocked by the fear that paralyzed her when a hand twined into her hair and yanked her head back. Her vision spotted as she gazed toward the door, praying for someone, *anyone* to save her.

CHAPTER FOURTEEN

KANE

Where the Silver and Gold Seas Meet

Late Redwind

Kane yanked his sword out of the gut he'd plunged it into. Blood poured out, splattering onto the deck as the Bonedog fell over, limp. Another man quickly took his place.

Kane blocked the attack with his blade, the clash of steel against steel thrumming through the hilt and into his hands. He leaned forward and shoved the Bonedog back. One of Kane's men cut in from the side, ending the opposing pirate with the slice of his axe. He moved from one opponent to the next, then to the next. He stepped over bodies, ducked under fatal strikes, and swiped men off their feet, plunging his sword into their chests. The battle became a blur of blood, smoke, and glints of steel.

Thanks to the endless bouts of training he'd endured as a child, instinct drove him through the haze. His father's fist in his face, his knuckles against his jaw, the way he smiled when Kane would hit him back—it was all preparation for moments like this. They'd never trained with wooden swords or padded fists. His father wanted him to feel the true pain of losing, to feel the blood leave your body, to feel your bones crack, so the next time you fought, you fought harder, so you wouldn't have to experience that agony all over again.

The Bonedogs pushed in, surrounding Kane and his crew in a circle of death. There was no time to think, no time to wonder where Rove was in all of this. As Kane caught his breath, another Bonedog barreled toward him with his sword raised. Kane stepped forward to defend himself, lifting his own blade.

The sudden shattering of glass made him turn to his cabin door, making him miss the timing of his block against the incoming attack. The enemy sword sliced his upper arm and he dodged away, toward the cabin, but his path to Lorelei was blocked by another Bonedog.

The smoke around him was suffocating. It burned his throat and stung his nose. His men pressed in at his sides, waiting for another command. Their blades quivered as they held them out, ready to defend themselves, but Kane's remained still as he pointed at the nearest Bonedog.

The man smirked at Kane and cocked his head to the side. "Rove knew you followed him to Port Barlow. Says he figured it was time you learned a lesson about meddling where you don't belong. What's your move now, Blackwater? Are you going to blow up more of your ship?"

Kane held his sword with both hands now. "If it would end all of you, then I'd *sink* my own ship."

The surrounding Bonedogs shifted closer, their dark laughter rumbling over the groans of the injured. He could break through their line and run to protect Lorelei, but odds were he wouldn't make it through in one piece. It was over.

Kane hadn't thought that before when facing the molten man, or when the Bonedogs boarded the *Iron Jewel*, but now he could see it, clear as a blue sky.

His father was right: he would die a failure.

The Bonedog in front of Kane moved forward, raising his sword to strike. He suddenly stopped as an arrow whizzed through the air and went straight into his throat. He gurgled as he swayed on his feet, then fell to the deck with a hard thump.

Kane turned in the direction the arrow had come from. Through the dying smoke crimson sails flapped in the wind and he could see a line of women standing at the ship's railing. Csilla Abado—Goddess bless her—stood in the middle, one leg hiked on a crate and hands gripping a rope. A red scarf was tied over one eye, a new addition since the last time Kane had seen her. Nara was next to her with a new arrow nocked in her bow.

"Maidens!" Csilla yelled, her voice carrying across the two ships. "Bury these Bonedogs!" Then she followed the group of women who swung to the *Iron Jewel*. As soon as their boots touched the deck, the clanging of swords broke out again.

With the Bonedogs facing new opponents, Kane had a chance to reach Lorelei—if she wasn't dead already. He prayed to the Sea Sisters she wasn't.

Kane rammed his shoulder into an approaching Bonedog's chest, sending him stumbling aside. The path to the captain's cabin was an endless stretch even though he reached the open door in moments.

"Kane!" Csilla's yell barely reached his ears.

He didn't turn to face her as he walked through the doorway of his cabin.

A pirate held Lorelei close to him, his hand fisted into her dark hair. One of Kane's swords dangled from her fingers, the tip coated in blood.

"Kane!" Csilla yelled again. She burst through the door behind him, growling under her breath as she slid in next to him.

The Bonedog's gaze flicked from Kane to Csilla before he pushed Lorelei from his grasp and readied his sword. Lorelei called out Kane's name as he lunged forward, catching her before she could hit the floor.

Csilla met the man's sword with her own.

Kane glanced down at Lorelei, who blinked up at him as if she was trying to clear her vision. Then his gaze trailed down to the sword Lorelei still held in her hand with an iron grip.

"You stuck him good," he told her approvingly. Perhaps she wouldn't be as helpless as he'd thought. In the background, Csilla gutted the Bonedog and his blood-soaked scream echoed in the room.

Lorelei opened her mouth to say something else, but fell limp in Kane's arms before he could hear what she was going to say.

CHAPTER FIFTEEN
CSILLA

Where the Silver and Gold Seas Meet

Late Redwind

Csilla wondered briefly what the stunned girl would have said had she not fainted on the cabin floor, but there was no time to ponder anything as the chorus of battle screams and gunfire continued beyond the door.

She'd left Crossbones days before with Nara, the twins, and nearly twenty other Maidens, heading due northeast, hoping to intercept Kane or Rove. The wind helped them travel swiftly—the sea setting course for the ship, almost as if the Sea Sisters were blessing their journey. It was the first cannon blast that drew them toward the battle.

Csilla watched Kane as he lifted the girl into his arms. She would've remembered any other girls her age when they all trained as recruits, and she'd never seen this one before. Kane wasn't known to keep a girl around for long, leaving Csilla curious as to who she was and why he seemed worried about her while some of his men lay dead on his deck.

"She's lucky she isn't dead," he said. He carried her across the cabin, stepping over the Bonedog's body. The edge of his boot dipped in the puddle of blood, leaving a trail behind him.

"She's the one who hurt *him*," Csilla replied.

"Good," Kane murmured as he carefully laid the girl down on his bed.

The moment Kane released the girl from his grasp, it was time for Csilla to return to her Maidens in battle. Yet she stood as still as a sandbar, watching his rough exterior handle something so gently, like the girl was made of glass.

"Since when do you have female crew members?" Csilla asked, eyeing his reaction.

"Since now," Kane replied, shrugging. She couldn't sense a lie, but Kane had always been difficult to read. His serious eyes were so different from Flynn's mischievous glint. She'd known Kane as a boy encased head to toe in a shield no one could see, blocking himself off from everyone who tried to get close.

"Is she your love?" Csilla asked, hoping he'd finally allowed someone into his life.

Kane whirled around on Csilla in a blink. "No. She's just a thief I picked up in Sarva."

"Fine then," Csilla answered, turning on her heel. "Don't tell me the truth even though I traveled all the way here to save you."

"Where are you going?" His footsteps echoed closer.

"Into the fray," she answered. "By the way, who blows a hole in their own ship's deck?"

Csilla didn't wait for an answer and stepped forward, glass cracking under her feet as she walked through the door of the cabin.

The *Scarlet Maiden* stood unscratched on the starboard side of the *Iron Jewel*. The *Bonedog*, on the *Jewel*'s port side, was a flurry of pirates. They battled around the two decks, swords crossing, guns shooting, bodies falling overboard.

The twins shimmied up the ship's rigging and dropped down on unsuspecting Bonedogs, their hidden blades piercing their victims' necks. Serafina's newest invention involved daggers that extended from arm plates attached to their forearms, and Rosalina enjoyed the embroidery on the leather sleeves of the contraption more than the actual blades themselves. Both of them struck like cats, a smooth feline grace accentuating the way they moved.

Nara perched on the railing of the upper deck across the ship, her bow in her grasp, arrows finding their targets among the chaos. Her lips moved with each release of her arrows. If Csilla knew her as well as she thought she did, Nara was counting how many Bonedogs dropped to the deck with her dead-on aim.

Rhoda would have been in the center of it all, tossing her blades and ripping them from bodies as she chased down the next Bonedog. But she wasn't there. She'd chosen to stay behind, wanting nothing to do with saving a competitor.

Csilla still wasn't entirely sure how she felt about that. She'd have to decide before their return to Crossbones, because only first mates could compete beside their captains. Her sister disobeyed orders openly in front of the other crews, making Csilla look like a weak captain. She had to make a point to the others if she wanted to be taken as a threat.

Two Bonedogs ambled toward Csilla, their blood-splattered blades aimed for her throat. But she was ready, despite her wandering mind.

The two pirates mirrored each other's movements, their blades arcing down. She countered, thrusting her sword up, blocking their blows and wincing as the reverberations trailed down her arm. The two men pushed harder. As they pulled back for their next attack, she reached to her side, pulled out her half blade, and slashed at the men's waists. They dropped to their knees, then face first onto the deck.

Clumsy footsteps clomped to her left. She hadn't seen movement from that side but she should've kept her hearing keen to her surroundings. As she whipped around to face her new attacker, she twisted her bad ankle. The throb nearly broke her.

She groaned as she lifted her sword once more.

She wasn't quick enough.

Someone jumped in front of her, shielding her from her attacker's strike. Nara's tall shadow swept over her as she swiped the attacker's sword down, her steel sliding against the other as she forced both their blades to point down at the deck. With one powerful kick to the chest, the Bonedog flew onto his back, his sword clattering to the wood.

Then Kane appeared and stepped forward, kicking the man's blade away before he could snatch it back up. Nara nodded at Csilla before speeding off, sheathing her sword and pulling her bow back out.

"Where is Rove?" Kane demanded, pressing the tip of his blade against the man's neck.

"I don't know," the Bonedog answered.

Csilla glanced to her right, eyeing the pirate wearing a Bonedog scarf. Her sword clashed into his, then she pushed him off. She ducked under his next swing and drove her half blade up into his gut.

"How can you not know?" Kane roared. "He's your damned captain!"

"I know *nothing*," he restated. He tried his best to inch his throat away from Kane's blade. His eyes darted left and right.

"He lies," Csilla interjected. "Your sword isn't the only reason he squirms." She crouched down next to the pirate and said her next words in his ear so she could make sure he heard her. "Spill your secrets or I'll carve them out of you."

Two more pirates ran toward them, swords raised. Csilla jumped to her feet and countered one attack while Kane blocked another. Steel clashed, a deadly rhythm that made Csilla's heart race. She lunged forward, despite the pain in her ankle, skewering the Bonedog's chest with her sword. Kane's attacker fell to the ground a moment after hers.

The pair rounded back on the pirate they'd cornered. He'd grabbed his sword but Kane stomped his wrist into the deck, pinning his arm while he writhed. Csilla didn't like Rove and thought him a disgrace to the fleet, but as she watched Kane's anger rolling off him in waves, she realized that whatever was between him and Rove was personal. Maybe the gossip about Kane's shadow deals was true.

"Last chance," Kane said through his teeth, giving his boot a twist.

The Bonedog yelped. "He's nearly to Crossbones by now."

"What?" Kane growled.

"He took a merchant ship from Port Barlow and left the *Bonedog* to us, so that we could slow you down, so that you'll miss the starting pistol."

"That pathetic swine!" Kane reared back his foot and kicked the Bonedog in the jaw, knocking him unconscious. Then he turned to look at Csilla, his eyes desperate, a shade of Kane she hadn't seen yet. "We can't let him win the Bone Crown."

"I know," Csilla replied. She glanced away from him and

toward the dying battle. She had every intention of winning so that she didn't have to live under the reign of Rove.

The scream of a hurt Scarlet Maiden pulled her away from her thoughts. She didn't have time for this—her crew needed her.

"Until we meet again, Kane Blackwater," she said with a crooked curtsy, and bounded off into the fight.

"I wasn't done with our conversation!" he called out.

"But I am!" she returned over her shoulder.

Csilla pushed over a barrel in her path and with a shove of her boot sent it rolling down the deck. When it collided with a man's knees, he fell onto his back. Csilla burst forward, despite the throb in her ankle, and swiped his sword from the ground, leaving him weaponless.

She rolled her wrists, arcing the dual blades in circles in front of her as she walked forward. Blocking, slicing, slashing until the cold of steel ran through her veins.

Leaving pieces of herself behind, she faded away during the blood spill, becoming a puppet to her instincts. She left behind the light of Macaya. She lost the warm memories of braiding hair and racing to the cliffs. She stepped away from the things that made her step into battle in the first place and became numb to the loss of life in front of her. If she didn't end her attackers' lives, then she would be the one lying on the deck. This didn't mean that guilt didn't eat away at her in the loneliness of the night. Her dreams remained haunted, her eyes raw from tears.

For now, she did what she had to do, and she did it with a wicked gleam in her eye. No one would know what they couldn't see. She kept up her shield until the Bonedogs retreated onto their sinking ship and hoped that her hold could withstand the storm when the stakes were even higher.

CHAPTER SIXTEEN
LORELEI

Gold Sea Due West
Late Redwind

Lorelei jolted awake in a dark room. She blinked, trying to clear the haze and let her eyes adjust. Candlelight dimly lit the teal canopy above her, and the comfort of the mattress against her back let her know that she was in Blackwater's cabin.

She'd somehow survived the battle.

The bedsheets were cool, but her body was on fire with the memory of her dream. Her skin was damp with sweat, her hair sticking to her neck and face. Breaths came in short, labored huffs as she loosened her grip on the thick blanket covering her legs. She'd had nightmares before, but this one didn't feel like anything she'd ever dreamed.

She'd been walking down a beach with the whitest sand she'd ever seen. It glistened with the sun's rays and made her feel as if she was walking on treasure. She'd blinked, and the serenity and light crumbled away like rocks falling off a cliff. The rip of it still echoed in her mind.

Flame and suffocating smoke, blood staining the white sand, and creatures that moved like lava. The scent of burnt skin hung in the air. Ships were aflame and embers rose into the dark sky. And there was Lorelei, on the ground with her dark hair strewn out around her dead, cold body.

Loreleiii, came a whisper on the sea wind, the same one she'd heard in the fire.

She hadn't said the words, but in her dream she'd thought them. *What do you want?*

I want to leave this prissson. The longer the voice spoke, the more malicious its tone grew.

What does that have to do with me? she asked.

Everything! The vicious yell trembled the ground. *You, Daughter of the SSStorm, Daughter of the SSSea!*

Then she had woken up.

It was just a dream. A terrible nightmare. Lorelei wiped at her forehead with the back of her hand, repeating the thought in her head over and over. *Just a dream.* But the gallop of her heart told her it was so much more. The whisper said her name, but the titles he also gave her rang true even though she'd never heard them before.

Lorelei sat up in the bed and reached for the candle on the end table. When her arm moved across her vision, she noticed the bandage that someone had wrapped around her burn.

Holding the candle in front of her, she let her gaze roam the room. She recognized Kane's quarters immediately but hadn't truly noticed the details before. It wasn't the doom and gloom she'd expected; instead it reminded her of the sea colors in her mother's paintings. Trinkets and tapestries of teal and gold spanned the room, dislodging the boulder in her stomach. It was strange to think that she felt oddly at home when looking at his decor.

She continued her gaze to her right. She nearly dropped the candle and set the whole damned ship on fire when she saw Blackwater sitting silently on the chaise in the corner of the cabin.

"How long have you been there?" Lorelei asked. ". . . in the dark."

"Long enough," Blackwater answered. His elbows were braced on his knees, and he was more still and calm than any man Lorelei had ever seen. Even with the dim light of the candle, she could see the blood that stained his hands.

"Well," Lorelei said, trying to break the tense silence. "We're alive?" She shuddered at how obvious her words were and the lack of strength in her tone.

Blackwater didn't seem to care. "Yes, we are." His voice was deep and warm—the kind of voice that could calm you down in the middle of a storm if used the right way. She couldn't imagine him using it to comfort anyone, though.

"What happened to the man?" she asked. "The one who broke into the cabin. I tried to stop him." *And failed,* she thought.

She placed the candle on the opposite bedside table, lighting up his side of the room. He wore a shirt now, but his hair crowded his face, the loose dark strands acting as a curtain for his expressions.

"Csilla Abado killed him," he continued. "She slaughtered him right there." He looked down at an empty spot on the floor. "Then I tossed his body overboard to the sharks." He paused, watching her. "Does that scare you?"

Lorelei was caught off guard by the question. She sat in the bed, clutching the blankets, silent, trying to come up with an answer that would be acceptable for someone who'd helped save her life. Because honestly, the fact that he killed so effortlessly and was so accustomed to blood that he still hadn't washed from his body *did* scare her.

"Thank you, Blackwater," she finally said. "Thank you for saving me."

His eyes widened. He must've expected a different reply. Clearing his throat, he rose from the chaise. "There are garments in the wardrobe that should fit you if you'd like to be rid of whoever's you're wearing. I'm going to run down to the ship's infirmary and find supplies to tend to the burn on your arm." He walked toward the door, then stopped. "My name is Kane, by the way."

When he left the room, Lorelei ambled over to the wardrobe. After some rummaging, she slipped on a dark-crimson tunic, letting it hang down to her knees, then pulled on a loose pair of brown trousers. As she returned to bed, she remembered peeling the bloody dress off her skin nights before and her face went cold. Where was it now? If anyone had found it, she hoped they'd thrown it overboard so that she wouldn't have to bear the sight of her mother's blood again. Then a part of her sank, wishing she could feel the fabric one more time, like when she and her mother would hang clothes on the line behind their cottage. Their clothes were always so soft because of her mother's handmade soap. She took a deep breath in through her nose and out through her lips to hold the tears at bay. The stray hairs that dangled across her brow blew with the gust of air.

Murder. Battles at sea. An evil captain who'd killed her mother for reasons still unknown to her. In a handful of days, her world had been taken and torn apart in a storm that she couldn't have predicted. A part of her trembled at the thought of what would come next.

A sudden knock at the door made her heart quicken all over again. She clenched the collar of the tunic as if holding on tight might bring her back down.

"Are you decent?" Kane asked from behind the curtain covering the hole in the door's window. The glass had been swept away. In fact, inside this cabin there were no remnants of the battle, aside from the song of the waves drifting in through the broken window.

"I am," she replied as she crawled back onto the bed.

All of this was so unexpected, so sudden, that she wasn't sure how to act or think. She wasn't sure if they were allies or strangers with the same goal. If she only knew where she stood with him and how far he was willing to take her—straight to Rove's neck if possible.

She still worried about Kane's crew, especially after the way they'd treated her when they'd found her pilfering through the food stock. Then she wondered where she would be sleeping and if she'd have to bunk with the rest of the men after they'd tried to make her walk the plank.

Kane must have read the worry on her face because when he walked into the cabin and his dark eyes fell on her, he asked, "Is something the matter?"

Her thoughts spewed out in fragments. "Nothing at all—I'm fine—I just felt warm—I—"

"You're worried about the crew."

Witchcraft. He'd read her mind.

"They're harmless," Kane continued as he set the infirmary

supplies on the bedsheets. "I'm surprised the twiggy brothers survived, if I'm being honest. You could've probably taken them all if you really tried, but don't worry, I won't make you bunk with them if that's what you're worried about. You can have my bed. If you do not mind, though, on the occasion that I have time to shut my eyes for more than a blink, I will sleep on the chaise in the corner." He had a particular way about setting each item down on the bed before moving on to the next.

Her lips parted to protest, to say he could use his own bed, but he continued before she could speak.

"I don't use the bed much anyway these days. I currently don't have enough men to have a full watch rotation. I lost them in a fire."

"Oh." Lorelei was unsure what to say. "I'm sorry."

"Don't be," he replied. "It was my fault. My lack of judgment. Is it all right if I dress your wound now?"

She nodded, offering her arm to him, and Kane sat on the edge of the bed, half turning to face her. His gunmetal gaze darted over her skin as he unwrapped the bandage.

"I'm not a healer," he said. "But I know a few things. You'll want to use this"—he eyed the bottle, searching for a name that wasn't there—"medicine until we dock next."

"How do I know you don't have the wrong medicine?" Lorelei asked, yanking her arm back. "You don't even know the name of it."

"Like I said," he answered. "Not a healer. Now, be quiet and watch so that you can do this yourself." She snapped her lips shut and observed him as he moved, uncorking a bottle of clear liquid with his teeth and pouring a bit of it onto a cloth.

"I knew I was right about you," Lorelei said quietly, unable to stand the silence. "I knew you weren't as terrible as the harbor-folk believe. I don't think there is a pirate anywhere in the world that isn't hated by Incendia, to be honest." She glanced up at him from under her brow, his features focused on her burn. Up this close, she noticed the sets of small scars scattered around his face. She briefly wondered how many battles he'd faced to receive all the marks.

Kane dabbed at her burn with what could only be poison, the medicine searing her skin. She held back her scream and distracted herself by wondering whether the sting was supposed to be retaliation for her words.

"Tell me, what do the *Incendians* say?" His voice was soothing, a tone he hadn't used with her yet, possibly a trick after the way he'd just set her skin on fire.

"They say you have no hearts," she answered. "That you carved them out and threw them into the sea." Kane dabbed at the angry red skin of her arm, his other hand softly cradling it as his callused fingers reminding her how deadly his hands must be with a sword. "They say where a pirate sails, you'll find bodies in their wake."

"Aye, there are those who tread through dark water, but the tide only rolls so far. Most of us only want Cerulia and our people to flourish, just like the first fleet captains who founded the island kingdom. We want Incendia to leave us and our gold alone. We do what we must to protect Cerulia, even if that means killing the Incendian Navy in battle or their wretched Scouts."

"And what about looting ships and stealing cargo?" Lorelei asked.

"We like to call it *controlling trade*. Does Incendia really need more guns and more ammunition? What do they need it for? Do you know how many weapon shipments we've halted at sea? And you're damned right we stole every coin and valuable on those ships because men who conquer other lands and people don't deserve any of it."

Lorelei was quiet as she watched him open a new jar of ointment. He dipped a clean cloth inside the container and brought it to her burn, dabbing the skin gently, spreading the smooth cream. Sure, it was kind of him to show her how to treat her burn herself, but she didn't know whether to have faith in him or to damn his words and throw them overboard.

She wanted her revenge, and right now, Kane Blackwater was her only way of getting even a taste of it. It didn't hurt to test him out, to see where he stood in the scheme, to see if he knew about her mother and why Rove killed her.

"Something doesn't add up," Lorelei said before she lost her nerve. "The day I ran into you in the tavern—"

"You mean, the day you stole from me?"

Lorelei sucked in a breath. "You know."

He shrugged, a gleam in his gunmetal eyes. "Figured it out."

"I guess I should apologize."

Kane shook his head.

"Rove . . . he came to the cottage that same evening," she continued. The words swelled in her throat and she didn't think she'd be able to say them until they tumbled from her lips, tasting wrong and still not real. Tears brimmed in her eyes, but she quickly blinked them away. "He killed my mother. She was defenseless and had been losing her mind, but she still tried to protect me. What bothers me the most about it was that she knew him somehow, and he knew her. He knew her name."

"And what *is* your family name?"

She narrowed her eyes, not fully understanding. She thought he knew her name already. "Penny. Lorelei and Genevieve Penny."

Kane's eyes widened at the mention of her mother's name. When he glanced away from her, she noticed the scar that cut through his brow.

"What's wrong?" Lorelei asked, suspicious. She almost withdrew from his grasp, but her burn needed treatment if she wanted to keep her arm. She'd have a hard time killing Rove if she was missing a limb. "Do you know something? Do you know why he'd want to kill my mother? Why he would want to kill me too?"

Kane fumbled the cloth he'd picked up from the bed and busied himself with wrapping her wound, his fingers skimming the open palm of her hand. For a few breaths, he seemed as if he was having a battle within himself, his mouth opening and closing, his gaze drifting from her arm, to her eyes, then back down.

If he didn't know or wasn't going to tell her what she wanted then maybe he at least knew something about the tainted whisper in her dream and what it had called her—*Daughter of the Storm, Daughter of the Sea*. Normally, she didn't pay much attention to the details of her dreams, but the whisper lingered under her skin even now, when she was wide awake. She'd heard of the Captain of the Storm in one of her mother's old stories, but she'd heard it when she was so young she didn't remember much aside from the title.

"The Captain of the Storm . . ." she pressed, keeping her voice soft and innocent. "Why was he so important to the island kingdom?"

Kane stopped wrapping her burn, his eyes rising slowly to meet hers. Her cheeks threatened a blush under his gaze, but she swallowed it away and focused on the torn material of his collar.

"Haven't you heard any stories of the Old War?" he asked, the smallest of smirks beginning to curl at the edge of his lips. Then he glanced back down and continued to wrap her wound.

"If I did, I wouldn't be asking you about it." A lie. She'd heard some from her mother, but she wanted the tale to be refreshed by a real pirate.

"Before there was a King of Bones, a Bone Crown, or even Cerulia, there were the mortals and immortals. It was during this ancient age that the Old War between fire and sea was won because of the Captain of the Storm. He was the one who united the pirate fleets and the islands into one kingdom. He was only a mortal fisherman before it all, but by the end of it, he was the first King of Bones. If it wasn't for him and the magic blessed upon him by the Sea Sisters to control the storm, then fire would've scorched the world a long time ago." Kane paused for a moment, adjusting the bandage on her arm, his fingertips little bursts of warmth on her skin.

"Many mortals were lost in a war of the gods that lasted too long, but with the Storm's goddess-given powers of rain and lightning, his magic could smite the creatures of lava and fire. Together, the Sea Sisters and the Captain of the Storm vanquished the Brothers of Flame and they've been cursed to imprisonment in Limbo."

Limbo. The in-between. The prison of monsters and the realm of lost souls.

Kane finished wrapping her forearm and tied the ends of the bandage in a knot close to her elbow. It felt better already. He reached over to gather the supplies he'd placed on the bed. In a moment, he would stand and leave, and then the darkness of the room would descend on her. Suddenly, she found herself wanting him to stay. Not because she longed for his company she told herself, but because she didn't want to be alone. She didn't want her mind to wander to dangerous places where her fragile heart cracked and more tears stained her cheeks.

There had to be more to the story than just that.

"Why did the gods wage war against the goddesses?" Lorelei asked. Her heart skipped a beat when he stopped and turned back to her. "Didn't they once rule in harmony?"

"You don't know this story either?" Kane asked, cocking one brow.

"I don't." Not a lie this time, but the more she knew the better.

He sighed. "Well, then. Yes, gods and goddesses once ruled together—Gods of the Earth and Flame from below and Goddesses of the Sea and Wind from above the sky. Magnus, the youngest god of the Brothers of Flame, was known for his fiery passion and often spent his nights in the rooms of mortal women. One day, when he was visiting Alannis, before the gods and goddesses blasted it to ruins, he saw the most beautiful sight he'd ever seen, one of the Sea Sisters, Anaphine, and his passion burned only for her from that moment on."

Lorelei hung on Kane's every word, his voice stringing her along like a song. She always loved a good story. "Did Anaphine love him in return?" she asked, her voice quiet enough to be a whisper.

"She did," he returned just as quietly.

"Then why the war? What happened?"

"Magnus loved Anaphine too much. His flame burned too bright. He couldn't stand the thought of never being able to touch her, hold her, love her completely. Although he could walk the earth, she could not. He asked her to give up her immortality so that they could be together, but she declined him, refusing to step away from the role she was meant to have in his world."

Kane's gaze fell on Lorelei, his shadow-dark eyes piercing. "Ravaged from the rejection of his love, Magnus's passion-fueled fire grew hotter, his flames higher, until there was no place in the world he couldn't reach. With the other elemental deities refusing to get involved, and confined to the open waters, the Sea Sisters could do nothing as Magnus and his army of molten men terrorized the land and made way for the Incendians to conquer the eastern free lands. Before they could turn their gaze to the north or south, the goddesses were able to bless a mortal with the power of the storm to strike down their enemies on land."

Lorelei's interest piqued at the mention of the mortal with power, hoping it would bring her more knowledge of this Storm and how he linked to her. She cocked her head to the side as she blinked up at Kane, her eyelashes fluttering, and hoped she looked innocently curious. "But how were the goddesses able to give that power if they could control only the sea?"

Kane smirked ever so slightly. "Everyone knows the strongest storms come from the sea."

Lorelei sighed, unsure what to make of all this and how it all spiraled back to her. *Daughter of the Storm, Daughter of the Sea.* The whisper kept ringing in her head, in the same slithering growl that had called her name through the flame in her cottage. There was something else, a piece that was missing; she just couldn't put her finger on it.

"Do you feel all right?" Kane asked, eying her carefully.

Lorelei cleared her throat, straightening her spine. "I'm fine, just fine. My arm is feeling so much better already. Wrapped up all nice and tight." She was so painfully obvious.

If she would have blinked, she would have missed the smallest hint of a smile that passed over his lips.

CHAPTER SEVENTEEN
KANE

Crossbones

Late Redwind

The *Iron Jewel* docked at the island of Crossbones during the last week of Late Redwind. By some goddess-given miracle, Kane's ship wasn't the last ship to arrive. The *Bonedog* didn't make it at all.

Even if Kane never found a way to kill Dominic Rove—the sneaky coward—at least he could now die having sunk the captain's gaudy golden ship. Rove had others, but it was still one less *Bonedog* on the sea. He briefly wondered what his father's reaction would have been, and for some reason, he found it bothered him that he didn't truly know if he would have been proud or angry. Did his action make him a black spot of a Blackwater?

Kane peered through the window of his cabin, watching the mob of pirates scuttle toward his ship like a swarm of crabs. They pushed and shoved at each other, fighting to be the first to uncover the gossip behind his late arrival, or attempt to stab him in the back—whichever came first.

But before he ventured into that pit of snakes, he had a separate issue on his hands.

Lorelei—the trouble he hadn't expected.

She stood nearby, watching out a different window with a determined gaze, her head held high. He hadn't entertained the thought that she might not be the fragile girl he'd imagined he'd find in Port Barlow. No, she was the opposite of that vision. *This* girl raised her chin and looked him straight in the eye. Some grown men wouldn't even think about doing that.

They'd fallen into a routine of sorts in the few days' sail from the battle to Crossbones. He would take the helm while she stood at the opposite end of the ship, staring out to sea, her mind wandering to places Kane couldn't imagine. His eyes were drawn to her, watching to make sure she didn't fall over the railing, he told himself, but if that was the case, then why did his gaze linger on the way her hair blew in the wind when she crossed the deck?

He'd avoided his cabin as much as possible in order to dodge the constant questions from her. She wanted answers—ones she deserved and ones that he didn't think she was ready for, no matter how much she protested. He never lied, he just avoided answering directly.

The best-case scenario for everyone involved was for Lorelei's identity to remain a secret to everyone, including herself. Not only was she the secret heir to the throne, she was an heir on both sides of her lineage. A Rathborne for a father, a hidden Storm for a mother. If who she really was became known to any Bonedog, Wavecutter, or any other cold soul with a greedy heart, they'd stop at nothing to end her if it meant an opportunity to make the Bone Crown their own. The fewer pirates who knew about her during the Trials, the better.

Even though he repeated these things to himself, his stomach sometimes felt uneasy, like he'd been out at sea too long. That's all it was, just a little seasickness.

Kane had come into his cabin to tell Lorelei they had docked at Crossbones, which only released a chorus of more questions. She was like a captain of her own ship, unleashing attacks when his shields were down each time.

"The Trials?" she asked, her crystal-blue eyes wide. She went to the bed and sat on the edge. She wore another one of his tunics with her hair swept over her shoulder. "You mean to tell me that I'm to witness the captains competing for the *pirate throne*?"

Kane wondered which stories Genevieve Storm had cherry-picked to tell her daughter, and why she knew of the Trials but not that her father was the dead king.

What had she heard about the Blackwaters, he wondered. *Focus.*

"You won't be witnessing the Trials." Kane watched the way her eyes squinted at his words, like they'd hurt her or she didn't understand. He thought he'd spoken clearly.

"Why can't I come with you?" she asked, dropping the piece of brown hair she'd been toying with in her fingers. "You promised me revenge."

Kane sighed, exhausted already. "It's too dangerous." He brushed his fingers through his hair. "Didn't I tell you to trust me?"

"Trust isn't all that simple." She crossed her arms over her chest, the calm blue waters of her eyes suddenly boiling hot. "You can't honestly expect me to fall over at every word you say. My mother always said—"

"—never trust a pirate," Kane finished for her. "I know the warning." He'd used it himself a time or two. Kane placed his hands behind his back to keep from wringing his fingers. He'd hoped she would see sense in his words, but now she'd left him with no other option but to frighten her.

Taking a step closer, he lowered his voice. "I'm not sure what details were included in the stories you've heard, but I'm sure it's only a taste. There are hidden pieces moving in this game, things I've seen that would have you crawling back to Port Barlow in an instant."

"Like what?" she asked, lifting her chin at him.

"Murderous, treacherous things that cause nothing but pain and regret. Things pretty girls like you shouldn't be worrying over."

"Pretty girls like me? What is *that* supposed to mean? I can't know pain because of the way I look?" Her cheeks flushed red, and he found himself instantly regretting his tone. He wasn't used to *this*—whatever this was. He ordered his men around every day, but she wasn't exactly a member of his crew. She glanced away and stared at the wall's wooden planks instead of at him.

Kane reached for the compass in his pocket and pulled it out, letting his thumb rub over the familiar weathered curve, thinking of the right thing to do, *the right thing to say.* When he looked up, he saw Lorelei watching him and his father's compass curiously. He quickly shoved it back into the depths of his pocket before she could ask any damned questions about it. Letting out a sigh, Kane approached Lorelei and knelt at the foot of the bed. He was close enough that she could kick him in the face and leave the ship on her own accord, and he was surprised when she didn't.

"Let me go down there." He hoped his voice was gentle—it

was what he'd intended, even if it sounded unnatural to him. She still wouldn't look at him. He imagined the way he'd once heard his mother trying to convince his father not to sail through a nasty storm, how she'd softened her tone to get him to listen to her. Now he tried to do the same. "Let me compete so that I can keep the Bone Crown away from the hands of Rove. Then I will let you have your revenge."

Lorelei broke her stance and turned her gaze on him. "Or we can cut his hands off and then he won't be able to hold the crown."

Kane blinked. Then blinked again, unsure of whether her words were real or a figment of his imagination. He couldn't keep this girl straight in his mind—she was everywhere. "As much as I like that plan, the Trials' code makes that a bit tricky."

"Then, before the Trials start?"

"Lorelei." He placed his hands on top of her fidgeting ones. He knew the pain of losing one's mother, but vengeance plagued this girl's mind. He doubted she'd even grieved yet. "Let me do this."

Lorelei was quiet as she watched him, as if she was deciding. Perhaps she was formulating a plan to do the exact opposite of everything he said. He had no idea what to expect from her and to be honest, it was steering him up the wall.

"Fine," she said abruptly. "I'll stay."

A lie or a truth, Kane wasn't sure. Her voice was steady and even, making him think she was honest about her word. Yet, as he rose from his kneel he could have sworn he saw a mischievous gleam in her eye.

For now, he ignored it. He just hoped it wouldn't come back to bite him in the ass. He turned to leave the cabin, but just as he reached for the door handle, her voice came back to him.

"I know you're hiding something else," she said, her voice oddly calm. "I'll find out what it is. One way or another."

He cleared his throat. "You are free to question me upon my return with the Bone Crown," he answered. "For now, *stay here.*"

Kane left the cabin, feeling ten pounds heavier from the guilt that Lorelei had tossed on him. He thought he knew all about women and their witty ways, but apparently, he knew nothing. As he crossed the deck toward the gangplank that led to the dock, he realized it wasn't seasickness that had him feeling ill, weighing him down like an anchor of iron and guilt—it was keeping this secret.

For the better of everyone involved, he reminded himself.

The gritty voices of pirates scattered around the edge of the island and the dock grew even louder as he marched down the plank. A few gray-haired men curled their lips at his busted ship and the lack of crew that followed behind him. He'd had what was left of them stay behind on the ship to protect Lorelei, promising to flay any one of them if they placed a hand on her.

"Where's your crew, Blackwater?" The raspy voice clawed its way down Kane's spine, just as it always did. "Did they jump ship rather than be stuck with you as a captain?"

Jarnis.

Kane wanted to throttle him, to beat him senseless, but he refrained. He ignored Jarnis's laughter as he beheld the cracked *Iron Jewel.* He wouldn't find it humorous when the *Bonedog* never arrived at Crossbones.

For now, Kane would sit on this information.

Pirates scrambled around him, badgering him for information on his whereabouts. He ignored the lot and followed the crowd as they moved toward the beach, congregating eastward. He moved through the bodies, suspecting most to be spewing about him and his last-moment arrival, but their conversations all revolved around a different captain.

"Csilla Abado has no control over her crew," a man in front of him said. He wore a rusted-orange scarf around his sweaty head. "When your first mate won't even follow you, that says something about you as a captain."

"Can you imagine having Rhoda Abado as a first mate?" the pirate following next to him replied. "Csilla's biggest mistake was putting faith in her. She's a loose cannon."

"It will be interesting to see who she names as her Trials' first mate."

Shit.

Trials' first mate.

With having to make sure the heir stayed alive so that an angry fire god didn't rise while also ensuring his path to competing in the Trials so he could finally end Rove, he'd completely forgotten about choosing someone to compete with him. He had to go back to the ship and find Doan, definitely not one of the twiggy brothers. Doan was the only one who could possibly keep up with him.

A loud crack ripped through the air, stopping him in his tracks. A hush fell over the gathered pirates. Kane turned to see who'd fired their gun, and spotted General Lockhart, standing atop a boulder with his legendary whip in his fist. He was stout as ever but his cropped hair had gone gray since the last time Kane had seen him and, and his eyes drooped with fatigue.

Four men, dressed in the black attire of the crown officials, stood in a line behind Lockhart with their hands clasped behind their backs. Kane was surprised they weren't leaning on walking sticks, considering how ancient they all looked. On their chests, over their hearts, they bore the symbol of the royal flag—a skull with a crown of gold.

"Shut your traps!" Lockhart commanded. "I've had enough of your squabbling and rioting over the past moon. The redwind season is coming to a close and the Trials are upon us now that everyone has decided to grace us with their presence."

This meant Dominic Rove stood somewhere in the crowd, smug, believing that he'd killed the heir to the throne. He did always seem to know more than Kane assumed, making him wonder if Rove knew the same thing the whispers had told him on that island, about the importance of the heir's blood. Kane could reveal Rove's planned attack on the sea right then and there, but with his late arrival, the cards already were stacked against Kane.

Lockhart's gaze roamed over the pirates again. After the silence, he cleared his throat. "Before we begin, I have news from Baltessa. The crown officials have declared the late King Rathborne's death an assassination. Incendia is suspected, but the crime is under investigation while the Trials take place."

The pirates burst into an angry chatter about the flame-worshipping kingdom, but Kane's immediate thought was Rove. He was the murderer, or he'd ordered the hit. Kane didn't have proof—he just knew it in his gut. He would bet five hundred gold pieces on it. Force the Trials, kill the heir, become the next King of Bones. The perfect recipe for a greedy soul like Rove. Kane knew more than anyone else the things that Rove would do for power.

Lockhart's voice drew Kane away from his thoughts. "I need all captains to the front, so I may speak directly to the crown candidates."

Everyone moved, bumping into one another, curses rising in

the air, but Kane stayed still. He had to step up right then. There was no time to return to the ship for his first mate. He'd have to enter alone, no comrade by his side, looking truly foolish among those who already believed him a black spot of a Blackwater.

"Blackwater?" Lockhart called out from atop the boulder. "Are you out there?" His eyes scanned over the four captains who lined up in front of him and lingered on the empty spot where Kane should be.

An elbow nudged Kane's side. "He's right here!" a man yelled.

Another voice took his place. This one from his other side. "And his face is white like he's seen his father's ghost. You ain't ready for this, Blackwater."

Kane lashed out, striking the bloke across his cheek. It was one thing to taunt him, but bringing Castor Blackwater into it was too far. Bodies pushed between the two, holding Kane back from attacking. Still he swung wildly, his fists craving contact, needing the release. Hands gripped him tightly, pulling him to the front.

"Captains," Lockhart announced as Kane stumbled out of the scuffle and into the lineup between Flynn and Csilla. "I know most of you have dreamed of this moment and want to get this ship sailing, but there are formalities in the Trials Code. When I present your name and your ship to the goddesses, you may enlist a first mate of your choice to join you in the hunt. Should you fall from a cliff or drown in the lagoon, your first mate will inherit your title as captain."

"Dominic Rove of the *Bonedog*." Lockhart fixed his gaze on the scum.

"I state Jarnis the Brute as my first mate," Rove replied. The gold buttons on his overcoat glimmered in the sun. His calm, cool smile beneath his ridiculous moustache was enough to make Kane grit his teeth.

Dear Goddess. Not Jarnis. Anyone but the Brute. The scarred slash across Kane's chest burned with the thought. If it came down to it, there was nothing Kane could do against Jarnis's strength. He snuck a glance at the man who was abnormally pale for a pirate who spent most of his days in the sun. Kane quickly looked away. He could show no fear.

"Tomas Stone of the *Wavecutter*," Lockhart announced, looking at the drunk captain with a white feather in his hat.

Despite Stone's feeble attempt to appear put together—blouse sloppily tucked in, unlaced boots—it just made him look as lazy as ever. Based on the glazed look in his eyes, he was still drunk from the night before. Truth be told, Kane felt sorry for the man who'd turned to the flask when he'd lost a child to the sea. Kane couldn't fathom the pain the captain had been through. Perhaps numbing it with rum was the only thing Tomas could do anymore. Why the crew hadn't mutinied against him long ago was still a mystery to Kane.

Tomas called out the name of his nephew, Rodolfo Stone, and the gangly young man teetered over, seemingly just as drunk as his uncle. Rodolfo stood a head taller than Tomas, his feathered hat crooked on his head.

Kane silently cursed in disbelief at the pair of them. It wouldn't be dreadful if Csilla or Flynn won the Trials and took the Bone Crown, but if Tomas won, Kane would assassinate the man and face a trial for treason before seeing the island kingdom crumble under his reign.

Kane's heart raced faster as the line neared him. Perhaps he could get Csilla to swap places with him to buy him more time to think.

"Flynn Gunnison of the *Anaphine*," Lockhart announced. "Who do you state?"

"I state Arius Pavel as my first mate," Flynn replied.

Flynn's choice of Arius came as no surprise. The two were practically brothers, since they had both been raised by Flynn's mother after Arius's father had died in action. A shoulder brushed against Kane's and he turned his head to see Arius's wide, white smile and the dimples in his light-brown cheeks.

"Kane Blackwater of the *Iron Jewel*." Lockhart fixed his gaze on Kane, then on the empty space next to him where his first mate would be. "Who do you state as your first mate?"

"About that," Kane said, his throat closing as his stomach churned. "I . . ." His father was probably watching him through the veil of Limbo, shaking his head, cursing him.

Black spot of a Blackwater. Always a disappointment to the legacy.

"I am his first mate."

The female voice caught him off guard. He recognized the feminine tone but he wouldn't believe it until he saw her. He whipped around, along with the rest of the pirates, to see Lorelei making her way through the crowd. They quickly made a path for her, all silent—which was a miracle around pirates.

She wore the same cream-colored tunic he'd last seen her in but she'd tied it in a knot at her waist. A baggy pair of trousers, rolled up at the bottoms, were secured with one of his ornate belts. She'd pulled her dark-brown hair away from her face with a black scarf and strolled toward him with a sway in her hips.

In that moment, he wasn't sure whether to be furious with her or thankful for her quick thinking, but he sure as hell didn't speak.

His chest flared with anger, yet somehow he was also relieved she had decided to come of her own accord. He watched as she slid into the position next to him, wondering who this farm girl truly was. His jaw went slack as she smirked at him—*like a damn pirate.*

All this time, he'd been trying to convince her to trust him, but perhaps he was the one who needed to place faith in her.

CHAPTER EIGHTEEN
CSILLA

Crossbones
Late Redwind

Csilla watched Kane's first mate carefully. With her delicate porcelain face and the baggy clothes hanging from her slight frame, she didn't quite seem to fit in. Yet somehow, she did—the lift of her chin, the small smile at her lips, the gleam in her eye. Csilla still wasn't quite sure what to make of Kane with a female on his crew. If his father was still alive, he'd probably drag Kane back to the *Iron Jewel* by his earlobe like she'd seen him do when they were children.

"You look familiar," Lockhart directed at the new girl, breaking formality. "Have we met?"

Kane turned back around. "Certainly not," he sputtered. "She's from . . . from . . ." For the first time in her life, Csilla thought Kane looked nervous as he shifted from foot to foot.

"From across the Frozen Gap," Kane's first mate answered. It was a smooth lie, impressive even, but she didn't fool Csilla.

"Are you from the air-worshipping kingdom then?" suggested Lockhart, tilting his head to the side as he waited to see if she was from Ventys. If she was, then maybe Nara knew of this girl. Csilla would be sure to ask her when they had a moment alone.

"Forgive me," Kane interrupted, the top of his ears flushing red. "But shouldn't we continue?"

"Hmm." Lockhart glanced around at the impatient group of pirates. "I suppose you're right. Kane, please state the name of your first mate for the goddesses to hear."

He hesitated and glanced down at his boots before facing Lockhart once more. "I state Lorelei Penny as my first mate."

Csilla glanced over her right shoulder, searching for other pirates' reactions or for any hints of knowledge of where this completely random girl had truly come from. Some seemed interested in Lorelei, but likely not because they found Kane's choice oddly out of character—she was a pretty little thing after all.

Dominic Rove, the slimy bastard, watched Lorelei like a hawk circling its prey.

"And Csilla Abado of the *Scarlet Maiden*," Lockhart suddenly announced, startling her. "Who do you state as your first mate in the Trials?"

She gripped the hilt of her sword with one fist to keep her fingers from trembling. A lump formed in her throat that she couldn't swallow; she scanned the crowd for her sister, not finding her. A deep part of her was glad to not have to look her in the eyes when she stated who she chose.

"I state Nara Esaki as my first mate," Csilla said, keeping her gaze hard and facing forward.

The pirates collectively gasped, and a breath whooshed out of her. When their murmur stilled to a silence, the boulder lifted from her chest.

Csilla had expected Rhoda to scream in a fit of rage, to cause an explosion of dramatics and have to be pulled away from the Trials in shackles, but when the hush fell over the pirates, somewhere, Rhoda was silent with them. Which was even worse, reminding her of the days after their grandmother had announced Csilla as her heir.

There was no doubt in this world that Csilla loved her sister. They were all each other had left, and although Rhoda was never the affectionate one, she had her own way of showing her love. Vowing to end the Ruin Witch for blinding Csilla. Forcing Csilla to stay in bed when she'd first shattered her ankle. Pummeling anyone who pushed Csilla around when they were younger.

Rhoda wasn't this same woman, though. She was changing, growing darker and more envious each day, always lost in her thoughts. Sometimes Csilla swore she had even heard her whispering to herself recently.

Being captain required having a firm hand and Rhoda had publicly disrespected her multiple times. If she was going to show these men that they could follow her, then she had to show she could separate love from duty and demonstrate some form of control over her crew *and* her sister.

"Out of my way," Rhoda ordered suddenly. Csilla turned to see her pushing through the crowd of pirates, leaving the meeting.

Dominic Rove chuckled from across the stage where they stood. Csilla's blood pumped so fast that she could hear it in her ears, and she curled her hands to hide the way they shook. Her face felt cold while her insides burned hot. If it wasn't for the sea breeze blowing across her skin, she would have broken out in a sweat.

Then Nara stepped forward, hesitantly, like she was stepping on broken glass. Her long, straight, raven hair was swept away from her face in a tight bun atop her head, her always-calculating eyes flicking from face to face as they watched her take her place beside Csilla.

Lockhart cleared his throat like he hadn't just witnessed the family drama unfold before him. "Captains and first mates, I'm honored to be officiating one of the rare occurrences of the Trials. As designed by the first King of Bones, our Captain of the Storm, one of the fleet captains will show they have the very same traits that deemed him worthy by the Sea Sisters—valor, wit, honor, and heart. Captains and their first mates will be collecting the four key pieces needed to open a chest containing the Bone Crown, buried in Skull Cave. While you might think these key pieces will be easy to find, there is a dangerous trial you must face before you can obtain each. All four pieces—wind, sea, earth, and fire—are needed to complete the key, just as a world with an imbalance of the elements would be no world at all."

The worry washed off Csilla with his words. It was real. This was Csilla's chance to reach everything she'd ever dreamed of. She envisioned the golden-tipped crown of bones resting on her head as she looked down from her plush throne. Her girls would be around her and they would no longer have to follow the orders of men.

"You didn't think it would be that simple, did you?" Lockhart chuckled. "I forgot to mention that each captain will be receiving a map with a route to only one location—one of the four key pieces or the Skull Cave. You will have to be crafty in order to retrieve all four pieces. The first captain with the Bone Crown on their head is our champion."

With that, a small group of boy recruits left the line of pirates and passed out parchments to the five captains. When one landed in Csilla's hand, she quickly unrolled it and scanned her eye across the ink. On the parchment was a map of Crossbones, from the sea cliffs to the lagoon and all of the jungle in between. An etched line trailed from their meeting spot on the beach toward the thickest part of the jungle. She wasn't sure if she'd follow the path, but at least she knew where one of the locations was. It might be more beneficial to follow Kane and Lorelei and find out another location first.

Lockhart's voice pulled her from her thoughts. "I know many of you spit on rules, but without rules there would be chaos. The code will be followed as law. If any of the code is broken, the offender will face trial and sentencing by the Trials official: me."

All were silent as Lockhart stepped down from the top of the boulder, now eye level with them. His gaze drifted around the group as he spoke, making sure each and every one listened closely.

"The first code of the Trials is that no pirate shall kill another pirate." Lockhart paused, letting the rule sink in. "Accidents do happen, fights happen, but if you strike down another with the intent to kill, you *will* face trial."

Csilla rolled her eyes. Dominic Rove and Jarnis would surely be the first to break the rule, though Lockhart would never know unless someone told him. None of them were snitches.

"The second code of the Trials is that no weapons, supplies, or any belonging other than the map or key, may be stolen during the Trials—only pieces of the key or map can be stolen." Lockhart shot a glance at Flynn, who was infamous for his thieving skills.

"The final code of the Trials is that only captains are allowed to touch the Bone Crown. If you aren't a captain and I see you with the crown on your head, I will bind your hands in the Traitor's Knot and you'll never be able to hold anything again after the flaming rope is finished with you. Do I make myself clear?"

"Aye," the pirates replied in unison.

Lockhart shook his head. "I said, *do I make myself clear*?"

"Aye!" the pirates yelled, some of them lifting their fists into the air.

Lockhart returned to his place on the boulder and clasped his hands behind his back. "When I shoot my pistol, the hunt will begin, and it will not finish until the crown rests with a new bloodline. I don't want to have to shoot a hole in anyone's ass, so just follow the damned code." He lifted his pistol into the air. "Let the Trials begin!" He pulled the trigger and the shot echoed across the beach, ringing in Csilla's ears as chaos began.

PART THREE

THE TRIALS

CHAPTER NINETEEN
LORELEI

Crossbones

Late Redwind

Before they could all take off across the island, the ground beneath their feet trembled, the scent of embers and smoke drifting in the wind. A rumble and rush of thunder rose in the air, but there was no storm to be seen in the endless blue sky. Lorelei looked at Kane, who gripped the hilt of his sword, the steel already partially unsheathed. The two Maidens stood steadily, their feet planted, their knees bent. Lorelei tried to mirror their ready stance, hoping she looked as prepared as the others did. The two other young men on Kane's side cursed and laughed together as they tried to remain upright. The drunken captain from the *Wavecutter* stumbled to the ground, his flask clattering against the wooden stage.

The ground continued to quake. The tremors rose, making it nearly impossible to stand. The trees across the beach trembled, the sand danced. The rumble in the air grew louder and louder until Lorelei heard it—the whisper.

Loreleiiii. The same wicked voice from the cabin and her dream scratched against her ear. She closed her eyes, wishing it away like it was a figment of her imagination.

The ground lurched beneath her and jerked her to the side. She reached for something to hold on to, but there was no structure besides the small stage they were standing on, so Lorelei clawed for Kane's arm and latched on tight. It was only a whisper, yet it was louder than the rumble.

"Did you hear that?" she asked, praying that the whisper wasn't just a voice in her head.

"Hear what?" Kane yelled, but she could barely hear him over the rumble. "The quake?"

You ssshould be dead, the voice continued. It rasped in her mind and echoed in her head. *You ssshould have died in the fire. You ssshould have died in the battle.*

"The voice!" Lorelei yelled desperately. She felt the hiss on her neck, on her shoulders, on her cheeks—it was everywhere. "Do you hear it?"

Kane's eyes searched hers. His head cocked to the side as he listened. The farther his brow furrowed in concern, the more she realized that the only things he could hear were the rumbles and the yelling pirates around them.

The pirate cannot protect you. The voice was louder now—on the edge of a scream. *You will die on thisss island. I will crush your bonesss into dussst. I will not let another SSStorm defeat me.*

Lorelei thought back to the dream she'd had and spoke back to the voice. She conjured a simple question in her mind and imagined saying it aloud. *Who are you? What do you want from me?*

A hiss echoed in her mind, but he didn't reply. Instead, a new, softer voice broke through the scraping darkness of his voice.

Magnus, the musical female voice said. *His name was once Magnus.*

"Magnus," Lorelei whispered. Then everything suddenly stopped. The earth stood still, the wind blew through the leaves of the trees, the waves washed up on the shore. The chaos ended as suddenly as it began, leaving Lorelei terribly confused.

"What dark magic was that?" Csilla Abado's yell ripped through the quiet air. For a moment, Lorelei thought that Csilla had heard the voices, too, until she realized that she was talking about the quake. Csilla cast her gaze in the direction of Dominic Rove, who hadn't seemed to move a muscle.

Lorelei had kept her own eyes from him during the entire introduction by Lockhart, a truly daunting task. She had battled with herself whether to damn it all and throw everything she had into stabbing him in the back with one of the knives she'd stolen from Kane. Then she remembered that her actual skills amounted to those of a pirate child.

"Why are you looking at *me*?" Rove said to Csilla. A strand of salt-and-pepper hair fell in front of his eyes, and he blew it away, his curled moustache twitching. He had to have an idea of who Lorelei was even though he'd never seen her. When he looked at her, did he see the eyes of the defenseless woman that he'd murdered in cold blood?

Whispers rose from the surrounding pirates as they argued over what the quake could have been.

"That couldn't have been natural," one of the men's mutters reached Lorelei's ears. "A witch has cursed this hunt!"

Flynn stepped forward. Lorelei could barely hear him over the rising voices. "Lockhart, perhaps we must hold off on the Trials. This is a sign."

Lockhart shook his head. "Pirate law states that once the Trials begin, it will not end until the crown is placed on a captain's head. If we leave, we will leave without a ruler. This is the way it has been done for hundreds of years and we will not change our ways because of a small quake."

For a moment the pirates were still. Their eyes slid over each other as they all waited for someone to make the first move.

Lorelei and Kane shared a knowing look, then he gave a nod and the two of them leapt from the small stage and ran down the beach. The pirate crews cheered as they left them behind. Lorelei had trouble keeping up with Kane as her feet buried themselves in the sand with each step, but Kane didn't run too far ahead. Every time she thought he might leave her in the dust, he was still right there in front of her, guiding them toward the jungle.

They neared the tallest line of trees Lorelei had ever seen. Her breath caught in her throat as she took in the sheer size of them, their trunks wider than the masts of Kane's ship. She snuck a quick glance over her shoulder, eyeing the captains and their first mates scattering in different directions, leaving Lockhart standing on the boulder alone. But someone followed Kane and Lorelei's footprints in the sand.

Csilla Abado was at the front, her lips moving quickly as she spoke to her first mate beside her. The shimmering white feather Csilla wore in her ear swayed back and forth as she ran.

Behind them followed two more figures. Possibly that Flynn fellow and his first mate, but they were too far back to make out clearly. Kane grunted for Lorelei to get a move on and she disappeared behind him into the jungle of trees and vines.

—

Lorelei had never seen so much green in all her life. No matter which direction she cast her gaze, green was everywhere. Giant leaves covered the sky, bushes and tangled roots sprouted from the ground. Thick vines coiled around tree trunks like ropes on the masts of the *Iron Jewel*. Already, Lorelei found herself wishing she was back out on the sea.

"Keep up," Kane grumbled ahead of her as he pushed a stray branch out of his way. "They're following us."

"They could just be going in the same direction." Lorelei knew she sounded naive, but for some reason she didn't want to believe that Csilla Abado meant her harm. She'd never forgotten seeing her flee with her Maidens that day in Port Barlow, and she'd saved Kane and Lorelei from the Bonedogs.

They'd already been trekking for a while, and Lorelei's legs were limp like boiled noodles.

Kane stopped and turned around to look at Lorelei. "No, you're wrong," he said sharply. "They're definitely following us." He faced forward again and continued walking. Lorelei stayed close behind. "Csilla is curious about you, I can tell. I'm still unsure where she stands. She's a dangerous player in this game." His fingers curled into fists at his sides. "You shouldn't have come here. You should've stayed in my cabin."

"You're welcome for saving you from looking like a complete imbecile," Lorelei reminded him. Staying on the ship would've been so dreadfully boring, and who knew how long he would've been gone.

"Now not only am I going to have to try to win the Bone Crown, but I have to try to keep you alive while doing it."

"Don't worry about me, then."

"I kind of have to," he said so quietly Lorelei wasn't sure if she'd heard him correctly. She didn't mean to be a burden, but he didn't have to be so rude.

Lorelei swatted at an insect that flew much too close to her face. "I can take care of myself, all right? I've done a decent job so far, I think." Then she tripped over a fallen log that blended in with the jungle floor, cursing the irony of the moment. Something snarled in the distance, followed by the cry of a dying animal.

Idiotic. This was completely idiotic. The voice was right. She was going to die on the island, perhaps from pure inexperience. Quickly, she caught up to Kane.

"My mother . . ." Lorelei said, trying to distract herself from the sounds of the jungle and ease the tension between them. "My mother heard these voices in the fire. I hadn't believed her . . . until now. This is going to sound like I've gone mad, but I heard them, too, during the quake."

"You hear the whispers too?" Kane asked, stopping next to a tree with a trunk blanketed with moss. A vine swayed behind him. He ran an empty hand down his face and sighed against his palm. What else did he know that she didn't? "Shit, you really should have stayed on the ship."

"She sacrificed herself for me, you know. She stood firm against Rove, and I *hid* while he gutted her in the room above me. I'm right where I should be, finding a way to bring pain to the one who inflicted it on me. Are you going to help me or not?"

Kane's gunmetal eyes softened when she spoke of her mother's death. In the end, he looked away from her, clenching his jaw. "For now, we must compete and must do it fairly. We can't give Rove a chance to call foul play or we will have to face sentencing from Lockhart. But when the time comes, we will finish Rove together. I swear it." Something was still hidden behind Kane's eyes, but there was truth in his words of revenge.

Lorelei hadn't realized how much hope she'd kept bottled up inside. The cork was sealed so tightly that she couldn't even glimpse it. She'd been caught up in the shift of tides, the change in her life. She rolled with the waves that crashed in on her, and she'd successfully kept her head above water so far. Perhaps trying not to drown in this new world wasn't as impossible as it seemed. Not with Kane at her side like a rope pulling her out of the deep water. With just a few words and a promise, he shattered her glass bottle and let her hope flood out in a pool of relief.

Revenge would be hers, and it would taste sweet.

"Now come." Kane turned and motioned for her to follow him. "The others aren't too far behind. We have to keep mov—"

A sudden rustle of leaves rose from behind Lorelei. She spun around instinctively and braced her legs, ready to run in the opposite direction should an enemy show their face. Kane gave her a push to the right and they delved farther into the greenery of the jungle. In just a few backward steps, they were surrounded by leaves that were bigger than their heads. Kane brought one finger to his lips as they crouched in the bush. Lorelei peered through the leaves as Csilla and Nara barreled through the same spot where she and Kane had been standing just a moment before.

The two female pirates stopped, chests heaving, sweat coating their skin. Lorelei and Kane watched silently, their sides flush together and Lorelei suddenly became very aware of his breathing, hers quickly falling in rhythm with his.

"Where did they go?" Csilla asked, hands on her hips as she

KIMBERLY VALE

leaned all her weight on one leg. "They couldn't have been too far ahead of us."

"Does it matter?" Nara turned to face Csilla. "Let them get to the cliffs first. We'll follow their wake through the jungle and snatch their map from them when they're sleeping. You need to rest your ankle."

Csilla opened her mouth, then closed it again. She looked away from Nara and right at the bush where Kane and Lorelei were hiding. Kane's hand moved to the hilt of his sword and the backs of his fingers pressed into Lorelei's side, warm and sending a buzz across her skin. Lorelei held her breath, afraid that one tiny brush of air might rustle the leaves. But Csilla glanced away, back to Nara.

"Rhoda wouldn't have let me rest," Csilla said. The way she said it almost sounded like she was saying it more to herself than her crewmate.

"Which is why your grandmother didn't choose her as heir," Nara replied. She dug into the small bag she carried and pulled out a water flask. After taking a long swig, she looked back at Csilla. "Rhoda is selfish and doesn't see clearly sometimes. A part of me worries she'll retaliate since I was chosen as your first mate instead of her."

"Rhoda is my sister," Csilla replied, her voice taking a much more authoritative tone. "Any retaliation won't be too drastic, but she probably won't talk to me for a few years. Be careful not to worry yourself over my decisions as captain, Nara."

"I'll worry about your decisions as my friend."

Quiet settled between them until a new sound made Kane curse under his breath.

The wild laughter of someone behind them.

CHAPTER TWENTY

KANE

Crossbones

Late Redwind

Kane sat crouched among the bramble of leaves next to a breathless Lorelei. He'd hoped Csilla and Nara would move on quickly, then he and Lorelei could quietly slip away, but he'd been so distracted by the surprising warmth of Lorelei next to him that he hadn't heard anyone sneaking up behind them.

When the laughter shattered the serenity, the rest of the world faded away. Csilla and Nara's conversation was replaced by a whirring in his ears.

Before Kane could unsheathe the sword at his waist, there was something sharp at his neck. His eyes drifted down, catching a glint of steel, recognizing the barreling waves engraved along the edges of the blade as Flynn Gunnison's. Kane hadn't realized they were following too. The Sons of Anaphine were too sneaky for their own good.

Next to Kane, Lorelei gasped. He turned to look at her, ignoring the sting against his skin. She, too, had a blade at her throat. He growled under his breath and clenched his fists at his sides.

"Would you look at what we have here?" Flynn said from behind Kane, his voice light, always sounding like the fox he was.

"Blackwater and his little pet," replied Arius, just as twisty as his captain. He stood behind Lorelei, his own blade at her neck. One of his honey-blond curls hung between his hazel eyes.

"I am no one's pet," Lorelei said, earning her an appreciative chuckle from the duo behind them.

"Are you sure about that?" Arius asked. "You look like a pet."

"Leave her alone," Kane said through his teeth.

Both swords were pulled back, then Flynn and Arius started laughing once again. "We were only joking!" Arius said. "Always so serious, Blackwater."

Flynn patted Kane's shoulder, but Kane didn't stand up. "Come on, old friend," Flynn said. "Don't be angry with us."

Kane brushed Flynn's hand from his shoulder and rose to his feet. He turned to Lorelei, whose ivory skin had gone even paler during the encounter. She either ignored or didn't see his outstretched hand to help her stand, ever adamant about doing things for herself.

He was slowly realizing that hiding her identity from her could be the very thing that would end up killing her. Guilt was something he paid so little attention to that he'd forgotten its long and hollow face as it tightened his chest. After the quake and her inquiry about that damned Brother of Flame, it was only a matter of time before something worse happened. He knew he had to tell her, but now he just had to wait until the right moment—not when they were surrounded by four other competitors.

An image of the Bone Crown flashed in his mind. With it, he could be so much more, right all his wrongs, prove that he was better than his father believed. He needed this more than the *Iron Jewel*. This girl didn't deserve it just because of the blood in her veins. This was *his* moment.

Kane shook his head, clearing the sudden selfish thought. He was different from his father. He was different from Rove. He didn't want power; he didn't want the glory. If he was being completely honest, he wasn't sure *what* he wanted anymore.

"You two are imbeciles," Kane told the two Sons.

"But good-looking imbeciles, right?" Flynn winked, but it wasn't for Kane. Following Flynn's line of sight, Kane could see that his question was directed at Csilla. She was watching the entire exchange with an unreadable expression.

"Did you hear the confounding news, Csilla?" Flynn asked. He sheathed his sword at his side. "Once again, we've failed to crack the Blackwater. I swear he hides his smiles in some secret locked box that he keeps with him at all times. Maybe in that compass of his." He slid a glance at Kane and chuckled, which made his counterpart, Arius, laugh as well, but Kane's expression remained grim, his pulse flaring at the mention of his father's compass.

"What do you know of feelings?" Csilla threw back at Flynn. She reached up and tightened the crimson scarf over her eye as she waited for his answer.

Flynn's smile fell and something passed between the two of them, making Kane wonder what the hell had happened between them since the last time all the captains had feasted together in Baltessa. Kane was sure the pair of them would've given in to each other by now, but instead tension simmered across the whole area, like a slow burn that creeps along paper, devouring everything in its path bit by bit. Kane wasn't the only one who noticed this. Both Nara and Arius looked back and forth between them, Arius rolling his eyes.

Flynn clenched his jaw before he answered. "I know more than you might think."

"You two together are such a headache," Arius groaned. From the look on Nara's face, she agreed. "Remind me why we followed them, Flynn. We should be trailing Rove, not running after these girls."

"Csilla followed Kane," Flynn replied. Kane was surprised to hear a hint of jealousy in his tone. "I want to know why."

"Why does it matter?" Csilla asked, seeming already tired of the conversation. "If anything, I'm curious about his first mate and where she really came from. I know I've seen her somewhere before." She glanced at Kane, a secret of her own hidden in her gaze.

Then, the rest of their eyes rested on Kane. Except for the blue ones that he could never read. He didn't turn to look at her and instead reached blindly for her hand. When his fingers brushed against thin air, something snapped inside of him.

Black spot of a Blackwater. You lost her.

"Lorelei?" His voice came out as a whisper.

He searched the spot she'd just been hiding in hopes that she'd ducked down into the bramble. He gripped the stems of the leaves, ripping, tearing at them. But she wasn't there.

"Lorelei!" He pushed past Arius and scanned the line of trees and bushes. "Where did she go?" Just one flash of her brown hair or the cream-colored tunic in the sea of green—that's all he needed. Yet, as he scanned the terrain there was nothing but the damned green, taunting him. "Lorelei!"

Kane remembered the molten man attack, the dripping magma, the earthshaking roar. Could Magnus find her alone too? If he caught her she stood no chance. Then what would become of Cerulia?

"Kane," Arius said. "Calm down. I honestly can't believe she got past all of us. Sly little fox." He placed his hand on Kane's shoulder but Kane shrugged him off. "Why are you so upset? She's a first mate. She can take care of herself."

Kane whirled around on Arius and drove his fist into his face. The crack of Kane's knuckles against Arius's cheekbone echoed off the trees around them. Arius stumbled backward, lifting his hand to his face. Before Arius's fingers could touch his skin, Kane hit him again under his chin, sending him falling onto his back.

Kane stepped forward, ready to lunge, but Flynn jumped between them. He held his hands out in front of him. "Kane," he warned. "Steady, mate. There's no need for—"

"You idiots have no idea what you've done!" Kane yelled. *What I did myself,* he thought. He took a step backward, clenching and unclenching his fists. He needed to do something with his hands to stop himself from wringing their necks right there on the jungle floor. He shoved his hand in his pocket, gripping the compass tight in his fist.

"What are you talking about?" Flynn asked, his brow twisted in confusion. "We were only having a bit of fun. We didn't hurt anyone."

Kane tore his eyes away from Flynn and turned to Csilla instead. She'd helped him before, maybe she'd help him once more.

"She'll die out there," he told her. "She isn't trained for this like the rest of us. She's different. This isn't about you or me or a crown anymore. Let me go and stop following me or help me find her."

Csilla gazed back at Kane intently, as if she was trying to decide what course of action to take. Her hand reached up to her earring, her fingers brushing over the glittering white feather.

"She's more important than any of this," Kane continued, hoping to push her over the edge he needed. At this point, he didn't really care if he sounded desperate. "Lorelei needs more than just me. I can't do this alone."

"Well, I'm thoroughly confused," Flynn said as he helped Arius to his feet. "Are we talking about a lover or your first mate? What was it? Lorelei Penny? Odd name. She sounds more like a baker or a nanny than a pirate."

"Csilla?" Nara asked, taking a step closer to her captain. "What do we do?"

Csilla took a breath before answering. "Let's go get her."

Kane breathed a sigh of relief, holding Csilla's gaze even after the others around them started moving again. Then he smelled something that made his blood freeze over.

Smoke.

And where there was smoke, there was fire.

CHAPTER TWENTY-ONE
LORELEI

Crossbones

Late Redwind

Lorelei heard Kane's call in the distance, but she kept her gaze straight and her boots forward. Even though her thighs ached and her calves burned, she pushed herself as far as she could. She leapt over gnarled roots, wove between tangled vines, and ignored the scratch of thorns against her skin.

This was her chance. This was her moment. While the pirates twiddled their thumbs, wondering where she'd run off to, she'd get that key piece before any of them and be one step closer to her revenge against Rove. She'd studied the map and their route to the cliffs; she knew the direction she needed to head if they got separated—even though the current separation was intentional.

She'd seen the opening—when they'd switched their attention to Csilla Abado and forgotten about Lorelei for those few golden seconds, she'd quietly slipped away. She was surprised that Kane hadn't seen her make her move. The concern in his voice as she heard him desperately calling to her left a knot in her stomach, but she knew he'd be close behind.

Nothing was going to stop her, especially not a group of squabbling pirates.

When the trees thinned out and more beams of light shone through spots in the canopy above, she slowed. Reaching behind her, she tugged at the parchment she'd stuffed into the pocket of her pants. The map was rough against her fingers as she unrolled it. Her fingertip traced a line from the starting point of the beach to the cliffs, a key piece location revealed on their map. She and Kane had trekked northwest through the jungle, and if she just made sure she continued veering to the left, she'd reach the cliffs eventually. Even if she reached the beach first, she'd just follow it until her destination came into view.

Seemed simple enough. Lorelei rolled the map back up and stuffed it back into her pocket, pleasantly satisfied with herself. She kept her pace quick, but slow enough to maintain her energy. There was no way she would let Kane find her sprawled out on the beach, too tired to move. Surely it was what he expected from her. But that was her advantage in all of this—she was unpredictable while the pirates followed patterns of slice and dice and twisted their words with hidden truths. She'd prove to him that she was worth keeping around, even if only to fulfill the promise of revenge.

She wasn't sure how long she trudged on, but the sun was still high in the sky by the time she broke through the trees, sweat rolling down her temple and her hair stuck to the back of her neck. Blinded by light, she raised her hand above her brows, squinting as she gazed out at the white sand and the sapphire water that swept up and down the coast. Tall, jagged cliffs stood at the edge of the beach and curved around the back side of the island.

Taking her first step onto the beach, she left the jungle behind. The heat of the sun stung her cheeks. She couldn't help but wonder how brutal the Trials would have been in mid-sunspur instead of late redwind. Back home, the first red and orange leaves might have fallen from the few trees that still stood. But here, redwind was still hotter than any sunspur she'd ever endured in Port Barlow.

As she neared the cliffs, she let her eyes trail upward. She searched for a glint in the sun, for something that didn't quite belong among the gray rock. The first key piece could be near. Her eyes combed over narrow ledges and the few randomly sprouted weeds and shrubs. She had no idea what the key piece might look like, but surely she should be able to spot it from the ground; that way the climber would know where to start climbing. Then again, maybe that was the point—to search *while* climbing. Nothing seemed to be easy with these pirates.

She stopped short when she smelled smoke. Her throat itched and she coughed as her eyes flicked around the beach and cliffs. Nothing. But the scent was so sudden and so strong that there had to be a fire close by.

When she turned back toward the jungle, she froze. Between her and the line of trees was a large, blackened splotch of sand, like it had been scorched. *Impossible.* Tendrils of smoke rose from the spot and into the air, snaking around each other before dissipating. The burning sand rippled and the stain spread, devouring more of the sand, like water on parchment.

Lorelei stepped backward instinctively as she watched the seemingly breathing spot. It rippled, sending more smoke into the air.

Sssilly little girl. The whisper scraped against the walls of her mind. *Running off on your own. Didn't Genevieve SSStorm teach you better than that?*

Storm? Her mother's name was Penny. It was trying to trick her, just like it had when it drove her mother mad. "Don't speak of my mother with your evil tongue!" Lorelei yelled. Her voice shook as she tried to move but couldn't, fear anchoring her where she stood.

The whisper chuckled—a rumbly, menacing sound. The waves of scorched sand grew, spreading farther as the voice spoke again. *I ssshould thank her. Your mother is the very reason I'm awake.*

"Lies!" Lorelei's eyes filled with tears. Her chin trembled. "You speak nothing but lies!"

You ridiculousss child. His whisper hissed like fire. *The ssspill of her blood allowed me to open my eyes and ssstretch my limbs. I would ssstill be confined to the flame if it wasn't for her.*

The memory of holding her mother's body on the floor of their cottage flashed in her mind, and her face went cold. The middle of the scorched sand rose, the grains falling. A faint sizzle drifted into the air, then angry red and orange lava spewed through the surface, molting, taking the form of legs, then a torso, broad shoulders, and hands with fingers that dripped liquid rock.

The ssspill of your blood will allow me to walk the earth again. When the last SSStorm fallsss, I will rise.

More charred sand rose from the ground, lava exploding from the mounds, shifting and morphing until there were five more molten bodies blocking her way back to the jungle, back to Kane. They were ever changing, constantly molting. An outer shell fissured into chunks of obsidian armor with orange lava glowing and spreading between the cracks. Lorelei blinked, realizing they looked exactly like the creatures she'd seen in her dream.

Air whooshed out of her lungs. The taste of smoke was on her tongue, and her nose burned with each breath she took. She almost tripped over her feet and fell into the sand as she stumbled backward. The creatures moved forward, their bodies hissing and sizzling as they moved. The sky above grew dark, when moments before she'd felt the sun on her skin.

"Why me?" Lorelei screamed. "Why my blood?"

She received only a hiss in return. She turned and ran in the opposite direction, sand flying with each step she took. The molten creatures followed. The crackle and sizzle of their movements echoed from the cliffs. Looking ahead, Lorelei saw the beach ahead narrow until ending completely.

Her feet fell heavy at the sight. There was nowhere to run. She turned back around, staring down the creatures that continued to stalk her.

"Why my family?" she pleaded. Her words were a cry as a tidal wave of regret washed over her. All the things she could have done but hadn't. All the things she longed to do but wouldn't have the chance to. She dug the toes of her boots into the sand and clenched her fists at her sides. "Answer me!"

The creatures stopped. The crackle and sizzle silenced. The world stood still, waiting for an answer.

You foolish girl. The voice taunted her, slithering up and down her spine. *Your blood controls the ssstorm. Your legacccy holds the key to the greatest treasure of all—the world. When the final desss-cendant of the Captain of the SSStorm falls, all I will have to do is reach out and take my treasure. You, Lorelei SSStorm, daughter of Genevieve SSStorm and Jack Rathborne, truessst heir to the pirate throne, you mussst die.*

Her legs went numb beneath her, but she somehow stayed

upright. Her blood rushed through her veins, burning her chest. The whispers remained in her head even when they left.

Jack Rathborne?

Heir to the pirate throne?

Her father was the fallen King of Bones?

No. Not only was she the heir to the pirate throne, she was also a descendent of the first King of Bones, the Captain of the Storm. She was more of an heir than anyone who came before her and she hadn't even known it.

These thoughts were followed by a vision of Kane's shadowed eyes and the secrets locked behind them—ones he'd chosen to deliberately keep from her.

The lava creatures hissed as they continued forward. Their dripping hands reached out for her as their pace quickened, closing the distance at a frightening speed. She moved back until there was no more beach and her hand scraped against the jagged rocks at the foot of the cliffs.

The cliffs.

Lorelei turned, her eyes trailing up the gray rock at what might be her only escape. With one last glance toward the molten beings, she reached up as high as her body would allow and curled her fingers around the curved edge of a protruding rock. Using the cliff wall, she dug the toes of her boots into a small gap and lifted herself high enough to grab another hold. In three movements, her ankles were out of reach from the creatures.

She climbed higher, ignoring the sharp rock against the palm of her hands and the holes tearing into the knees of her trousers. Blood smudged around her fingers and trickled down her legs but she didn't stop. Her arms shook and her legs trembled while she held herself momentarily, trying to catch her breath.

Her heart hammered in her ears, drowning out the growls and hisses of the creatures below.

Yet still, even as she climbed a cliff to escape lava monsters, she burned inside with anger. Kane kept this secret from her—she could have claimed the throne for herself if she'd known. It was no wonder now why he didn't want her to come to the Trials with him. He was the same as the rest of them—just another crooked pirate. She was wrong to have even thought about trusting him.

Lorelei shouldn't have glanced down. She should've kept her eyes upward, eyeing the next spot or groove to fit her hands and feet. When she heard the grinding of rocks against the crackle of flame, she couldn't resist the urge to look at what was happening below.

She watched in horror as the creatures became one with the cliff, their bodies disappearing into the rock. The cliff wall turned obsidian for a moment, smoke rising from their spot of entry. Then all was silent, aside from Lorelei's labored breathing.

Keep moving. The new voice in her head was feminine. It was soft and soothing, like water on a cool day, calming the dread that boiled hot in her veins. *Don't stop climbing.*

Lorelei didn't hesitate. Suddenly feeling stronger, she listened, and reached up for the groove she'd picked out a moment ago. She lifted her foot to move up to the next ledge but stopped when pain seared at her ankle. Her screams echoed off the cliff side.

Looking down, she saw a molten hand sprouting from the rock, which had swiped at her ankle. She gripped the rock tighter and kicked her leg back, trying to keep the creature from grabbing her and searing straight through her flesh and bone. Her hands couldn't take much more. She hung from her fingers and used her free leg to kick the arm, driving her heel down into one of the obsidian-armor plates until a shriek rippled through the air and the hand let go.

Another arm took its place, reaching for her again. She climbed higher and higher until she reached a point of no return. If she slipped or let go from this point on, she would fall to her death on the beach. Molten hands continued to explode from the rock, their fingers dripping with lava as they reached for her. Her body was done, exhausted and drained, but she wouldn't stop until she either reached the top of the cliff or fell.

Who am I? she asked herself. *If I'm this Storm, then who is it that I'm supposed to be?* She was going to die on this island before she ever received an answer to that question. If only she really had the power of this Storm she kept hearing about.

If she could, she would summon the rain.

A streak of lightning bolted across the sky, followed by a crack of thunder. As Lorelei looked up, a raindrop fell on her forehead, cascading down her face. She wondered for a moment about the storm, and the skies that had been clear a moment ago. Then she closed her eyes, breathed in the scent of the rain, and embraced the storm.

CHAPTER TWENTY-TWO

CSILLA

Crossbones

Late Redwind

The lucky zhacia feather had been light when Csilla had first put it on. She'd forgotten she was even wearing it at times, until she stepped foot on Crossbones. That was when everything changed. It was even heavier now as the group of them trudged through the jungle together. The hook tugged at her earlobe.

It had to be the luck magic being spent. It seemed possible that the Ruin Witch had cursed her again because being stuck with Flynn didn't feel like luck. She'd learned from the feather by now that when it warmed, she was making the right choice, and the heavier it hung, the more luck was spent. She assumed quite a bit had been used up during her interception of the *Bonedog*. She only hoped the earring's weight wouldn't eventually tear through her lobe when the magic ran out.

Csilla was the one who led the hunt for Kane's lost first mate through the tangle of earth. The girl left no mystery as to which direction she'd run in, a trampled path leading straight to the cliffs. The broken twigs, torn-through thickets, and smattering of small boot prints made for easy tracking. But Csilla was still impressed that she'd kept her route so straight.

Kane scowled as he searched through bushes. Nara swung her machete left and right, attempting to cut away some of the overgrowth with Kane muttering about how she should be careful where she swung that thing. Flynn and Arius lingered behind. They spoke in hushed voices, but every now and then Csilla caught a few words.

". . . expect us to just follow along . . ." Arius's broken-up whisper reached her ear. ". . . chasing after a girl . . . really?"

"She can't be *just* some girl," Flynn murmured. "Not if the Blackwater is so interested in her."

"Oh come on," Arius groaned. "This is as much of a waste of time as searching for the lost bride."

"You know, rumor was Genevieve Storm didn't want to marry back into the throne. I mean, who would want to after your bloodline was shafted for not bearing any male heirs? I'd bet a whole chest of gold pieces that's why she stole one of the ships."

"No, I heard she married an Incendian prince," Arius argued. "Or was it a lord?"

"She was murdered," Kane cut in. "And Rove's the one who did it." The growl in his voice sent a shiver down Csilla's spine. He must've known something about the heir, too, perhaps through one of his many shady deals with Rove, and he'd tried to keep the secret from the rest of them.

Csilla stopped and hooked her leg over a fallen tree. Bracing her hands on the trunk, she lifted herself up and jumped to the ground on the other side. On impact, a sharp pain shot up her ankle. The others climbed over the log after her. She stood straight, not wanting to draw attention to her injury.

"How do you know so much about it, Kane?" Arius asked. "Did you scare the information out of someone with that scowl of yours?"

Csilla looked over her shoulder. Flynn stood between Kane and Arius, hands on Kane's shoulders as he tried to hold him back from pummeling an entertained Arius. Blackwater stood a head taller than Flynn. He could've walked right through Flynn if he wanted to, but for some reason he resisted doing so, which wasn't like him at all. She'd seen Kane fight many times in the pits of Grisby's tavern in Baltessa and he never lost.

"Tell your friend to keep his mouth shut," Kane said, ripping himself from Flynn's grasp.

"He used to be your friend too," Flynn said, fixing his tattered vest, which had ridden up during the scuffle. "Or were we never your friends to begin with? We just want to know what's going on is all."

"Friends?" Kane asked like the word was one he hadn't used very often. "I don't have any *friends*."

"Aye, and maybe that's the problem, mate."

"We need to keep moving," Csilla said. The group continued, as did the bickering. Csilla rolled her eyes as she pushed a dangling vine out of her way.

"So, Csilla, what do you think?" Arius called.

She ignored him as she stepped over a moss-covered rock that she almost didn't notice. She hoped Arius tripped over it. She bit her lip, holding back her smirk when she heard Arius's curse followed by a thud and groan. Perhaps the feather truly was lucky after all.

But Arius's fall didn't stop him from bothering her again.

"Csilla." He sang her name like he had when they were all kids. "How did it feel to betray your sister? I must say I was shocked you didn't choose Rhoda as your first mate. Some would even question your honor."

Csilla stopped. Is that what everyone thought? That she'd betrayed Rhoda? Her gut twisted. No, she'd made the right choice. Arius was only provoking her. His mouth would get him killed one day, and today could very well be that day. She reached across her body and grabbed the hilt of her sword, pulling it slightly out of its sheath. Nara took a step closer to Csilla, ready to defend, always loyal to the end.

Csilla didn't look away from Arius as she spoke. "You can question my feelings, or even my actions, Arius Pavel, but you don't get to question my honor. Don't bait me with your questions, nor tease me with your ridiculous taunts."

Flynn's eyes were on her but she didn't dare look at him or she risked losing face in front of them all. Sometimes she wished for nothing more than to scream and cry about the cards she'd been dealt in life—an ill mother she couldn't save, a blind eye that she kept covered, a betrayal by someone she thought she cared for. She hadn't shed many tears through her pain and she intended to keep it that way.

"It was just a joke," Arius said after the silence. The smile had fallen from his face.

"Jokes are supposed to be funny," Csilla answered and turned back around to lead the dysfunctional team through the jungle.

When the group finally reached the tree line, the sun had vanished and dark clouds had rolled across the sky. A fierce wind slapped against Csilla's cheeks. There were boot prints in the sand that led from the very spot she stood and down the beach. She narrowed her eyes curiously when she noticed a patch of sand that looked burnt—strange, since sand didn't catch fire. Lorelei wasn't on the beach, but there were no returning prints.

"Dear Goddess . . ." Flynn's voice trailed off from behind Csilla.

"She's climbing!" Kane yelled as he pushed through to the front of the group. "What is that . . ." Without another word, Kane burst into a sprint toward the beach.

Csilla's gaze found the cliffs and Lorelei. She was climbing fast, but something wasn't right. Lava sprouted from the jagged rock, moving like it had a mind of its own. Csilla ran forward, and as she got closer, she realized that the lava had morphed into arms and hands, reaching for Lorelei.

"What . . ." She stopped short. The scent of burnt skin filled the air, making her stomach churn.

"Molten men." Flynn answered the question she hadn't asked. "I never thought I'd live to see the day."

"If they're after her," Arius chimed in, "is this a part of the Trials? What the hell is happening?"

"Ask questions later," Csilla said quickly. "She needs our help!"

Rain fell as they raced to the bottom of the cliff. Kane was already there, his large frame climbing up after Lorelei, who'd stopped and was kicking at an extended, molten arm. Kane took the wrong path up the cliff, missing ledges and footholds that would make his climb easier.

"Hold on!" he yelled up to Lorelei. Her knees wobbled and sweat shone on her skin. She'd stopped, but not at a spot where she could adequately rest. The only reason she had lasted this long was because she was so slight, unlike Kane, who had to hold up his own weight.

A faint sizzle reached Csilla's ears as the rain fell harder. Smoke rose from the molten arms, rain extinguishing the flame that burned inside of them. The arms trembled as pain-filled shrieks filled the air and the limbs hardened until they were nothing more than smooth obsidian.

Kane moved too slowly up the cliff. Csilla sensed how unsure he was as he backtracked and attempted to climb a different route. Craning her head back farther, she saw a clear path to Lorelei, and she was going to take it.

"Nara, did you pack that rope?" Csilla asked. Nara nodded in reply, her lips set in a thin line. "Good, take the slope up by the tree line and drop the rope down to us."

"To *us*?" Nara asked. "You're climbing up there?"

Csilla couldn't save her mother, but maybe she could save this girl.

"I can get up there quicker than Kane." Csilla reached up and curled her fingers around a groove in the wall of rock. "Rhoda and I grew up climbing cliffs like this in Macaya." She lifted her leg and placed the ball of her foot on the first ledge.

"This isn't Macaya," Nara argued. Csilla moved so fluidly up the cliff Nara had to raise her voice to ask, "But what about your ankle?"

"To hell with my ankle!" Csilla yelled down. It throbbed, but the fierce pumping of her heart and the thrill of danger running through her veins numbed the pain. "The rope!"

In just a few movements, Csilla had passed a struggling Kane. The captain could very well beat her in a duel, but everyone had their weakness. Csilla already knew what her weakness was. She looked straight down at Flynn, focusing on him with her left eye, his eyes fixed right back on her. It could have been just an illusion, but when their gazes locked, she swore that he looked worried for her. Goddess, she hated the way her heart raced more from that simple expression than it did from climbing the cliff.

The rock was slippery as Csilla continued up. The heavy rain made it hard to see as she scoped out her path. She blinked away the raindrops, but it didn't help. The storm was odd, having come from nowhere on a clear day.

She had to be quick. She'd learned that the hard way as a child in Macaya. Rhoda had always sung, *Climb quick and true, or it'll be the end of you.* Her song had echoed off the cliffs. One day, before their grandmother had come to collect them for training, Csilla had frozen on the cliff side. Her muscles had tensed up like she was made of rock herself, and the longer she waited in that one spot, the more her muscles ached. Fortunately, she had fallen from a safe enough height, but she still had to endure Rhoda's taunts and ridicule until the day that Csilla finally beat her to the top of the steepest cliff on Macaya.

This cliff wasn't as grand as the ones back home, but the rock was jagged and sharp, cutting into her palms and tearing at her shins when they collided with the wall. Below her, Kane grunted out a curse. She glanced down at him quickly, noting that he hadn't made it much farther than when she'd started climbing.

"Go back down!" Csilla shouted as she moved up. She wedged her foot in a small gap and used it as a step. She latched onto the next ledge.

"No!" Kane yelled back. "I won't!"

"Fine. Then let your pride be your death!"

After another string of curses from below, Csilla looked back and smirked as Kane backtracked down the cliff. Above her, Lorelei held on for dear life. The arms surrounding her no longer moved thanks to being hardened by the rain. White smoke rose into the air.

The rain tapered off the closer she got to Lorelei. Kane was running across the beach to the spot where Nara and the others had disappeared to get to the top of the cliff, but they hadn't made it yet or there would have been a rope dangling. She was completely alone with Lorelei.

A dark, dangerous thought seeped into her mind.

You could end this pessstilent girl, a voice whispered in her head. She wasn't sure if it belonged to herself or not. It was a flutter of wings, a bristle of leaves, barely even there. *It would be easy.*

The rain stopped, allowing her to gaze upward clearly and climb faster. Csilla shook her head, pushing herself up higher, almost to Lorelei.

But the dark whisper didn't leave.

No one would sssee you, the whisper continued. *No one would know her fall wasn't an accident. One lessss competitor to deal with.*

Csilla eyed the first set of molten arms. Heart pounding, she climbed through the narrow space between the obsidian limbs. She watched them out of the corner of her eye, waiting for them to burst with movement and grab her, burning through both her sides. After she passed them, she gave one a rough kick with the heel of her boot, just to see how hard and sturdy they were. Steady as a rock. Her attempt didn't even make a mark. She decided to use the arm to her advantage and rested her weight on it for just a moment so she could breathe.

You could have your dream. Csilla smelled smoke even though there was no fire. *You could be queen and prove your ssstrength onccce thisss girl is out of the way.*

She was so close that she could reach out and wrap her fingers around Lorelei's ankle. The whisper was right. It would be incredibly easy to pull her down and send her free-falling from the cliff. Kane would be furious, but she was nothing to Csilla—nothing more than a problem.

Wait. Why would she think something so terrible?

Do it. If you don't, she could take away everything you've dreamed about. The whisper was a desperate plea.

Csilla shuddered and looked up at Lorelei, who was already gazing down at her through the gap between her arm and chest. They watched each other for a breath before Csilla hiked her leg up to the next edge and pulled upward, her legs shaking. Her body begged her to stop; her teeth were clenched so tight that she was afraid they might crack.

This girl couldn't be the heir. Csilla would know it.

DO IT.

Perhaps this was it—this was the moment the witch had been talking about. This girl could've been an assassin sent by the flame the Ruin Witch had mentioned—maybe this had been Csilla's role to play all along and that's why Csilla had never seen her before. The moment was here, and Csilla couldn't let her kingdom down. She lifted her arm, her fingers reaching toward Lorelei. There was no edge or handhold to grab, only Lorelei's ankle.

DO IT NOW.

Csilla swiped her hand, but her fingers didn't graze Lorelei's ankle and instead found something different. A small warm hand wrapped around Csilla's and pulled.

Her gaze drifted upward, unbelieving. Lorelei's face was pale, her chin trembling as she held on to one of the rock limbs. Her other arm reached down toward Csilla. She was risking a fall, risking her life, for someone who had just debated whether or not to toss her from the cliff.

Csilla couldn't hide the smile that peeled across her lips. It shattered the dark wall the whispers had built around her mind and lit something inside of her, warming the bitter cold layer she always wrapped around herself to keep everyone far away.

It was one simple act of kindness. Just one reaching hand was all it took. Lorelei tugged and Csilla wrapped her other arm around one of the limbs, pulling herself up.

For a moment, they were both safe with their feet planted firmly on the rock limbs. Csilla gripped the stone even though her palms burned with fresh blisters. She felt Lorelei's eyes on her.

Csilla knew she should thank Lorelei for reaching out to her, but her lips remained sealed while Lorelei spoke.

"I'm going to kill him," Lorelei said.

Csilla almost laughed, but she didn't have the energy. She didn't think there was a murderous bone in this girl's body, if she was being honest. "Who are you going to kill, and can I help?"

Lorelei's eyes widened, her cheeks blushing scarlet. "Oh, I hadn't realized I said it out loud."

"Who did you wrong?" Csilla asked, giving it her best effort to sound gentle when she was anything but. "I'll gut them for you."

Lorelei was quiet for a moment, as if contemplating whether or not to confide in Csilla. She wouldn't blame Lorelei if she kept her mouth shut. After all, you bring about your own demise when you put your trust in the hands of a pirate.

Csilla bent at the knees, giving her legs a much-needed rest.

"Kane lied to me," Lorelei said finally. "He lied to me about something really important." There was a true sadness in her voice, the kind that Csilla avoided at all costs. There was no escaping this, though—what separated her from the ground was a fall to her death. "Well, I guess he didn't lie precisely. I knew he was keeping secrets. But keeping this from me? How could he do that? I'm such a fool. I can't believe I trusted him."

"I don't know what secrets he has kept from you, nor do I have the answers," Csilla said. "But Kane has a reason for everything he does, the good *and* the bad." She glanced up, hoping that the rope would be dangling down for them. She needed to get out of there; she needed the pressure of consoling this girl lifted away from her. Csilla could barely even comfort herself—how was she supposed to give Lorelei a shoulder to cry on?

"Why am I even still hanging here?" Lorelei asked. Tears filled her eyes as her voice cracked. Kane's betrayal, whatever it was, must've really done something to her, or maybe there was a deeper reason. "I'm no pirate." She laughed at herself then, a tear rolling down her cheek. "I'm not cut out for this. I should've stayed in Port Barlow. At least I knew who I was there. Who was I kidding? I'm no match for these creatures or men like Dominic Rove."

Csilla snorted. "Let him attack. Let them all attack. Regardless of where you came from before, you're a pirate now. We don't show our fear—we embrace it. The next time someone or something threatens you, you let them know you will not accept defeat or death on that day. Show them that you are not a damsel to be trifled with."

Lorelei watched her for a moment, her chest rising and falling, her chin still wobbling slightly. She blinked her tears away and cleared her throat. "You're right," she whispered. "I don't have to be afraid. I can choose my own path."

The Ruin Witch's words recited in Csilla's mind. *Consider this your path to fate. Which direction will you take?* The feather in her ear warmed, letting her know this girl was worth keeping around.

She noticed movement from above. Nara leaned over the edge of the cliff, sliding the rope down the side. It wasn't long enough to reach them. Lorelei would have to climb up, but her hands were bleeding and her ankle was singed. It was odd for Csilla, worrying over someone else who wasn't a part of her blood or crew. She didn't like the way it made her stomach feel queasy and her pulse pound in her ears.

"Nara has arrived with the rope," Csilla told Lorelei over the wind. "But you must climb higher to reach it. Can you do that?"

Csilla saw Lorelei cringe at the word *climb*. She didn't answer, but they couldn't stay on the cliff forever. Either she had to climb or Csilla would have to resort to other, more painful measures. She did have an idea of how to get her moving, though.

"If you don't climb now," Csilla said, "your fatigue will set in deeper. Your legs will start to tremble, and the ground will seem farther away each time you glance down. You won't be able to move. You won't be able to hold on. You will fall and you will die." Lorelei still didn't answer, so Csilla reminded her of what she wanted. "If you let that happen, then you can't kill Kane."

Lorelei shut her eyes and nodded. "I can do it."

"That's the way! Once you start climbing, don't stop, no matter what." Then she remembered her sister's rhyme. "Climb quick and true, or it'll be the end of you."

With arms and legs shaking, Lorelei climbed, reaching, pulling, lifting herself up. The girl had more strength than she gave herself credit for. It didn't take long for her to reach the rope and grip it with both hands.

"Hold on as tight as you can!" Nara yelled down from the top.

"Use your legs to walk up the rock while I'm pulling the rope!"

Nara started pulling and Lorelei did exactly as she had asked. After a short time, Lorelei reached the top and Nara helped her crawl over the edge before sticking her head back out.

"Do you want the rope, too, Captain?" she yelled down. A playful smirk tilted at her lips. Csilla never asked for help. Nara knew that, but it would benefit Csilla to save her strength. She had to choose logic over pride.

"Toss it down!" Csilla yelled up.

As she watched the rope fly over the edge, something caught her eye. It glinted in the sun, shimmering like it was laughing at her for not noticing it before. Kane's first mate hadn't been wandering the jungle—she'd headed here for a reason.

A key piece.

Csilla climbed sideways along the cliff, past the cluster of rock arms to the spot where the key piece was wedged in a crack in the wall. She gripped it and pulled it out, almost falling backward with the momentum.

What were the odds of her finding the key piece after she'd chosen to save the girl instead of tossing her to her death? Pure luck. The feather at her ear suddenly seemed heavier, weighing down her lobe. More magic spent, and another step closer to the Bone Crown and what she'd be sacrificing for these moments. The Ruin Witch had reminded her that you can't take from the earth without giving something in return. She still didn't want to think about what she'd be losing.

The silver key piece she pulled from the cliff was smooth on one side and jagged on the other, where a second piece would connect, then the third and the fourth. Engraved at the top was a cloud, its edges tufted by a gust of wind. Csilla gave it one final look before shoving it inside the pocket of her pants and climbing at an angle toward the rope.

But Nara wasn't at the cliff's edge anymore. Flynn was. He held the rope end and glanced over his shoulder. His pulling was faster than Nara's, frantic even.

It seemed Lorelei wasn't joking about killing Kane.

CHAPTER TWENTY-THREE

KANE

Crossbones

Late Redwind

This mess was all Kane's fault. His mean old crow of a father laughed from the grave. Kane could practically hear the cruel man's deep, throaty cackle, which used to wake him up in the middle of the night when Kane was a boy. There was nothing worse in Kane's world than realizing that he was still a disappointment to a man who was long gone from the sea, who was only waves on the shore, yet still shaping Kane's entire existence like he was wet sand.

His selfishness to take the crown for himself had him keeping secrets that had put someone's life in danger. He was just so sure if he could make it his, that he would make the fleet better, *Cerulia* better, leading them to vanquish the fire god like they had all those years ago. This wasn't better though. This was destructive in itself, even if he couldn't see it before.

When Nara hoisted Lorelei up over the edge, regret hung over his head, a dark gathering cloud. Her bloody hands, her torn-up trousers, her pale face as she huffed for air. When her eyes found Kane's, her brow creased and her eyes narrowed. Her gaze tore into him like a thousand knives.

"You," she said, her voice low and dripping with accusation. She pointed at him with a shaking finger as Nara lowered the rope back down the cliff. "You are a liar!"

Kane moved back, confused by the sudden accusation and wondering what had happened on that cliff side. "Liar?" he asked, trying his best to keep his voice calm while his insides flurried in panic. "I've *lied* about nothing."

Then she ran toward him, her hands reaching, her nails clawing at the air. Arius grabbed her around the waist and pulled her back. She threw her elbow back and caught Arius in the temple. He let go, stumbling backward as he cursed, but Nara took his place, holding Lorelei back and leaving Flynn to pull Csilla up the cliff alone. Lorelei squirmed and kicked, her face fuming red, her eyes glazing until they were filled with murder-fueled rage.

Throughout it all, Kane went completely still. His palms were cold despite the heat. He tore his eyes away from Lorelei, unable to look at her while she glared at him with such hatred. Instead he watched Nara, who held fast and whispered something in Lorelei's ear.

Kane opened his mouth to speak, to tell Lorelei to calm down and that she would understand if she let him explain himself, but his tongue had gone dry as sand, scraping against the roof of his mouth. How had he let this happen? How had he let things spiral out of control so quickly?

Nara continued to comfort Lorelei until she breathed deeply in and out. Her scarlet-flamed cheeks faded until they were only slightly flushed with sunburn. Another hand rested on Lorelei's shoulder. Kane cringed when he saw the captain of the *Scarlet Maiden* appear on the cliff edge.

"You're in trouble, Blackwater," Csilla sang like a scolding elder sister. She gave Lorelei's shoulder a squeeze before letting her hand fall. "Keeping secrets from someone who trusts you. From your very own first mate. Shame, shame, shame."

"Don't act like you have the faintest clue what's going on," Kane fired back. He shifted uncomfortably. They all crowded around. Even Arius and Flynn looked at him suspiciously, Csilla judging him with her gaze.

"Here's what I *do* know." Csilla began counting on her fingers. "I know you hate rum. I know you're forever scarred from your duel with Jarnis. I know you're still afraid of your dead father."

"What does my father have to do with any of this?" he yelled. He was tired, *so* tired, of the games these pirates played. No one ever gave a straight answer. The truth was always hidden in riddles.

"The point is that I always know more than you think I do. *Much more.*"

Kane growled under his breath, wishing he could pick at her brain and find out what she knew. Csilla hadn't even chosen her own sister as her first mate, but *he* was the bad guy? Perhaps she was purposely sowing division between them for the purpose of winning the crown.

Lorelei nodded in agreement with Csilla. "You didn't think for one moment that maybe I should know the truth?"

Kane fumbled to explain himself, his fingers curling into fists at his sides. He stood on such unfamiliar ground, which was why he favored the loneliness of the sea. Managing functioning relationships with others was not a skill he'd mastered yet. "No, I didn't think—"

"Oh, you had plenty of thoughts," Lorelei's voice was bitter and so cold it made him shiver. "You kept from me that—"

"Lorelei," Kane said, quieting his voice, but everyone still heard him. "Please. Can we talk about this alone?"

"Absolutely not," Flynn said with a devilish grin. "This is way too entertaining."

Lorelei glanced back at Kane. She looked at him like he didn't matter, like he was sea scum under her boots when she spoke. "Whatever you have to say to me you can say in front of them."

No, he couldn't—he was plagued by pride.

Surprisingly, it was Csilla that spared him. "You should let him explain," she said to Lorelei. "Hear him out."

They all turned on Csilla, confusion filling their features. "What?"

"Give them a moment," Csilla continued. "The rest of us will go gather wood for a fire. The sun will be setting soon."

The group moved away from Lorelei and Kane. As they walked off, Flynn said, "So Csilla, does that mean you're going to hear me out too?"

"Possibly," she said, their voices drifting farther away. "Depends on what you have to barter."

"Barter? I have to buy your time?" His voice trailed off as they walked out of hearing distance. Flynn would be lucky if he came back in one piece.

Then it was just Kane and Lorelei with an entire sea of silence between them. He'd never felt so distant from her, even when they'd barely conversed on the ship. At least he'd known where they stood then. At least he'd known that she was slowly begin-ning to trust him. But all of that was now slashed and lying in ribbons at his feet.

Lorelei spoke first. "If you're not going to say anything, then I'm going to go with them."

She moved to step around him, but he stopped her. They both glanced at where his hands were placed on her shoulders. He pulled his hands back.

"I was going to tell you at some point," he started. He had no confidence in himself, but looking at her made him lose even the thought of it. He gulped. Were relationships always this hard or was he the problem?

"Before or after you were named king?" Lorelei crossed her arms over her chest.

"You are right. I was going to wait until I had secured the Bone Crown for myself, but you don't understand. I've been training my whole life for a moment like this. Until a few weeks ago, I didn't even know you existed."

She turned on him, her anger flaring brighter. "Why did I have to learn about my claim to the throne from a monster, rather than you?"

"Magnus spoke to you again?"

"Of course he did! He sent his lava monsters after me! My blood is the only thing trapping him in Limbo . . . or did you already know that too?" She raised her brows, waiting for his answer.

"To some extent." His voice hitched at the end, making it sound like he was questioning himself, and damn, he was.

Lorelei looked as if she was ready to roar at the sky. "The worst part is that my mother knew too." She took a deep shuddering breath like she was trying not to cry. "She knew! I thought my mother was mad, but it all makes sense now. Magnus had been talking to her through the fire for years, breaking her down. I never believed her, yet I wasted belief on *you* in a heartbeat. I'm so pathetic. I thought . . ." She shook her head like the thought was silly, a smile that wasn't truly a smile pulling at her lips. "I thought I could trust you."

Every word was a dagger.

"You *can* trust me," he said, although she probably didn't believe him. The words surprised him yet rang true. "You deserved to know the truth, but I never lied to you. I will still help you get your revenge."

"Omission of truth is just a lie in disguise. If I had known who I was, I could've spoken up before the Trials started. I could've taken the throne and punished Rove for what he's done."

"How do you know they would've even listened to you? Don't you think I thought about these things? Or do I just have a black heart because I'm a Blackwater?" He didn't mean to raise his voice or lightly grip her shoulders again.

"I don't know!" she said through her bared teeth, the sunburn on her cheeks deepening the more heated she got. "I don't even want this throne, nor do I care about it. I only wish I would've known because then I could've chosen my own path!" She turned away from him but he scrambled, following her, gently pulling her to a stop.

"I can't go back and change my selfishness," he said, wishing she'd look him in the eyes. He took a deep breath, knowing that the conversation was edging dangerously close to his even deeper confession. "It is a weight that I've been carrying, growing heavier each day."

"That feeling is called guilt."

"I'm quite aware what it's called." He struggled to keep his voice even as she pulled at his sails. "Yes, I felt guilty, but the truth is, the longer I held your secret in, the more fearful I became."

"Fearful?" Lorelei asked, her tone mocking. "What could you possibly be afraid of?"

"You."

"Me?"

"Yes, you."

She scoffed at him. "You're so full of lies, you can't even think up good ones anymore."

He could have screamed, he was so frustrated with her. "Look at you. Of course, I'm scared of you. All you've known your whole life is your farm and your mother's stories, yet you didn't hesitate to join a deadly competition among pirates while an angry fire god taunted you in the meantime. You look so innocent, but you could wield a knife, stab me in the back, and I wouldn't even see it coming. How do I know whether you hate me or not when you're so unpredictable?"

"Why does it even matter whether or not I hate you?" She watched him, unblinking.

"Isn't it obvious?" He laughed, almost cruelly. "I don't want you to hate me!" He'd yelled the words but hadn't meant to say them aloud.

Lorelei was silent with her delicate brow cocked.

"I was a selfish cod," he continued, pleading his case. "But I was also trying to protect you. The only reason I came to Crossbones instead of going halfway across the world with you was to keep Rove from the throne. I can't let him win, not just for myself, but for the island kingdom. If the majority of these pirates knew who you were, if Rove figured out you'd survived that fire, there would be a bounty on your head. I'd be surprised if Rove didn't already know and had Bonedogs scouring the jungle, looking for you *right now*." He stopped and took a breath. "I'm telling you again, even though you already know. You are Lorelei Storm, daughter of King Rathborne and Genevieve Storm, heir to the pirate throne. And you . . . you are my friend."

She was quiet, her face unchanging, so Kane continued.

"If you couldn't tell, I'm not very good at friendships, but that doesn't mean I don't want to try harder. I do."

Lorelei raised her chin slightly, her expression unchanging. He wasn't sure what to do, but he didn't want to face the Trials alone anymore. He needed someone on his side.

"I am sorry," he said. Words he rarely said but he meant them.

"Today I have lived through an earthquake, had a sword to my throat, argued with a god, and climbed up a cliff while running from his monsters. If I have learned anything after nearly dying, it's that I can't do this on my own." But then her eyes flashed. "I'll forgive, but I won't forget."

"What can I do?" Kane asked, stepping even further into unfamiliar territory. "To make it up to you?"

"Don't betray me again." Her voice lowered, her tone darkening like storm clouds. "Ever." It could've just been the sun, but Kane swore her eyes flickered the blue of lightning for just a moment.

"It was never my intention in the first place—"

Lorelei raised her brow at him.

"—but it won't happen again. I swear it."

Lorelei smiled then. It was a small gesture of peace between them, but at least she'd stopped scowling. "It seems that the captain of the *Iron Jewel* needs a lesson or two on friendship."

"Perhaps you'll have to teach me," he replied, breathing easier for the moment.

CHAPTER TWENTY-FOUR
CSILLA

Crossbones
Late Redwind

Csilla watched the fire carefully that night. The newly assembled group of pirates gathered around the flames with jugs of water opened and ready to be used on any lava creature that might spring up from the ground or the campfire. The rest of the Maidens were camped back at the northern edge of the island. She briefly wondered if they were mingling with the Sons and Jewels just as she was. Was Rhoda with them all too?

She tore at the small loaf she'd packed in her bag and popped a piece in her mouth. Nara had cut off a plug of tobacco from the cured twist that she'd braided herself. She quietly shredded it with her knife on the rock beside her, then loaded her curved pipe. The pipe was engraved with mountains hidden in clouds, representing her home, Ventys. Although she'd been born in the wind-worshipping kingdom, she'd left the north in search of adventure and joined the ranks of the *Scarlet Maiden*. Csilla was thankful now more than ever that she was here.

The others ate, enjoying the peace as they all warily watched the fire dance in the night's shadows. But Flynn was never one to embrace silence.

"So, Csilla," he said from across the fire. "I've been wondering for a while now, why did your grandmother choose you over Rhoda as captain of the *Scarlet Maiden*?"

Csilla swallowed the bread she was chewing and took a good, long look at him before answering. "I'm still asking myself the same question."

"Oh come on!" Flynn rolled his eyes. "You're telling me she just said, 'Csilla, you're captain,' and that was the end of it? You Maidens are always much more complicated than that."

"She made them duel," Nara said, betraying her.

Eyes around the fire widened. Flynn smiled wickedly and leaned forward, resting his elbows on his knees. A strand of sandy hair fell in front of his eyes. Arius stopped stuffing his face for a moment, a piece of dried meat falling from his open mouth. Kane looked amused for once, and Lorelei watched Csilla like she was waiting for a story to be told. Everyone had their eyes on her and she wanted to curl into a ball under a rock and wait until they all went to sleep for the night. Since she couldn't do that right then, she reached over and shoved Nara, making her fall off the boulder they were perched on.

"What was that for?" Nara yelled through her laughter.

"You know exactly what that was for," Csilla answered through her teeth, trying not to laugh herself. She couldn't show any of them her softness or they'd take advantage of it the first moment they could.

"So, Csilla beat Rhoda in a duel and became captain?" Flynn asked incredulously, prompting the discussion to continue even though Csilla longed for it to end. Heat rushed to her cheeks.

"No, she lost," Nara said as she sat back down.

"Well, everyone knows Rhoda is better with weapons than Csilla," Arius said. He took a sip from his flask and burped. "That's common knowledge."

"Shut the hole that you call a mouth." Csilla seethed, which only earned her a chuckle from Arius and Flynn.

"You're right, Arius," Nara said, and Csilla raised her fist. "Don't hit me! Let me finish first!"

"Fine, just get it over with. But I expect to hear your stories, too, Flynn and Kane."

"Ours won't be nearly as interesting as this," Flynn argued. "But if you insist."

"Rhoda nearly killed Csilla," Nara continued. "She beat her to a pulp."

"You're that bad with a sword, Csilla?" Arius teased.

"No," Nara answered for her. Then with wide eyes and more theatrics than Csilla had ever seen from her, Nara wove the story of that day. All eyes were on Csilla by the time she finished.

"You make it sound much more honorable than it was," Csilla mumbled.

"No," Nara argued. "It was inspiring. *You* are inspiring. Every day. But Rhoda . . . Csilla, you have got to be careful with your sister."

"I second that," Kane said, piping in for the first time in their conversation. He raised his hand as if casting a vote for despising her sister.

"Aye," Arius agreed. "There's something wrong with that woman."

Flynn elbowed his first mate. "Just because she won't sleep with you doesn't mean there's something wrong with her."

"Who doesn't want a piece of *this*?" Arius flexed his muscles.

"I don't," Csilla and Lorelei both said at the same time.

"Honestly though, Csilla," Flynn said after the laughter died down. "I don't think you can trust her."

Csilla's stomach tightened. She suddenly didn't feel hungry anymore. She felt like throwing up everything she'd eaten. "She's my sister," Csilla said. "Sure, she beat me in the duel, but it was our grandmother who put the swords in our hands in the first place. Rhoda was just doing as commanded. She's my family—all I have left."

"You have your friends," Lorelei offered quietly. The girl's cheeks held a tinge of scarlet, a burn from the sun. "I know I haven't been around very long at all, but even I can see the strings that tie you all together."

Csilla could've agreed with her. She could've smiled and opened her heart to the group, but she didn't. She'd been broken too many times by people she thought had good intentions. Never again would she let her guard down around anyone else.

Although the fire glowed brightly, the area around them felt dark. Smiles fell from faces, the banter died, and Csilla was cold even though the flames warmed her skin. She was surrounded by company, yet she'd never felt more alone.

Flynn watched her closely. She could feel his eyes all over her face, observing her insecurity and sorrow from across the fire. She avoided his gaze for only a few moments before he shattered the silence again, almost as if he knew how Csilla was feeling and wanted to provide a distraction. If that was his plan, it worked.

"That's certainly a lot more interesting than how I became

captain," Flynn said. "Right, Arius?" He nudged his friend, who nodded eagerly.

"Aye," Arius said, slapping his hand against his knee. "When our captain, Seamus, died—merry rest his soul—we took a vote and Flynn won. I know, I know, such a disappointment. I'm sure you ladies would have loved to see Flynn and myself duel it out."

Csilla snorted. "I'd rather see chickens duel."

"But what if our chests were bare?" Flynn winked at her, knowing that she remembered what he looked like underneath his tattered cream shirt and worn leather vest.

"Not. Even. Then." Csilla bit out the words, trying to keep her face stoic despite her lie.

Nara smirked as she leaned in to the conversation. "I would, if it was also raining. What about mud? Would mud be involved? Let's throw Kane in while we're at it, call it a real good time."

Csilla couldn't help it. She laughed. She laughed loud and long, even though it wasn't the funniest thing she'd ever heard. Flynn's eyes were on her again and when she looked at him, his lips curled up into the type of smile usually saved for private moments. She was so used to seeing his devious grins and his sly smirks that she was taken off guard by the brilliance of his true smile. She sighed, then swore to herself she would choke anyone who noticed.

"Lorelei," Arius slurred, his eyes hazy from whatever was in his flask. "Do you have a lover waiting for you back home?"

Kane cleared his throat, quickly changing the subject. "We didn't have duels or votes on the *Iron Jewel*," he said. "When my father died, the ship passed down to me." He honestly sounded a little pained to talk about it, but he still did. "I was the one who found him in his bed, drowned in a puddle of his vomit. *That* is why I hate rum, Csilla." She felt guilty for bringing it up now.

She could have apologized, but not in front of an audience. Instead, she asked Kane a question that had been lingering on her mind. "When you became captain, why did you make deals with Rove?" It had been so unlike Kane when she'd first heard of the things he'd done in the night. He'd always been a broody one with a quick whip of anger, but he'd still been good, he'd been *one of them*. During his tread down the dark path, it was like watching him disappear in front of her eyes, but now, parts of him were reappearing again.

"The ship was mine," Kane said, his voice dropping low. "But that didn't mean the men thought of me as their leader. They'd seen the way my father tossed me around on the deck like a child's plaything. They saw the doubt in his eyes when he looked at me. So instead, they followed Jarnis the Brute and I had to duel him for my rightful spot. I won, but his axe nearly cut me in two."

Kane pulled down the collar of his shirt, revealing the angry, jagged scar marring his chest. Csilla looked at it for too long, guilt creeping in around her heart at the thought of him facing all this pain alone.

"I kept the ship," Kane continued. "I kept a part of the crew, but my father didn't leave behind much gold, having spent it all on booze and whores in his final days. The ship was my home and it was falling apart. I didn't have much of a crew left. I felt like I had no choice but to go to Rove, so I could restore the *Iron Jewel* to its former glory." Kane shrugged. "I swear I have the rottenest of luck."

Csilla's fingers absently went to the zhacia feather hanging from her ear.

"Well," Flynn said. "Now that I'm depressed, I guess we can discuss other depressing things. Such as me never becoming king."

"You would have been a shit king anyway." Arius laughed, his eyes dancing in the firelight. "You can barely even command the men of the *Anaphine*, much less an entire nation."

"I suppose you're right." Flynn glanced at his friend, then back at the rest of them. "I would have looked dashing with that crown though. Don't you agree, Csilla?"

"Do you live to torture me?" Csilla asked, groaning. Just one day. One day of not hearing his voice and she would get over him. Or would she? The more she thought about it, the more she realized that she might actually miss his shenanigans when all of this was over. Maybe she'd even let him explain himself in time.

"I live for much more than that." His voice was serious, no double meaning in his words. Flynn was more than a mystery. He was a hidden treasure. If she just kept digging, maybe she would figure out what made his heart beat—or she would open the chest and it would be as disappointingly empty as she'd expected it would be.

"Are you denouncing your search for the key pieces then, Flynn?" Kane asked. "Will you align and fight for us against Rove should the moment arise? We can't let him or Tomas win."

"Well," Flynn mused. He linked his hands behind his head and stretched his legs out in front of him, crossing them at the ankles. "I don't know if I'll fight for *you*, Blackwater. After all, my jaw still tenses up from the last time we brawled."

"You deserved it," Kane argued. "You were cheating at Aces in that tavern and you know it."

"Aye, I was. But no, I don't want to see Rove with the crown either. Teaming up against the scoundrel sounds like a bit of fun, to be honest. To see the look on all of their faces when they realize we've bested them all."

"What about the *Scarlet Maiden*, Csilla?" Kane asked as Flynn watched her carefully. "Are you willing to ally to take Rove down?"

Csilla thought for a moment. If they worked together, they'd have greater odds against Rove, Jarnis, and the men of the *Wavecutter*. There would be the inevitable confrontation between her and Kane over who would get to open the chest, but she would worry about that storm when it rolled in.

"Aye," she agreed, earning her a cheer from the group. Except for Nara.

"Rhoda would be furious," Nara whispered. "I worry what she has been up to since our departure and what she will think when she knows you allied with other contenders."

"She'll understand." Csilla had faith in her words.

"But what if she doesn't?"

"Then she'll face the consequences like any other Maiden would." She wasn't sure if she believed herself. If Rhoda did rebel, did Csilla have it in her heart to punish her? She didn't want to face the answer to that question. It had already hurt enough when she'd stripped Rhoda's position as first mate.

"What about the molten men?" Flynn asked. "Does anyone know why they've made a return?"

Csilla noticed Kane and Lorelei share a glance before Kane spoke. "Before the Trials, I was attacked by one. It spoke to me as Magnus, one of the Brothers of Flame, threatening destruction to Cerulia, offering me the Bone Crown."

"In exchange for what?" Csilla asked. Her heart quickened at the mention of the destruction of Cerulia, reigniting the Ruin Witch's warnings of the spreading darkness and flame.

"Nothing," he said. "I ended him before he could offer me a deal."

A terrible lie.

"The details don't matter." His words rushed out. "What's important is that we finish the Trials and gather forces, ready to fight when he helps Incendia finally claim the islands. The first step is finding the key pieces." His eyes roamed over the group. "In the morning, we continue our search for the pieces. Since the other two crews are still searching, we need to cover more land quicker than them. Lorelei and I had a map that led us to these cliffs, so we can search the area at dawn for the key piece on the cliff once we've had rest."

The silver piece was a sudden weight in Csilla's pocket. She could keep it a secret from them then steal the pieces once they collected the rest. She could remain honest and loyal on the outside until the very last minute.

Something dark inside of her purred.

But then her eyes fell on Flynn again. His smile was small, but effective.

"I have the sky piece," Csilla said, stuffing her hand in her pocket. She pulled out the silver in her fist. "Lorelei found it on the cliffs. I grabbed it on my way up."

Lorelei locked eyes with Csilla, both of them knowing full well that her words were a lie.

"Saves us more time." Kane nodded at her appreciatively.

Flynn cleared his throat. "Our map leads to the lagoon. Here, take a look." He rummaged around in his small sack and handed the parchment to Kane.

"Ours to the thicket of the jungle," Nara said, revealing their map.

"Lorelei and I will venture to the lagoon for the water piece then," Kane announced. "Csilla and Nara, find the earth piece.

Flynn and Arius, you two find Tomas and Rove. Steal their maps or their pieces—whatever they have."

"I don't think these pairings are of the most logical sort," Flynn mused, his voice holding the same lilt of humor that it did when he was hatching a plan. "Shouldn't we rather split up based on skill, considering that we're all in this together for the time being? Nara and Arius are two sneaky devils—together they could scour more than myself and Arius. Plus, I'm a fantastic lookout and can be of service while Csilla shimmies up the trees for the earth piece."

"You have to be joking," Csilla said, taking her wrath out on the loaf in her hands. She tore viciously at the remaining bread and shoved a piece in her mouth.

"For once, your plan makes sense." Kane cocked one curious eyebrow.

Flynn nodded, appreciatively. "I know it does. My mother always told me I had a brilliant mind."

"Fine. You and Csilla can get the earth piece, and Nara and Arius go after the other crews."

"No!" Csilla tossed the last chunk of bread into the fire. Embers sparked into the air and the entire group flinched away from the flames, waiting for creatures to be unleashed. When nothing attacked, they all breathed again.

"I always knew you were reasonable, Kane." Flynn was smiling wildly now. "These pairs are going to work out swimmingly."

"Ayyyye," Arius slurred, his eyes drooping. He'd be as useless as a gull if they were ambushed right then.

"On that note," Nara said. "I think it's best if we all get some rest."

"Don't tell me you're okay with this," Csilla whispered harshly. "We shouldn't split up."

Nara kept her voice quiet as she replied. "Don't tell *me* that you trust those two enough to go out on their own. Can you imagine the ruckus they'd cause together? We can keep an eye on them separately."

Csilla had nearly swung from the gallows because of that back-stabber. All she'd been trying to do was stay away from Flynn, yet Nara was pushing them together. Nara must've noticed Csilla's hesitation because she suddenly stood straighter. "Unless that doesn't sit well with you. It's your call. You're my captain."

Csilla glanced at Flynn, watching the way he tenderly pried Arius's fingers from his flask. He always took care of everyone else, so why didn't he take care of her? Why had he let Incendia take her away?

She was ready to know the answers now, however much they might hurt.

"The plan is a clever one," Csilla said, giving Nara's shoulder a squeeze. "I always value your opinion."

"Until morning then," Flynn said as he stood and pulled Arius's arm over his shoulder. He helped his mate stand up and stepped away from the fire. His voice echoed in her mind that night as she tried to fall asleep under the stars.

CHAPTER TWENTY-FIVE
KANE

Crossbones
Late Redwind

Kane made sure Lorelei stayed close as they trekked around the back side of the island. Her muscles had to be sore, a fire blazing on her hands. He'd carefully wrapped her fingers and hands after the argument they'd had, both of them silent, the tension between them too thick to slice. She'd warmed up a bit during their time around the campfire with the others, but after, when he lay next to her on the grass to get some rest before the sun rose again, he watched her as she watched the stars until he finally fell asleep.

He just wished she'd say something to him, *anything* at this point. She hadn't said anything the whole morning and it was driving him up the mast. Silence was a friend of his, but he found himself wanting to be rid of it.

After what seemed like hours, he finally stopped at an edge, Lorelei brushing against his side as she joined him. He heard her gasp above the whip of the waves nearby. Below, a lagoon sparkled in the sun, the teal water separated from the sea by a long stretch of sandbar. The lagoon was quiet, calm, and without a ripple, but he knew the deadly danger that lurked beneath the surface.

Something shot out of the water before flipping and diving back in. It happened so quickly that they were only able to catch a glimpse of deep-green fins disappearing back into the water.

"Was that a . . ."

"Mermaid?" Kane finished for her. "Yes, it was."

"A mermaid!" she said excitedly, her eyes shimmering like the lagoon. "They're in the lagoon? Oh, to swim with mermaids! I just can't believe it!"

Her wide, wondrous blue eyes looked at Kane, then she cleared her throat, composing herself and straightening her belt. The grudge she held against him must've lifted for the moment because she spoke to him like she had before she found out he'd kept secrets from her. "Every little girl in Port Barlow dreamed of being a mermaid," she said, her voice soft as she traced memories with her words. "With their flawless skin, their beautiful voices, their glittering tails. And when their call reaches the one they love, their kiss binds their souls forever, their love everlasting." She sighed dreamily.

"These aren't the mermaids from Incendia's fairy tales," Kane said grimly. "These mermaids may seem beautiful, but on the inside there is nothing but sea foam and rot. Their siren calls lure men during their darkest and loneliest moments, and the mermaid's kiss steals the wanderer's soul so the mermaid can maintain their beauty." He cocked an eyebrow, waiting for her answer.

"You mean . . ." Her voice dropped, her fingertips barely touching her lips. "They steal their beauty?"

"Yes. The purer the soul, the prettier the outcome. Which is why you won't be swimming with them today, or ever, for that matter."

"And you don't think your soul has anything to offer?" Lorelei asked, blowing a piece of hair from in front of her eyes.

Kane tore his gaze from her and glared straight ahead instead. "No, I don't. My soul is marred with the acts of my past."

Lorelei was quiet for a moment. Great. Her silence returned now that they were done talking about mermaids.

"What have you done?" she asked, taking him by surprise. "You've mentioned your past, but you've never told me why you're punishing yourself."

How did she see him so clearly? Her attempt at a connection nearly made him confess, but then he remembered the things he'd be telling her, and witnessing her face crumble back into hatred of him was something he'd rather avoid. There was no easy way to tell her about the things he'd done for Rove's gold. If he told her that he'd silenced men in the dark of night and dumped their cold bodies in the sea, she'd never look at him the same. He'd done those things to rebuild, he always told himself, but what kind of man had he been building himself into?

An echoing crack ripped through the air. Kane quickly dropped to the ground, pulling Lorelei down with him. They both lay flat on their stomachs, his hand on her back, her heart thumping wildly under his palm.

They waited, peering over the edge. Another crack echoed in the air, followed by a wail of pain.

Just when Lorelei was about to ask Kane what was happening, someone burst through the line of trees below and fell to their knees in the sand. He wore no shirt and his pale skin was burned by the sun, his trousers riddled with holes and tears. He hunched over, curling into a ball on the sand. The skin on his back revealed two long, red gashes.

"Borne," Kane said. "The witch's son."

"He needs help," Lorelei whispered to Kane. She moved to get up, but he gripped her wrist tightly, holding her down in the grass.

"Wait," he whispered back. "Watch."

Another person exited from the trees. Rove, with a long whip in his hand and a sinister smile stretched across his face. "Get up!" he shouted at the boy on the ground.

The boy stayed where he was.

"I said *get up!*" Rove yelled the last two words and kicked at the ground in front of him, sending grains of sand flying onto the boy's injured back. Kane clenched his jaw and curled his fist into the grass, his hatred for Rove growing by the second.

The boy grunted in pain and rose with his knees shaking. His frame was slight and even from where they watched, his golden eyes flashed. They glimmered in the sun, holding the same deal-binding magic as his mother.

Kane's gaze locked back on Rove, who circled the boy with a predator's prowl, his eyes dark, his smile cruel.

"What is he doing?" Lorelei whispered. "How did he know to come to the lagoon?"

Kane was quiet for a long moment before answering. "He must be using Borne as a map of some sort."

"How do you know Borne?" Lorelei asked. "We have to help him. We can't just let Rove get away with this."

"Rove introduced us at your father's funeral," Kane replied. "I wish I could have saved him then, but don't worry. I won't let Rove leave this island with Borne. I made a promise."

"What if we claimed he broke a Trials code." She proposed, her eyes narrowing as she schemed. "I thought only the captains and their first mates were allowed to search for the pieces."

"How will they know he broke the code if no one saw him do it?"

"But we saw him do it."

"He'll lie and he'll get away with it."

Lorelei cursed under her breath, something he'd never heard her do before. "Well, we have to stop him somehow. We have to kill him. No one will know if they don't *see us*, right?"

Vengeance seemed to be a fire that burned in her veins. If Kane wasn't careful with her, that flame could become a wildfire.

"In time," Kane said, trying to calm her down. "We don't know how many of his men might be waiting in the trees. For now, we watch and we wait."

"I can't watch this. I won't." She closed her eyes.

Rove did not strike the boy again. Instead, he pointed at the lagoon and gave Borne a command. "Get me that water piece."

"But sir," he whimpered. "The mermaids."

"I know very well about the mermaids, Borne. Do you really think I intend to swim with those vicious creatures when I have you to do it for me?"

Borne didn't answer.

"You'll speak when spoken to!" Rove yelled, gripping the whip tighter in his hand.

"Yes, sir. I will get you the water piece."

Rove smirked "You witchbloods learn fast. The struggle is always easier when you don't fight." He turned his back to the shaking boy and faced the jungle.

Borne cast his gaze straight in their direction, looking right where Lorelei and Kane hid atop the cliff. His golden eyes sparked in the sun like his gaze was on fire, his red-orange hair blowing in the sea wind. It was almost as if he had heard them speaking. Kane thought Borne was looking at him, but Borne gazed next to him, straight at Lorelei.

Lorelei lifted her hand from the ground and subtly waved her fingers, but then Borne glanced away, back at the jungle, purposely ignoring them. Who else was he waiting for?

A silver glint spun through the air and Kane cursed. A dagger arched over Borne's head, so close that it nearly grazed his scalp, and landed in the sand in front of him.

"Oops," said a female voice from behind Borne. "Don't know what happened there. Dagger must have slipped from my fingers." Her voice lacked all sincerity. Her dark hair was pulled back from her golden-brown face, every strand perfectly in place, unlike her sister's fierce curls. Body lean and toned, she moved like someone who'd been training their entire life. There was no way that dagger had accidentally flown in Borne's direction. She was messing with him for sport.

"Rhoda Abado," Kane whispered furiously.

Borne glanced at them one last time before turning to face Csilla's sister. Kane was relieved that the boy did not reveal their hiding spot, but he couldn't bury the anger rising in him.

"What is she doing?" Kane hissed. "Of all the idiotic things she could have done, why would she team up with Rove?"

Rhoda pulled another dagger from the satchel at her hip and directed the tip at Borne. She then pointed it at the lagoon and motioned for him to start walking in that direction. "We don't have all day," she said to him. She followed as he trudged through the sand. "Or you know what? Maybe you should fail so that I can carve something into you. I'd love to pay back your mother for sealing my lips closed with her magic. Pulling them apart felt like I was ripping my skin open."

"Enough, Rhoda," Rove reprimanded.

"You have no *idea*—"

"Enough! It's no wonder your own sister didn't want you as her first mate. You are incapable of shutting your trap. Now, we were both brought together by *him* and as much as I don't want you here, I have to put up with it because he tells me so. But if you don't learn how to shut up, I'll have Borne seal your lips like his mother did."

Borne crawled to the edge of the lagoon and peered down into the teal pool for a long moment. With the tip of her boot, Rhoda pushed him in, the water swallowing him.

"We can't let them get that piece," Kane whispered. A bead of sweat rolled down the side of his face. "If Rhoda gets her hands on it, stealing it will be near impossible."

"How will we stop them?" Lorelei asked, shivering next to Kane. "They'll see you if you dive in."

"I hope they do." Kane smirked.

"And you want me to just stay up here?" Lorelei asked, her whisper a harsh hiss.

"Please," Kane whispered. "If you could listen to me just once, let it be this time. If Rhoda is aligned with Rove, she won't hesitate to kill you."

Kane rose to his feet as Lorelei tugged at the legs of his pants. He tried to ignore her pleas for him to stay there with her, but someone had to get that piece before Rove did. Without a second glance at Lorelei, he jumped forward, his arms arching over his head as he dove toward the lagoon below, his fingertips slicing through the water. He didn't know whether Rove or Rhoda saw him dive, but now that he was submerged, he had to get that key piece before Borne . . . and before he ran out of breath.

The magical lagoon water allowed him to almost see clearly as he swam farther down into the deepening blue abyss. Coral of all colors lined the walls and glowing fish chased each other in and out of the stalks. Borne and the silver key piece were nowhere to be seen. If he didn't find some sort of clue quickly, he'd have to emerge for air before trying again.

Movement below suddenly caught Kane's attention. He swam deeper, toward an edge where a figure waved in the water. As he got closer, he soon realized it was the tail of a mermaid fluttering softly as she hovered over something. An arm that wasn't hers stretched from beneath her, reaching and grasping in the water.

Borne. The mermaid was sucking out his soul.

Kane kicked faster, his arms stroking wider until he plunged into the back of the mermaid, her screech so loud it ripped through the water. She turned on him then, her gaze finding his as Borne slid out from under her. He swam away freely and Kane turned to follow, but the mermaid snatched his wrist, her sharp nails digging into his skin as she pulled him to her.

Her white hair fanned out behind her, the strands waving together, dancing to the ripples of the water. With a face sculpted from marble and endless silver eyes, looking away from her was a feat in itself. She was beautiful. So achingly beautiful. She was everything he needed. He would willingly drown in this lagoon time and time again if it meant an eternity with the most gorgeous being in the world.

No. The thoughts were not his own. Kane kicked his leg in defiance, the only thing this trance would allow, his fight pointless. He *had* to swim back, get away before he became too entranced by her, but his limbs wouldn't move; his lungs tightened.

If only he could bring his lips to hers, feel the velvet of her skin, taste a glimpse of eternity, then he'd be fine. The corners of his vision spotted as the mermaid beauty brought her face closer to his. When she kissed him, the need to breathe slipped away. He could drown in the lagoon a happy man.

Except for something . . . there was something he'd miss.

The mermaid's claws dug into his back as she kissed him deeper.

Someone he'd miss . . .

As the world around him went black, a name circled his mind like a whirlpool.

Lorelei.

CHAPTER TWENTY-SIX
LORELEI

Crossbones
Late Redwind

Lorelei watched as Kane dove into the water, her heart in her throat, her breath a rush in and out. When Kane's body completely disappeared into the lagoon, she dared a glance at Rove and Rhoda to see if they noticed, but the Abado sister was already looking at her with a look that could kill. She scrambled to her feet. From the way Rhoda smiled at her, it was as if she'd known Lorelei was hiding there the whole time. She was like a python, waiting for the perfect moment to strike.

Even though her legs ached in protest from climbing the day before, Lorelei ran as hard as she could toward the trees. At the sound of rocks clattering down the slope toward the beach, she knew Rhoda was quickly climbing up after her.

If Rhoda moved anything like Csilla, then Lorelei was in deep trouble.

Twigs and branches scraped at her skin as she crashed through the jungle. She wove through the trees, bumping against the trunks she wasn't swift enough to avoid. She knocked her knees against fallen limbs as she attempted to leap over them. The rustle following her proved Rhoda was dangerously close.

"You can't outrun me, Lorelei!" Rhoda yelled. "I grew up chasing rabbits faster than you."

Lorelei's face went cold. She pushed harder, barreling through bushes, ignoring the thorns that tore at her hands and cheeks. Pushing aside vines, she trudged farther into the sea of green. She kept track of the directions she turned, trying to lose Rhoda in the tangled mess. *Left, left, right. Right, left, left, right.*

But she couldn't lose her. Rhoda was hot on her trail, gaining on her with every step.

Lorelei's sides pinched. Her lungs failed her and were no longer able to push enough air into her body. She had no choice but to stop against a tree trunk for a moment. A whirring sound buzzed past her ear before a dagger embedded itself in the trunk next to her head. She yelped at how close it had come to finding her temple and shoved herself away from the tree.

Rhoda cackled from somewhere behind her. When Lorelei turned to spot her, she saw nothing but the green of the jungle.

"Little Storm," she called. "Little Storm, come out, come out, wherever you are."

Lorelei almost stumbled when Rhoda said her true name. How did she know?

She couldn't run anymore. She'd get herself lost and killed before she could get away. She knew the only way she would get out of this was to fight. It was foolish to think she could take on someone as skilled as Rhoda, but Lorelei was a pirate now—she didn't have to fight fair.

She spied a rotted-out, fallen tree not too far away, sprinted to it as fast as she could, and found haven in the mess of tangled roots that had shot into the air when the tree fell. She scooted back until she was sure she wasn't visible to the naked eye. Her trembling fingers wrapped around a hefty rock, and she fit it snug against her palm.

It was only a few moments before Rhoda made her presence known.

"Little Storm." She sang like a child playing a game. "Did you think I didn't know who you were?"

A twig snapped as she inched closer to Lorelei's hiding spot.

"He has told me everything," Rhoda continued. "He's offered so much just for your blood. When I end you, I will finally bring respect to the *Scarlet Maiden* and we will bow to no one."

Lorelei's heart raced like it never had before. As quiet as she was, she was sure that the frantic beating in her chest would give her away. The rhythm echoed in her ears as Rhoda taunted her.

"I *will* kill her!" Rhoda suddenly shouted at no one, ripping at vines, stomping over branches.

She whispered a few more phrases under her breath, but they were alone in the jungle.

"Get out of my head!" Rhoda screamed. "No one tells me what to do!"

Rhoda stepped into view, her legs bent as she crept along. She stabbed one of her daggers into a bush next to her and continued to search for her prey. As she stalked through the area, she sang the same song Lorelei's mother had sung when they were playing hide-and-seek in the wheat fields. But this time, the song had a whole new, eerie meaning.

"*The gull flies overhead,*

"*The mouse treads over ground,*

"*The fish swims undersea,*

"*The fox, it makes no sound.*"

Rhoda pulled a second dagger out of her satchel and wielded them both at her sides. She prowled nearer, her blades sharp and ready, her eyes darting around the area. With her golden-brown skin and her beauty, she looked so much like Csilla. But where Csilla's features were soft, Rhoda's were as sharp as her daggers.

"*The wolf howls at the moon,*

"*The hog eats its fill,*

"*The rabbit scurries home,*

"*The fox stalks its kill.*"

Rhoda moved closer and stopped at the opening, turning so that her back was facing the fallen tree.

Lorelei took a shaky breath, gripping the rock tighter in her hands. She shifted her weight onto her feet and stood slowly as Rhoda continued her song.

"*The snake slithers by,*

"*The owl flies at night,*

"*And when you least expect it,*

"*The fox will strike.*"

Lorelei surged forward, jaw clenched, and rammed the rock into Rhoda's temple. Rhoda's body went limp, falling to the ground like a doll, head rolling to the side and blood trickling from where Lorelei had struck her.

The rock slipped from Lorelei's fingers as she stood, dumb-struck, watching the blood roll down Rhoda's cheek. She looked peaceful with her eyes closed and her jaw slack. For just a sliver of a moment, guilt crept into the back of Lorelei's mind. She thought of the brave Csilla and what she would think of her cowardly actions.

She shook her head, trying to be rid of the guilt. She hadn't killed Rhoda, only knocked her out, and if she hadn't protected herself, Rhoda would have murdered her. Csilla would understand. If she didn't, Kane would help make her see reason.

Kane.

Lorelei suddenly remembered where Kane was and the danger he might be in. She tore her eyes away from Rhoda's unconscious body and ran back in the direction she'd come. Her heart raced so quickly it was hard to tell each beat apart.

No matter how fast she thought she was going, it wasn't fast enough. Pain was nonexistent. Fatigue was an illusion. Nothing—not trees, vines, or thorns—would slow her down or keep her from reaching Kane. She tried her best to follow a familiar path, remembering the pattern of turns she'd taken earlier.

Light shone through the canopy as the trees thinned out. She was close. But what would she find when she returned? Her stomach flipped over as she imagined Kane floating lifelessly on top of the turquoise water—or worse, drained of his soul at the bottom of the mermaid pool.

The image in her mind pushed her farther, faster, until she broke through the green and burst into sunlight. It was so bright that Lorelei had to shield her eyes as she glanced across the beach toward the lagoon. She stopped at the edge of the jungle, hiding behind the trunk of a tree, her face suddenly cold and clammy when she had been sweating just a moment before.

Rove stood on the beach, his fists at his hips, his back to

Lorelei. She could sneak up on him the same way she'd snuck up on Rhoda and hit him with a rock. At least with him, she knew she wouldn't feel guilty.

The water was smooth as glass—much stiller than it should've been with both Kane and Borne swimming beneath the surface. What if Kane was . . . she couldn't bring herself to even think the word.

Then the water rippled as something rose, hazy at first in the deep. It edged closer and closer. Borne emerged from the water, gasping for air as he struggled with someone in his arms. Lorelei almost cried with relief when she saw Kane, but quickly put her hand to her mouth. His dark hair was flattened against his face, his eyes closed, and his body still.

Borne pulled Kane halfway out of the water. "The mermaids," he said between breaths. "He saved me. From them."

"Who cares?" Rove bellowed. "Did you get the piece?"

Borne glanced away from the Bonedog captain. "Yes," he replied quietly.

"Then get up." Rove kicked at the sand. "I want to make it back to camp by nightfall."

"But what about Captain Blackwater?" Borne asked, rising onto wobbly knees, his flaming red hair an auburn shade as water dripped from him.

"Leave him for the vultures," Rove spat out.

When Borne made no move to leave, Rove cracked his whip in the air. Borne winced at the sound. He softly pulled his arms from under Kane and followed Rove. He gave one sad look back, just before disappearing into the jungle.

It felt like an eternity, waiting for them to leave. The moment they disappeared into the jungle, Lorelei burst forward. She knew right away Kane wasn't breathing. Panic poured through her, cracking at the surface, threatening to send her overboard. But instead, she closed her eyes and took a deep breath before tilting Kane's head back to open his airway.

Lorelei remembered watching her mother save the lives of drunken sailors who'd fallen into the harbor. She mirrored her movements. Placing one hand over the other, Lorelei linked her fingers together and pressed the heel of her palm against the center of his chest. She rose on her knees, straightened her elbows, and started compressions.

Water spilled out of his mouth as she pushed against his rib cage. Her fingers shook as she moved her hands to his face and plugged his nose. Pressing her lips around his, she blew out, watching as his chest rose. She gave him another breath before starting compressions again.

She repeated her movements another time after, losing hope in a steady stream. He had to take a breath. He *had* to. She pushed harder, harder, until she was sure his ribs would crack. More water spilled from his mouth, but no movement.

It wasn't working.

Tears welled up in Lorelei's eyes as she held back her cry. But she didn't stop pushing on his chest.

He's dead. Magnus's dark taunting whisper was in her head. *The Blackwater is dead.*

"No!" Lorelei screamed angrily as she continued to pump his chest. "He isn't!"

And to think I'd once wanted him to fight for me. His laugh was raspy. *He's weak. His father was right. Kane Blackwater is nothing.*

Lorelei didn't waste her energy arguing with him. She bent forward and gave Kane two more breaths.

Please, she begged the Sea Sisters. *I don't want to lose anyone else. I'll be your Storm. I'll fight for you, I'll do whatever you want. Just don't let him die. I can't do this alone.*

A flurry of coughs rose from under her. Lorelei looked down to see Kane sputtering water. She pushed him onto his side as he coughed up the fluid from his lungs.

When she glanced back at the lagoon, there was someone else in the water. Only cold eyes and white hair were visible—the rest of the watcher remained submerged. A mermaid.

Lorelei reached for the sword at Kane's hip. But it wasn't there. He must have taken off the belt before diving into the lagoon and she hadn't noticed. Her frequent watching of him paid off when she found the knife he always tucked in his boot. She gripped the handle and pointed the blade toward the lagoon. The mermaid was gone without a ripple in the water.

A splash sounded to the right. Before she could turn, something cold wrapped around her wrist and tugged her back. She pulled away from the mermaid that gripped her, but with a strong yank, Lorelei was forced to look directly at her.

The mermaid's white hair glistened in the sun, blowing in the wind even though it should have been dripping wet. Her eyes were cool pools in the sweltering heat. Drops of water fell from her lips. She was magic. She was beauty. She was so mesmerizing that Lorelei couldn't look away. She could look forever, and ever, and ever.

Kane coughed again, pulling Lorelei out of the trance. Her gaze stayed locked on the mermaid as she gripped the knife tighter.

Lorelei counted to three then plunged the knife into the mermaid's hand gripping the edge of the lagoon. She howled in pain, tossing her head back to scream at the sky. Her white hair fell back from her shoulders, revealing a chunk of silver attached to a chain around her neck. Waves were engraved in the silver.

The sea key piece.

Borne had lied. He didn't have the key piece after all.

Lorelei yanked her arm out of the mermaid's grasp and swiped at the necklace. The chain snapped when she tugged, sending her falling backward. The mermaid hissed and clawed for Lorelei's ankle but she quickly crawled out of reach. When she turned back around, the mermaid was gone, along with Kane's knife. She quickly tucked the key piece in her pocket before turning to her captain.

"Kane," Lorelei said, leaning over him so she could see his face. His eyes found hers and blinked. "We have to get off the beach."

"Rhoda?" Kane's voice was nothing more than a rasp.

"She'll be coming back here soon. We have to get moving." She rolled him flat onto his back again and grabbed his arm to help him up but he groaned in pain when he sat.

"My ribs," Kane said, flinching. "They must be cracked."

"I would apologize, but it saved your life."

Once he was on his feet, Lorelei positioned herself at his side. As she slipped under his arm to give him support, he grinned at her.

"My hero," he said.

CHAPTER TWENTY-SEVEN
CSILLA

Crossbones
Late Redwind

Csilla was going to kill Flynn Gunnison by the time they reached their destination in the middle of the jungle. He led the way with his compass in hand, glancing back at her every now and then with that smug smile of his. If he kept looking at her like that, then maybe she wouldn't feel guilty about his untimely death by her hand.

That morning, before the group had gone their separate ways, she'd pleaded with Nara to trade places with her. At least Csilla wasn't attracted to Arius. But Nara only looked down her nose at Csilla and told her to confront her demons.

"If you keep looking at me," Csilla warned Flynn, "I'll cut your damned smile from your face." She'd rather be anywhere else with anybody else. She didn't trust herself around him.

Flynn feigned hurt and gripped his chest as he turned around to face her. "Do you kiss your mother with that mouth?" As soon as the words left his tongue, his smile fell. "I'm sorry. I wasn't thinking—"

"Do you *ever* think about what you say before it comes out?" Csilla asked, brushing past him. She pulled her own compass out of her pack, refusing to follow him any longer.

"I'm sorry," Flynn repeated as he rushed up behind her. "I forgot. How are you holding up since she died?"

Csilla swallowed and glanced down at the arrow of the compass. She'd look anywhere but at him. "Why do you care?"

"Because I know it's hard to lose your mother." Flynn's voice took a soft tone that he rarely used. It was smooth and soft, like velvet.

"Then why did you joke about it?"

"Because that's what I do." Flynn walked next to her. "I joke around. Not much of an answer, I know, but I didn't mean to offend you. Truly."

Csilla kept her gaze fixed on the path ahead. "I don't understand you. I don't know if I ever will. You can't make a joke out of everything."

"But I do." He paused for a moment. "It helps hide the pain." The realest words Flynn had ever uttered.

Csilla wished it was that easy for her—to just laugh away the ache in her heart. "Pain is necessary. If you don't know pain, you'll never know true happiness. Think of each day as a canvas, fresh and new. You can't paint every day yellow without leaving one for gray."

"But what about you?" Flynn was closer, his arm nearly brushing against hers. "How many days do you even paint yellow? You leave *too many* gray. Maybe you're the one who needs to lighten up."

"We weren't talking about me though, were we?"

Arguing. It was what they did best.

"But—"

"I think I've finally figured you out," Csilla cut him off. "You paint over your feelings with coat after coat. If the world can't see them, then they must not exist. Because Flynn Gunnison has no emotions and the world must see it that way. We should rename your ship something more masculine. What about *The Manly Man*?"

"Not true." Flynn's fingers swept against hers, perhaps accidentally.

"Then what are you hiding from?" Odds were he wouldn't give her a straight answer. It was just like him to skirt around the truth.

"A combination of things." Flynn kicked at a rock in their path. "Pain. Fear."

"Fear?" Csilla was shocked that he didn't twist her words again. "You're captain of the *Anaphine*. You're the most confident man I've ever met."

Flynn didn't answer for a moment. Either he was thinking of the right way to phrase it, or he was brewing up a lie. "I fear for my mother."

"Your *mother*?" Csilla looked at him then. A strand of his sand-colored hair hung over the right side of his face, hiding his eyes. When he didn't continue, she probed him further. "Is she sick?" Memories of her own frail, sickly mother tugged at her heart.

"No," he answered.

"Then why do you fear for her?"

He took a deep breath before answering. "She's a prisoner of Incendia."

"A prisoner?" Her voice was shriller than she intended it to be. "But why?"

"My mother was on board the *Anaphine* when we were attacked by the Incendian Navy." Flynn curled his fingers into a fist so tight that his knuckles turned white. "We weren't in their territory. We weren't committing any crime. I was just taking my mother back to Ravana, but we were overrun quickly, and they took her when I wouldn't give them the locations of the fleet captains. They took my mother, offering her safe return if I gave them the locations of the fleet captains."

A trade, she realized. The Incendian fools probably thought breaking her would be simple just because she was a young woman, and when it came to Flynn, she was made of glass.

She remembered that night like it had happened just hours ago. Flynn's smile as he watched her from across the tavern. The sweet taste of rum on her tongue. The way his fingers felt like fire on her skin as he pulled her into the booth with him. After resisting his pull for so aching long, the moment was everything in a world where his touch should mean nothing.

She remembered the flurry of clothes and desperate kisses when they were finally alone in his room at the inn. The sharp yet delicious pain when he bit her bottom lip. His hands as they felt every single inch of her body. The way he made her a goddess to be worshiped, only by him.

When she had sighed against his chest afterward, he had breathed her in. Euphoria. That was the only word to describe it.

But, just like every other time that night played over in her mind, the dark silhouettes came for her and swept away her happiness like a wildfire, leaving her in ashes. She remembered their hands scraping against her skin. The whip of the bedsheet they tossed at her to cover her naked body. The cold bite of the shackles they locked around her ankles and wrists.

If Flynn had said or done anything during her capture, she hadn't heard him over her screams of rage. She hated him more than anything in that moment—more than Incendia, more than any pain, even more than the death that had claimed her mother only moons before that night. But as she looked at him now, his hair longer than when she'd run her fingers through it, his eyes hiding so much more than she'd assumed, that hate faded.

Would she have done the same thing if it meant saving her own mother?

Without a doubt.

"Your betrayal . . ." Csilla tried to say what she was feeling, but it was impossible. How could fickle words describe the hurricane of emotions inside of her?

"I never betrayed you," Flynn said so quietly that she almost missed it.

"Flynn, you don't need to lie anymore. I suppose I understand why—"

"No." Flynn's voice lowered, his gaze firm. "I never betrayed you. I knew you wouldn't believe me. Why would you, after all? I know what it looked like, but I let the navy take my mother so I didn't have to give up my kingdom, so I didn't have to give up *you*!"

"What?" Csilla had been so certain it was him. All the threads had led to the same conclusion. How had she been so wrong? "Why didn't you tell me sooner?"

"I tried, but you wouldn't listen." His voice softened then, like he was telling her a secret. "I fought for you, you know."

"You did what?"

"I fought for you, after they dragged you away that night. I tried to tear my way out of that room but they knocked me in the skull before I could reach the door." He shifted his weight on his feet, avoiding eye contact with her as he spoke. "I acted too late to make any sort of difference, but I thought you should know that."

"But you were in the crowd that day," Csilla argued, trying to make sense of it all. "You smiled as I was about to be hanged."

"When I heard news of you not being rescued from your cell by the Maidens, I knew Rhoda would wait until you were out in the open. I watched the door into the fort. I watched the court-yard walls. Sure enough, they came. I had provisions in place if they didn't. Do you believe me? Do you forgive me for letting them take you from me?"

Taking a deep breath, she gave his hands a light squeeze and dared to look him straight in the eyes. She could get lost in the waves of his sea-colored gaze, but she let her words anchor her. "There's nothing to forgive."

He smiled, allowing her to paint her canvas yellow instead of gray, except for the furthest corners of her mind that left her mind racing. If Flynn hadn't betrayed her to Incendia, then who had?

—

The trees grew taller toward the middle of the island. Csilla had to stay close to Flynn as they wound through the maze of trunks and vines. The next key piece was close, Csilla knew it, but it was diffi-cult to stay focused on searching when her mind was preoccupied with thoughts of Flynn.

She'd never considered herself the romantic type. She never saw herself lusting after anyone, especially someone like Flynn, but her eyes kept finding him. As he cut a path through the jun-gle, his muscles moved under his thin, cream-colored blouse, having discarded his vest before they began their trek. With his hair tied back, beads of sweat trickled freely down his neck. The glory of him was hypnotizing, but her gaze wasn't involuntary. She found herself *wanting* to watch him, as foolish as it was.

"Surely we're close," Flynn said over his shoulder. "How many paces do we have left?"

"I lost count," Csilla mumbled, hoping he wouldn't hear.

"Speak up, love." Flynn slashed at another bush. "I can't hear you."

"I said, I lost count."

Flynn stopped and turned around, laughing the whole time. "You lost count? But you were the one who took control of the map while I thwacked my heart away on all of those bushes."

"I was a bit distracted." But she would never say *why*. She'd rather die first. Quickly, she diverted attention from her last comment. "Rhoda was always the tracker anyway. She's an ace with maps."

"What do you think she's up to now?" The smile fell from his face. "How long will she stay angry with you?"

Csilla sighed. She had no idea what Rhoda was up to, but she didn't like the way everyone was taking shots at her. "I will be fine, Rhoda will be fine. Don't worry about what I do with my crew. Worry about your own, like Arius. He'd better not try to hurt Nara or I'll break his face."

"Nara is a big girl," Flynn argued. "She knows full well how to handle him."

"No, she doesn't. Nara seeks out the best in people. She's impressionable, kind, and loyal. Everything Arius isn't."

"If she seeks the best in people, then why doesn't she have anything good to say about Rhoda?" Flynn leaned against the nearest tree trunk and crossed his arms over his chest. She was beginning to think that making her angry was a game to him. What was his prize if he won?

"She doesn't have to like Rhoda. None of you do. She's my sister—the only family that I have. Now, will you get back to thwacking, or shall I take over?"

Flynn's eyes flickered, as if he was trying to see into her soul, but she wouldn't let him see past her scowl. "You know, Csilla," he said, his voice lilting. "You should rid yourself of the scarf." His sudden change of conversation took her by surprise. Perhaps there was a crack in her shield and he'd figured out how uncomfortable she was talking about Rhoda. Then Flynn shocked her even more. "Don't hide your scars. Brown eye or silver, you're still just as gorgeous."

Csilla absently touched the crimson scarf, right over the spot that covered her blind eye. She wasn't sure if he truly believed what he said, or if he was creating a distraction from their previous conversation. "You're just saying that," she said.

Flynn chuckled, almost looking a little shy as he rubbed the back of his neck. "No, I mean it. Any man would be lucky to have you."

Csilla shrugged her shoulders. "I wouldn't know. I've fought more men than I've kissed."

"And *those* men were lucky to be blessed with the grace of your touch."

"How many times have you practiced *that* line?" Csilla joked, and damn—it felt good when he laughed. She smiled, Flynn smiled back, and the tides between them shifted whether they were ready for it or not.

It was like when Csilla was ten years old, and her grandmother forced her overboard from the *Scarlet Maiden*. Csilla knew how to swim, but that didn't mean she was an expert, and her grand-mother knew that she secretly feared the seemingly endless depth of the dark-blue water. The only way to conquer fear was to face it head-on—at least, that was what her grandmother believed. With the ship anchored, Csilla was made to walk the plank. Before she frantically saved herself, she had sunk down into the dark abyss of the sea. It seemed never ending, so vast, yet excruciatingly suffocat-ing around her. She felt that same hopelessness when the tension between her and Flynn shifted. She knew she was only going to get her heart broken, but she couldn't fight this battle anymore. Her smile was her white flag of surrender and he knew it.

Flynn opened his mouth to say something doubtlessly clever—she could tell from the gleam in his eyes. His lips snapped shut when voices sounded through the trees. Flynn darted behind a tree, Csilla close behind him. The voices came closer, so close that she could make out what they were saying.

"—earth piece should be somewhere around here," a man said. The voice was scratchy and not one she recognized.

A loud smack followed, then another man spoke. "If you'd stop looking at the ground and start looking up in the trees, maybe we'd find it." His voice was incredibly deep and she felt like she should be able to recognize it. "You Incendians know nothing about the elements. You just burn everything away."

Incendian. What was an Incendian doing at Crossbones? Csilla peeked around the edge of the tree trunk, desperate to get a glimpse of who spoke. An older man stepped into her vision, dressed in a simple shirt and trousers, but from the strict way he stood, he didn't seem like a pirate to her. Something was off.

The man whimpered. "Well, you didn't have to hit me for it." He lifted his arm to rub his head and that's when Csilla spied it—a branded emblem of flame and sword.

"A Scout," Csilla whispered to Flynn hurriedly. "Where there is one there's bound to be more. They're dressed as pirates. But why?"

"Shut your whining," grumbled the deep voice from before.

"Why are you always so angry, Jarnis?" the man asked.

Jarnis?

Csilla's breath caught in her throat and Flynn stilled beside her. She prayed to the Sea Sisters that there was another Jarnis with a deep voice and not Jarnis the Brute. Her heart raced as she peered around the edge of the tree trunk again. She questioned the power of her lucky feather when her eyes fell upon Jarnis's pale, bald head not too far away. Of all the people they could have encountered, it had to be the giant one.

"Aye!" a new voice called from behind. Csilla turned around. Her heart jumped in her throat as three more men emerged from the bushes. She couldn't tell if they were Rove's goons or disguised Scouts. "We found some spies over here! The blind girl and the miscreant!"

Flynn snorted. "Why am I the miscreant?"

Csilla's legs tensed to run, but Flynn pressed in close at her side. They wouldn't make it. She would never be able to outrun them with her ankle and leaving the key piece behind was out of the question. With her hands behind her back, she felt the vines that wound around the tree. Another advantage of growing up in Macaya was the abundance of trees. If she couldn't outrun the pirates, she would outclimb them. The key piece was also likely up there somewhere.

"Buy me some time," Csilla said to Flynn in a quick, hushed voice.

Before he could respond, she reached for the highest vine she could find and pulled herself from the ground. Below her, Flynn burst into action. The sound of him unsheathing his sword was just as comforting as if it was one of her Maidens. Climbing the tree was much easier than the cliff side, and soon she was perched on a thick branch.

Glancing down at the ground, she checked on Flynn to see if he was all right. The three men had closed in on him, their swords slashing through the air. Flynn blocked each strike effortlessly, sending one of the men's blades flying out of his hand.

"Get her!" Jarnis boomed from below, spurring Csilla into action. "Don't let her get the key piece!"

Jarnis and the Scout he'd been arguing with climbed up after her, making the vines around her sway.

"Csilla!" Flynn yelled as the swords continued to clang. "They're coming up the tree!"

"Obviously," she muttered to herself as she stood to grab the next branch. As she hauled herself up, she noticed a glimmer in the sea of green. She wasn't sure what it was at first, but when she crossed over to a closer branch, she knew it was the key piece. It wasn't going to be easy to reach.

A man screamed out in pain, and she couldn't help but glance down, past the scowling Jarnis and the old Scout. One of the men on the ground staggered away with blood pouring down his arm. She breathed easier when she realized it wasn't Flynn who'd screamed.

Jarnis drew closer, his speed surprising for how big he was. It was a lot of weight to haul up a tree. Csilla scrambled for her next move, gazing out at the neighboring trees and their branches. She wondered the fastest way to get to that piece and slip away from

Jarnis, but each direction involved having to climb back down. She couldn't do that. Jarnis's huge, meaty hands would crack her neck with one simple squeeze.

Then Csilla smelled it—the thick tang of smoke.

A small flake drifted down from above and landed on the back of her hand gripping the tree branch. Softly, she touched the gray blot and it fell apart, smudging into her skin.

Ashes.

Csilla glanced up, expecting to see a fire raging in the canopy above her, but what she saw was somehow more haunting. The leaves had blackened, their edges glowing with embers, pieces drifting down like snow. The wood of the branches was charred, yet through the grooves in the bark, tendrils of flame snaked outward as if the tree was burning from the inside.

She couldn't climb up or down. She was trapped between two evils.

Csssilla, came the whisper she'd been desperate to be rid of. *Join me.*

She glanced down at Jarnis, who climbed closer despite the burning tree.

Be sssmart about thisss, like the othersss. Isn't it a beautiful sssight to ssee piratesss and Scoutsss come together at times like these?

She shook her head as she climbed, trying to be rid of the hiss.

The Bone Crown can be yours. You can be the firssst pirate queen. Let the SSStorm fall and I can make it happen. I can even bring back your mother if you wish.

Her mother.

To see her again. To thank her for teaching her how to remain strong despite her weaknesses. To apologize for letting Rhoda stray from her heart. To hold on and never let go.

But when she remembered her mother's warm smile as she lay frail and broken in her bed, Csilla realized she couldn't do it. Her mother had taught her more than to just be strong—she taught her how to love and how to remain good and pure among the crookedness of pirates, of the world.

The feather warmed, tickling Csilla's neck.

Her eyes landed on a thick vine that dangled from above. It swayed slightly as if beckoning her to grab it. Was this her luck? She didn't have long to decide as Jarnis growled from just a branch below.

Csilla reached out and grabbed the vine, giving it a firm tug to check its pull. Jarnis's fingers brushed the heel of her boot. She stomped on his hand, earning a growl.

"You won't make it across!" he yelled. "Don't be a fool! Rove, the Incendian king, Magnus—they'll all make you a deal!"

"I would never make deals with men like them," Csilla said, bracing herself to jump.

Ashes continued to fall, coating her curls and her skin. The smoke grew thicker, scratching her throat, burning her eyes.

"Then it's your funeral!" Jarnis yelled. He pulled himself halfway onto the branch. With one hand, he pushed her to her death.

Or so he thought.

A shove from a man of muscle was just the momentum she needed to propel her across the gap. Flynn yelled her name from somewhere below, a loud, panicked sound. But she could barely hear him over the rush of wind in her face and through her hair. She was flying, like a bird with wings, her stomach gone and left behind on the branch.

The tree across the gap came much too quickly. When she was just over the nearest branch, she let go of the vine, and landed in a crouch. She remained on the balls of her feet and twisted to face Jarnis, who was staring back at her like she'd slapped him in the face. She wished she had.

The vine swung back to the far tree and Jarnis swiped it into his grasp. He rolled his shoulders once and stretched his neck before gripping the vine with a fist that could break bones. Csilla stepped back toward the trunk of the tree.

Jarnis jumped. He soared across the gap quicker than she did, but his weight was more than he could bear. He hadn't wrapped his legs around the vine the way Csilla had and it cost him. The farther he swung, the farther he slipped down the vine. Csilla peered down between branches as he swayed over a thin limb below her and landed on his feet.

He looked up and laughed—cold, dark, triumphant. But his smile fell quickly when the snapping of wood cracked through the air.

"Looks like it is *your* funeral," Csilla said with a wave of her fingers.

Jarnis screamed, his veins bulging in his neck. The branch below him snapped, sending him falling to the ground. The thud of his body echoed sickeningly. Either he was dead or every bone in his body was broken.

Kane would be pleased.

Her earring weighed heavier, stretching her earlobe. More magic spent.

Csilla turned her face back up to the canopy. The strange fire spread as the wind blew, gnawing on wood and shriveling leaves up like parchment. She didn't have much time before the fire touched this tree, leaving the earth piece lost in flame.

She searched for the glimmer she'd seen before, moving along the branches like the jaguars back home. When she spotted the silver close to the top, she climbed for it. The branches grew thinner and thinner until Csilla was sure they wouldn't be able to bear her weight and would crack. But they held fast until the key piece was dangling in front of her face. She ripped it from the limb, holding on tight even though the heat from the fire had torched its surface, singeing her palm. She shoved it in her pack and shook out the pain in her hand.

As she raced down the tree, the fire chased her, following her every move, trailing her like her shadow. Once her feet touched the ground, the fire hissed out all at once, filling the jungle with an eerie silence.

Gone were the clanging of swords and the raging heat of the fire. When Csilla glanced up, the canopy was black, ashes blowing in the wind, drifting down to the ground.

The sudden sound of clapping made her spin around with her hand at her sword. Flynn was there, leaning back against a tree, one foot crossed over the other. Blood streaked down his cheek from a gash below his eye, but he was still in one piece. She breathed a sigh of relief.

"Well done," Flynn said. He stopped clapping and hitched his thumb over his shoulder. "I might have fought off a few recruit Scouts, but I also found a dead Jarnis. Did you push him from up there? If so, I'd commend you, but then you'll have broken code."

"Why are you still talking?" Csilla asked. "You're making that cut on your face bleed even more."

"Do you think it will scar?" Flynn asked with a smile as he pushed himself from the tree. He rolled his sleeves up as he walked next to her. Their stroll was so casual after the action they'd just been a part of.

A pirate's life.

"It will leave its mark," she answered.

"And what will you think? Will you still think of me as handsome with a scar on my face?"

He was asking the question on purpose, after he'd told her not to hide her eye anymore. She reached up and untied the scarf from her head, letting her sacrifice show without shame. She'd given her eye for more time with her mother, and her mother wouldn't want Csilla to hide it. It was time to stop thinking so calculatingly with her mind and feel with her heart.

"You'd still be dashing either way," she told Flynn. "With or without that scar."

"And what about the Scouts?" Flynn asked, humor leaving his eyes. "What do we tell the others about them working with the Bonedogs?"

"What if they're here for me?" Csilla asked. She wiped the sweat from her brow. "We can't let the rest of them know I led Incendia to our most sacred island. I'd be labeled a traitor by the elders in a heartbeat."

"So we keep it a secret for now?" He shrugged. "I don't really care, but they'll find out eventually."

"And we'll act like we had no idea. Maybe it won't even matter by then."

"Sure, love. Just be careful you don't cross bones too far or they're bound to break."

CHAPTER TWENTY-EIGHT
KANE

Crossbones

Late Redwind

Kane had let his impatience get the best of him once. He'd regretted it.

He remembered every moment of that day on the deck of the *Iron Jewel*. He could still smell the sweat of the crew, taste the salt on the sea air, hear the sails flapping with the rhythm of the wind, feel his father's knuckles against his cheek as he knocked Kane backward onto the deck.

Get up, his father had growled, nudging Kane's bruised ribs with the tip of his boot. *You get knocked down, you get back up. Blackwaters don't sink, we always rise.*

The deck was slick with sea spray, making Kane's hands slide out from under him as he tried to stand up. His wrists ached from the way his father had blocked his strikes and twisted his fists behind his back. With his left eye swollen shut and his other blurry from tears, he could only see the crimson of blood on his hands, but not where it had come from. Breathing felt like dying as his ribs protested against him.

The shadow of his father blotted out the sun when he loomed closer, crouching next to him as Kane struggled to get to his feet. Kane could smell the rum on his breath as he spoke.

It hurts, doesn't it? his father had asked, his voice a thick rasp in Kane's ear.

Kane had only grunted in response as he'd tucked his knees under him and pushed himself up. Eye level with his father as they both knelt on the deck, Kane glared through the tears. He damned them because they only proved his weakness.

Use that pain, his father had continued. *You'll need it one day. Let it drive you to never feel it again. Let it sink in your bones and become a part of you so that when pain comes once more—and it will—you'll be able to fight the urge to give up and succumb to it all.*

Kane had curled his hands into fists to regain control so he could prove to his father he was more disciplined than his father believed, that he could persevere while being patient. But he still hadn't mastered the art of restraint.

He had lashed out, striking his father with such ferocity that his head had snapped back and he'd crumpled to the deck. Kane had never attacked him without his guard up, not like *this*.

He'd expected his father to leap up and pummel him so hard he would have to eat mush for three months, but he didn't. Instead, he'd gotten up, straightened his coat, taken a long gulp from his flask, and walked away.

Somehow, it was worse than a beating.

For days afterward, Kane had constantly glanced over his shoulder, waiting for his father to enact his revenge. But it never came. The cold eyes that always set Kane on edge were even colder after that, frozen with guilt and regret until the day they closed forever.

Those eyes often woke Kane in the middle of the night, but for some reason when he awoke this morning, for the first time in a long time, he didn't feel the weight of his father's cold stare. It was almost as if the choices he'd been making recently were separating him from the loneliness of his father's shadow.

Kane shifted his back against the tree trunk where he sat, cringing at the pain that shot through his ribs. A restless night on the jungle floor hadn't done much to heal his injuries, even though Lorelei had urged him that sleep would do him good. His wrist still ached from the mermaid's deadly grip as she'd pulled him deeper into the lagoon. His other arm hurt from when Borne had pulled him in the opposite direction, and his chest was sore from being almost ripped in two. His ribs ached from the cracks he'd received during Lorelei's compressions. Even his throat was raw from coughing up water. Drowning wasn't pretty. He was still drained even though he'd gotten some sleep while Lorelei insisted on keeping watch.

Or perhaps the mermaid almost stealing his soul was what had him feeling so tired.

He couldn't deny it—he wouldn't be doing much of anything, especially killing Rove, until he was healed. He would let Csilla handle Rhoda's betrayal. Rhoda was still out there, most likely fuming about Lorelei's escape, and was a danger to them all. She was reckless, destructive, and ruthless—the complete opposite of her sister. He didn't even want to think about what she and Rove were scheming. Knowing the captain of the *Wavecutter*, Tomas was probably aligned with Rove, too, not even aware what was going on as he tipped back his flask.

Every possible outcome was terrible—which was why Csilla and the others needed to complete their missions as soon as possible and *get their asses to the meet point*. Kane slammed his fist back into the tree trunk behind him.

"They'll get here," Lorelei said quietly, as if she'd read his mind. "Please, don't strain yourself."

"Maybe they've fooled us," he said. He'd thought of the possibility so many times it gnawed a hole through him. "Maybe they've betrayed us."

"Csilla wouldn't do that." Lorelei's voice was firm, sure. She'd been sitting next to him the whole while as the sun rose higher in the sky.

"Would you stake your life on that claim?" Kane asked. Thoughts of all of them acting against him were hollow things, but the doubts lingered, pushing him further over the edge. He couldn't take the paranoia and panic anymore. He just wanted the Trials to be over and done with.

"Sometimes you know what is in someone's heart," she explained. She played with a piece of her long, dark hair, twirling the end of it in her fingers. His gaze lingered over the tip of her nose, the blossom in her cheeks as she spoke, her words only for him, more mesmerizing than the magic of a mermaid. "Anyone can speak a lie. Their lies can paint the most beautiful picture, but when the rain comes the illusion is washed away, never truly there to begin with. Sincerity, however, remains. The picture they paint may not be what you want to see, but their truth remains despite any storm."

She was quiet for a moment, as if pondering the depths of the seas.

"Csilla always speaks with sincerity," Lorelei continued when he didn't speak. "She means every word she says." Then she smiled like a fox. "When she arrives, maybe I will tell her that you doubted her."

At her words, Kane straightened his spine. "Don't you dare." She dropped the piece of hair she was toying with and turned to face him. If she was any other woman and he was any other man he'd kiss her right then, but he'd only screw everything up.

He needed a distraction. Reaching into his pocket, his fingers grasped for his father's compass, itching to rub his thumb along its side, but his hand came up empty. He dug in his pocket again, then the other, scrambling onto his knees as he searched the ground around him.

The compass. His father's legacy. He'd lost it.

"Kane?" Lorelei asked. Her eyes were on him, cutting into him as he dug desperately through the grass. "What's wrong?"

"It has to be here," he said. "It has to be."

"What? What are you missing?"

"My father's compass. Have you seen it? It means everything to him and if he finds out I took it again without his permission he'll—"

He stopped, realizing what he'd just said, his chest and shoulders rising and falling, hunched over on his knees just like that dreadful day on the deck of the *Iron Jewel*. The compass was probably at the bottom of the mermaid lagoon, a trade for the sea piece, forever forgotten. Tears sprang up in his eyes and he damned them, hating their existence.

Soft hands cupped his cheeks, lifting his face to look up. Lorelei was on her knees with him, her stormy gaze finding his like a compass of its own. "It's okay," she whispered. "You're okay."

The bare-boned truth was that he wasn't okay.

"I'm not," he admitted.

"And that's okay too." Her hands slid past his face and around his neck, drawing him into an embrace. "If it's any consolation, you're going to find your way with or without your father's compass."

He sat in her arms for a moment, her warmth spilling into him, fracturing the darkness that had clouded over him for so long. She scratched her fingers down his back, a feathered comfort he didn't know he needed. He wrapped his arms around her, pulling her closer, having forgotten what a hug felt like. He wished he could bottle time, if just for this small moment.

"Someone's coming," Lorelei said, letting go and spinning around, taking the warmth with her. She glanced at Kane, then looked back out at the trees.

Kane gripped the blade at his hip as the leaves trembled. Four people emerged from the jungle. Csilla was in front with Nara close behind her, both looking strong and rested. But Flynn had a large gash across his cheek. And Arius . . . Kane had to look away from him before he started laughing.

"You've made it." Lorelei sighed as they approached. "We were beginning to worry something might've happened to you." Good. No mention of Kane doubting loyalty.

"We're all in one piece," Flynn said with his fists at his hips. "But what happened to you, mate?" He glanced down at Kane.

"Mermaid," he answered, hoping that was a simple enough answer. "But we got the sea piece. What happened to *you*?" He eyed the long gash that tracked below Flynn's cheekbone.

"Pirates," Flynn answered with a grin.

Then Kane looked at Arius and pressed his lips together, trying not to smirk. Half of Arius's sun-kissed curls were blackened and singed, making him look like he'd been struck by lightning or left too long in the skillet. "And what in Goddess's name happened to *you*?"

Arius scowled, and Nara answered for him. "We were trying to steal a map from Tomas and Rodolfo last night and he fell into their campfire."

"How does one fall in a fire when sneaking around?" Flynn asked. "The whole point is to be careful of where you're stepping."

"You lot try creeping around in the dark with drunk men sprawled out in your path," Arius argued. "I'm lucky I didn't burn this face off."

"You would have done us all a favor." Flynn laughed and Csilla laughed with him. It was then that Kane noticed she was no longer wearing the red scarf across her blind eye.

"Csilla," Lorelei said, rising to her feet. Her eyes shone with regret as she looked over at the *Maiden* captain. "There's something we need to—"

"Wait," Kane said, interrupting her. He stood as quickly as he could without hurting himself more. He knew Lorelei was about to enlighten Csilla about her sister's betrayal, but right then was not the most opportune time. They still needed Csilla to act accordingly, to stick with them until the chest was out of Rove's hands. If they accused Rhoda of treachery and Csilla didn't believe them, then they lost one more sword on their side. He turned his attention to Nara. "You said you were *trying* to steal a map?"

All eyes cut away from Lorelei and to Csilla's first mate. Precisely what he needed.

"Yes," she said, her cheeks flushing from the sudden attention. Typical of Nara, she collected herself in a blink. "We were unsuccessful. Once Arius fell in the fire, every pirate within shooting distance probably awoke from his scream."

"There was fire on my head," Arius scoffed. "Screaming seemed to be the only option at that moment."

Kane ignored Arius and continued prompting Nara. "Did they have a key piece already?"

She shook her head and fiddled with an arrow she'd pulled from her pack. He noticed she always kept one at the ready at her fingertips. "They don't have a piece, but while Arius and I were staked out we learned something."

"And?"

"The *Wavecutter* is giving the throne to Rove. Heard Tomas say it myself. They had nothing. Anything they did have, they would've handed over to the Bonedogs. Someone is plotting something. I can feel it in the wind. It's getting colder, and not because we're on the cusp of frostfall. This is different."

Kane had forgotten that Nara had been an orphan from Ventys, the air-worshipping kingdom in the north, past the Frozen Gap. What else did the wind tell her?

He felt Lorelei's gaze on him then, waiting for him to provide their own evidence of treachery afoot, but it wasn't time to open that chest yet. It was too private for the moment.

"Flynn and I found the earth piece," Csilla said, dangling it from her fingers for everyone to see. "We had a tangle with some Bonedogs but not much damage done aside from the cut on Flynn's face."

"Well, then," Flynn said. He clapped his hands together once. "I'd say we have a camp to loot tonight."

"I suppose we have no other option," Kane replied.

"The crews are camped together near the falls," Nara said, tapping her arrow with her forefinger as she spoke. "From what I gathered from Tomas and Rodolfo's conversation last night, Rove is keeping the key piece there for protection until he can get the rest. We wait until nightfall. Then we search."

"Isn't that against the rules?" Lorelei asked.

"Not necessarily," Kane answered. "His crew isn't involved directly in the search, so it's more of a loophole."

"Where do you think the key piece will be?" Csilla asked, noticeably shifting her weight off of her left ankle. "If they have it."

Kane didn't have to ponder over it. "Rove will have it with him. No doubt about that."

"It's settled then," Flynn said. "When the moon is high, we do what we do best—except for Arius, who falls in fires. Sea Sisters, please forgive him for his blight upon our craft."

"To hell with you, mate!" Arius yelled.

"I'll race you there." Flynn kicked dirt in his direction before running off with Arius chasing him.

"Am I the only one who finds them strange, yet terribly endearing?" Nara asked as she watched the captain and first mate—more like brothers—chase each other like children into the trees.

"I think Csilla might understand how you feel," Lorelei said with a cheeky smile.

—

Navigating to the falls wasn't difficult with the map they had. It was the waiting that was tedious. Crouched in the bushes, lurking in the shadows of trees.

Kane kept Lorelei close. Truthfully, he was scared to look away and find that she'd run off again—or worse. Cerulia depended on her and her blood, because if she died and that unleashed Magnus, there might not even be a throne to sit on in the end.

Nara and Arius were right. Pirates he recognized from both the *Bonedog* and the *Wavecutter* crews stumbled around together, finding spots to sit around one of the many fires scattered throughout their camp. From their slurred curses at each other and their slouching bodies, Kane knew they'd all had their fill of rum and ale and would soon be passed out cold on the ground.

Csilla's shadow passed through the trees on the other side of the camp, followed by Nara close behind. Flynn and Arius were hidden somewhere else, most likely bouncing on their toes with anticipation, fingers twitching at their sides, finally in their natural sneaky habitat.

Kane's gaze searched the area for Rove, finding him leaning back against a boulder, his clothes in pristine order. His eyes drooped farther with the rising moon, but he still twirled a gold coin between his fingers, never letting it drop. Kane was surprised Rove wasn't flaunting the key piece his heathens had found for him. He continued to watch between the leaves of the bush he hid behind with Lorelei, until his eyes fell on the boy he'd been searching for.

Borne did not sit with the pirates. He was on the ground at the edge of their messy camp, his golden eyes flicking from man to man as if he was contemplating which ones he would kill first if given the chance.

The bronze band that rested on his collarbone shone against the light of the fires. Why didn't he run while they slept? He could have escaped from the island and returned to his mother. She could have removed the band with her magic, yet he remained on Crossbones.

Whatever his reasons, Kane had made himself a promise and he fully intended to fulfill it. While the others would search the sleeping pirates, Kane's path would lead directly to the boy who'd helped save his life.

They didn't have to wait too much longer. Soon the Bonedogs and Wavecutters were asleep, their snores rising over the chorus of insects in the canopy above. A few remained on guard, their pacing sluggish, their faces dreary with exhaustion.

Only one more thing to take care of before they were free to forage through the camp.

Csilla and Nara emerged from the trees, moving like shadows in the night. The two pirates on watch didn't hear them coming. At the same time, the two Maidens leapt onto the men. Wrapping crimson scarves around the pirates' necks, they squeezed, muting their yells until they passed out, then dragged them back into the jungle.

On the other side of the camp, Flynn and Arius took care of the two Bonedogs on watch with a blow to the temple with the buttstock of their pistols.

"I'd tell you to stay here," Kane whispered to Lorelei, "but we both know you won't do that, so stay close."

She only nodded in reply, her lips set in a firm line, her eyes wide and restless.

Kane stepped out of the bush first, surveying the crews for ones who had seen him. No one moved. He took two steps forward, his hand at his sword, ready if necessary. When the pirates remained sleeping, Kane motioned Lorelei forward with his empty hand and she quickly joined him at his side.

His comrades made their moves through the sleeping pirates. The two Maidens rummaged through their stock, moving from barrel to barrel, crate to crate, while the two Sons of Anaphine dug through the pockets of higher-ranked elder pirates quickly and stealthily.

Kane led Lorelei along the edge of the camp. They passed in front of Rove, who was hunched over asleep in front of the boulder he'd been leaning against earlier. His gold coin had fallen from his grasp, lying discarded on the ground beside him. The tips of his moustache fluttered with his breaths.

Kane's gaze found Borne's as they neared the spot where he sat. The boy's golden eyes seemed to glow against the shade of night, watching Kane and Lorelei like a cat in the dark. When they approached, Borne didn't hesitate to scold them like a parent would their child, even though he was the youngest one present.

"You are fools to come here," he said quietly. "You are vastly outnumbered."

"And that," Kane replied, "my friend, is the reason we came at night."

"Fools nonetheless."

"We must hurry," Lorelei whispered, tugging on Kane's sleeve.

"Borne," Kane said, drawing closer to him. "Come with us. Be free of this."

The boy shook his head, remaining seated. "I cannot go. The band will not allow it."

"Then let's be rid of it." Kane stepped forward and placed his hands on the band around Borne's neck. The bronze burned his skin at the touch.

"Only hands of magic can remove it." Borne's eyes drifted to Lorelei. "Let the girl try."

"Lorelei?" Kane asked, unsure.

"I have no magic," Lorelei argued quietly. "If I did, my life would be much different."

CROSSBONES

"You're a stormblood," Borne replied. "Of course you have magic."

Lorelei stepped forward, her cheeks reddening as she took Kane's place behind Borne.

The click of a pistol's trigger echoed among the quiet.

"Blackwater," came Rove's raspy voice. "Risen from the dead."

Kane turned around slowly, his hand finding the end of his own pistol. "You should have known better than to leave a Blackwater out to dry."

"You've become a hassle to kill," Rove continued, his gun remaining pointed at Kane. "First, you manage to slip away from the *Bonedog*'s attack at sea. Then you come back to life when I was sure you had drowned in that lagoon. Now, here you stand. Let's see if you can escape a bullet to the skull."

Rove's hand tensed as he pulled the trigger. The pistol never fired.

Borne brushed past Kane, the band no longer resting on his neck. Kane glanced back to see the bronze glinting in Lorelei's hands.

"I . . . I did it," Lorelei said, her shaky hands gripping Borne's collar. "I got it off."

Borne stepped between them, his hand held out in front, his elbow tucked in at his side. He approached Rove, fingers bent, clenching the air as he spoke a curse under his breath.

"No more talking from you, Rove," Borne said, continuing forward.

Kane gave Lorelei a quick glance before following closely behind the witchblood. The others drew in at the commotion until Csilla, Nara, Flynn, and Arius were there with blades and pistols at the ready. Pirates who had been sleeping began to rouse, rubbing their eyes before gazing over at the group and springing to their feet.

"Stay where you are," Kane ordered. "Or we'll kill Rove."

The lie was easy because he felt like doing nothing more than sliding his blade across the Bonedog's throat. The Trials Code stayed his blade, but the Bonedogs and Wavecutters were dumb enough to believe his bluff.

Rove stood still, his pistol pointed forward. Paralyzed by Borne's magic, his finger remained on the trigger. Sweat rolled down his temple.

"The fire piece is in his left jacket pocket," Borne informed them as the gold in his eyes flickered and the color in his lips paled. "The map to Skull Cave in his right."

Flynn and Arius quickly stepped forward and picked through Rove's pockets, pulling out a silver key piece and a rolled parchment.

Before Borne dropped his spell and they made their escape, Kane wanted Rove to be fully aware that he'd been beaten by the very captain he'd doubted and underestimated.

He stepped close to him and whispered in his ear, "When I serve the queen and am swimming in more riches than you could ever imagine, you will no longer exist. Your days are numbered, Rove." He bumped Rove with his shoulder as he passed him.

But he noticed Lorelei wasn't following. He quickly turned to see her halted in front of Rove, her chin quivering, her hands curled into fists at her sides.

"Lorelei." Kane warned, taking a step toward her.

"He killed my mother," Lorelei whispered harshly at him. "If I can't end him now, then when?"

"Not here. Not now."

She groaned in frustration, then without warning, lifted her arm and drove her knuckles into Rove's face. Rove grunted, his head whipping to the side. Lorelei winced as she rubbed her knuckles.

"Lorelei," Kane urged, an unease creeping down his spine at the darkness that flashed across Lorelei's eyes. "We must go."

She turned back to Rove again, hopefully for the last time. "Don't forget me," she told him.

Then she turned away and followed Kane, the others close behind as Borne's spell held Rove until they disappeared through the trees. Then they ran even though no one chased them. Kane's chest ached and he stayed at the back of the pack, but relief and triumph coursed through him, filling the void, numbing his pain.

They'd done it. They'd collected all four key pieces and had the map to the location of the buried Bone Crown.

There was nothing that could stand in their way, except deciding who would take the completed key to Skull Cave.

Kane or Csilla?

CHAPTER TWENTY-NINE

LORELEI

Crossbones

Late Redwind

The rising sun set the sky on fire the next morning.

They'd run through much of the night, stopping for rest once they were sure they weren't followed by any Bonedogs or any other fake Incendian pirates. With the others readying themselves for what they hoped would be the last leg of their journey, Lorelei and Borne sat in the grass, the four key pieces laid out in front of them as they tried different combinations to complete the puzzle. So far, they'd figured out the pieces connected in two separate grooves along the shaft, but from that point on they were stumped. Lorelei thought harder, biting the inside of her cheek, trying to envision what the key should look like when it was all together. They would all connect to each other in the end like a circle, a never-ending cycle.

"That's it!" Lorelei exclaimed. "A cycle!" She snatched the air piece from the grass, her gaze roaming over the engravings at the rounded top with a cloud, tufted by the wind. "Borne, if we started with air, which element could it best?"

Borne thought for a moment, his gold eyes squinting. "Air can aid the push and pull of the tide, and when cold enough, it can freeze the sea to ice."

"Okay, so let's try the sea piece next." Lorelei snatched the silver that was decorated with cascading waves. When she lined the edges and grooves together, there was a click and the two pieces became the front side of the key. The Powers Above. She glanced at the next missing space, the one that would connect to the sea. "Water extinguishes flames, cools its burns."

Borne handed her the fire piece, its flame engravings evident under her fingers. It locked into place easily. "Fire scorches the earth, new life found among the ashes."

Lorelei swiped the last silver piece, leaves decorating the shaft with a mountain at its top. "And when the wind blows, the earth remains." The final piece clicked in, the cycle complete.

Lorelei quickly waved everyone over, but Borne continued watching Csilla with cautious eyes. While the group was marveling over the Crown Key, he addressed her. "Csilla Abado, I have news for you."

Lorelei's pulse quickened. She turned to Kane, whose face had gone white. Csilla was bent over, retying her boots, but now she straightened, her eyes curious, a small smile pulling at her lips.

"Your sister has betrayed you," Borne said. "She has betrayed us all."

The smile fell from Csilla's face.

Well, that was one way to open a chest of secrets. No one breathed as they waited for Csilla's reaction. It was as if even the wind stopped to listen. Lorelei's heart pounded in her ears.

Csilla narrowed her eyes at Borne as she drew her sword and pointed its tip at him. "You're lying."

"I speak nothing but the truth."

"What proof do you have of Rhoda's betrayal?" Csilla didn't pause long enough for Borne to answer. Instead, she turned on everyone else. "I'm sure you're all happy. You've been dragging my sister's name through the mud the whole time. Now you have nothing to say?" She turned toward her first mate, lowering her sword as she eyed her friend. "Nara?"

Lorelei's gaze flicked between the two of them.

"Csilla, I—" Nara snapped her mouth shut and looked away from Csilla, her cheeks flaming.

"She tried to kill me," Lorelei said. She hadn't meant to intercede, but her heart was beating too fast and her mouth had opened of its own accord. Csilla's shoulders tensed, her sword lifting again to point at Lorelei's neck. Lorelei gulped. "She chased me into the jungle while Kane was diving for the water piece and threw her daggers at me with every intention of killing me. She has a partnership with Rove, Csilla. I heard it straight from their mouths."

Csilla was still for a moment, her chest rising and falling with quick breaths as she glared at Lorelei. She took a step closer, her blade still ready. Kane rose to his feet, grunting in pain, and stepped in front of Lorelei. He panted, exhausted from the sudden movement. With one arm across his chest, gripping his ribs, he used his other to pull the half blade from his belt. He held the steel firm, angling the blade in Csilla's direction. Nara responded by grabbing her bow and a spare arrow from her back, sliding next to Csilla. Lorelei reached around Kane's hip, fumbling with the snaps on his weapon-heavy belt, unsheathing a long curved dagger. This was the moment then, the moment the comfortable balance between them tipped.

"Rhoda wasn't at their camp," Csilla argued, "so why should I believe a word you say, *Lorelei*?" Her eyes were cold where they once had held such warmth. She took another step closer, tension rising as Nara nocked her bow, ready for a sign from Csilla. "Why should any of us believe *anything* you say? We don't even really know you."

"Be careful, Csilla," Kane warned, his low voice menacing. "Don't do anything reckless like Rhoda would do. There's more at work than you know."

"Was it you, then?" Csilla asked, her anger spinning on Kane, her features sharpening, making her look much more like Rhoda. "Were you the one who gave me up to Incendia? Trying to rid yourself of a competitor?"

"What? I'd never do such a thing."

Lorelei stilled, wondering if this was the dark secret he'd kept from her, the one always hiding behind those metal-black eyes of his. He always seemed like he admired Csilla's honor though. Surely, he had nothing to do with her capture.

"Are you happy?" Csilla asked Kane. "Because of you, the Scouts are after me. They've trailed me here."

Flynn coughed. "I thought we were keeping that little bit a secret, love. Now isn't the best time to come clean about that . . ."

"Scouts?" Kane's yell scratched. Birds in the branches nearby fluttered away, rustling the canopy. "There are Scouts in Cerulia? Here. *On Crossbones?*"

Flynn shrugged as if it wasn't a big deal. "They were new members, if anything. Not their best squadron by any means."

Kane turned his blade on Flynn then. "Are you lot *trying* to end Cerulia?"

"Don't you all see what's happening?" Lorelei interrupted, their gazes pinning her. "You're playing right into their hands when you turn against each other. While we're bickering, they're planning Goddess knows what because it's obvious they're all working together—Magnus, Rove, Incendia, and whoever else they've tangled in their web."

Csilla turned back to Lorelei, her sword following her like an extended arm, her gaze narrowing. "Hold on a minute . . ." Csilla mused. "Now I remember. I *have* seen you before. You were there when I escaped Port Barlow that day. I saw you in front of that little house on the hill. You . . . you're not even a pirate."

All weapons turned on Lorelei then, except for Kane's, which he still held firm. He let go of his ribs, his arm reaching back to protect her.

"Who are you?" Nara asked, watching Lorelei carefully from behind her bow. Just one slip of her finger and there would be an arrow in Lorelei.

"I thought you already knew." Lorelei donned a smile, but her heart climbed up her throat. "My name is Lorelei Penny and I'm Kane's first mate."

"Who are you, *really*?" Arius asked. He was the only one besides Borne without a weapon drawn, but his fingers still twitched at the pistols in his holster.

"I—I am Lorelei." She hated that she stuttered, that she looked weak in front of these pirates she'd grown to admire. "That part is not a lie, but you're right, I'm not who I've said I am."

Kane let out a gust of air, his blade lowering.

"I suppose my true name is Lorelei Storm." She paused, watching the faces around her twist with confusion, but Csilla's face remained unchanged. "I am the daughter of Jack Rathborne and Genevieve Storm, though I didn't even know this until two days ago."

"So why are you here?" Csilla seethed, though her eyes brewed like troubled water, torn about something. "Did you come here to take the crown from us? You know nothing about us or what we stand for. You're basically an Incendian from the fish-reeking Port Barlow. You're only here because of your blood, not because you deserve to be. Take a good look at us, take a good look at *me*. The Trials mean a lot more to some of us than just getting to wear a pretty crown on our head."

Lorelei feared this girl who was more skilled than she could ever be, but she didn't back down from her even though she was practically snarling.

"Do you think I asked for any of this?" Lorelei asked calmly, holding her ground. "Do you think I wanted to watch as Dominic Rove murdered my mother? Or that I wanted an angry fire god to burn down the only home I've ever known? I don't want to be hunted by molten creatures who want me dead. I know you don't want to believe any of this, but I don't want your throne. Your sister, however, *does*. We can help you through this, Csilla, if you'll let us."

Lorelei stepped around Kane and lifted her hand to reach for Csilla and offer her embrace, like when she'd offered her hand on the cliffs, but Csilla didn't take a step toward her.

"What do you want from me?" Csilla yelled, her eyes shone with unshed tears. She finally lowered her sword. "Am I to disown the only family I have left in this world? How can I cast her out? How can I accept that? How can I live with myself knowing that I let go of the last person who will ever love me?" A sob escaped from her lips. She bit them, holding in her cry, her chin wobbling, tears spilling onto her cheeks. "How could I let this happen?" She asked the question quietly.

"We can help you through this," Lorelei repeated as she reached out. "There's so much that we can do, if we face it together."

Csilla flinched away from her. "I don't need you." She spun around and faced everyone else. "I don't need *any of you*!" She turned forward again and dug into the bag she carried. She pulled out the Crown Key she'd shoved in her bag for safekeeping and threw it into Lorelei's hands. "Take your key. Take your crown. But you won't be taking me with you."

Lorelei's hands shook as she watched Csilla turn onto her frail ankle, twisting it. She whimpered in pain, straightened herself, and limped away from the group, her head held high.

"Stop," Lorelei pleaded. "Csilla, we need you."

Csilla laughed darkly. "You don't. No one needs me." She ignored the pleas from the others as she passed, but Flynn grabbed her wrist to stop her.

"Csilla . . ." he breathed.

"I don't need more than one traitor in my life," Csilla seethed. Flynn cringed and dropped his hand, but he still watched her as she limped into the jungle without a second glance.

"I'll follow her," Nara said. "I'll talk to her and make her see clearly. She's just upset."

"What's done is done," Kane said. "We have to get to Skull Cave now. Bring her if you can. It doesn't feel right opening the chest without her. We can decide who gets the crown then."

"I'll do my best," Nara said. She spun on her heel and walked up to Flynn before she followed Csilla into the jungle. "You could have done more to stop her," she told him. "From the way she was looking at you earlier, she would have listened to anything you said if you'd tried."

"What was I supposed to say?" Flynn asked, the look on his face truly confused. "I tried to tell her about Rhoda."

"No, you idiot!" Nara shoved his chest. "Maybe the truth about how you feel? That you're in love with her? She needed you to say those words."

Flynn looked as if someone had slapped him. His face went pale and his eyes looked everywhere but at Nara. Then he tucked a stray hair behind his ear and nodded. "I'll talk to her. I'll bring her back. I'll drag her down to the cave if I have to."

"Good."

Then he was off into the jungle, chasing a woman who might eat him alive.

"Great," Arius groaned. "Now I'm stuck with all of you." Nara looked saddened for a moment before Arius spoke again. "Except you, wildcat."

Lorelei's brows raised, and she glanced at Kane. He was just as surprised as she was at hearing Arius's nickname for Nara.

Nara unrolled a map and walked past Lorelei, leading the way. Arius followed closely, looking at the parchment, pointing out which way would be best to approach the cave.

Kane rolled his shoulders. "Are you ready?"

Lorelei stole another glance back at the trees where Csilla had gone. "I suppose I'm as ready as I'll ever be," she replied. "But what about Csilla?"

"She'll . . ." Kane's eyes moved over the jungle where Csilla had gone. "She'll be okay."

Then they followed Nara and Arius in the opposite direction. Borne trailed close behind, his eyes searching the trees. Lorelei thought he might be using some sort of tracking magic to scan for unwelcome visitors.

"Flynn will bring her back with his declaration of love I'm sure."

"What's wrong with that?" Lorelei asked. "Is there something wrong with declaring love?"

"There's nothing wrong with love, but loving a pirate? *That's* a dangerous notion."

"But isn't love always a risk? Isn't that the point?"

"I suppose you could say so." The path sloped down, making them slow their pace to keep from tripping. "Are all risks worth taking, then? Even if you're bound to be hurt in the end?"

Borne spoke from behind them, startling them both. "My mother taught me that there are three kinds of people in this world. The ones scared to love, the ones who embrace it, and the ones who seek to destroy it."

PART FOUR

THE STORM

CHAPTER THIRTY
CSILLA

Crossbones

Late Redwind

The feather in Csilla's ear felt cold for the first time. It was like the tip had been frosted, biting the skin of her neck and shoulder, spreading up her ear and across her cheek. The magic was telling her she was making the wrong choice, but to hell with the magic. It only knew what its maker desired, not what was best for Csilla.

She had no idea where she was going as she pushed deeper into the wild of the jungle; she just knew it was far away from *them.*

She'd been feeling something special, something new that she hadn't known she needed. She'd been high on it, soaring like she was still swinging from the vine. She hadn't seen the fall coming, but she should have. Happiness never lasted long enough for her to enjoy it. It was like dew on a hot morning—gone before the sun hit high noon.

She tripped over a gnarled root as a sob escaped her throat. The words were there in her head, stabbing her over and over. *Your sister has betrayed you. A partnership with Dominic Rove. She betrayed you.*

There had to be some misunderstanding. The same person who'd taught Csilla how to climb, how to fight, how to look strong when you felt weak, couldn't just betray her for no reason. Something else had to lie below the fog. There had to be another truth.

But Csilla knew her hope was pointless.

She'd seen the honesty in Borne's eyes the moment she looked at him. Yet she couldn't accept it. She wouldn't believe that another person she cared about would turn against her, leaving her to be swept away by the wind like a fallen feather. She'd done this. She'd pushed Rhoda down this path when she hadn't named her as first mate.

To top it all off, the heir had been right under her nose the entire time, taunting her with the royal blood that Csilla didn't have. What a sickening fate it was for the heir to be known just when Csilla had a real chance at the crown.

Tears blurred her vision as she continued into the jungle, never once bothering to check if anyone was following her. She told herself she didn't care if they did or if they didn't. She didn't need them or their judgmental gazes.

A snap of a twig made her whirl around with her hand at her sword, ready to slice through anyone that dared come at her.

"Always so quick to pull out the sword," Flynn said as he stepped out from behind a tree. "Kill first, ask questions later. Brutal, but effective."

He's come to rub it in. Magnus's voice crawled back into her mind. *He's come to put sssalt in your wound.*

"I told you not to follow me," Csilla said menacingly. She didn't let go of her sword as Flynn stepped closer.

"Oh, you did?" He smiled as if it was an honest mistake. "I'm sorry. I must have not heard you."

Liar. Liar. Always lying. The voice was sharp and persistent. She tried to shake her head clear of it but it lingered. Was she losing her mind?

"I know you heard me," Csilla said. "You looked me right in the eye when I said it."

"What was that?" Flynn placed his hand behind his ear. "I didn't quite catch it."

He sitsss on a throne of lies with you as his footsssstool. She shook her head again, harder, like when she tried to force water out of her ears, but her action did nothing. His voice was still there, breathing in the back of her mind.

"You. Heard. Me." Csilla bit out each word. She wrapped her fingers tighter around the hilt of her sword.

"My ears must be shot." Flynn shook his head, playing more of his endless games. "What was it you said?"

SSSilence him. SSSilence his liesss forever.

Enough. She unsheathed her sword and pointed it at Flynn, daring him to come closer.

"I hate you!" she screamed, letting her anger pour out of her in a tidal wave. "Your games and your tricks, and your reckless abandon. Your pretending that nothing affects you when everything should. Your smile and the way it twists the deepest part of me, making me feel alive when I'm walking this world half-dead inside. I hate it all! And the worst part is, Flynn Gunnison, is that even though I have every reason to hate you, I can't!"

Flynn pushed the sword away and closed the distance between

them in a few strides. "And why can't you hate me, Csilla?"

She would *never* give him the satisfaction of knowing the answer to that question. She put the tip of her sword back against his neck in response.

Do it. SSSlit his throat open. He's just like the ressst of them.

Flynn glanced down at her blade. He chuckled nervously. "Did you sharpen your sword? I swear it looks much sharper than the last time you had it pressed against my neck."

Csilla gave her sword the tiniest of nudges, making Flynn squeal. The voice in her head laughed darkly.

Yesss. Make him sssqueal like the pig that he is.

"Okay!" Flynn yelled. "Okay, I get it, love. You're done with the games. I won't play them any longer."

"Why did you follow me?" Csilla asked. She tried to hold her sword still, but it trembled in her hand. She blinked away the tears that dared to show themselves.

"To bring you to Skull Cave with the others," Flynn answered simply.

"I'm not going anywhere with you, or with them. You're all so quick to judge my sister for her faults, but I can't. What's the point, anyway? The heir is here now. It's hers. It was never mine."

You can never trussst a pirate. Claws latched onto her mind. A thick, choking smoke clouded her thoughts. Embers and the musk of scorched earth filled her every sense. The voice lowered to a whisper, a grim seduction. *Let me guide you. Let me help you reach your full potential, Csssilla Abado.*

"You misunderstand," Flynn said. His throat bobbed against her blade as he swallowed. "None of us meant to hurt you, Csilla. That was never our intention. We've spoken ill against Rhoda only because we wanted to protect you from this."

Liesss. His lies conccceal the truth. They don't truly care about you, Csssilla. Look into him. There's ssstill ssso much he's hiding from you.

She looked deep into Flynn's sea-colored eyes, trying to see past the curtains he kept drawn close, hiding what was truly behind.

"You're still not being completely honest with me," Csilla said. "You're still lying!"

"Fine!" Flynn yelled. In one swift movement, he swung his shoulder down under her blade, swatted the dull edge of the sword away, and grabbed her forearm. He pulled her close and wrapped his other hand around her wrist, making her drop her sword to the jungle floor. "You want everything from me? Then take it!" His words were fire on her face, flaming her cheeks.

"You may hate me," he continued. "You may curse the air I breathe, but I don't hate you. I love your fire and independence. Your will to push harder when the odds are against you. Your laugh and the way it makes me want to be a better person, just so that I can hear it more often. Your pure heart that gives me more to live for, more to *fight* for in this treacherous world.

"I love you, even if you hate me because that's what love does, Csilla. It endures through every dark night, through every passing shadow. Go ahead, let your fear and despair devour you whole, but I'll still love you through it all."

Csilla's chin trembled. She wouldn't cry. Flynn's fingertips trailed down her arms like drops of water until they found her fingers and intertwined with hers.

Don't fall for his lies. The voice was angry, rattling inside her head. *It's jussst another one of his games. He'll betray you one day, jussst like your sssister.*

Csilla clenched her jaw and shoved at the thing inside of her mind. Flynn's hands gave hers a squeeze, reminding her that he was there—that she wasn't alone. She imagined the wind of a hurricane blowing away the shadows, sweeping away the darkness. The voice hissed and ripped its claws from her mind, leaving her alone once more inside her head.

Csilla closed her eyes and leaned forward, resting her forehead against Flynn's chest, finding what she'd craved most—love. It washed over her like cool water on a hot day, ridding her of the weight that kept her anchored to the bottom of a dark and lonely sea. She'd lost her mother. She'd lost her sister somewhere along the way too.

But hope was a beacon that lit her way to the surface—a light against the darkness.

She had friends. She had those who would stand by her side and fight when she was buried so deep in her head she hadn't seen what was right in front of her. She could have so much more if she took a chance and reached for it. So, she did.

Csilla untangled her hands from Flynn's and placed them on his jaw. She rose onto the tips of her toes as she pulled his face down to meet hers. When their lips touched, the world around her was set ablaze, her skin on fire, their kiss demanding every drop of their souls as the jungle fell away. His hands found her hips, pulling her closer until the rapid rhythm of his heart beat against her chest.

A flame danced between them, more passionate than ever before. In that moment, she was certain. If love was a dream she wanted to chase, she would take the journey for him. The words weren't there on her tongue, but they lingered behind her lips, waiting to be spoken. It was like hearing a new song or opening the pages of a new book and letting herself get completely lost in it. He was the trap she'd been waiting to fall into, the cradle she'd needed for her broken and fragile heart.

But just because she was allowed this small moment of happiness didn't mean all the extra weight that she carried washed away. There was still an entire mountain of pain and problems to climb. She only hoped that she'd come out alive on the other side.

CHAPTER THIRTY-ONE
LORELEI

Crossbones
Late Redwind

Skull Cave lived up to its name. It stood alone among the trees, its rock smooth and muddy brown. Lorelei had expected a gaping hole in a hillside, but when she looked upon the perfectly rounded sphere, she knew the cave wasn't natural—it had been crafted to look exactly like a skull. There were two holes toward the top for eyes; a gaping hole for a mouth was the entryway. She was sure if she looked close enough there would be sharp teeth glimmering at anyone who dared pass inside.

A shiver shot down Lorelei's spine. She suddenly wanted to be anywhere else but walking toward the skull that looked like it wanted to devour her whole. One big bite and it could crush her to pieces.

A string pulled inside of her, begging her to turn back and find anywhere but here. Back on board the *Iron Jewel*. Around the fire with new friends. Anywhere but this place. The string tugged harder with each step she took toward Skull Cave. It constricted her ribs so tightly she could hardly breathe.

"Lorelei?" Kane asked at her side. "Are you all right?"

"No," she said, tearing her gaze away from the foreboding skull. "Something . . . something doesn't feel right."

"What do you mean?" Kane stepped closer, placing his fists on his hips. "We're almost finished. All we have to do is dig up the chest, then it's off to the beach where we started. The look on Rove's face when he finds out we bested him, no matter how many alliances he forged."

His dark eyes flickered with light and she wanted to hold on to it and bask in it with him, but there was no denying the rot twisting the air.

"Do you not feel it?" Lorelei's knees shook beneath her as her gut twisted itself into a knot.

"Feel what?" Kane cocked his head to the side as he watched her, his brow creasing in confusion.

"Darkness," Borne answered. Lorelei looked at him, noticing his golden eyes and the way they stared warily at Skull Cave. "It's waiting for us."

Nara and Arius stopped up ahead when they realized the three of them weren't following. She hustled over while Arius rolled his eyes and dragged his feet.

"Everything all right?" Nara asked, surveying them.

"I don't know what it is, but I just know if we go in there, something bad is going to happen," Lorelei said as the dread built inside her.

"What?" Arius laughed. "So, she can predict the future now? What next? She sprouts wings?"

Kane shoved him hard. "Stop being such a plague."

"If I'm a plague then you're a scourge." Arius pushed Kane back.

"That's the same thing, you imbecile!"

"Can you both stop?" Nara yelled. She put each of her hands on their chests, keeping them apart. "Enough with the pissing battle between you two. There are much more important things at stake than which dog's piss ends up on top."

"My mother once said," Borne offered, plucking the thought from thin air, "the man who places himself atop the tower is the one who will make it crumble."

"Your mother is full of analogies, isn't she?" Arius asked. "Perhaps she should write a book."

Lorelei ignored the arguing. Skull Cave was a sight she couldn't tear herself away from. It sat there like a dark cloud against the blue sky. The slick shine of the rock taunted her, daring her to come closer, yet warning her to stay far away.

She swallowed. "We have to go in, darkness or not. That's how we win the Trials. That's how we end this." As much as she wanted to argue against entering the cave, what other choice was there? She looked at Borne, wondering why they were the only two who could feel the darkness awaiting. The memory of the buzz she'd felt in her fingers when she'd removed the bronze band still lingered. It twitched at her fingertips even then as she stood there.

Magic.

Was it really hers?

The group fell back into step, moving toward the cave. Lorelei could barely lift her foot as the rock skull loomed closer and closer, but she knew she must, so she pressed on. Its surface shone in the light of day, water dripping off the sides as if the skull was somehow sweating. The air changed. The last remains of the rich jungle faded into the reek of mildew.

"Have your swords ready," Borne whispered as the group approached the opening. "The darkness is here."

Those words were ice in Lorelei's bones. The slick cacophony of multiple swords unsheathing was enough to freeze her in her tracks, but Kane tugged on her arm. She closed her eyes as they passed through the skull's mouth. Fear greeted her, a snake that slithered up her spine and wrapped around her neck. The rock walls were close enough to reach out and touch, but instead she wrung her fingers like a wet rag.

A soft trickle reached her ears, like there was a creek up ahead in the cave. Step by step, the trickle grew into a roar and she realized what she heard wasn't water.

Voices. They echoed off the walls, rising in crescendo the farther they moved into the cave. Lorelei knew Lockhart would be waiting for whoever arrived with the key pieces, but there were too many voices. They yelled over each other, screaming curses and death threats.

Kane stopped. Maybe he realized what she'd felt before they walked in—that there was one more trial left to face. She stepped around him and walked through another opening, her friends following, this time into the center of the cave, where a bright light bombarded her. The top of the cave had crumbled in, letting the sun illuminate the floor. Lit torches lined the slick rock walls that sparkled with the flicks of the flames that glowed against it. In the very center, surrounded by the shimmering rock, was a circular area of earth. But where the chest should have been buried, there was only a gaping hole and a dug-up pile of dirt.

"There they are!" one of the pirates yelled from the opposite end of the large cave. He pointed his finger in their direction, bringing every pair of eyes to land on them. Everyone shushed. It was so quiet Lorelei heard water dripping from the top of the cave.

"Ah, perfect!" Lockhart said, stepping away from the crowd of pirates. "Now we can settle this dispute!"

"Dispute?" Kane asked. He stepped in front of Nara and Arius. "What is the dispute? And where is the chest?"

"The chest has been dug up, as you can see," Lockhart said matter-of-factly. Behind him stood the row of crown officials, their faces masks of no emotions. "We know that you have all of the key pieces, and we know that you've teamed up with the Maidens and Sons of Anaphine to achieve it. You've surprised me, I'll admit, connecting with your old friends again. But it seems that we have a bit of a problem, Captain Blackwater. It has been reported that one of your crew members broke a Trial Code."

The pirates behind him burst into chatter again. The aggressive ones looked to all be Bonedogs and Wavecutters, and there were a lot of them. It turned out her group's stop to rest had been much too long, but in their exhaustion, they hadn't seen the possible fault in their actions until it was too late.

Familiar faces turned in their direction. A pair of twins with curly, wood-colored hair flocked to Nara's side. A few young men joined Arius. Doan and the small crew of the *Iron Jewel* trailed behind. The cave was divided. Bonedogs and Wavecutters on one side; Maidens, Sons, and Jewels on the other. They might have had more crews on their side, but the Bonedogs had the numbers.

"What is all of this?" Kane's voice rose. The cave was so quiet, so tense, that Lorelei was afraid to move. "What has Rove done now?"

Rove laughed loud and long. Lorelei finally spotted him off to the left. He was leaning back against the rock wall with his arms crossed over his chest, looking like he hadn't been held captive by magic the night before, but his cheekbone held the purple tint of a bruise from where Lorelei had struck him. His coal-colored hair was slicked back into a tie at the nape of his neck, revealing the line of stubble along his jaw. He resembled Kane in a way, but a version of Kane without a soul—dark and empty. There was no amount of good looks or moustache that could cover the rot inside of Dominic Rove.

"There you go again, always blaming me," Rove said. He unfolded his arms and placed his hand over his heart. "*I* am not the one who has committed a crime."

"You're the guilty party almost every time." Kane countered. "You had your crew attack me at sea!" His last word echoed in the cave.

Lockhart turned to Rove. "You didn't tell me this."

"Aye," Rove said. "I lost my pride when I lost my ship." He hung his head, feigned grief sagging his frame. "I was separated from my men after a run-in with the Incendian Navy at a free-trading port. They must've taken over the ship and pretended to be my men so as to lure in another of the pirate fleet. Say what you will about Incendia, but they are as crafty as they are fiery."

"You *liar!*" Kane roared, the veins in his neck throbbing.

"Calm down, Blackwater," Lockhart said, nearing Kane. The Trials Master shot Rove a warning look. "This is a separate issue and we seem to have a more present problem. One of your crew members broke a code, Kane, and they must stand trial."

"That's absurd!" Kane yelled. "My men have done nothing."

"It isn't one of your men who broke a code, it's *her*." Lockhart looked around Kane and the pirates behind them and gazed directly at Lorelei, making her blood run cold in her veins. "It's your first mate, Kane. She's the one we want."

Everything stopped. Lorelei stopped breathing. The world stopped spinning. The water she'd heard earlier might have even stopped dripping. Shock burned through her stomach as every pirate in the room turned their head to look at her. Unable to think straight, she fumbled through her memory, trying to figure out what she'd done wrong, what code she'd broken. She'd left Rove alive for this very reason. They had to be wrong.

"Lorelei is innocent of whatever crime you accuse," Kane spat out. "She's been by my side the entire time."

"You sound so sure of your words," Lockhart said. His wrinkled eyes looked sincere as he spoke, and he frowned in disappointment. "But how can I believe you when the proof is here with us in this cave?"

"Proof? Any proof you have is folly. Who is the accuser?"

"The accuser is not the point. It is the accusation."

"Who is the accuser?" Kane asked again, his voice on the brink of a yell.

"Kane," Arius warned from behind him. "Calm down, mate. You'll only make things worse."

"No," Kane argued. "If these idiots knew *anything*, they wouldn't be wasting our time."

The click of a loaded pistol sounded, then Lockhart spoke. "I didn't want to have to do this." He had his pistol pointed at Kane. The officials behind him watched closely but said nothing to stop the Trials Master. "If you don't shut your trap, I'm going to put one of these bullets through your kneecap and you'll never walk again. The accused will stand trial at this moment and you will not stop it from happening. Do you understand me, boy?"

Kane didn't reply. Lorelei wanted to smack him, push him, beg him to comply and walk away unscathed. She would not allow him to get hurt because of something she might have done.

Lockhart pressed the barrel of the pistol against Kane's heart. "I will ask one more time. Do you understand me?"

Kane growled. "Yes, sir."

"Fantastic," Lockhart sighed. "I really didn't want to have to kill you, Blackwater. You're one of my favorite contenders for the crown."

The tension in the room pulled away slightly as Lockhart relaxed, but it still hung in the air, waiting for what would happen next. Even though the cave was large and open, the walls felt incredibly close. She'd done her best to be brave during the past weeks, stowing away on a pirate ship, facing fire and lava creatures, climbing a cliff. But as she stood there, waiting for Lockhart to call her forward and face whatever fate they had planned for her, her bravery faded away like it had never been there in the first place, like a spot washed away with the laundry.

Lorelei didn't hear Lockhart when he said her name. There was a whir in her ears, pulsing in rhythm to her rapid heartbeat. She was there, but she wasn't. She was lost inside of herself, swimming through fear like a blind fish. Kane's voice was in her ear but his words were garbled, like she was underwater.

Kane pulled on Lorelei's wrist, bringing her back above the surface. "Come."

She didn't fight it. She let Kane pull her through the crowd of pirates, passing Nara and Arius until she stood in the middle of the cave. They faced Lockhart, which put the two opposing groups of pirates on either side of her. Kane stood to her right, closest to the Bonedogs and Wavecutters.

"Kane," Lockhart said, swinging his head toward his allies. "You can go back now with the rest of them now. This isn't your trial."

"I'll stay here and await the accusation as well as your verdict," Kane replied, before turning to Rove. "Then we will be taking that damned chest and you'll be lucky if we don't hang you for treason when we get back to Baltessa."

Rove cleared his throat from the wall behind Lockhart. "That's assuming your *first mate* survives the trial."

"I've told you she's innocent." Kane directed his words at Lockhart. "This is just a waste of time."

"Enough," Lockhart said. "Lorelei Penny has broken the second code of law—no belonging may be stolen from a rival crew except for a key or map piece. Your first mate has stolen something else from Dominic Rove."

"What?" Kane screamed.

"Sir," Lorelei said, her voice burned in her throat. "I did no such thing."

"Then why did you walk in with his witchblood?" Lockhart asked. He glanced over at the crowd. "Rove has informed me you stole him after an attack on his camp last night. I didn't want to believe that a Blackwater would have a code breaker as a first mate, but the proof is undeniable. There that boy is, and here you are, guilty as a wolf eating its kill. I have no choice. My hands are bound."

"No," Kane said, taking a step closer to Lockhart. "Don't do this. You have no idea what you're doing. She's not who you think—"

Lockhart backhanded Kane so quickly, Lorelei barely saw it. The force of the hit jerked Kane's head to the right. When Kane slowly turned back to look at Lockhart, his jaw working, his left cheek was already red.

"Interrupt me one more time," Lockhart warned. "Stop making a mockery of this trial and let me do my job as Trials Master. Do you think I wanted this role? Being a wet nurse for you babies in this ancient, ritualistic treasure hunt? I'm too old for this shit! Your first mate will face trial by combat." Lockhart tore his eyes away from Kane and turned his anger on Lorelei. "Prepare to duel or *prepare to die.*"

CHAPTER THIRTY-TWO
KANE

Crossbones

Late Redwind

How quickly the tides changed.

Kane's heart had been racing during the confrontation with Lockhart and Rove, but after Lockhart declared trial by combat, his heart stopped completely, leaving him hollow as driftwood.

A strangled cry left Lorelei's mouth. One of her hands reached up to her throat while the other tangled into her hair. Kane whispered promises he couldn't keep into her ear, anything to keep her composed right then.

The crowded Maidens, Sons, and Jewels shifted, parting as Csilla burst through, breathless and huffing. Flynn followed close behind, riding her wake.

"Csilla," Lorelei said, sighing her name. "Thank Goddess you're here."

"What happened?" Csilla asked. She cast her wary gaze past

them all across to the other side of the cave where a mixed group of Bonedogs and Wavecutters stared back. She scanned their faces, clearly looking for someone, but Kane hadn't seen Rhoda in the cave at all.

"They refuse to give us the chest until the verdict is final," Lorelei said. "When Borne came with us, we didn't think we were breaking a code."

"Rove pinned this on Lorelei purposely," Kane said from behind Lorelei. "He has to know who she is. He knows the stakes in trial by combat."

"Stakes?" Lorelei asked, panic filling her eyes all over again. "What are the stakes?"

"If the accused fails to defend, then their sentence is death."

"What?" Lorelei asked, her face ashen.

Kane took a deep, shaky breath. "Lorelei, trial by combat is a fight to the death."

"Yeah," Arius agreed. "Rove is going to kill you after all." Nara reached up and swatted him in the back of his head. Kane would've started another fight with him had the moment not been so pressing.

"Great," Lorelei said, smoothing the stray hairs away from her clammy face. "Why does everything have to be so dramatic with you pirates?" She closed her eyes and tilted her head back. "Anaphine, Talona, Iodeia, please give me the strength to—"

"Is she praying right now?" Arius asked in disbelief. Flynn took his turn smacking him in the back of the head, but that didn't stop him. "Wake up, Storm! You have to fight!"

Storm. That was the answer to this mess.

"Lorelei," Kane said, pulling her out of her prayer and back into the cave with the rest of them. "Tell them who you are. Tell them you're a Storm and you're Rathborne's daughter. They can't follow through with this if they know you're the heir to the throne."

Lorelei stared at Kane blankly. "Right now?" she asked. "Just walk out there and say it? The starting pistol already shot. I forfeited my right then. I told you I don't want the throne. It isn't mine to take from either of you."

"If giving up the Bone Crown means keeping you alive," Kane said, "then I forfeit it in a heartbeat."

"Aye," Csilla added. "I think it's the only way. Listen, I was wrong, Lorelei. Yes, your blood brought you here, but that doesn't mean you aren't one of us. Dominic Rove took away your mother. Are you going to let him take your crown too?" She smiled as she continued. "Remember? You are Lorelei Storm. Show them you are not a damsel to be trifled with."

Lorelei squeezed Csilla's hands and nodded as she bit her lip. Her eyes shone when she let go. She looked at Nara, then Arius and Flynn, before looking back at Csilla. "The harbor-folk used to tell me pirates were scoundrels without a loyal bone in their body. I was always told to never trust a pirate, for their treachery knows no bounds. I was wrong. You lot may pride yourselves on being ruthless buccaneers, but I want you to know that you're all so much more."

Someone sniffled. Kane cast his eyes around the group. "Arius?" he asked. "Are you *crying*?"

Arius wiped his eyes with the back of his hands and then scowled at him. "No!"

Lorelei turned away from the group and held out her hand to Kane, offering a handshake.

"I'm sorry for stealing your gold," she said, to which he smirked. "And thank you for getting me here in one piece."

"You did that all by yourself," he replied, not wanting her to go, afraid of what might happen to her.

Unexpectedly, she threw herself into him, wrapping him in her embrace. She rose onto her tiptoes to whisper, her lips brushing his collarbone. "You're not a black spot of a Blackwater. You're the one who changes the tides."

Lorelei's words filled him like wind filling a sail. He gripped her tighter and rested his chin on the top of her head.

Without another moment spent, she whisked herself out of his arms and walked to the center of the cave alone. His chest swelled with pride as he watched Lorelei face the jeers of the taunting pirates and lift her chin to them, but that didn't mean *he* didn't want to slay them all for even looking at her wrongly.

"Are you ready?" Lockhart asked her, the cave falling silent.

"No," Lorelei answered. Her voice was much stronger than it had been earlier. "But I have something to say."

"More theatrics from your captain, I presume?" Lockhart rolled his eyes and pulled out a flask from his belt. "Get on with it. The young ones are always so theatrical. So *dramatic*." Lockhart lifted his flask to his lips.

"I am not who you think I am," she announced to the entire cave, not just Lockhart. "My name isn't Lorelei Penny, it's Lorelei Storm. I am the daughter of Jack Rathborne and Genevieve Storm."

Lockhart choked on his rum, spewing it from his lips as he coughed. The officials behind him suddenly weren't statues anymore.

"I was born in Incendia after my mother left Cerulia and King Rathborne when she was pregnant with me. I am here because Dominic Rove killed my mother, leaving me as the last descendant of the Captain of the Storm. Magnus, a Brother of Flame, is rising once more and burned down my home because of the stormblood that runs in my veins. I came here not knowing who I was, but now I know who I'm supposed to be. The Trials didn't need to happen. There has been an heir this entire time, and that heir is me. I am the rightful heir not only by my father's side, but by my mother's as well. I, Daughter of the Storm, claim my right to the Bone Crown and the pirate throne."

Kane let out the breath he'd been holding. If Genevieve Storm hadn't run away and Lorelei had been raised as a pirate princess, how different would things have been? She was a puzzle piece that no one knew was missing.

Whispers rose from the allied crews behind them, wondering if Lorelei was who she claimed to be, but across the cave, snickering turned into outright laughter. They pointed at Lorelei, clutching their bellies as they roared and howled with amusement. Lockhart chuckled and shook his head. Kane growled under his breath, his hands clenching into fists. Damn them all.

"Enough with these games," Lockhart said, silencing the pirates with a wave of his hand.

"No," Lorelei argued, balling her hands into fists at her sides. "My father was Jack Rathborne. My mother was—"

"Genevieve Storm died at sea," Lockhart corrected. Everyone knew the rumor, but not many knew the truth. Even though the truth was standing right in front of Lockhart, he was unable to see it. "Jack had no children. Your claim doesn't exist. *You* don't exist, Lorelei *Storm*."

"No, I—"

"Even if you were who you claim to be, you have no proof," a man wearing the *Bonedog* colors yelled.

"My friends know who I am, and so does Dominic Rove."

Lockhart whirled around on the devilish man, waiting for his response to her accusation. Rove wore no expression on his face and told no tales with his eyes—already dead on the inside. He was neither surprised nor outraged. Rather, he seemed to be amused.

"Dominic Rove killed my mother," Lorelei continued. "He tried to have me killed. No one knew that I existed but him until he told Kane."

"What do you say, Rove?" Lockhart asked.

Kane desperately wished that Lockhart would see sense, that asking Rove to play fair was like asking Incendians to stop burning things.

Rove chuckled grimly and shook his head. This would not end well. "Tale after tale seems to spill from this girl's mouth. I only wonder what story she will come up with next to avoid her trial."

"Rove," Lockhart called out, cutting off Lorelei's last chance. "Are you ready?"

"Oh, I won't be fighting," Rove answered. Of course he wouldn't fight—the coward. Kane had never seen him use a weapon. Other hands always did the killing for him, including Kane's own. Rove moved away from the group of pirates he'd been standing with and stepped forward. "Instead, I choose Rhoda Abado as my fighter."

Beside Kane, Csilla wobbled, nearly falling to the ground, but Flynn and Nara were there, supporting her from behind. Pirates across the cave parted, revealing Rhoda at the very back, having been present the entire time. She sat on a large, smooth rock, with her elbows resting on her thighs, daggers flipping over her fingers in a dangerous dance. Her hair was pulled away from her face and tightly braided, revealing the large gash on her temple from where Lorelei had struck her.

Not Rhoda, Kane thought. *Anyone but Rhoda.*

Rhoda tossed both daggers up into the air as she stood, then caught them by their handles and slid the blades into her belt. She walked through the opening the pirates had made for her, each stride confident and quick, like a cobra. The Maidens didn't curse her—they didn't throw their words as stones. When Kane glanced back at the twins and the other Maidens, the glares they shot Rhoda meant more than any words they could ever say.

Rhoda stopped next to Rove as if she was his champion, and maybe she was. Kane wondered if Rove and Magnus had offered her the power she craved. Rhoda looked at Lorelei as if she was going to rip her limbs off one by one. Her face was vicious, seething with rage as she glared at Lorelei.

Rhoda would tear through anyone and everyone to kill Lorelei. Her blazing eyes told a deadly future.

Lorelei didn't stand a chance. She *had* to name a fighter in her place.

Lockhart cleared his throat. "And you, *Lorelei?*"

"I fight for myself," Lorelei answered, her voice shaking as she stared ahead at Rhoda.

Kane wasn't in any shape to fight Rhoda, but he still stood more of a chance than Lorelei. Her blood could not be spilled. If the pirates wouldn't listen to them, then he'd make them listen.

"No," Csilla said at Kane's side, her hand on his shoulder. "This is my fight." She stepped forward, ignoring the pirates' confused murmurs. "I'll fight for her," she announced.

CHAPTER THIRTY-THREE
CSILLA

Crossbones

Late Redwind

A collective gasp echoed around the cave. Captain against first mate. Sister against sister. Csilla remembered what happened the last time she'd dueled her sister, but if there was anyone to stop Rhoda's madness, it was Csilla.

"No," Lorelei argued, shaking her head. "I won't let you."

"I'll take orders from you *after* you're queen," Csilla replied.

"You can't do this," Nara said, yanking on Csilla's arm. "Your ankle. Your eye. Rhoda is so quick you won't see it coming. She'll kill you and she'll get the *Scarlet Maiden* when she does. She will ruin the legacy you're building in an instant."

"She can do this," Flynn said. He grabbed Csilla by the shoulders and turned her to face him. "Don't let her get on your left side and keep her where you can see her. She's reckless, so let her strike first. You can parry and attack when her guard is down. But most importantly, don't let her get inside your head. She's going to—"

"I thought you said I could do this," Csilla said.

"And you can. Just thought I'd give you some pointers." He winked and smiled, but Csilla still saw through it. He was worried too. No amount of rambling or charming was going to cover it up. "Just . . . stay safe."

Before Csilla could leave them, Kane reached for her. "Thank you," he told her. "I'm sorry I kept secrets from you when you needed a friend. I—"

"I'll see you on the other side," she cut in.

Csilla stepped forward, leaving her friends behind. The icy chill in her feather earring melted away, growing so warm it nearly burned. Whispered words of encouragement drifted from behind her as she walked toward her fate. Their words were water against her dry tongue—shade against the blinding sun. Rhoda, however, had no kind words for her. She snatched away the water and shade with her sharp voice.

"Little cub," Rhoda said, her nickname for Csilla sounding more like a taunt. She shifted her weight onto her hip. "I've missed you." She pouted, pretending to look distressed, then twisted her lips into a cruel smile.

"I see that." Csilla stopped next to Lorelei and placed her hand on the girl's trembling shoulder. "You've missed me so much, you've sought out the company of devils."

"Devils?" Rhoda laughed. "We're pirates, Csilla, or have you forgotten while you were playing pretend with the children behind you? Besides, we all have a devil inside of us." Rhoda tapped the hilt of her sword with her pointed nail. "I can't wait to see what brings out yours."

"Not all of us have to lie and kill to get what we want."

"No, some of us don't do anything at all. Some of us give up our dreams to fulfill the desires of others."

"And what about Mother?" Csilla watched Rhoda flinch at the mention of the woman they both had deeply loved. Rhoda could wear the world's thickest armor, but Csilla would never forget the sound of her broken cry when their mother died. She didn't show her heart much, but it was in there, somewhere. "What would she think of your betrayal?"

"Mother wouldn't have understood any of this," Rhoda hissed. "She was too frail to be a Maiden. She didn't know what this life took and the sacrifices you have to make."

"Mother didn't have to understand being a pirate to realize that you are a disappointment to the Abado name."

Csilla barely had time to react to Rhoda's fury. In one swift movement, Rhoda unsheathed her sword and lifted it high above her head, lunging toward Csilla and Lorelei. Csilla shoved Lorelei back and whipped around to clash steel with her sister. The crash of their blades ripped through the air.

She held her cutlass in a perfect horizon, leveled with the nose, her stance undaunted. Most of her weight rested on her weak ankle, but despite the throbbing ache, she pushed against Rhoda. She moved her hand down the dull edge of her sword for even pressure and thrust forward, sending Rhoda stumbling back.

"Go!" Csilla yelled to Lorelei, who scrambled to the others.

"I'm not the disappointment," Rhoda growled. Her blade flashed in the light as she brought it over her head. She struck again, and Csilla blocked it. "You're the one who's weak."

Csilla held her sword in front of her with its tip pointed at Rhoda. "My weaknesses don't define me," she said as she rocked her weight forward, giving her ankle relief. She couldn't switch stances with her strong leg in front because then she'd be fighting blind. No matter what, she had a disadvantage against Rhoda.

Csilla retreated step by step with each strike of Rhoda's sword. Her sister swiped left, then stabbed right and left again. She clanged and clashed against Csilla's sword with each movement, the music of their deadly duet rising in crescendo.

Rhoda struck again. Csilla parried her attack, but she wasn't quick enough. Rhoda lashed out, smashing Csilla's nose with her fist. The crack of bone reverberated in Csilla's head as hot blood trickled down her face, dripping from her chin. A metallic tang filled her mouth. She spat as Rhoda laughed.

"Poor Csilla," Rhoda sang as she twirled her sword at her side. "The half-blind, half-crippled girl who was named captain instead of *me*." Rhoda thrust her blade forward, straight toward Csilla's gut, but Csilla knocked the sword away. Again and again, Rhoda attacked, relentlessly thrashing.

Csilla couldn't keep up anymore.

She cried out in pain as Rhoda caught her on her blind side and slashed her arm. Her hand went to the wound as she stumbled back. Blood seeped between her closed fingers. She lifted her hand and glanced underneath it, watching as crimson spread down the sleeve of her blouse like ink spilled on paper.

"You think you're better than me," Rhoda said, angling her sword for another attack while Csilla's guard was down. "But you're not. Grandmother was wrong."

Csilla heard her name being called by more than one voice, urging her to carry on, to raise her sword and defend herself, but her arm, her ankle, her shattered nose all begged her not to. She blocked Rhoda's next attack, but barely.

"I never should have saved you from that noose," Rhoda said through her teeth. "You're too weak to be captain. Too weak to be a queen."

Csilla stumbled back for a second, stunned with realization. Deep down she'd always known it was true, she just hadn't wanted to admit it to herself.

"It was you!" Csilla yelled. "You're the one who gave me up to Incendia!"

"And I should have taken the *Scarlet Maiden* for my own then, but I was blind, weak with love for my sister."

"You made me believe that too," Csilla said, holding on to one last shred of hope that her sister could be saved from herself. "But you're wrong, love makes us stronger. It gives us something to fight for."

Their swords clashed between them. As they both leaned forward into their stance, baring their teeth at each other over the glint of steel, Csilla could finally see the stark differences between them. The darkness in Rhoda's eyes swallowed her whole. She was full of hatred, fear, and pain, plunging into an inescapable void of destruction. Csilla feared there was no way to bring her back. She'd strayed too far.

Rhoda's gaze turned to the side, eyeing Csilla's feather earring, which swayed back and forth. Her eyes widened as a triumphant smile lit her face. She brought her sword back and curved it down so that Csilla had to block her from the side. With her other hand, she reached out and snatched the feather, ripping the hook through Csilla's earlobe, splitting it open. Csilla's scream sliced the silence. Rhoda kicked Csilla's chest, sending her flying back onto the rock and dirt.

On impact, Csilla bit her lip clean through, blood instantly pooling in her mouth. As she sat up, she spat on the ground and wiped her chin with her sleeve. Blood from the tear in her earlobe dripped onto her shoulder, pain searing through the whole side of her head. Her vision blurred as Rhoda crossed the cave and retrieved a torch from the wall. She stalked back, eyes blazing their own fire, whispering to no one under her breath.

Stopping in front of Csilla, Rhoda stilled. She held the crackling torch in her right hand, the zhacia feather in her left. From her fingers dangled the bloody hook, tiny flecks of light speckling across her skin as the feather shimmered against the light of the flames.

"Where's your luck now, Csilla?" Rhoda asked. She held the feather above the torch, letting the feather blacken and curl in on itself, its glimmer fading to ashes in an instant. She let go of the hook and tossed the torch aside with a triumphant gleam in her eyes.

No. Csilla would not let her win. She would not let Rhoda break her again.

Csilla rose to her feet, gripped her sword with both hands, and growled. "I make my own luck."

She lunged forward, catching Rhoda by surprise. She kept her strikes unpredictable and quick. Curving her blade, she slid her feet fluidly with her movements. *She* attacked. *Rhoda* retreated, their duet changing tone. Csilla was the one orchestrating now.

Rhoda countered swiftly, but her timing crumbled. Csilla changed her rhythm. She paused, stepped, then thrust. Lunged, struck, then paused. Rhoda couldn't stop her. Csilla's blade slashed her cheek, and Rhoda roared, letting her sword hang loose at her side. Rhoda took a few steps back, her chest heaving, her eyes never leaving Csilla's.

It all happened so fast then.

Rhoda smiled, blood coating her teeth. Csilla blinked and Rhoda had pulled a dagger from her belt.

One breath. One step. One second.

There was no way Csilla could have stopped it.

Rhoda threw the dagger, the blade glinting as it circled over itself through the air. It struck its target. Rhoda never missed. A gasping croak lifted into the air as Lorelei fell to her knees, blood streaming from the dagger protruding from her chest.

The cave was silent at first. The whole world was silent. But Csilla's heart was screaming.

"No!" Kane roared, dropping to his knees. He caught Lorelei as her body fell to the side. He cradled her head and rolled her onto her back. "No! *What have you done?*"

Csilla didn't think. There was nothing in her head but a thick cloud of wrath. Rhoda was so blinded by her own sick vengeance that she didn't see Csilla lunging toward her.

Rhoda blocked her strike just in time, their blades like crossbones between them. Their gazes connected over the steel.

A familiar look passed over Rhoda's eyes, reminding Csilla of the moment they'd both found out their mother was ill. Her eyes shone with unshed tears, her chin wobbling as she struggled to keep Csilla's blade back. Then Csilla's hand slipped and the blade pierced Rhoda's stomach. Csilla cried out, grief filling her, yet still she stood firm, held her sword ready. Rhoda's sword clattered to the cave floor, her hands rushing to hold Csilla's sharp blade.

"End it," Rhoda said quietly. "End the whispers, please. I didn't mean for any of this to happen."

The whispers. Magnus.

Csilla's grip loosened, her brow turning down at her sister.

"End it!" Rhoda begged again, her face twisting in anguish, her hands grasping for the sword and pulling it deeper into her own belly. "I can't take it!"

Csilla nodded, trying by everything that was holy to keep it together for a moment longer. Her shaky hands gripped the handle and pulled back her sword, then with all her might, she drove it through Rhoda's stomach. Rhoda looked down at the blade, then back up at Csilla, color draining from her cheeks.

"Thank you," Rhoda said as she fell forward, gripping Csilla's shoulders. The darkness faded from her eyes as her chin trembled. Csilla held her, their foreheads touching, warmth leaving Rhoda's skin.

"I'm sorry, little cub. So sorry."

"Find peace," Csilla whispered to her, tears filling her eyes. Then she ripped the sword away and took her sister's life with it, paying the Ruin Witch's price.

CHAPTER THIRTY-FOUR
LORELEI

Limbo
Late Redwind

The world was white when Lorelei opened her eyes.

The cave had vanished. The pirates had disappeared. The clanging of swords had silenced.

Lorelei lay on her back, gazing skyward at an endless sea of white clouds. When she sat up straight, she saw she was on an island, but the trees were white. Crystal clear water washed across the ivory sand of the beach. Her trembling hand reached for the dagger in her chest, but she grasped thin air. When she looked down at her body, there wasn't any blood. Gone were her dirty, torn clothes; in their place was a white dress of lace and ribbon.

She investigated the rest of her body. There was no wound in her chest. No blisters on her hands. No burn on her arm. Even the scar on her finger from learning to cut vegetables was gone. It was like she'd never been hurt at all.

The last thing she remembered was watching the dagger spiral through the air and plunge into her. It hadn't hurt at first, but then she couldn't breathe. She remembered the horrible croak that had left her throat as she'd tried to swallow air, but none would enter her lungs. Then the fire had started in her chest, spreading through her arms and down her legs. The flames were so hot, so consuming that they seared her heart, her mind, her soul. She couldn't scream; she couldn't cry. She had fallen to her knees, but after the fire had burned through her body, she felt nothing.

She didn't feel Kane's fingers as they brushed a stray hair out of her face or when he kissed her forehead, but it was the last thing she had seen before she closed her eyes and faded away from the world.

Where was he now? Where was *she*?

"You're in Limbo," a voice answered. It was strikingly familiar.

Limbo? Her soul wasn't lost.

"Isn't it though? You carry the weight of your mother's death and it fuels your revenge because you think it will make you feel better. There is no doubt you are lost."

Lorelei whipped her head toward the white palm trees, toward the voice, but there was no one there. Until the trees moved. The long trunks curved, bowing away from something below.

A man dressed in white like her stalked through the trees toward the beach. His hair was gold, shining and flickering like fading embers. His skin was even paler than hers, his jaw strong and nose straight. He wore no shoes as he left the magical trees and crossed the beach to her. She rose to her feet and held her hand out to stop him when he neared too close.

"Don't take another step," she said, moving back toward the crystal sea. The cool water lapped against the heels of her bare feet.

"Or what?" the man asked. The brown of his eyes was flecked with orange, reminding Lorelei of burning wood. "What are you going to do, Lorelei Storm?"

"How do you know my name?" she asked. "Who are you? What is this place?"

"I've already told you where you are," the man answered. He placed his hands behind his back, not drawing any closer to the sea. "You're in Limbo—the place between places, the harbor for lost souls. As for your name, all of us know your name."

"Us?"

"The gods and goddesses, the elemental deities, the Powers Above and Powers Below—whatever you mortals call us nowadays."

"You're Magnus," Lorelei said. Anger balled her hands into fists. "Why are you here? What do you want from me now? You've already taken everything!"

"You mortals ask so many questions." His voice turned mocking then. "*Why do wildfires keep ravaging my crops each sunspur? Why was I not blessed as an emberblood? Why can't I find love?* You, Lorelei Storm, are about to release me from all of the *relentless* hounding."

Lorelei stepped back farther into the crystal sea. Her feet were submerged, the skirt of her dress skimming the water.

"You've been quite the slippery little mortal." Magnus smiled. To others, he might have looked genuine, but a firestorm cracked and cackled behind his mask. "Every time I thought I had you in my grasp, you wriggled away. I had help, of course. My whispers reached more ears than just yours. Dominic Rove heard me first. He was so quick to follow my commands, to kill and plot by my will, like he'd been waiting for me."

"You told him to kill my mother," Lorelei said, wishing this was just a dream. "You're the one who started it all."

"I was surprised he could hear my whispers—Kane Blackwater too. My voice was so quiet, so *weak*, and their hearts were already dark. Kane was a tricky one, though. He left the shadows behind and journeyed toward the light, toward *you*. You ruined his potential."

"Kane chose his path before he knew me."

"But it was the idea of you that had him pretending to be a hero."

"He *is* a hero." He'd protected Lorelei when he hadn't had to. He could have easily won the Trials had it not been for her.

"Heroes don't commit terrible acts for the price of gold." A smile twisted at Magnus's lips.

"I don't know what you're talking about." She tried her best to seem unshaken, but she wasn't sure if she was successful or not.

"Of course you don't." Magnus feigned sympathy toward her, his lips pouting, his gaze softening. "No one has told you about the man Kane Blackwater used to be, especially not him."

"It matters more who he is now."

"Does it? What would you think of him if you knew of the deals he used to make with Dominic Rove? The lives he ended for gold."

Lorelei's heart sank, a burning ship at sea. Even though she was dead, Kane had to keep steering toward the light on the horizon; he had to fight for the good in the world or it would fall like ashes.

"Once Rove killed your mother, it opened a door and gave me the strength I needed. I'll admit, I've been impatient." He stepped closer. Lorelei stepped back. "Using my powers while still trapped in Limbo is exhausting. But thanks to Rhoda Abado and her deeply conflicted mind, I will walk the earth again. I tried to lure her sister into my bidding, but she fought against me. Rhoda just needed a push in the right direction, and she found her target *perfectly.*" Magnus smiled full tooth, his teeth as brilliant as the world around them.

Flakes of white drifted from the sky. At first Lorelei thought it was snow, but when a flake landed on her arm, she touched it. It smudged into her skin, leaving a streak of gray. *Ashes.* The thick woody scent of embers drifted in on the wind. Beneath Magnus's feet the white sand blackened, tendrils snaking out like they had minds of their own.

Magnus's laugh amplified, echoing as the falling ashes stained his white blouse. He opened his hands in front of him, collecting ashes in his palms. "The more blood that spills from your body, the stronger I become. I'll burn my way out of this realm and find my brothers. Then together, we will scorch the sea."

CHAPTER THIRTY-FIVE

KANE

Crossbones

Late Redwind

Kane held Lorelei in his arms as the warmth left her skin. He said her name until his lips were dry. The pirates were a blur of noise and chaos around him, but he stayed on his knees as a pillow for her head, a casket to hold her cold body.

He watched as Csilla laid her sister gently on the ground. Flynn ran over to her, pulling her under his arm as he shouted curses at Dominic Rove. Everyone was yelling, screaming across the cave at the opposing side.

He gazed down at Lorelei's soft, peaceful face, hating himself the longer he looked. He never should have brought her to Crossbones. The only reason she was there was because of him. If he had taken her somewhere else, where she could have been more protected, she wouldn't be dead. Cerulia wouldn't be at stake.

His fault. Always his fault.

"Lockhart!" he yelled. Even though his words were too late to make any difference, the world needed to know. The pirates fell silent. They watched Kane warily, as if he would explode. Maybe he would. "She truly was the heir. Genevieve ran away to Port Barlow when she found out she was with child."

"How could you expect me to believe such a claim without proof?" Lockhart asked, pain in his eyes.

"Sometimes you just need to have faith. That's what your queen needed from you. That's what the island kingdom needed from you. Now, because of your stupidity and the stupidity of the men behind you, Magnus will rise. Her death, her stormblood, was the last thing he needed. The Trials were supposed to be about saving our nation, but you've only condemned it."

Then Kane was surrounded by faces just as troubled as his own. Nara's chin trembled as she lowered herself to her knees in front of Lorelei. Arius knelt next to Nara, his hand finding hers. Flynn bowed his head as he dropped to his knees.

Csilla's eyes were just as broken as her body. "I couldn't protect her," she whispered as she knelt. "The Ruin Witch gave me one job, and I couldn't do it."

The ground below them trembled, rattling the cave. Then just as suddenly as it started, it stopped.

"It has begun," Borne said at Kane's side.

Kane clenched his jaw. "So that's it then? It's all over?" His voice didn't even sound like his own.

Borne knelt beside Lorelei's still body. "There's a chance I could bring her back. A long shot, but—"

Nara stopped sniffling. "There's nothing else to lose."

"I'm not as strong as my mother," Borne explained. The gold in his eyes shimmered as the light reflected off them. "It will require all of my magic."

"Then, let's get her to the Lost Isle," Csilla said. Her eyes were still empty, but there was hope in her voice. "Your mother can do it."

"That's too far," Arius said. "Her body will stink up the ship."

Everyone turned their angry gazes on Arius.

"What?" He shrugged. "It's true."

"He's right," Borne said. "We don't have time. She may be gone from this realm, but her blood still drips. Magnus is still trapped."

"Do it then," Kane commanded, squeezing Lorelei in his arms. "Now. *Please.*"

Borne leaned closer to Kane, lowering his voice so that only he could hear. "I have to reverse the bleeding. But she's not in this world anymore. She might not come back as the same girl you knew. Are you fine with that?"

"She's become dear to me. Do whatever it takes."

The ground quaked again, but this time it was stronger.

"We must pull out the dagger to let her body heal during the spell," Borne said as he settled himself by Lorelei's head. "But once it is out, the blood will flow quickly until every drop is gone. We won't have much time. Are you ready?"

Kane nodded, gripped the handle of Rhoda's dagger, and yanked the blade from Lorelei's chest. Blood flowed freely, dripping onto the rock floor beneath her.

CHAPTER THIRTY-SIX

LORELEI

Limbo

Late Redwind

Lorelei waded deeper into the crystal water. The white clouds above darkened as ashes fell heavier. Trees burst into flames, which spread as a roaring crackle rose into the air. Black smoke plumed into the sky.

Magnus threw his head back and laughed as the white world burned behind him. He lifted one of his bare feet and stomped once into the sand. The ground shook. A crack resounded from above. Lorelei glanced up and stumbled backward into the water at the sight of the sky being ripped apart like paper. Magnus stomped again, and another crack tore through the sky.

"Stop!" Lorelei screamed. When the sky split in two, nothing good would come of it, allowing Magnus and other evil creatures locked away in Limbo to escape. "You can't do this!"

Magnus turned his attention back to her. His eyes were flames, burning with the trees. "Stop?" he mused. "Who's going to stop me?"

When Lorelei didn't answer, Magnus turned his back to her. She had to do something. She had to stop this from happening. If he succeeded, if he burned through Limbo, what would happen to her friends, to the world? His fate had been tied to hers this whole time, so it had to be her that could end it.

But how was she to stop a god? She didn't even know how to hold a sword properly.

You're not alone. The soft, female voice caressed Lorelei's mind as a hand found hers in the water. A woman stood at her side, her amber curls hanging loose over her shoulders. Golden flecks edged along her light tawny cheeks like freckles. When she smiled warmly at Lorelei, the gold shimmered. Lorelei knew it in her heart. The woman was Anaphine—Goddess of Grace.

You have the power within you. A new voice, rich and warm, filled her senses. On Lorelei's other side stood a tall woman with umber skin that glowed in the light. Gold flecked above her brow, her lashes sparkling as she blinked. She rested her hand on Lorelei's shoulder and squeezed. Talona—Goddess of Strength.

Show him who you are, stormblood. The third sea goddess appeared in front of Lorelei. Her white-blond hair was cropped short and swept across her ivory brow. Her golden lips smiled as she reached forward and grasped Lorelei's empty hand. The final Sea Sister, Iodeia—Goddess of Justice.

The Sea Sisters whispered one word together: *Listen.*

Behind the crackle of the flames and the rumble of the earth, a quiet song drifted on the wind. She recognized Borne's voice as he sang in cadence through the crack between worlds. He sang in a magical language that Lorelei had never heard, yet somehow she understood each word.

"*Ahr, Ernil, Sabah, Jahrr.*" Air, earth, sea, fire.

"*Karsa Mehno, Karsa Eto.*" Powers Above, Powers Below.

Warmth grew in Lorelei's chest as he sang about the elements and powers beyond her comprehension. It sprouted like vines, swimming through her blood.

"*Shirei komiinera naskarren ento.*" Soul trapped in darkness.

"*Vriina la shasarren err eto.*" Journey back to the light.

Magnus continued to burn the trees and rip at the sky. There wasn't much time left until he broke free of his cage. She hadn't fought for herself before her death, but now she could. The words that Borne spoke filled her with the same buzz she'd felt earlier. With it, she could do anything.

"I am Lorelei Storm," she said, her voice booming with power. Magnus stopped and jerked around, the flames still blazing in his eyes. "Daughter of Jack Rathborne and Genevieve Storm. Last descendant of the Captain of the Storm. *I* am the one who is going to stop you."

Magnus scoffed. "You foolish girl! You're dead!"

Yet she felt very much alive.

Then Magnus's eyes fell on the Sea Sisters around her, pausing on the Goddess of Grace.

"Anaphine?" Magnus asked, his voice soft. The flames in his eyes died, leaving them burning embers.

"Yes, Magnus," Anaphine replied gently. She recognized the voice immediately as the soft lyrical tone which had spoken to her before this. "It is I."

"How many years has it been since I've seen your face?" Magnus seemed to forget about the raging fire behind him as he gazed upon the beautiful Anaphine.

"You must stop this chaos," Anaphine said, ignoring his question.

"In my years of entrapment in this forsaken realm, I've done nothing but think of you." Magnus took a step forward as if pulled by his love for the sea goddess.

"Cease the fire. Stray from this destructive path and learn from your mistakes. Serve your sentence, then take your place once more as a god below the mortal world."

Her words went unheard by Magnus. "Your face has never left my mind. It's been present in every dream I've had of killing you. The best part is when I watch the life leave your eyes."

Magnus threw his arms forward, sending a ball of fire cutting through the air like a cannon. The flames roared as they neared. Heat singed Lorelei's cheek as the fire struck Anaphine in the chest, sending her flying back into the sea.

Magnus attacked again, summoning more fire into the palm of his hand and throwing it directly at Lorelei. Iodeia jumped in front of her, a blur of white. She shot her hand through the air in front of her, slicing the ball of flame in two with a blade of water.

Talona grabbed Lorelei and pulled her behind her tall frame. Then with her fingers dancing, she raised her hands at her sides until they were near her chest. A wall of water rose in front of them, shielding them from more fire flying in their direction. As the flames collided with the water, a hiss rose into the air.

A wave washed Anaphine's charred body to Lorelei. The goddess's eyes struggled to remain open, her mouth fighting to form the words Lorelei's mother had said before she'd died. "Follow the storm inside of you."

Then Borne's voice once again carried on the wind. He sang the same cadence, but this time it was louder, stronger. Magnus glared up at the sky with fury as liquid gold seeped through the crack between dimensions, snaking through the sky.

"*Ahr, Ernil, Sabah, Jahrr,*

"*Karsa Mehno, Karsa Eto.*"

More power filled Lorelei. She thought of the waves and the wind, and it lifted her up and out of the water, holding her suspended above the crystal sea. The liquid gold swam toward her from the sky, reaching for her, and she reached back. The gold seeped onto her fingertips, spreading over her fingers like honey, across her hands, halfway down her arms. It coated her skin like gloves and shimmered in the light.

"*Shirei komiinera naskarren ento,*

"*Vriina la shasarren err eto.*"

Borne ended on one last, strong note. The world went silent aside from Lorelei's rapid breathing as she hovered over the water, her body glowing with powerful magic. Her dark hair whipped in the wind, the edges of her white dress ruffling.

She glanced down at the Sea Sisters below her, struggling to keep Magnus's blazing rage at bay. She had to help them.

Rain. It was a simple thought, but in one breath it poured down, torrential and unforgiving. The flames of the Limbo jungle hissed as they shriveled, revealing charred trees that were once unworldly white.

"It can't be possible!" Magnus screamed, his golden hair stuck against his forehead. Rain dripped down his face, his jaw slack as he gazed upon Lorelei. "You're dead! You have no power here!"

The warmth of Kane was suddenly everywhere, cradling her body, tracing over her cheeks. Then came the light of the others around her as if they were right next to her. Kane's heart and Csilla's strength. Nara's loyalty and Flynn's optimism. Borne's selflessness and Arius's . . . whatever he had. Lorelei's voice echoed over Magnus's when she spoke. "I have a power you'll never have. The love of friendship."

"That's the most ridiculous thing I've ever heard."

The Sea Sisters smiled up at her, then blinked away, leaving a shimmering gold dust floating on the waves where they once stood.

The light inside of her grew, burning hot yet cold at the same time. Her chest arched up as if someone were pulling her by a string. Her arms and legs dangled below her as she rose above the sea. Her body glowed brighter and brighter until Lorelei had to close her eyes against the sheer brilliance of it.

"Wait!" Magnus roared. "No! This isn't possible! You'll never be able to escape me!" His yell carried over the wind as Lorelei rose higher toward the clouds. "I'll find a way out! This scar will never fully heal!"

The light eclipsed for a breath then exploded out of her, sending her soul flying through the crack in the sky and into the unknown.

—

She awoke to Kane's worried gaze, hidden behind the dark hairs that escaped from under his black head scarf.

"You're back," he said, letting out a gust of air he must have been holding in.

"You're alive!" Nara yelled from Lorelei's feet.

Lorelei tore her gaze from Kane and glanced down to see the raven-haired Maiden smiling. Arius knelt at her side, smirking, but his eyes were puffy and red like he'd been crying.

"The Storm lives to fight another day," Csilla said, but her voice sounded so far away even though she knelt near Lorelei's legs. Since Csilla was there, did that mean Rhoda was dead? Lorelei didn't have the heart to ask.

Then she remembered the voice that had brought her back from Limbo.

"Borne?" Lorelei called. "Where is Borne?"

"I'm here," Borne said at Lorelei's other side.

She turned to look at him. His red hair was now the only thing that stood out about him. The gold of his eyes was gone, replaced with a muddy brown.

"Your eyes," Lorelei said. "Your magic."

"It's gone," Borne said, his voice hollow. "The spell channeled all of it into you. My magic is yours now."

"You gave up your gift for me?" Lorelei asked, unbelieving.

"We had to bring you back. Magnus was rising. The ground was quaking. Guiding your soul back into your body was the only thing that could have stopped him. Besides, it was my destiny."

The gold dripping through the sky. It must have been his magic.

The battle in Limbo flashed into her mind, making her heart pound fiercely in her chest. Her blood had been spilled, the slickness of it still beneath her. Was bringing her soul back really enough to keep Magnus trapped?

Then she remembered the man allied with the fire god.

"Rove!" Lorelei yelled, her throat burning. "Where is that bastard?"

"The coward and his men fled when the quakes began," Kane replied. "Some of the Maidens and Sons tried to stop them, but there was too much chaos."

"Lorelei Storm," came a new voice. Lorelei glanced up to see

Lockhart standing on the edge of their group, gazing down at her. The officials loomed behind them, ever silent. Did they ever speak at all? "An apology isn't enough for what I've done to you."

"You did not throw the blade," Lorelei replied.

"But I put the blade in her hand when I forced the trial." His face was grim and filled with regret. The corners of his eyes turned down. "The chest is yours."

"You mean . . ."

"Yes," Lockhart answered before she could ask. He dropped to one knee. "Only a Storm could unite the pirate captains under such circumstances. You gave me all the proof I needed when the Sea Sisters allowed your soul to return to your body. You are to be queen of Cerulia, Lorelei Storm."

The words were passionless to Lorelei. She didn't want the throne. She doubted this was who she was meant to be.

"If it's all right with you," Lorelei said, hoping no one would argue with her. "I'd rather wait to open the chest until we are off this goddess-forsaken island."

Kane laughed as he scooped her into his arms, but Csilla eyed her curiously. The half-blind captain always seemed to see much more than most did.

CHAPTER THIRTY-SEVEN
CSILLA

Baltessa
Early Frostfall

Csilla never slept well anymore. Even when she was curled into Flynn's side, she still tossed and turned in the night. Rhoda's face was always there, pale and pained, begging her to make the whispers stop, make the whispers stop, *make the whispers stop.* Csilla sat up sweating each time the slick slide of her sword emptied Rhoda's insides onto the ground. This time when she bolted upright in the middle of the night, hands shaking and legs trembling, there was no possibility of her falling back asleep.

"Don't leave," Flynn groaned from the bed, reaching out for her. "It gets so cold when you're gone."

"You'll survive without me," Csilla murmured, giving his hand a squeeze before she pried his fingers from her wrist.

"Barely," he whispered. Then he was snoring again, sprawled across the sheets.

Csilla shook her head and smirked as she slipped on the patterned silk robe she'd bought with some of the gold she'd acquired since their return to Baltessa. During most of their sail back, Csilla had locked herself in her cabin, letting herself heal in solitude as she mourned her sister. When they'd arrived back in the capital, life became a flurry of changes for everyone. But now, the coronation was only a day away and there was hardly time to breathe.

Flynn and Arius had taken charge of the special crews with the Sons of Anaphine. For the most part, their role kept them inside the capital, sending out patrols and strategizing defensive plans, but they still sailed out with the *Anaphine*, searching for lost treasure among the scattered islands. Flynn's newest, most important mission, however, was to find a way to pass the Frozen Gap and call on Ventys, the northern air worshippers.

Nara's new role was to train recruits, and she enjoyed it a little too much. Csilla heard her yells and quips from across the courtyard every day that she made the recruits run her impossible drills. Borne assisted Nara with her lessons and learned quickly. He'd gone to see his mother, then surprised them all by joining them in Baltessa.

And Lorelei . . . Lorelei was . . . Csilla didn't know anymore. After Lorelei awakened, they had all rejoiced, but every now and then Csilla heard her mumbling to herself about cracks between worlds. When Lorelei had first opened her eyes, they were blue as lightning, electrifying with gold sparks. Csilla had never seen anything like it. But Lorelei had blinked, and the cobalt in her eyes had disappeared. Csilla and Kane were the only two who'd noticed.

She left her bedroom in the south wing of the palace, closing the door behind her and stepping into one of the many hallways. She still got lost in the maze of corridors and spiral staircases even though this had been her new home for the past moon.

The night air chilled her bare legs as she treaded down the dark hall, her feet stepping lightly on the long crimson rug that adorned the polished floor. Paintings of ships and heroes lined the wall, the moon casting them in an eerie glow. She hated being trapped inside with all of the delicate decor of royalty. She wanted to be out on the sea with the rough wood of her ship under her fingertips. The balcony at the end of the wing was going to have to make do.

Csilla stepped through the glass doors and into the night. But she wasn't alone on the balcony. Lorelei stood at the railing with her back to the doors. Her hair waved like sails rolling in the wind, but her body was still.

"Csilla," Lorelei said, without turning around. How had she known it was her? "You can't sleep again?"

Csilla stepped forward so that she was side by side with her friend. She reached out and gripped the wooden railing, pretending she was on the deck of the *Scarlet Maiden* instead, staring out at the open sea. It didn't make her feel any better. "How did you know I haven't been sleeping well?"

"You're not the only one who walks the halls at night." A small smile lifted the corner of Lorelei's lips, but then it was gone.

"Lorelei?" Csilla asked.

"Hmm?" But Lorelei didn't look at her. She continued to stare out at the copper spires of the city and the sea beyond.

"Lorelei," Csilla said more firmly, grabbing her attention. "Look at me."

Lorelei turned to Csilla. The moon reflected the tears in her eyes. One shimmered as it fell in a lone trail down her face.

"When are you going to talk about what happened in Limbo?" Csilla asked, hoping that maybe if Lorelei finally told them what happened, they could help her through it. She'd kept her secret wound tight. Csilla wasn't sure if Lorelei had even told Kane what she'd been through yet.

"I can't—" Lorelei started, then stopped herself. She shook her head and wrung her fingers. "I can't stop thinking about what happened . . . in there."

In Limbo, she meant. Csilla's brow turned down in confusion. She cocked her head to the side and touched Lorelei's shoulder. "Whatever it is, I'll help you. Kane will help you."

"When I was there I had this . . . magic," Lorelei said, something similar to fear swimming in her eyes. "And when I came back I thought it was gone, but I don't think it is. It scares me a little bit."

"Lorelei." Csilla grabbed her by both shoulders now, staring at her grieved expression, trying to figure out what in the world was going on inside the girl's head. "You're not in Limbo anymore. Everything is going to be okay."

"You don't understand," Lorelei said, turning her head to the side.

"Let's get you back to bed." Csilla gently pulled Lorelei forward to get her moving toward the door, but Lorelei pulled out of her grasp.

"No," Lorelei said, shaking her head back and forth. "The magic is still there. I know it."

"It's okay." Worry twisted in Csilla's gut. Something wasn't right. Perhaps Lorelei was sleepwalking. She'd shown no sign of magic or even spoken of it in the past moon.

"In Limbo, the magic consumed me entirely," Lorelei said. It was the most Csilla had heard her speak about Limbo since she'd opened her eyes in Skull Cave. "I was glowing, my arms were golden, I could control the sky. The sheer power that coursed through me . . ." She stopped for a moment and took a breath. "I've never felt anything like it." Her eyes brimmed with unshed tears. "It was dangerously powerful. *I* was dangerous. If this magic does still rest inside of me and the power becomes too much, promise me you won't let me hurt Kane. Or you. Or anyone." Her voice cracked. "Please."

"I promise," Csilla agreed, even though she had no idea what was happening. She didn't ask any more questions. Instead, she wrapped her friend in her arms and let her know she wasn't alone.

—

The coronation was extravagant.

Ships from across Cerulia sailed into the port to witness the first pirate queen and celebrate her defeat of Magnus. The capital flooded with people, its streets bustling, red and gold banners swaying with the sea breeze. Music drifted into the air from every corner of the city, following the procession of pirates and their crews down the main road to the palace courtyard. The four captains led the march. The *Wavecutter* captain was still allowed to participate with his crew, but the Bonedogs had been exiled from the islands. A new crew would form a banner and take their place.

The parade stopped at the steps of the palace. The crowd quieted when the pages blew into their horns, their deep blare signaling Lorelei's appearance on the balcony above. Csilla glanced up, but there was no queen.

The horns blew again, yet Lorelei still didn't emerge through the doors.

"Something's wrong," Kane whispered at Csilla's side. "What if an Incendian Scout somehow slipped inside?"

There was that possibility. The navy had been pushing farther into the island kingdom the past moon. However, with the number of pirates in the capital today, she thought the scenario unlikely. Could Lorelei be having another mental breakdown?

"Incendia wouldn't dare send a Scout today," Csilla whispered back. "We'd slaughter them. I'll bet Lorelei is just nervous."

"I'll go check on her," Kane said, but Csilla stopped him with her arm.

"Let me. Maybe she needs help with her dress." Even though Csilla knew nothing about clothes except what felt comfortable, she had to keep the promise she'd made to Lorelei. Kane looked like he wanted to argue with her, but she ignored him and hobbled up the steps as the crowd chattered curiously behind her.

Csilla found Lorelei in the artifact room by the balcony doors. Her boots echoed as she stepped across the marbled floor, making Lorelei's shoulders jump. She stood in the center of all the treasures scattered around the room, looking like a jewel herself with her sparkling gold and ruby dress. Her hair was spiraled up in a pile on top of her head with tendrils that curled down. When she glanced over her shoulder to see who'd come in, Csilla saw that her eyelids were painted gold and her lips blood red.

"Wow," Csilla said. "You look like a queen."

Lorelei sighed and shook her head before turning back around. "I don't feel like a queen." The chest from Crossbones sat on the ground in front of her. "The Bone Crown is still in there, you know."

"It is?" Csilla asked. She figured Lorelei would have taken it out and tried it on at least once.

"I opened the chest," Lorelei continued as she wrung her hands, twisting the rings on her fingers. "I thought that maybe if I saw the Bone Crown, then this would feel right. I thought I'd have this moment where I saw it and I just knew in my bones that this is who I'm supposed to be. But I'm not a queen, Csilla."

Csilla stepped forward until she was at Lorelei's side. "You were quite literally born for this."

"That doesn't mean anything. I may have Cerulian blood, but I was raised in Incendia. I tended a farm with my mother and sold rolls to the traders in the harbor. I know nothing about how to lead, or about the people I'm supposed to rule. When Kane came to Port Barlow, I went with him because I had nothing left, but now I just have to figure out what I have within me. I'm not queen of the pirates, but I can still be queen of my own destiny—not the one that's been chosen for me."

"If you aren't queen, then who is?" Csilla shifted nervously. There was going to be an angry crowd of pirates if this coronation got canceled. Lorelei bent down, placed her hands on the lid of the chest, and pulled it open. Light shimmered off the golden Bone Crown inside.

"It's you, Csilla," Lorelei said quietly. She looked up at Csilla while she continued. "It isn't my fate to rule. It's yours."

Csilla couldn't speak. Her throat burned and her legs tingled numbly. No. There was no way after everything that this was her fated path. But then there was the whisper of the Ruin Witch's words and the reward she'd seen. Could it be? Was it possible?

"Me?" she asked as she bent down beside Lorelei. Her fingers trembled as they touched the edges of the chest. She'd dreamed many different versions of this moment, and it felt like she was still sleeping.

"What do you say?" Lorelei placed her hand on Csilla's shoulder. "Will you accept this?"

"I don't know." Csilla's voice was only a whisper. "I don't think that—"

"Technically, the Trials never concluded." Lorelei nudged her. "A captain has yet to put the crown on their head. You spend so much time trying to help others, trying to help *me*. Do something for yourself. Take the Bone Crown."

Csilla didn't move.

"Fine then." Lorelei snatched the crown. "You've given me no choice." Before Csilla could stop her Lorelei lifted the crown above her and gently placed it on Csilla's head.

For a moment Csilla forgot how to breathe. The weight of the crown pushed on her skull and her fingers itched to rip it off before someone saw. But then it was as if the missing piece of her shattered life clicked into place. Her blood thrummed, her heart warmed, and she felt like she could walk ten thousand paces without a limp and see clearly with both eyes.

"Lockhart said the Trials weren't over until the Bone Crown sat on a captain's head." Lorelei shrugged. "Loopholes."

Csilla chuckled, then smiled at Lorelei. "Our enemies will be terrified of us, you know. The queen and the Storm, protecting the world from scoundrels."

A guard suddenly appeared at the door. "Your Grace. The crowd is restless—" His voice trailed off when his eyes fell on the Bone Crown atop Csilla's head.

"We're ready," Lorelei said, breaking the uncomfortable silence. "Csilla Abado, first of her name, captain of the *Scarlet Maiden*, winner of the Trials, is ready to face her people."

"Can she do that?" the puzzled guard asked.

"Do you want to know what happens to guards who ask questions?" Lorelei cocked an eyebrow, then turned to Csilla. The fear Csilla had seen in her eyes the night before was gone for the moment. "How was that? Was that an adequate threat?"

"It's a great start," Csilla said. "Add in higher stakes, such as which body part they might find themselves missing. Then you'll have their knees trembling."

The two of them laughed together as they exited the room and faced the doors of the balcony. Csilla could hear the crowd's shouts through the doors.

"I can't do this," Csilla said, shaking her head.

"You can," Lorelei said, pulling open the balcony doors.

"Lorelei?" came Kane's voice from the shadows of the hallway. "What's going on?"

"Kane," Lorelei breathed. "You scared me. I—I couldn't do it."

The corner of Kane's lips twitched as if he'd known this was going to happen. He pulled Lorelei into his arms and gave Csilla an accepting nod. She smiled at him before turning toward the open balcony doors and stepping through.

Csilla had never seen so many eyes on her at once. The crowded courtyard fell silent.

They scrutinized the Bone Crown on her head. Their gazes lingered over her blind eye. They judged the pants she wore when a queen should wear a dress.

Flynn's ecstatic voice broke through the silence. "Long live the Queen of Bones!"

The crowd burst into applause, their cheers rising until Csilla was beaming.

She turned and looked at her friend, who had backed into the shadows of the hallway behind her. Lorelei's relief shone in her eyes, but Csilla knew that the power her friend feared—the same one she craved—couldn't be kept a secret for long, and there was no way Csilla was going to be able to keep Kane away from her after everything the group had been through together. And perhaps there was more to Lorelei's frenzied murmurs about the cracks in the world. Maybe they weren't as safe as they all assumed. What else was in Limbo, waiting to be released, waiting for their moment to slip through the cracks?

Csilla took a deep breath and pushed the thoughts out of her head for the moment. Whatever came, they would all face it together. But right now, she would enjoy this moment of peace and happiness for as long as it lasted.

ACKNOWLEDGMENTS

Publishing this book was a dream that I never thought would become a reality. The support from many I received during this journey is something I would've been lost without.

First, I'd like to thank my husband, Derek. I wrote this book during the most chaotic period of our lives while I was working full time and going to college at night. You were and continue to be my biggest supporter, and you didn't let me give up when I wanted to. Thank you for staying by my side and loving me through it all. To my parents, thank you for raising me with a heart strong enough to chase my dreams, even when people doubted me. You are the real MVPs.

I'm also immensely grateful to the many friends I've made in the writing community throughout the years. It is so important to have a group of people who understand your goals and your struggles, and who don't let you hit the panic button when everything feels upside down. Francesca Flores and Sonia Tagliareni, you are a blessing to me and I wouldn't even be writing these acknowledgments if it weren't for you. You've cheered me on throughout the years, told me truths I needed to hear, and you are always there for me, ready to listen with compassionate hearts. Thank you.

I owe an enormous debt of gratitude to Wattpad, the Wattpad Books team, and the Wattpad community. I started writing on Wattpad in 2009, and my life changed because of it. Through Wattpad, I found my closest friends and my love for writing. To every reader who read my incredibly messy first drafts and supported me over the years, thank you is not enough. When I thought no one cared about my words, you were there to prove me wrong, and you inspired me to keep going. Thank you Deanna McFadden, Rebecca Sands, Rebecca Mills, and Jen Hale for helping make this book feel like a real book. Also a huge thank you to Monica Pacheco, Samantha Pennington, and Alessandra Ferreri for always believing in me. To the rest of the Wattpad staff, thank you for providing a space for readers and writers around the world to come together and discover their love for reading and writing.

Last, but certainly not least, I want to thank my two children, Kaylee and Jaydon, for putting up with a mother whose nose is sometimes buried in her laptop, especially when she's on a deadline. You two are my biggest inspirations in this world, and I'm incredibly grateful and proud that you are both mine. Don't forget about this when you're grounded one day, okay? I'll be sure to remind you.

Thank you is just a phrase, but my feelings of gratitude will last a lifetime.

ABOUT THE AUTHOR

Kimberly Vale is a reader, a bit of a hopeless romantic, and started writing on Wattpad as a teen. In the years since then, she has accumulated millions of reads online and has volunteered her time to mentorship programs and other efforts in the writing community. With a BA in education, Kimberly teaches remediation and dyslexia intervention in public schools and lives in Arkansas with her husband, two children, and two dogs. She also enjoys playing video games, trying new recipes, and coming up with ridiculous theories about her current tv obsessions. Don't even get her started on the last season of *Game of Thrones*.

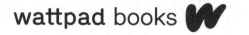